WELCOME TO

The Abyss line of cutting-edge psychological horror is committed to publishing the best, most innovative works of dark fiction available. ABYSS is horror unlike anything you've ever read before. It's not about haunted houses or evil children or ancient Indian burial grounds. We've all read those books, and we all know their plots by heart.

ABYSS is for the seeker of truth, no matter how disturbing or twisted it may be. It's about people, and the darkness we all carry within us. ABYSS is the new horror from the dark frontier. And in that place, where we come face-to-face with terror, what we find is ourselves.

"Thank you for introducing me to the remarkable line of novels currently being issued under Dell's Abyss imprint. I have given a great many blurbs over the last twelve years or so, but this one marks two firsts: first *unsolicited* blurb (*I* called *you*) and the first time I have blurbed a whole *line* of books. In terms of quality, production, and plain old storytelling reliability (that's the bottom line, isn't it?), Dell's new line is amazingly satisfying . . . a rare and wonderful bargain for readers. I hope to be looking into the Abyss for a long time to come."
—Stephen King

"The quality of the Abyss line really is remarkable. Right from the start, I was impressed with its distinction and ambition. It's wonderful to see this excellent line continuing."
—Peter Straub

Also by Kathe Koja

THE CIPHER

BAD BRAINS

SKIN

KATHE KOJA

Delacorte Press

Published by
Delacorte Press
Bantam Doubleday Dell Publishing Group, Inc.
666 Fifth Avenue
New York, New York 10103

Library of Congress Cataloging in Publication Data

Koja, Kathe.
    Skin / by Kathe Koja.
        p.   cm.
    ISBN 0-385-30899-X
    I. Title.
    PS3561.0376S58   1993
    813′.54—dc20   92-1639   CIP

Manufactured in the United States of America

Published simultaneously in Canada

March 1993

10 9 8 7 6 5 4 3 2 1

FOR RICK AND AARON

Always mine

I would like to thank Jim Pallas for his technical advice, and especially my father, Bruno Koja, for his endless patience with endless questions.

I would also like to acknowledge a special debt to Re/Search Publications, whose *Modern Primitives* and *Industrial Culture Handbook* were invaluable resources for me.

And as always, my great and special thanks and love to Rick Lieder, for all the indefinables, for everything.

1

METAL

FATIGUE

Every idea is an incitement.
—Oliver Wendell Holmes, Jr.

Dust. Above a party store, LIQUOR, LOTTO, keno machines fed by the poorest of the poor with coins rattled black by pocket tumbling, machine sounds nervous as a nervous cough. Grit-rimmed eyes, grit beneath her nails like powdered bone, fresh solder burn on her inner wrist a party-red, still too sore even to bandage. Dirt like sugar between her teeth.

Already dark, and she thought about going downstairs, scraping change for a sandwich, a bottled drink maybe. She had been working all day, sweaty and burned, heavy pants stuck ragged to the backs of her legs. On the worktable the sculpture's long arms lay maddening in static; beautiful; what difference did that make? Her arms were long, too, knotty with muscle, throwing metal around had made her strong. Now away from the table to stretch, bending awkward to tug at her body, a little Oh of pain when a joint pulled wrong; stretching harder.

The whole room was less than three meters wide, absurdly long from door to fencing wall: floor scraped to splinters past the overlay of her workspace, hemmed by the inscrutable orange wall of the welding panels oblique as any antique screen. Near the worktable a green metal rack, half-drawered, hung deft and messy with tools, cables, filter masks, welding helmet and goggles; forming a bandy L, a battered couchbed, table with cooking tools, an empty sink. In the farthest corner wavy green plastic, chest-high to partially shield a toilet and stand-up shower box reminiscent of a Porta-John, with the same faint chemical flavor; stripping as she crossed the room, into the instant sting, leaving it cold to soothe her burned wrist, faint pepper of burns across her cheek.

Strings of wet hair in her eyes, towel as bright as her burn; someone had stolen it for her, hotel name stenciled into the heavy fabric. A rich person's towel. The casement windows were chicken-wired but she had found a way to open them; no breeze tonight, somebody's radio harsh with distortion. Drunk laughter, a girl, somebody else saying, "Squeeze me, chita, come *on,*" as if the act might be completed there in the street; the girl laughed again, the glossy humor of denial.

Long legs stepping into cotton pants torn off at the knees, thin T-shirt and hair scooped heavy into a wet topknot tied with a jaunty twist of speaker wire. Scuffed steel-toed ankle boots thick on the risers, kicking gently at the paint-skinned door separating the stairs from the party store's entrance, where the manager was now counting half-smashed cartons of cigarettes.

"Hey, Tess," coolly, still counting. Still mad about the smoke, probably; her complaints were getting more frequent, but then again where could she find a tenant so oblivious? Tess moved past her into the dirty warren of the store, everything leaky or cheap or plastic, half-crushed boxes and dusty greeting cards, keno machines loud and blurry and two white guys in black T-shirts ceaselessly pumping quarters. Half a liter of white grape juice cool in

her hand, a box of crackers, two handfuls of change and
the girl behind the counter scowled, big hair, big fake earrings shiny with scratched gold. "Whyn't you try paying
with real money?"

"Want me to count it for you?"

A deeper scowl, scraping it across the counter into her
hand. "Bitch," underbreath but just loud enough to be
heard, but already Tess had turned, past hearing and up
the stairs again to sit in the circle of white, juice and crackers and new sweat already trickling down her forehead
before the moveless sculpture lying in its trench of spatter
and shine.

Showering again, spurts and gurgles of unpredictable
heat, she had slept for less than four hours and felt it.
Today was her day for the scrapyard, jagged landscape and
you needed those steel-toed shoes, sturdy beggar with a
heavy bag, reinforced canvas and sometimes it ripped anyway. Her sunglasses hung on a black vinyl string around
her long neck; she put them on as soon as she got outside,
almost ninety and not even noon.

She had no car now, had sold it to get breathing room
on the rent, missed it more each trip to the scrapyard—
small harvests, without a car—and now not much room
left to breathe, either; she would be out of money soon,
out on the street maybe, or maybe her piece would sell at
the show: THE ART OF STEEL. What a joke. Five guys with
dayjobs and two professors, metals used as just another
tool in the larger service of introducing one's name to the
art journals, *New Art Quarterly, Art NOW.* Needless angles,
curlicues and avant bobbing birdfeeders, the ones who
thought a jagged weld made the whole piece gritty; as if to
name it real would make it so. Worst of all no one did their
own work, their own welds, she had asked enough ques-

tions to get sure. She was the only woman in the show: maybe they were getting state money and had to let her in. Tonight was the opening. She did not want to go but would, for the food, and to see if, maybe, maybe, somebody would buy her piece. Which was ridiculous. Empty bag against her shoulder like a flopping flap of skin, skirting the back of a moving bus, halo of fumes. Dry eyes burning behind her sunglasses, dark as welder's goggles.

The scrapyard was not far but seemed so. Burn on her wrist chafed by the too-tight bandage, she had to jockey for entrance, the manager in the mood to charge double and said so. On the counter was a disassembled eight-gauge nibbler, the parts runny, frozen like cooled lava. "I can fix that for you," Tess said. "Got a glue gun?"

"You got half an hour," the manager said. "That's it."

Landscape of iron and rusty teeth pointing at the sun, she climbed carefully, doubting each step; tetanus shots were expensive. Once she had tumbled through an unstable pile, incongruous whoop of surprise as something grabbed, ripped, tore; she still had the marks on her right arm, long spiderweb scarring thin as machine lace. —Here a flotsam of something black, very much like the nibbler but webbed in sagging cable and the blistered strips of some heavy plastic casing; it was nothing she recognized but she took it anyway, its heft was good in her hand. Beyond that the false glitter of chrome, a fan crippled bladeless, she left it for a sullen slick of unwarped plastic that looked good from a distance but turned out to be nothing. Step and bend, step and bend, the red dirt of rust on her fraying work gloves, sun on her head and the back of her neck, burning, burning. Step and bend. She was there for over an hour before a guy on a hi-lo hollered her down and back to the office, where she haggled for her finds, paying more than she meant to for the nibbler-thing;

its weight in the canvas bag banging hard against her hip, long legs in long strides, eyes big and dark and busy behind the black sunglasses: scanning the street, discards, you never knew where you might find something good.

Even the stairs were an oven, going up. As soon as she got inside she pulled off her T-shirt, gray with sweat, tossed it to the couchbed to maybe dry, then changed her mind and took it into the shower with her. The shower was her one luxury, the only thing free and now in its cold drench she felt her sunburned neck, the ache of her wrist gentle down, her nipples grow pleasantly hard. She was almost out of soap so was careful with the sliver, small and pink like an animal's tongue, faint smell of flowers that would never grow here. It was nearly two; time to get to work.

Almost at once she saw she had been right about the nibbler-thing: its ruined cables hung like seaweed about the blistered arms of her sculpture, its warped shaft the piece's new throat. Faulty heat gun to melt a pink scum of bubblepack across the shaft; thinnest leaves of solder where the skin would be.

The opening was at seven; she worked till six, cleaned up, chose clothes from the zipperless husk of a three-suiter hung from the gibbet of a railroad nail: short black pants, long black T-shirt, the soiled white of her bandage bright as found jewelry against her skin. Sandals instead of steel-toes. She let her hair hang, coarse, long, half-auburn and half-brown, it was beautiful hair and she knew it and she wore it the way another woman would have worn a favor-ite dress. Snapping the elastic keyring on her unburned wrist, slamming the door on heat to more heat, sweat on her upper lip, on the pale ridge of skin behind the bridge of her sunglasses. On the bus two boys tried to pick her up, cute boys, ten years too young for her. She joked with them a little until they got off, watched with half a smile their brisk extravagant postures, hips cocked big-man as the bus pulled away.

The opening was crowded, Gallery Isis, hieroglyphic entryway in overdone reds and golds. Big plastic letters made to look like iron; pig iron; THE ART OF STEEL. She had to pass all the pieces to get to the food table, pass men in linen suits and women with heavy gold bolts hung from gold neckchains, pass the two professors and the five guys with dayjobs, none of whom noticed or spoke to her. She already knew where they had placed her work, one piece in a corner, poorly lit, she had argued about it for most of an afternoon before abruptly giving in; why waste breath.

Mineral water and cut-up lemons, lots of rye bread squares and little cheeses sliced into shapes. One was dark and sharp and tasted like liquor, loose and heavy in her mouth; she spit it into the tiny red fanfolded napkin, balled it up in her hand and kept it there as the gallery director paused in passing: chunky jewelry, heavy brown lipstick on a thin white smile.

"Isn't it a terrific show?"

She said nothing. The spit-out cheese had begun to soak through the napkin, touch her skin like the moisture from a leaking boil. Let's shake on it.

"I think your pieces look wonderful."

"I only have one." Pointing with the napkin hand. "There in the corner." It was one of her best, too, *Archangel,* and how she had struggled to transmit the sense of motion: wings like knives, the churn of flayed metal sheet stock, the mouth all teeth like God's own engine come back to earth to burn. The teeth alone had taken a week. She wasn't asking much for it, much less after the gallery's cut; in the end it would probably work out to a dollar an hour, but if you calculated things that way, why bother? You did it to do it. Everything else was extraneous.

"—and Matty Regal, too." The director was talking, apparently had been. "So we're very pleased with that as well."

Her mouth still tasted sour from the cheese. "Excuse me," and stepped away, back to the food table, more flat mineral water that she drank as if she were dehydrated, three plastic cups one after the other. After she had eaten as much bread and cheese as she could stand she left, through chatter and wine and the shine of fake gold bolts and nuts beneath aimed light less bright than her Spartan circle, talk so cheap a week's worth would pay her rent for a year; and the heavy glass door with its gold-stenciled icons closing silent on its own behind her, night and heat and work safe on her side.

She still had an answering machine; sometimes people wanted her for pickup jobs, missing a call might mean missing half a month's rent. Tonight there was a message, some guy, Crane somebody. Want to talk to you, maybe I'll see you at the opening. He didn't sound like anybody who would want to buy anything from her, but you never knew.

Back into work clothes, sweaty-hot but being burned was hotter and took longer to go away. She remembered her real school, welding school: truck bodies and they had let her watch, they thought she was cute or something, had not driven her away. Hot, always, and the big ventilators going on and on and on, the endless revolution of blades big as bodies, rod and arc and the fountaining shine like stars ground to pieces, the endless eclipse one must not watch. Fascinated, silent, in roll-down pants and her hair skinned back, baseball cap and wanting to make the fire, make the metal run; she had never gotten over it, the idea of liquid metal. She remembered the smell of scorched clothing, heavy coveralls burned straight through, everything seen through the underwater gloss of welder's goggles, the helmets most exotic: round-headed spacemen with flat square eyes, the world's most faceless mask. She had seen men—it was all men, only men—hurt, burned, once she saw a man drop the fluxless tail end of his welding rod into his low-cut shoe: hideous and funny his screaming dance; he had danced her into taped-up pantlegs as an article of faith. Liquid metal and so much to learn, and then the shop closed down, moved to larger quarters where the only access was through an air-conditioned office with a big red OSHA notice taken as lawsuit gospel; no trespassers at all.

So. Get your own gear, melt your own metal. No one would hire her, the welding shops she applied to thought she was hilarious, so: fast food, and to speed it up she started barmaid moonlighting, still underage but nobody cared since she didn't drink. After a month she quit the dayjob, worked all the hours no one wanted: saving, saving, busy as a little beaver, wise little underage ant. In a few months she had enough for a welding-cutting outfit and the space in which to use it. Another three months' worth bought her time.

First embarrassing works but she got that out of the way fast, quick study, learning that what she made could be called sculpture, actual art. You could apply for grants, too, but to Tess taking somebody's money was just carte blanche for taking their shit, too, and she got enough shit as it was, nobody wanted a welding shop on the premises, even in the places she could afford. So. A year here, there, cinderblock storefronts getting shabbier all the time, earning the rent at pickup jobs: they quit laughing when they saw she had her own gear, but still she wasn't certified so no real-money jobs, no municipalities or building tanks for her. Just keep moving, further down the food chain, all the way to this shithouse where Grace downstairs was so greedy she would rent to anybody. Even a welder. She was probably hoping Tess would burn the whole place down one day so she could claim the insurance and leave town. No such luck; there was too much work to do.

This piece, now, was reaching completion, with the addition of the nibbler parts. Little left, but *something,* not sure what but she would know when she found it. In the green metal rack was a dishpan jumbled sharp with small parts. Picking through it with the care of a carrion crow, big anonymous bolts skinned with grease, a broken baffle for an old heat gun, the springless trigger from something, a thin strip of Lexan the width of a bookmark. A blindfold. Holding it like a microscope slide, she placed it before the sculpture's headless neck, a little higher. Higher. There. Not a smile but an inward nod: now how to hold it?

Hot in the white light, and downstairs the tingling chitter that meant a payoff on the keno machines, some guy yelling "Yes! Yes!" over and over again. Careful crack of last night's empty juice bottle, slivering the glass to insert three slim splinters into the Lexan, just where a mouth might be. Her burn ached less. Sweat under her breasts, salt in her mouth. Solder on the floor, a cooling drop that spread unnoticed like silver rain and dried at last to the unseen thickness of a tear.

On her way downstairs to buy breakfast and on the phone, Crane; picking up while he was in the middle of his message, "Hello, yeah, I'm here."

"I called yesterday." He sounded like he had a cold, a wet cold. "I want to come by and see you."

Silence. She didn't like people in her workspace. Finally, "How about I meet you somewhere?"

"No, I need to see you in your workshop." Workshop; Santa's littlest metal-grubbing elf. "I'm a sculptor, too— you've probably seen some of my work. Crane Kenning, I do aluminum constructs, I just had a show at the Gerry Hilbin last—"

"Right. Listen, I don't do much aluminum, just steel and iron, I don't know if—"

"I'm sure you can help me, I mean the differences are not that great."

Asshole. "Look, I'm really busy today."

"How about tonight then?" and he talked her finally into a place from which she could not escape without great rudeness; he would be brief, he promised, though sounding somewhat aggrieved that he need promise this at all. Brief and succinct and maybe she could learn something from his methods, too. She hung up angry at herself, clomped downstairs to the street, to another and what called itself a farmer's market but was more like a jumped-up fruit stand; Tess bought two oranges, the luxury of a peach, and stole a handful of cherries when no one was looking, chewed them stones and all as she paid then spit the stones and stems on a straggly stand of weedy grass. The rest she carried home, sat outside just past the party-store door to dissect with her thumb one orange, careful of the juice. Two women started pushing over who would board a bus first. A passing radio advised that temperatures would be a little cooler today, lows tonight in the seventies. Hurray. Her hair was sticking to the back of her neck. She sucked the orange thoroughly, down to chewy rind, the other orange between her knees, the peach beside her on the pavement like the firm and thoughtful heart of a liberated beast. Across the street one teenager yelled "Suck me!" at another; Tess licked her fingers slowly and as slowly went inside.

* * *

Crane was six feet tall and all in black, steel-rimmed glasses with tinted lenses round as the little juice bottles she bought downstairs. He started talking as soon as the door opened and worse yet had not come alone: a woman with him, behind him, hanging a little back in the hall but not shy; waiting. Waiting, Tess saw, for her and not Crane to say it was okay.

"Come on in," she said, and the woman stepped forward, past Crane; not quite as tall as him, not quite as tall as Tess: younger but more muscled, athlete's legs, or dancer's, smooth bare skin like Teflon over steel. Her handshake was very strong but she did not squeeze the way a man might.

"I'm Bibi Bloss," she said.

Foxface bones, pale bright hair and eyes the same: incanescent, less broken glass than the sheer act of breaking. When she smiled Tess saw her teeth were very small, milk teeth, strange childish grin.

"You do all your own welding, don't you?" Crane was looking around the room, moving to the pieces she had pushed in a corner, sculpture forestry about his legs and waist. "This one's kind of interesting," he said, careless hand above the razored ribs of *Mater Intrinsecus,* fierce her crown of sheared bearings and Tess pushed his hand brusquely away.

"That's really sharp," she said. "Listen, why don't you tell me what you need."

"Fine," he said. "I don't even know if you can help me at all. What I need primarily," and Bibi now to where the toilet was, the green wall of the shower, moving as if through a particular silence of which no one but she was aware, "is information. I have a special piece in mind," and off on some weird impossible tangent, he worked with aluminum, he should know better. Maybe he didn't. She tried to explain why there was no doing what he wanted to do but he wasn't listening, he was talking about layers of metal mimicking layers of meaning, talking about metallurgy as metaphor and the intrinsic *barbarism* of iron in such a way that she felt like striking an arc off his steel-rimmed glasses; and looking past him to see Bibi beside another piece, *Dolores Regina* and her fingers loose and deft on half-deliberate spatter, the flat fillet weld, street-light from behind less halo than warning light and chicken-wire shadows on her face like the solemn etching of tattoo. Standing there she was sculpture, strong iron bones and solder muscles, the tilt of her head a construct so subtle that Tess stared, the flat appraising stare of the scrapyard as with the grace of gears meeting Bibi's head turned, to watch Tess watching her.

Crane just noise in the background now and Bibi's gaze calm and calmly thorough, Tess and the room and the sculpture both harbored, everything plain to those eyes. Tess still as metal in her own silence and Crane finishing up, so what did she think? How long would it take to do?

Shaking her head, can't be done and his irritation immediate, "Why not? It seems easy enough to me."

Then go do it, asshole. "Look, all I can tell you is I can't do it. All right?"

"Well, then," a busy man in pursuit of his art, "can you recommend anybody? I have to get—"

From across the room, still in that posture: "Tess. Why haven't I seen your stuff before?"

Glance down, reluctant now to meet those eyes straight on. "I don't show much."

"Why not?" Nodding inclusion, the sculpture, the work-table. "It's brilliant work. Don't you have an agent or anything? Are you represented by a gallery?"

Tess's smile involuntary, and Crane again, excluded and annoyed, "She's showing right now at the Isis," and again Bibi ignored him, or rather accepted the information as if it had dropped like a pearl from the bodiless air: "The Isis? You don't belong there."

"I don't belong anywhere," and wondering as she said it why she had, it sounded so sophomoric, so moronically proud. "I just, I don't really show much."

"Listen," Crane louder, dragging back attention, one hand full of keys impatient, "can you help me or not?"

"No. I can't."

Before his answer, Bibi's smile: "Thanks," as if it had been on her errand they had come. "I'll see you." And gone that moment, out the door and Crane pausing to watch as she did Bibi's silhouette, one long-stepping muscle in tension and his irony, "Well *thanks,*" and graceless down the stairs. Tess watched for a moment longer, to see if she would come back. Nothing. Closing the door, slowly, strange strange eyes and then forgetting it all in the turn and step, back to the workspace and taking up her mask, flipping the grounded switch to start the final burn.

Sleeping in to wake sweaty and muscle-sore; the piece was done. Scrap steel and Lexan, glass and the warped plastic throat, it was better than she had expected though still not where she wanted to be; where was that? who knew? She would know when she got there. Still the piece was good: textures all a-mesh and it almost seemed to move, to twitch when not watched, calm semblance of silence in the moment of attention. Smiling a little to think of it creeping loose around the room, trying the windows, trying the door, peering eyeless to clear its plastic throat; dry in self-mockery: anthropomorphizing; watch it. She knew people, artists, who liked to gurgle about their "babies," their "children": "Every one of my pieces is a child of mine," who had said that to her? Horseshit. Children were children and work was work and people were ass-holes when they started believing their own arty bullshit. They should all work with metal, get burned once in a while: keep them grounded.

In the shower, the last of the soap in her eyes and some-body knocking, not banging but hard, Tess heard it plainly over the water. Determined. *"Shit,"* hissed between her teeth, eyes burning. Loud: "Who is it?"

Indistinct.

"Who *is* it!"

"Bibi Bloss."

Dripping on a T-shirt, the towel around her head, shoot-ing back the dead bolt: "Come on in."

Alone, smile and ripped leggings, slipping off her black sunglasses to hook them in the stretched neck of her T-shirt. "Hi," closing the door. "If this isn't a good time, please say so."

"No, it's okay." Stringy wet bangs, dripping onto her cheekbones. Crane's errand? or her own?

Unerring toward the worktable, she had little feet, Bibi, bony ankles above disintegrating sneakers, she cocked her head like a listening animal and said nothing at all. Exam-ining the new piece for literal minutes, a long time to stand staring but her eyes were busy as a bird's, she left nothing out. Finally: "It's ready to move, isn't it," not a question and Tess nodded, pleased with more than the pleasure of surprise.

Glancing at the metal rack, tools still in last night's or-derly scatter; sun through the chicken wire, endless burn holes and dust. "Tess. Why do you live here?"

Surprised, "It's cheap. Why?"

"I just wondered." There was definitely more to it than

that but no more was coming now. Silence; Bibi's dirty finger on the piece's throat.

"What?" wiping at her wet neck, water in her eyes. She felt no footing here, was unsure what to say until she did. Bibi saw, or seemed to; seemed to understand because she nodded, once and brisk.

"I know; what do I want. Listen, today I made a pilgrimage to that creepy Isis Gallery. —Without Crane, incidentally, who's back at his place with two other guys trying to figure out what you told him last night."

"Doesn't he do his own welding?"

"Crane doesn't know shit about welding. Why else do you think he came to you?" A pause. "I'm glad I came with him."

It sounded rude; she said it anyway. "Why?"

"Because of your work." Full stare, her eyes washed marble light and fingers unconscious on the piece before her. "I wanted to talk to you last night, but not in front of Crane. You must have noticed he's a size-eleven asshole, once he gets started you can't shut him up. And besides, it's none of his business."

"Are you, is he your—"

"I used to live with him, if that's what you're asking. He's part-time in a dance group I'm in—he's a much better dancer than he is a sculptor. Which still isn't saying a whole hell of a lot," and that strange little grin again, dry as the curve of a bone. "No, what's mostly wrong with Crane is that he doesn't have anything I want."

Tess smiled, as much in surprise as discomfort; at least she was honest. "Do I?"

"Yes. I want to see all your stuff."

"Why?"

"Show me," shark's grin, "and I'll tell you."

* * *

She ended up showing everything, all the way back to *Mother of Sorrows,* the oldest piece she still had. Beginner's work, not even good enough to be called crude but Bibi inspected it as she did all the others, attention severe and severely focused, all of her there in her eyes. Hot crouch in the endless turn of the fan, windows empty of any breeze and both of them sweaty, spotted with the floating grime from moving between pieces, moving the pieces themselves. Some were painfully heavy, but Bibi was strong as she looked, and stronger; she held up her end with ease. The afternoon passing in a running catalog of material, place, title, then on to method and juice drunk standing, cookies eaten crumbling from the box. The theory and practice of welding, her own experiences, dreary and not, keno accompaniment a chatter and grind to the rod-tip-in-the-shoe story and Bibi's shut-eyed laugh, really funny.

More talk, Bibi's questions and they were good ones, ancient to modern history now and asking why this place, why not more shows; why the Isis? One dirty hand light on the swollen iron back of *Lay Figure,* its hideous humps like bones distorted, the face one howling O of blackened wire: "And this is one of the pieces you were going to show there?"

"That, and *Delta of Silver,*" nodding to the riverine figure of solder and charred iron bone, melancholy line of shine beneath the overhead fluorescents. Night coming on and this day gone purely in talk, when had she done that last? Past memory, loner weeks and months, plenty to do; still did; always did. But no one to talk about it with since, what? All the way back to Peter? Sweet ugly Peter, last lover, almost-best friend with his found sculpture, plastic milk jugs and detergent bottles, and sidewalk paintings that took him finally where it was warmer, where, he said, the sidewalks stayed dry all year. Two letters, one long awkward phone call, already long gone but she was stubborn, she had to be hurt hard to let go. He ended by obliging her, poor Peter, she had not meant to cause such pain to either of them; he was not a monster, he did not want to wound her so. What would he think of her work now? What would he think of her? Strange to think of Peter, now; she had not in so long.

A sigh, and back all at once to Bibi's quizzical gaze, there was something she should be saying, explaining. The Isis show, right, the pieces they wanted and didn't want. "They only took one," sitting up straighter. "The one you saw, *Archangel.*"

Impossible to read those eyes, washed to nothing but light. "Why didn't you show them all?"

"They didn't want them all." The painstaking slides rejected, half an explanation half a month late but she had not wasted time with anger, she had been through this before. Leaning on the toilet wall, pinch of green plastic against her sweaty back. "You were there, you saw what they show. They don't want stuff like mine, that's not what they're interested in."

The exposed tines of *Lay Figure*'s bones denting the bare skin of Bibi's arm, she did not seem to feel or notice. "What are *you* interested in?"

"Metal."

At once, like a teacher, a cop: "What else?"

"Making it . . . work." Her hand moving in half a circle: frustration's symbol, the answer incomplete. "Making it do what I want."

"What do you want?"

"I don't know," flat and honest, out before she could think or rethink to call it back. "I guess I'll know it when I see it. If I see it."

"You won't. Unless you build it yourself." And trapdoor sudden, little meat-eating grin and "Hey: come on. Come see what I do, now," keys without looking, open door and on the landing to stop: and wait for Tess.

Who stood, waiting herself. "You never said," scarred hand poised on the light switch, the light from the stairway a greasy yellow, cloudy with the tiny blunderings of flies trapped by false eternal daylight, around and around. Downstairs the sounds of big kids yelling, the dumpy thump of a loaded handcart over the uneven threshold.

"Said what?"

Hitting the switch, sudden black and Bibi clear, then shadowed as she moved closer, half-back across the threshold. "What you want." Want to give. Or share. Or take.

Very close in the dark, one hand on the jamb and a smell to Tess like sugar, like sweat, distinct and oddly nameless, your own secret scent found inexplicable on the flesh of another. Her eyes could have been marbles, or bearings, or Lexan chipped cold with scavenged glass, eyes that wait and see in any dark, the eyes of sculpture ready to move when no one watches, ready to crawl and buck and scratch slow paint from the shivering walls like skin from the shrinking lines of tender bone.

"I don't think I need to tell you," Bibi said. Voices up the stairwell, the jitter of empty bottles like tumbling coins, somebody's curse and her closeness, close enough to touch, her stare to Tess as vivid as taste in the mouth. "I really think you already know."

Rivertown, the area fancifully named, warehouses mostly empty and the real estate cheaper than almost anywhere; too intrinsically shabby to gentrify, scored forever like burned skin with industry's effluvial and ghostly stink.

Streets not like caverns but the bottom of cans, trash cans, looking up into rust and darkness and the soundless progress of decay.

Now before them, GRANT CHEMICAL in heavy red caps, BLDG 2 in shy green, a stenciled afterthought. Prison-bright lights, high noon at night; there were two cars there already and one rusty black scooter, so heavily chained it seemed at first to be scrap. Inside the sound of heavy blowers, and beneath that the shrill of a radio turned up far past its capacity for clear sound.

Following Bibi toward the noise, Tess looking around at the huge cardboard drums, the heavy labeled sacks. "They let you use this place for free or what?"

"Yeah, they want somebody here at night," turning left past a glassed-in foreman's booth, NO ADMITTANCE on the door. Jumble of clean-up tools in a corner, fat mops and raveling cloth pushbrooms like the wigs on old-fashioned clowns. "They think if we're here no one will break in and rip them off. Besides they don't use all the space anyway."

The radio louder, more space between the cardboard drums, waist-high pyramids of sacks and a few of them ripped to spread fine bluish grit like beach sand across the floor. Scent in the air like warm bleach. "What kind of chemicals are they?"

"Soap. Industrial detergents and cleansers, stuff like that—I checked. Believe me, I checked. They have another building, it's a lot bigger but the stuff they keep there can give you cancer just looking at it." One more turn and now the music was very loud, the space empty; two women in sleeveless T-shirts and spandex shorts sharing water from a bicycle bottle, a bare-chested man in a blue bandanna perched on a hi-lo. "Hey, baby," the man said, sliding upright from his seat to come nodding to Bibi; on his chest a black tattoo as stylized as an Aztec glyph;

one of the women was tattooed as well, fat black bull's-eye circles on her left biceps. The man came to Bibi, kissed her cheek. "I thought this was a closed rehearsal."

"This is Tess Bajac," Bibi said, an unsmiling gravity that stilled them: may I present the queen; it startled Tess. "Tess, this is Sandrine, and Raelynne, and Paul. They're the only decent dancers in the troupe."

"Troupe, shit," said the shorter woman: Raelynne. Sandy hair, pure frizz in a ponytail; her accent was all Tennessee. Both ears lined with little rings, slim and shiny as needles in the garish overhead light; the other woman had one ear multiply pierced. "'S more like a dance club for people who can't dance."

"It's a mutual masturbation society," Paul now. "For jerkoffs." Rubbing Bibi's neck, the hard muscles of her shoulders, his stare as much as his touch said Hands off. Bibi did not seem to fully notice he was there, turned to Sandrine—dyed red hair chopped chin-length, ragged T-shirt reading GENITAL COMBAT in scissored sans serif— saying, "Flip that," and to Tess, "You watch, okay?"

"You can sit over there if you want," Raelynne nodding helpfully toward the hi-lo. "It's not really clean, but at least the seat's padded."

The plastic beneath her still warm from Paul, Tess settled to watch their formation, Raelynne's swagger, Paul's humorless grace; he was very beautiful, Paul, maybe he was Bibi's lover. Sandrine changing the tape and now the music began, a spare rhythm, simple drum beat slow but somehow unsettling, a moment's close listening to discern why: deliberately uneven, it ran 3/4 then skipped, a stuttering but no pattern even in that. Bibi in front, the others scattered triangular around her, all four heads down, arms hanging bonelessly loose. Tess saw a muscle moving in Bibi's thigh, was she consciously keeping time and how

could she, there was no time to keep. And a keening, for a
startled moment she thought it was coming from the tape
but no, it was them, all three of the women in the same
painful note, only Paul silent and then it was Bibi moving
forward, still keening, still bent and now crouching, half
her body frozen like a stroke patient, like a corpse, the
other women swaying silent on their feet, arms like wind-
cracked branches and Paul crablike, mouth open in
Kabuki grimace as he crept sideways to Bibi, still in her
terrible stasis, still keening like the warning of disaster un-
avoidable and then as Paul's outstretched arm reached the
barest periphery of her skin, the flat landscape of her belly,
she struck him, not in pantomime, not with an actor's false
violence but truly hit him hard, Tess wincing instinctively at
the dull meaty sound. Struck him on his tattoo and again,
still that keening but louder, air-raid whine joined now by
the other women mimicking the circular sound of the
drums, off kilter, off balance, almost pain in the ears and it
grew louder, louder, Bibi striking again and again, full
punches, *uh, uh,* little whuffing grunts of effort, she was
putting everything into it, *uh uh uh* and all the rhythms
increased at once, the keening grown to screams and the
sound of Paul being beaten and the hideous boneless sway
of the women's arms, *uh uh uh* and Paul's body jerking,
now, like electroshock, the hooked-fish leap of a cardiac
jumpstart and Bibi's face contorted, spit in the corners of
her mouth and *uh uh uh* and from Paul a horrifying sound,
a cry as primal as that of a murdered baby, it took Tess by
terrible surprise and she found herself half on her feet,
one hand pushing instinctive on the hi-lo's greasy skin to
launch herself to the rescue and the *uh uh uh* become the
sound of the drums and the wave of the women's arms like
the undersea sway of drowning grasses and Paul's cry, cry,
Bibi's relentless battering arm and Paul fell to his knees

and then onto his face, Bibi striking now at his head, his
back, the two women beside her, the movement of their
arms mingling with hers, fearful grace and ferocity and the
cry again from Paul, but much muted, as if the infant was
now dying, dying under the savagery of Bibi's beating and
she struck a tremendous blow to the back of his neck, as if
she would decapitate him by sheer force; his body bucked
once and then the cry tiny as a tear, informed with a nauseating gelatinous undercurrent as if the infant had finally
strangled on its own blood. The keening dwindled to a
hum, a whistle, stopped entirely. The women's arms
stopped moving, lay like the empty skins of snakes across
Bibi's torso, her shoulders and breasts moving strongly,
hungry for air. The drums leapt into a dreadful sprightly
beat, almost a march beat, and then abruptly stopped.

Silence. Bibi's fierce breathing.

And then everyone relaxed, Paul pushing up, seemingly
unhurt but groaning, a little, Sandrine bending to help him
stand upright. Bibi took one last big breath, let it out, and
then turned expectantly to Tess.

"Well?"

Raelynne in pirouette—"I can tell it's good, our director
would've *hated* it"—and to Paul Tess said, "How in God's
name did you make that sound?" to the brief endlessness
of his silence, deliberately turning his back and Bibi's nar-
rowing stare: "Oh, Paul can do all kinds of stuff, he used to
be an actor."

Paul's body tightening as if being beaten again, this time
with weapons more shameful and Bibi, loud cruel cheer,
"Yeah, Paul used to do dinner theater, *Kiss Me Kate* reviv-
als. *The Music Man.* Didn't you, Paul?" and then swiveling
in dismissal, back to the others who stood passing the water bottle: their fast dancer's argot meant nothing to Tess
who instead was watching Paul, very busy now by the tape

player; rewind, fastforward, rewind, useless busywork so he would not have to turn around.

Bibi clapping, "Okay, okay, listen you guys, once more," and, incredibly, again: the same keening, beating, the same hideous infant-cry but this time Tess held herself on the outskirts of drama, watched each, component and individual: Raelynne's back muscles taut as pulleys, Sandrine's thin lips twisted crooked in a snarl unconscious, the deliberate closed-eyed concentration of the slack and beaten Paul. And Bibi, more dervish than ever, eyes so wide and white all around, the enormous energy of each action, the perfect structural economy, her moving body precise and precisely there in each motion as the picture lies entire in each splinter of a sundered hologram. At this ending Tess applauded instantly and hard, Bibi's little chorine highkick and bouncing to a stop before her: "You want to go get a drink with us?"

"Are you—is it over?"

"For tonight, yeah." Wiping her sweaty face with the hem of her T-shirt, hair stuck straight up in corona above her wet forehead as if even at rest she continued to move. "Hey," louder, "you guys coming?"

"Bar H?" and at Bibi's nod Raelynne nodded back, yeah, she was coming. "Gotta go easy though," sitting to pull on her shoes, unraveling hightops that had once been red. "I have to work tomorrow."

Sandrine off to meet her boyfriend and Paul said nothing, gathering up tapes and tape player, pulling on a black mesh muscle shirt that enhanced rather than hid his tattoo. All at once fast toward the exit, Raelynne calling out to him but Bibi raised a warding hand, shook her head.

"Leave him," she said. "If he wants to be an asshole let him go. He'll probably show up there later anyway," and they were walking past bags and the dry scatter of soap,

crashbar bang and outside the day's heat gone at last into
night's fetid humidity, street moist and Bibi had to open
the car door for her, battered blue subcompact with the
passenger side bashed in. Tess watched her drive, greased
bearing roll of her ankles, the way she toed the brake.
Looking up to the slam of physics, forward and back
abrupt against the seat and Bibi saying, "Here we are."

BAR HERNANDEZ in ice blue, graffitied brick and the whole
building smaller than the cleared area in which they had
danced: twenty tables, dry smoke and scuffed linoleum a
bare square yard for jukebox dancing. Raelynne instantly
feeding change and Bibi at the bar, asking in pantomime
What do you want?

"Any beer," and finding miraculous a table, man and
woman bickering their way to the door, spilled drink and
one soggy lime wedge speared on a tiny red plastic pirate's
sword. Bibi back, one beer, one shot of sour mash, one
clear lime-wedged glass: Tess guessing vodka, Bibi shaking
her head.

"Tonic water," and Raelynne's solemn drawl, "That's a
fact. She doesn't need no mood-altering substances 'cause
she *is* one."

"Fuck that altered-mood shit. I have a good enough
time on my own," and nodding toward the door, "See?
Didn't I tell you?": a dispirited Paul, yelling his order as
one of Raelynne's selections came on and she out of her
seat at once, dancing alone on the dirty linoleum. Bibi
took a drink, Paul forgotten, and said, "Well? What did
you think of us?"

"I liked it." The beer strangely sweet in her mouth. "I
don't really know enough about dance to—what?" to
Bibi's vigorous headshake, bright eyes rolling, no no no.

"Don't give me that. You have eyes. Tell me what you
saw."

"I—all right. All right," and what had she seen? Not even grace, first, but action, motion, the pure violence of a body through space subsuming the lesser, more showy violence of the beating, the aural violence of the keening and the shrieks and the tempoless drum, the whole not even testament but document, one moment enacted with rigor and pain. And Bibi's judicial nod, so.

"Have you ever heard," big pale eyes bright, bubbles in her drink in tiny upward formation, minuscule spheres like drops of blown glass, "of kinetic theory? Kinetic theory states that the particles of all matter are in constant motion. *All matter.* Did you know that the origin of the word *kinetic* is *kinētikos,* Greek for 'putting in motion'? Did you know that when I was ten years old I wanted to be a ballet dancer, but the skin of my toes wouldn't harden, it was constantly bleeding, and my father said no more lessons? And I heard him, and I sat down on the back steps with a kitchen knife and cut off the tip of my right big toe and I carried it back inside and threw it on his dinner plate, right when he was eating and I said if he cut off my lessons I would cut off my toes. One by one."

For a moment Tess was silent, knuckles light against her lips as if to silence spoken thought, Bibi half-smiling as though at a pleasant memory. "Well?" and irrepressible, strange dry smile welling up, "then what happened?"

"Nothing. He kept on paying for the lessons. I didn't really have an aptitude for ballet, though; I quit the next year. —What's so funny?"

"Nothing," shaking her head; picturing Bibi, bloody blackmail knife in one hand, knob of flesh in the other. Quitting ballet the next year. "Then what?"

Then modern dance, "whatever that is," two years of it before a move to Seattle with friends of the family—"it was beautiful there, but I got really tired of the rain"—and a long time spent in the South, New Orleans, Nashville, slowly moving upward like mercury in the heat. Dancing, always, or performing in some way: "I used to do street theater, like acting out people's poems at art fairs, or just improv, playing off what people were doing or saying." Guerrilla theater for a while, but that proved too harsh for too little return: "People used to *stone* us, can you believe it? And plus most of the stuff we did was shitty, just rants, how can you perform a rant?" North again, living with a loose shifting partnership of friends and sometimes-lovers, a particle in random motion and now, for the past two years, here. In a loft for a while with Crane, who had swiftly become very boring—"Do you know what it's like to live with someone who uses himself as his only frame of reference? All the time? Plus he can't cook"—and dancing now with this larger troupe for rent and gas money while time-off rehearsing with Paul and Sandrine and Raelynne.

Who plopped down, legs stretched sweaty and "Whoo! You'd think I'd get enough dancing, wouldn't you, with the Marquis of Queensberry here? Shit, I got to get another drink," pushing as if to rise and Bibi motioning her back, "Same again?" and Raelynne nodded; Bibi out of earshot and Raelynne turning at once to Tess: "You smoke?"

"No," and Raelynne sighing, "Shit. I love to smoke, but Bibi throws a fit when I do, says it cuts my wind. Which it does. Smart bitch," with obvious affection, sipping a little of Bibi's tonic water. "She's really something, isn't she? Have you known her for long?"

"We met yesterday."

Raelynne's pleased nod, a notion confirmed. "I thought she was showin' off a little tonight. Must be for you," and waving a finger, no no to Tess's protests, she doesn't chew that much ass usually, "especially not on a night this hot. Shit, I'm from Tennessee and even I can't stand it," and

Bibi back again, Jack Daniel's and water and another beer for Tess who was beginning to feel the first and Bibi telling Raelynne about Tess's sculpture, saying they ought to have a show around it and a thought in Tess's head, inarticulate, trying to swim for it through the twisty maze of beer and heat and no dinner, saying something half-aloud and Bibi's voice, "—incredible textures. You ought to go down to the Isis, see her piece there. Actually you ought to go to her place, she lives in a rathole, too," showing those little teeth, "all this sculpture crammed into a tiny little space like half your place, Rae."

"She can have my place," drinking down her drink. "I'm movin' next week, I can't stand those dogs anymore, yap yap yap all the time."

The idea in motion, eluding her still: something about Bibi, the image of her violence, swath of metal like the endless edge of a knife. Posturing steel, the notion of her last piece in secret dance: something there. What? With it under her hands she could tell, or grow at least closer to the knowing.

"Listen, excuse me," pushing away from the table, "I have to get back. No, no," as Bibi rose, "you stay, I'll just grab the bus or something."

"Buses've already quit running." Keys out, moving through the puzzle of tables, past the bar and Tess watched Paul's head turn, tracking, staring at Bibi with a look so bare she felt shamed in the seeing; Bibi did not see, was already pushing outside. A rain as fine as pure humidity, distilled on cars and skin and the sullen lights so dim the insects would not dance in their weak lumination. Dancing insects, Bibi dancing. The sculpture in motion. What?

Speaking only in directions, eyes inward in the timed swipe of the wipers and they reached her place more quickly than she knew; still thinking hard when Bibi hit the brake, swerved to the curb beside a rusted black Jeep with peeling Oi! decals and the motor running. Stinky gray smoke, the store's double door pushed open and two teenagers on the threshold kissing in the drift of the rain. Bibi's strong hand forcing the broken door.

Tess through the window, half-apology and Bibi shaking her head, forget it. "Just let me see it when it's done," and smiling. And gone. Up the stairs double time, banging the door behind her and she worked till morning, till noon, burning, burning, Grace downstairs screaming up about the smoke, you can smell it in the *cooler* for fuck's sake *Tess!* Big new burn on her right arm, close to the old scars, hair clubbed back in a filthy knot and the heat monstrous under the mask, breathing her own sweat like some rare vapor. The new piece disassembled before her, plastic throat slashed vertical to her surgeon's fire, inserting in the running melt the corkscrewed filigree of metal strips as falsely bright as chrome. She left the throat hinged open, worked next on the Lexan eyes to ladder them blind with the broken brown glass of an empty beer quart stolen weeks before from downstairs. Now the arms. Steel sharp against the scarred palms of her gloves, the fleshy reek of burned plastic beneath pale gray smoke like the breath of ghosts, the rod in her hand burning, burning, white at the core like the beating heart of a star. The arms twisting under her assault, *running,* running *metal,* one drop on her boot burning into the leather, round black instant scar. So hot. Light-headed, sick-hungry; keep going. Keep going.

When she was done the piece stood spraddled, rough hard bubbles of spatter from her hurried weld, flayed throat and sightless eyes, rusty steel arms rich with a menace not before possessed, not only suggestion but the active threat of motion, not only motion but violence black and pure and ultimately irresistible in its surety. Pulling off her gloves one finger at a time, slumped hard against the worktable and too tired to shower or even think of eating, too tired finally to do anything but sleep, stretched out on the couchbed, burns and boots unlaced and dry eyes closed at once to small and instant dream as outside an afternoon storm formed and broke, heavy rain on chicken wire puddling tiny on the floor amidst the other shines and slicks, the smell of wet wood and captured mist suspended ephemeral in the empty air.

Sandrine had a pierced nipple and eight holes in her right ear and was more than happy to show them all to Tess. Cross-legged on the couchbed beside her, Bibi guiding Raelynne quiet among the pieces, Sandrine smelled like cigarette smoke, like hair mousse and damp perfume. The three of them had appeared, black cotton and beer and heavy cream pastries making grease spots on the bag, Raelynne hollering up the stairs with a voice bred to summon the Valkyries: *"Hey Tess! You home?"*

Tess awake less than an hour, pop-pop-pop outside her window, something sharp as firecrackers or gunshots, the rimshot of a car. Shaking in the shower, hands unsteady on the soap; too long this time without eating. Hurried downstairs and out to avoid Grace, found the first kiosk still open to eat hugely, big sloppy fried-pepper sandwich and two bottles of soda, hurrying back and Grace's big-haired daughter like statuary in the wait: "My mother says," long red claw fingernails around the helpless shaft of a broom, "that you're a fucking fire hazard. Hear me? You're gonna burn the whole *store* down, we're gonna wake up and the whole fucking building'll—" Closing the door, taste of peppers under her tongue, in her nose like some folk medicine.

Now, half-empty quart bottle of Kicker beer by San-

drine's bare ankle, matte pink nail polish and red hair
pulled back to show each golden trinket bobbing in explanation: "This is an ankh, that's Egyptian for life, the life
force. This is a cross and anchor, that's for faith and hope.
My sister got it for me, she's like a Catholic or something.
This is a heart, for love, and this is a heart with my birthstone, opal, which is the moonstone. Tides, and all that,"
and so on, each piece had its own tiny history, its signifi-
cance, sweet as charms on a charm bracelet. The nipple
piercing was a delicate gold ring, a banded snake eating its
tail. "That's for eternity," and Raelynne plopping down
beside them, contradicting, the figure-eight is for eternity
you dumbass, that's just a snake. Sandrine flicking the ring,
pierced where the nipple joined the areola, her nipple
quickly coming erect. "See?" she said. "It's pretty, isn't
it?"

"Ouroboros," Bibi still beside the new piece; distracted
look, her fingers cautious and sure on the split throat.
"That's what that snake is called."

Sandrine drank beer, pulled down her shirt; this one
said LIEDERNACHT above a graphic of a cave. Raelynne
lifted her mop of frizz to show her earrings, "Mine don't
mean anything, they're just rings. I once had my nostril
pierced, but I let it go." Drinking some of Sandrine's beer,
leaning back against the couchbed. "I used to go with this
guy who had an ampallang, that's like a pierced cock, you
know, a little bar through the head on either side? And
once when I was giving him head, I felt this pain, right? In
my mouth? And I felt around in there and sure enough,
one of my teeth was cracked right in two! On the ampallang!" Her clumsy crowns, big horse mouth opened wide
in a big dry smile, isn't that something. "Hey," nudging
Tess with the bottle's neck, glass sweat on her upper arm.
"Hey, I like your stuff. It's real raw."

"Thanks," and Sandrine shrugging, no offense but she wasn't into sculpture, she didn't *resonate* with anything static, anything that didn't move.

"But that's what Tess wants." Bibi and the new piece, the new improved piece in its agony of near motion. Chicken-wire light; the oracle who speaks your dreams speaking now in daylight just to you. "She wants them to move."

Tess, very still.

Sandrine and Raelynne, talking around her, before her suddenly Bibi looking down into her face. Not speaking; her own mouth a little open, as if she would break the silence herself; but did not.

She wants them

Sandrine's laugh unexpected and unexpectedly high, shrill as a little girl's.

to move.

"Well," Raelynne's rising bounce, her weight gone from beside Tess and "Are we goin' or not?" Hands on her knees, unfocused eyes staring and suddenly Tess looking up to see all of them looking at her. Go where? They had probably already said, maybe more than once. "Sure," off the couch and burned arm newly smarting in the motion, gaze at once to the worktable: the black primary shapes of tools, solder loops, bolt cutters and tinsnips and crack-handled chipping hammer in a scattered rebus telling more than she could read. For now. Tonight. "I'm ready."

On the stairs, Sandrine's deft clatter and Raelynne's howl, "Hey, they got keno machines!" skittering inside the store to Tess's glimpse, Grace and her daughter. Talking. Bibi touched her upper arm, very lightly. Her fingers were hot, and she said nothing at all.

* * *

The club was called Infexion; Tess remembered it as the Eldredge Theatre, she had gone there a few times to see thrash bands. Now the seats had been eliminated in favor of an endless dance floor, endlessly tight: the beer was cheap, the lights the hectic flash of Xenon; on the walls industrial signs in red and black: CHEMICAL: GOGGLES RE-QUIRED. DANGER: ACID. DANGER: DO NOT WATCH THE ARC; that one made her smile. Raelynne and Sandrine danced every song, flying hair and long-muscled legs; Bibi at the table drank ice water and said very little. Tess said less, watching the dancers, thinking of the rhythm inherent in metal, in corroding iron, in the slick long limbs of steel. Could it be found? Could she find it? She had heard of the performing machines, the war machines of Survival Research Labora-tories, the *ballet mécanique* of Denmark, Duchamp's bach-elor machines, the robot terrorists of Hunter-Graves. Branches of mastery, hints and feints and driving piston hearts, the drip of machine oil, the stutter of living flesh mechanically enabled; what she wanted—what did she want? Machines that were not robots, moving sculpture that did not mimic the organic but played, somehow, both with and off that distanceless dichotomy, the insolvable equation of steel screws and aching flesh, that wanted peo-ple not only as operators but as co-conspirators. See those dancers now, and imagine them locked in ballerina combat with the grip and clench of metal, the sweet smoke of rosin solder like incense around their dripping faces, imagine them lit with a hundred strobes and the subsonic growl of bass-heavy music like the throb of an engine running hot, burning hot, burning like the white heart of the arc.

Burning. All of it burning.

The music now a fast pop babble, she realized Bibi was talking to someone, someone sitting at their table. A man, head shaved austere and long earlobes with eighth-of-an-inch grommets glowing gold around the empty space, his front teeth missing in a surprising childish smile. Bibi saw her looking, smiled a very little but did not include her by introduction, spoke only to the man in a slangy slur of names and times Tess did not recognize or place. Her beer gone flat before her, pale gold between locked fingers; the moving dancers like a hot and living frieze before her eyes.

And coming home, she and Bibi, to find her door broken open, its obvious gape seen from the bottom of the stairs and she scrambled, half-falling, to the landing, slammed inside; a moment's dumbstruck terror—robbed —but no, pushing past her ludicrous stall Bibi found a note spiked hard to the couchbed: evicted. And now she saw the tools jumbled in cardboard boxes, FRITO-LAY and SUNBELT JUICE, saw her three-suiter wardrobe balled like a bedroll and set conspicuously by the door.

Bibi read the note out loud. " 'Tess. This is not a factory it is a store. I am charging you for all the burn holes.' —What a *cunt.* Let's see her charge you for a fucking thing."

Tess, still frozen, all ideas quivering now, now with no place to work. No place to go. She went to her worktable, tried sorting through, moving the tools through her hands as if their familiar heft might slow her moving mind, too fast to sort ideas, one question only like a mantra, where where where. And Bibi, drawer by drawer, pulling empty the green metal rack, looping the cables into tight circles.

"One of Crane's friends has a truck," she said.

For a minute this meant absolutely nothing, as if Bibi had begun to speak backward; then it made some sense but not enough. "Bibi," louder than she meant, "I have nowhere to *take* this shit, I don't—"

"Raelynne's already moving." Hands balancing two rolls

of solder, acid flux and a Grainger's catalog thick as a phone book. "She can just move a little faster."

Big windows, long and thin like an old-fashioned church; they opened with cranks, cool air higher than before, third floor in this warehouse half-restored and then abandoned. Room, ventilation, wired to handle what she needed; there was even a service elevator. One of the downstairs dogs in the doorway, black-spattered beige and cocked ears and a woman calling, "Cocoa! Cocoa, come down here now! Cocoa, *now!*"

The dog ignored her. Bibi silent in the window, Tess pacing out the floor space, pacing one way twice, confused: she had not slept, sat out the night guarding her broken door. Coffee, more coffee, wordless and knowing she could not afford Raelynne's place; but that could not matter, she would have to hire herself out, let the new ideas burn internally; not good, but no help for it. Bibi, helping her pack, working until near dawn, when she left for Crane's; Tess could not question this help, did not in brutal fact have time. Grace had come up with the sun to ask when she would be gone.

"Tonight," in flat bravado, slamming the unlockable door in her face. Her stomach hot and burning, thinking, thinking.

Now the woman at the door, "Cocoa, you bad girl. I'm sorry," leash in hand, another puppy under her arm. Her sweat shirt read I'M OWNED BY A with a dog's head, breed indeterminate, wash-faded and huge beneath. She took the dog away. Less than a dozen of Raelynne's boxes still building-block scattered, Tess's reflection exponential in Raelynne's left-behind mirrors, cranking wide the windows to the sonata of barking dogs.

The first few days were transformation, dance studio to

workspace, it was not so hard; she used the ballet barre to hang scrap pipe; she tried not to think what she must sell to keep this place. Bibi stopped by, once, twice, perched still while Tess ran cables, hung lights, positioned panels; sere and brief in her conversation, apparently the troupe had become intolerable.

"Some director," chewing at her lip, sharp little teeth. Head wrapped in black like a mourning mother. "He's just a drug addict, he's hardly ever there anymore and when he is he's so fucked up he can barely watch the show. We had a big fight about it. Again." Silence. "I want to break away; it's time." More silence. One leg swinging back and forth, tight metronomic motion. "And I'm taking those guys with me."

Nailgun in hand, sunlight in long rows across the concrete. A curious resin smell here, as if the space had recently been used to store wood. "Who?"

"Rae and Sandrine. And Paul. And you."

"What?" Gracelessly loud, pivoting gun in hand to stare at her; saying it again, what?

"I want you to come with us." Crossing to the worktable, one hand in a stop-sign gesture: "Wait, I know, I know what you're going to say. But see, it doesn't matter if you're not a dancer. I don't want to just dance anymore, it's a dead end. It's empty," fists opened to show nothing but the retreat of clenched blood. "I'm sick of being empty, Tess. I want to do my own work, and I want us to work together. As partners."

Confused, gazing down like a child abashed, the nailgun hanging from her hand like a bizarre prosthetic. On some dry level unsurprised, there was buildup aplenty and the offer made sense: Bibi's drive was surely her own, ambition expressed through another medium like blood through a sister vein. But Tess had never worked with anyone else, distrusting collaboration, suspicious of the inherent sublimation. In theory, two wills worked unto symbiosis, creating a third independent; but what if both wills were very strong?

Gray marble eyes staring at her, a muscle jittering slow a tempo in the length of that long thigh. Ambulance noises through the window, the endless barking reminiscent of the keno machines. Bibi, waiting for an answer; Tess knew she would not ask more than once.

Two strong wills.

The sensation of motion. Bibi juggernaut, that colliding body; and steel: what collision might it make?

"Okay," and Bibi's widest smile, bright feral teeth and hugging Tess one-armed, "I knew it, I *knew* it! I saw your face, I saw the way you were in the bar. You had the idea then, didn't you," not a question and Tess gave no answer, shrugging with the gun, smiling in tandem with Bibi's exhilaration, already plans, plans. "We'll start today, tonight —I'll call you," and gone, and Tess, smiling, not sorry but curiously regretful, raising up the nailgun, hollow thump into the framing wood of her new worktable, nails counterpoint and the stately movement of the sun across the floor, gentle as flowing water, slow as flowing blood.

Partnership: Tess had not known it would mean Bibi moving in, but: two months' rent already paid, gripbag and toothy smile. Boxes, the long splintery bed, heavy black garbage sacks trussed full of clothes, piles of magazines and books like blocks to build a city of their own. Tess had not had a roommate since Peter, but that was different, they had been lovers. Now half the living area was partitioned off, for now with crude cardboard walls that Bibi herself did not strictly respect, moving quick and silent in the mornings past Tess on her couchbed, the shower's blurry sound the static border between sleep and consciousness, head still heavy with dreams of the night before, their talk, plans like scaffolding blended with the images they aroused: Bibi a long fierce spider, made of metal and moist rag, herself crouched on some swaying catwalk, blackbox in hand and some demanding vision etched just beyond waking memory's reach. They talked late, sketching, planning, no idea too complicated or grotesque: "It's all seeds," Bibi's nod, "just seeds, we'll see what grows." We. It was *fun*, talking to Bibi, planning; there was no one like her: a pair of eyes, a hungry little mouth that kept saying More, more.

Still much to adjust to: Bibi's dawn returns from one of her endless forays, dance clubs and street theater, under the underground and bright eyes, whispered reports to half-wakened Tess, too much fun to hold till morning. Bibi on the phone for an hour at a time: to Sandrine, Raelynne. To the ex-director, yelling so loud it spooked the dogs below to whining. To Paul, who came without warning, "just stopping by" each time, dour and silent, Bibi's barkless dog. Listening to them fuck behind cardboard; listening to them argue, Bibi quick, so very quick to plant the knife, Paul's exit always with a virulent slam of the door. It was not always fun, after all.

But, again: Bibi silent as Tess struggled, never intrusive, never disrupting either Tess's schedules or her frustration when the work went poorly; which was often, this new discipline so clumsy in her hands she must learn everything all over again, even the things she took for granted. Modification was more than this here, and this here, and this gone altogether; it was an art in itself, demanding a new eye: scrapyard scrounge was, here as well, the first step, but she had to be able to see motion as well as line, inherent and possible. Sometimes in frustration she paced, worktable to her makeshift metal rack, again and again

through the manuals that could no longer help her, study-
ing the new books designed for disciplines she did not
need; sometimes sat staring at the pieces scattered before
her as if by sheer rage she would force assembly. And the
muscular spectacle of Bibi, silently stretching, bending,
long legs in positions asymmetrical, seemingly arranged to
rack bones from flesh, they had horrified Tess when she
first saw them but now she saw them differently, as sculpture, a template of sorts for her machines; or, as now,
curled into that peculiar graceful C-shape—fetus-bent,
wrapped arms and legs bound each to the other by hooking ankles—an insect mummified in silk, she could sit like
that for hours, Tess called it hedgehogging—keeping others away with a peremptory "No: Tess is working."

Still curled, glancing at Tess, "Trouble?" and Tess's instant litany, hands on the worktable as if she would push it
like Titan through the floor: she had no idea what she was
doing, she was fumbling like a tyro, she was making it up
as she went along.

"Did you want it to be easy?"

"No. I just want it to *work.*" Glaring down at the small
elementary being, thin cable ligature and drops of oily
blood. "It doesn't even walk like a person. *When* it walks.
Which is never." Glancing back at her sculpture, rowed
now before the windows, wry notion of informing *them*
with motion, at least they were already built. At least
they—

and silent, staring, Bibi saying something but she ignored it, rising to touch the sculptures, feel them roughly
up and down like a soldier or an athlete, do you have the
blood? Do you? Hands scraped and pinked by their varied
surfaces, blind-eyed to see them covered in the white arc
of flying sparks, ranked onstage in full dark and the dancers, Bibi, between them, roped claustrophobic with cable

and chain, struggling, struggling, Tess behind spraying that continuous fire in the air. And the small human figure, not made to walk, not made to do anything but what it already did, jerk. And twitter. And spasm. Lit from above like the last live human caught by God's wandering eye.

And Bibi, beside her, "What? What?" and grinning, little teeth in bare excitement. "What?" and Tess turning, her own smile—she felt it—long and sharp across her face like electricity itself, archangel in motion with the message of constant light.

Dressed in metal, faked from beer cans and duct tape, Raelynne making Tin Woodman jokes as she wrapped her feet with Ace bandages and long swaths of pewter-colored cotton, her head in a black turban; they all wore turbans, Raelynne, and Paul, and Sandrine. And Crane. And Bibi, ribbons of black and silver like the skin-scraps of a flayed machine, gray gauntlets of webbed plastic and a neckpiece of splintered boring bits, all eyes penciled heavy black like a traveler from the land of the dead. Tess herself wore black from head to toe, hot in tight cotton, hair braided back and tucked into her collar; hair shirt. Her hands were sweating on the pinpoint tip of the button mike: her job to start the show.

Naïveté, maybe, but she had expected the whole process to take longer, grow more slowly from idea to expression. But Bibi was in a hurry, Bibi kept pressing: wilder ideas of motion, not only web-caught strugglings but acted violence at the hands of the sculpture itself, the bristle of *Mater Intrinsecus,* the paired grotesqueries of *Lay Figure* and *Dolores Regina,* the rusty shark's jaws of *Sister Jane, Mother of Sorrows:* all ragged and roped with heavy black cables at which the dancers would claw and scramble, push and bite; and die, Bibi's character especially beneath the hooded wings of *Archangel* (unsurprisingly unsold and returned from the Isis) bitten to blood-capsule death by its vicious teeth. They had the basic idea in place within hours, Bibi choreographing and Tess sketching placement of the pieces, of herself behind with the white spray of fire, both talking at the same time, gleeful override, look at *this*—no, wait, look at this! Bibi's laugh like an arc itself, sparkle like burning metal; Tess's little metal figure in triumphant lounge across her worktable, limbs in perfect sprawl the way they would be under purest watts of holy light.

"We don't want it too perfect," over her shoulder, sweet breath on her neck. "We want to put all this stuff in place and let shit *burn.*"

Location was Bibi's problem; her angry sigh, "It's the welding part that scares them off, the fucking sissies, they think we're going to burn down their dumb galleries or—"

Galleries; shit. Without real thought, still eyeing the sculpture: "How about here? The place's half-empty anyway."

Bibi's thinking silence, then, "There's plenty of room. And we wouldn't have to truck the sculpture." Punching her shoulder, very lightly. "You're pretty smart, John Henry."

"It's my job."

So: their name in bold black electrical tape on the building's gray-pitted wall: SURGEONS OF THE DEMOLITION and beneath a plastic sheet with day and time, their phone number and suddenly constant messages, what was Surgeons of the Demolition and what was "an instructive series of tableaux"? Xeroxed flyers of a backlit *Archangel* and Bibi's staring eyes nailgunned everywhere, hyping word of mouth in the clubs, at Inflexion and Bar Hernandez, carefully worded teaser for the alternative papers, even the pirate radio station whose all-night DJ Sandrine used to date, everyone's friends recruited to push the word.

Tess sweating at the scrapyard, buying yards of split and dirty cable, "That stuff won't work" and getting it cheaper. Moving the sculpture piece by slow piece down the service elevator, Paul a surly helper, cables strung and restrung with obsessive care. Nerves everywhere, nerves and dust and dead bugs, hurried work and Crane's loud objections to some piece of business, calling it melodrama, calling Bibi a dictator and "You," swinging on Tess crouched sweaty with duct tape fat as a manacle around her wrist, "you're worse, you're Himmler, you're—"

"*You're* the asshole," Bibi's glare, "asshole. And you better find this out now, and that goes for all of you"—voice like a siren over the bass-line roar of the tape and with one hand she slapped it silent—"me and Tess are in charge here. Got that? No democracy. Got it?"

Head down, Tess kept working, loud the sound of the ripping tape and around her the dry quiet of a drawn line.

"Tyranny, huh," Raelynne lacing dance shoes, legs canted in a broken V. "'S cool. Turn the music back on, okay?" and Sandrine coming in late with a bagful of blood pellets, got 'em at the costume shop, man, aren't they great? Look! and a sudden spatter, laughing blood leaking from her mouth and everyone had to try, the floor a stained mosaic and Bibi yelling Leave it, leave it: it looks good that way. Crane in a sulk, refusing to join in the play and Tess saw his gaze on Bibi, did not turn as he turned on her: flat-eyed: her own stare as level and as cold. Go ahead, asshole—and she's right, you *are* an asshole—go ahead. Say something.

His silent pivot, back to the tape machine, and Tess pulled another length of tape, long and slow.

The last rehearsal and sleeping to wake early and alone,

sitting up to crank the windows and let in the end of summer. Did this place get cold in the winters, with its church
windows and concrete floor? She would find out. Would
anyone come to their show tonight? Would things work
the way they were supposed to, would anyone like it? She
would find that out too.

And now: sweating in black, the locked room huge and
hot and ready, the pirate DJ outside keeping some kind of
order while they placed themselves. Tess looked at no one,
dry-mouthed, nervous in a way she had never been before
but yet strangely buoyed, loner finally part of a pack. Hers
the final word through an earbutton speaker mike jury-
rigged from a kid's walkie-talkie set: "Go," and the doors
opened from deliberately overbright light to disorienting
blackness, shapes of people—lots of people, my God, *lots*
of people—moving in, slowly, blinded eyes groping and the
music on, *loud,* the pencil spot hitting the splayed ma-
chine-figure and behind the membrane, yellow vinyl and
Tess started arcing, goggles on, welding a slow burn on
scrap and Raelynne's banshee scream—no one could
scream like Raelynne—as the sputtering firelight found
her, wrapped like a slave and screaming, screaming, the
others steeped in groans and cries like rehearsal but
louder, much louder, crazy, and the second pencil spot on
Bibi, eyes wide like on the flyer, her face seemingly caught
in the snarl of *Archangel*'s teeth.

A girl's shriek, and from Bibi a groan, struggling with
Archangel and Tess kept burning, burning, her view distorted by distance and goggles, someone yelling and it was
hot, behind them, hot in her tight black turban, hot in the
screams and the fountain of fire, the dogs barking now in
faraway alarm and Paul wriggling past her like a snake,
pure bucking torso and he was way too close, sparks on his
bare back, mouth wide in one mad grimace and gone, trail-

ing cable like intestines. Some guy yelling *"Fuck, man!"* and Tess saw Bibi seemingly atop *Archangel,* holding on to the razored wings: slashed plastic gauntlets and the first of the blood pellets running down her arms, strange pudding-black to Tess's shielded gaze.

Louder. Hotter. Welding a rough spattered line, current too high and the line bubbled with wet metal, the smoke getting bad now, this place was not as ventilated as she had hoped or else someone had forgotten to open the windows. People yelling, she could not turn to see what they were so excited about, must be Bibi. Shrieks as loud as the music and Tess found she was shouting, too, wordless in the heat and the noise, Bibi rushing past her in the thirsty dance of fire and she was all blood now, smeared across her clothing, she was blood and Tess was fire: burning.

And someone crying, very close, "Hey! Hey!" over and over and it was some stupid girl right next to her, white T-shirt and open mouth, "Hey!" and Tess shoved her away with one foot sideways in her ass, get *out* of here, what was the flash doing to her eyes? And now, already? the crescendo, she heard the tape turn from the bass-heavy groan to the sounds of explosions, one after the other, louder and louder and the current all the way up, burning, metal wet and slippery as blood and the whole cable-web shaking, the sculptures trembling, what was making it move like that? Turning to look in the scattering sparks and the people in the front were pushing back, pushing the others, it was hard to see how many in the twice-dark and it was Bibi shaking the web, her costume ripped and bloody, howling into the explosion sound and falling backward as if poleaxed, curling onto her side to spew a long gelatinous ribbon of blackest blood like a curling finger at the feet of the crowd.

And then no motion, *perfect,* just the way they had re-

hearsed it: the drop abrupt into stillness. Stillness, and silence, except for the endless soundtrack barking of the
frightened dogs.

And then applause. Over and over, applause.

They could not stop congratulating themselves, yelling
like a winning team in a locker room Did you *see* that and
Shit, man! Tess leaning hard against the wall, a curious
light-headed glee and Bibi beside her, still bloody, her
smile a little too wild.

"How'd you like it?" and Tess laughing, hugging her
one-armed, there were no words for it, it had been the
strangest fun she had ever had. To work like that in front
of people, to have them so close, to be so close to others:
again. Let's do it again.

Talking too loud till too late, all of them still jittery, Bibi
finally waving them gone with her sticky arms, the fake
blood dried now to an unpleasant dirty brown. Into the
shower, and to Tess, impatient in her own sweat and stink,
it seemed she took forever. Stepping out with curious
modesty, wrapping the towel tight and Tess's sudden stare.

Warding Tess off, hand out: "It's okay. Method acting,"
showing teeth but Tess pulled at the towel, turned her left
and right like a mother with a child: on her arms ragged
marks red as burns, big V-shaped gouge bright as a brand
on her neck. Her back one long abrasion the color of raw
bacon.

"You're all cut up. *Bibi,* you're all—"

"I know, I know. Stop yelling," kicking away the towel to
skin into an oversized T-shirt, settling it carefully across
her back. "It's not that bad, anyway. Shit, it's only blood,"
and now her smile was back, but narrow, red as the
scratches running up and down her arms. Tess waited,
wanting to say something, wanting to ask how did it hap-

pen but she knew how it happened, Bibi climbing the sculpture, the sheared edges and the ragged hasp, not all of the blood from pellets, dark and sweet. Bibi was still smiling at her, pale eyes blinkless and bright with some fathomless hilarity that Tess did not, all at once, want to see; in silence turning away, to the shower where she stood in water as cold as she could stand it, stood for a long, long time. When she emerged, Bibi lay in sleep too still to be honest, scratches covered, the gouge hidden behind the innocent white of a fresh bandage. On her back the drying puzzle of bloodstains, seeping through the T-shirt, red to brown like the inevitable slow corrosion of metal to broken rust.

The next show had a title—*In the Service of Motion*—and a date too close, Tess was fighting with a new piece, blunt chassis modification, building not from scratch but someplace further: working simultaneously with and against the function, as if one might engineer a bird to fly backward and upside down. Bibi was gone somewhere with Paul, and Tess was glad; the aftermath of the last show was still a topic unapproachable, it was awkward to know it was still there, like a big bag of shit on the floor that no one will touch, let alone clean up.

Empty scrapyard sack; Bibi had left her car keys. It was so much easier to drive there, much less limiting in her scavenging choices and she needed no limits now; she had to have everything she could carry, could afford. This new way of working was demanding a new way of thinking as well, an expansion, a blending between static and kinetic, between sculpture that did not move, was not meant to move, and machines that were created for nothing but. And it all had to be viewed through the lens of its eventual use, the performance, big loud vortex into which it would be thrown to scratch and batter its own way out; or deeper in. Bibi called it *tanzplagen,* literally "plague dance" though she chose to translate it as "torture dance": "It's not like anything anyone's done before, all that pretentious performance art shit, like Jimmy Castro, or those jerks in Boston with their Projekt Skullpture. Or Antique Chorines, although they can be funny, sometimes."

Tess, amused, "Come on, Bibi, we steal, too," but Bibi's passionate denying headshake, no no no, this was different, different at its heart. Unable to articulate, erupting at last into gestures, nails hooked in the air and "It's where you are when all that other shit runs out, when it leaves you. When it turns out to be too *weak.*"

"I build," slowly, "with the metal there is. I don't demand a new kind of metal for every piece I make."

Now, driving back from the scrapyard, the radio on loud and remembering that talk, remembering Bibi's clawing hands. Thinking of the hole in her neck. Soon the new performance, bigger and better and louder, at least they were agreed on that. Bibi called it hardball evolution; to Tess it was just the expected lengthening of the stick, you always needed a bigger stick. And there was that to it that was just plain fun, the hard-work fun of trying to see just how well you could build, to set your own limits and then surpass them. Her boundaries now were further; she was learning the new way to see.

The service entrance was on the building's west side: easiest to unload straight onto the elevator. Pulling up and almost onto a kid, busy with some kind of tool and he tried to run as soon as he saw her. Out the car window in one swooping jump and she slapped him breathless against the wall with her scrapyard bag, jumbled plastic and metal thumping his meatless belly: "Hey! Hold it—I said *hold* it!" and taking the tool from him: a slim-jim, a jimmy bar.

"You want to break into my place?" Holding the bar in front of his eyes, oh he was young, sixteen or maybe not even that. "I ought to make you eat this, you little shit." An inexpert job, all he had managed to do was scratch the metal jamb. She stuffed the bar into her bag, pushed him backward with one stiff hand; he did not resist her, grimy jeans, bare toes sticking out of ragged Keds, a tangle of bones and dirty hair.

"Out," pointing back to the street, turning her back to him; she was ready for him to jump her but he did nothing, only stood where she had pushed him; watching. Opening the service door just wide enough to back in, in the car and he said, "I'll help you unload, if you want." She did not answer. "I saw the show," he said.

He saw the show. "You did, huh," and his smile, his teeth were terrible. "Why were you trying to break into my house?"

Shrugging, staring down in that adolescent embarrassment as evident as heat. "I just, I wanted to see the stuff again. I wasn't going to take anything."

Tess revved the engine slightly. "Come back tomorrow," she said. "I have to work now."

And he did. Outside the service entrance at the same particular time, a cloudy noon and Jerome, he said his name was Jerome, he would not tell his age. Bright and nervous and tactless, fumbling metal savant who stopped grail-still when he saw Tess's worktable, her books and tools: "All this is *yours?*"

"A friend lives here with me, but the tools and stuff, yeah, they're mine." He was still beside the doorway, shifting foot to foot, those big dirty toes sticking stranded from his sneakers. "Go on, you can look at it if you want. Just don't break anything."

He didn't stay long, that day, left Tess working but he

came back the next day, to touch the tools, to sit silent with the sculpture, touching it, too. On his third visit he met Bibi, who thought he was cute; as soon as he left, "Why don't you use him for the shows? He can help set stuff up or something, run cables."

"Altruist, huh," but Tess had already had the same idea. It would be good to have an assistant other than Crane, or Paul; and Bibi's frown, "At least Paul can dance. That Crane, he better shape up a little bit and I don't mean his fucking pecs that he's so proud of. Know what it was today?" and talking as working, as both turned to their larger tasks, how to make the metal arms clench and twist without breaking, herself a twist of flesh, bent and hedgehog frowning, oblivious as she spoke.

"We are priests," Raelynne's voice amplified, witchy and hoarse, "in the service of motion," and a crash like God's sky opened, the tumbling rush of half-inch bearings down the curve of a makeshift ramp, cataract fall onto a sheet of thin aluminum to scatter haphazard among the audience: twice as many, this time, they filled the room nearly to the doors; ready.

This time it was louder, rattle and thump and the fat blades of an amped-up blower poisonously a-clatter over the bass subsonics, over Raelynne's whoops and Paul's wet growls through a borrowed throat mike, their simulated sex atop a blistered landscape of sheet metal and the others circling like buzzards, masks made hasty of old welding helmets, the twin planes of safety glass, clear and heavy green, slid free to be replaced by thick blinding broadcloth, raveled and black. And Tess again in back, burning, this time working on a piece, right there, through the shriek and clatter, the off-balance pulse of strobes above and the new metal arms mounted high atop a stolen stop-sign pole, grabbing and pulling, fantastically jury-rigged but the people watching did not know, did not suspect just how rigged they were. The sign itself had been stenciled DON'T across its age-blistered face and nailgunnèd to the top of the bearing ramp.

The piece absorbing Tess's attention, burn and spatter and smoke, running her own slippery edge, working hard and looking up only rarely, to see where she was in the show: now Sandrine's butcher-dance, hacking at plastic hands; now the lovers in combat, clumsy gauntlets of corrosive-grade plastic and Paul had knocked Raelynne to the ground, not in the script, and Bibi leaping like a crazy lizard from the top of the bearing ramp, landing with a hideous thump on the sheet metal, eyes wide in the surprise of great injury and a fat bubble of blood bursting red from her mouth and Raelynne rising to be struck from behind, Crane and Sandrine hand-to-hand, Sandrine's tattoo ringed with a shiny gloss to make it sparkle, exotic prosthetic in the flexing flesh.

Tess through the mask, smoke around her head and the panels occluding, it was getting harder and harder to see; Bibi on her knees and crawling in a broken way toward Paul, who was not looking, people yelling and her fingers strangely tight in work gloves, into the burn again, legs braced and somebody crashed into her, her fire hitting plastic and the flare of poison stink, instant and dire: we need air. "Air in here!" and the smatter of glass, somebody else shrieking, Tess struggling back to see Raelynne rise again bloody-mouthed to deliver an enormous suckerpunch to Paul's unprotected belly, doubling him up, striking him again in the moment of his fall. More broken glass. The tape looping back onto itself like the birth cries of giants, the groans of the dinosaurs in their pits and plastic still afire, fumes, Tess dizzy in the shadow of her

own fire and someone hit the crashbars, the doors wide
and people stumbling out, coughing, the entering air feeding the plastic fire and Jerome, suddenly, wide eyes and
extinguisher spray, fat gobbets of foam from atop one of
the sculptures, just to the left of the grabbing arms which
threatened to push him from balance. And the tape still
booming, and the fire out, and the room empty except for
the performers, two of whom were vomiting, Tess light-
headed and sick to the door and arms around her, helping
arms taking her to safety and to air.

"—just stupidity, that's all it is. If they're supposed to be
in *charge,*" a dark pause, "then maybe we ought to rethink
this whole fucking *enterprise.*"

Tess, scrubbing her face for the third time, plastic stink
indelible down her throat: slow turn, water running to a
stop. Listening to Crane, outside on the stairs, Crane who
could not see her: presumably as well the others just up
from the show's debris, and Paul's voice: "I got no problems with them being in charge." A pause. "Either one of
them."

Her hand on the faucet: listen to Sandrine: "—to admit
it, she gets a little crazy sometimes, she's got her own
ideas—"

"We could get *sued.* Has anybody thought of that?"

Raelynne, dry, "No, Crane, only you would think of that.
Who the hell's going to sue us?"

"Who?" His voice swooping, deep registers, the world's
last sane man. "How about the kid who got all cut up?"
What kid? "He's going to need stitches. And that woman,
last time, yelling about being blinded, she—"

Tess, eyes closed in memory: the girl behind the panel;
not blinded, no, but the flash would bring pain worse than
a migraine, endless crying eyes and the cure for that was a

raw potato, cut in two; put it on your eyes and let it sit. She had learned that in the truck shop, too. But that girl didn't know, though, did she?

And Crane still talking, "—Tess's stupid welding torch, what about her? What—"

"What about her, Crane?"

Bibi's voice, so flat even Tess froze, then from behind the green screen to the door to see the four in tableau and Bibi half a landing down. And rising: smoke-smeared, hair fantastic with sweat, black gauntlets shredded to the wrist. Staring.

"What about her?" Closer. "What about *me,* Crane? Are you going to sue me?" Even her voice stalking. "If I threw you down the stairs right now, would you sue me?"

Hands on him now, her fingers flexing hard against the thin slick of his silver vest, the others stepping back; instinct; away. Crane far larger, far heavier, Crane's slitted eyes and no attempt to move, or even move her hands, scratching deeper now, she had torn the fabric, her hands all at once in gripping motion and he was tumbling, abruptly off balance as the others flattened startled to the wall and Bibi aloof above, smiling? And Tess, instant past the door her lunge to grab him back, yank his arm hard to keep his fall contained; something hurting in her back, the stress of his descent arrested.

Everyone staring; everyone silent. And Bibi, breathing through her nose, twin lines like scars deep and sudden in her forehead: "You asshole. Go home."

Crane on his feet, shaking sudden and enraged away from Tess, her guarding arm and down the stairs, not looking back: the ferocious slam of the fire door setting the dogs to yelping. Bibi's arrowed shoulders loosening, just a little, the tiny sound of her breath released.

"Go on," Tess to the others silent around them, "go on

in," and waiting out their motion, Bibi where she was; waiting too. Tess closed the door, then quietly, to her alone: "I saw you hook his leg."

The barking dogs. Bibi shrugged.

"Did you want him to fall?"

Shrug.

"Bibi, answer me. Did you want him to fall?"

Another shrug, a step closer and "Did you see me jump off the ramp?" next to her now, linking arms. "Boom! I thought I broke my foot. Wasn't it cool?" and the smile tempered with something both hideous and sweet, something that made Tess close her fingers about the trusting arm, squeeze it lightly; and for an instant's darkness close her eyes.

Crane was out, back to the old group Raelynne said: "Back to his dumb toe-shoe shit," but Bibi's sneer was more succinct—"He was never what you'd call simpatico" —and also final, as if Crane had ceased existing in the instant of his departure. There was talk about replacing him, mainly from Sandrine and Raelynne, both of whom believed the group needed another male presence: "For balance," Sandrine said. "For balance and to fuck me," Raelynne said, "and to carry the heavy shit, right, Tess?"

Hot-wiring under surgical light, brief distracted nod; Jerome blushing beside her; he was learning not to, learning a lot. Jerome had found the buckets of bearings, had showed Tess where she could acquire a surplus army smoke machine, other toys less obvious, one's greasy guts now delicate before her like an anatomy lesson. Hungry, Jerome, hungry all the time, what does this do? What's this for? How many amps, how sharp, how fast? He found her workspace endlessly enticing: the cardboard cartons of welding rods, menagerie of files, solder pencils, chipping hammers, double-sided filter masks like twin insectile snouts, even the endless sound of the ventilator a flat bassless music, work's own harmonic voice. Living on air, sleeping, when he slept, on a pallet-bed on the disused second floor—the show floor—so he could be close, and need not take the long trudge back to wherever he was squatting these days from his rapt tutelage with Tess.

Who found him more than useful, in many ways, not least a bright protracted shield when she needed it; Bibi's infrequent immersions in Paul, for instance, or now, let them talk to each other, she had work to do. Anyway dance was Bibi's preserve: who, what, how many; though scrupulous, always, to inform Tess of her choices, ask opinion, ask advice and often take it: "You don't think like a performer," Bibi would say. "That's invaluable."

Their talks: Bibi coiled loose on her broken-down bed, sucking tonic water through a red straw, and Tess, legs drawn up and a handful of bent hinges, telling them like rosary beads, one by soundless one. Before even the shows themselves was the intricate fun of this; there was no one like Bibi, no one who could speak so sharply, listen so full. Partner in the best way, right hand and left, each what the other was not. So many ways a joining like this could fail, and they had avoided them all.

So. Tess was content to leave dance to Bibi; if she needed another body she would get one. Meanwhile Jerome would move the sculpture, splice wires, ask a million questions and apparently be satisfied to sleep on splinters for the privilege of working with the Surgeons; already, a reputation.

It was true—renown both antic and frantic, *anything*, said the buzz, could happen at a Surgeons show. How far, in such a short time; once started, the buzz went under its own power, obeyed its own acceleration. Fed by the wet excesses of *Infections and Their Uses,* its slippery near nudity, its buckets of costume-shop blood splashed wild counterpoint to the strangely foodlike odor of smoking rosin solder, by the ominous theatrics of *Hysterica's* mimed balletic cannibalism beneath a swaying frieze of plastic masks made to mimic the dancers, features heat-gunned to distortions too gross for mere caricature, as if those huge twisted faces were the outward manifestation of souls too ugly to contemplate for long: each show brought louder crowds, larger crowds, word of mouth urged by more and less than truth, rumor running like too much current until *Slave to the Burn,* where for the first time they had to turn people away, had to pay with beer two steroid cases to hang on the crashbars until the show was ready to begin. Even Bibi's ambitions had not prepared them for this.

Nervous in a new way, cold outside but the room already too hot and half-whispered curses and quick bickerings as if unwilling to be overheard by those they heard outside: in the hall, against the door, their susurrations endless as a cage of moving snakes: skin against skin. Bibi reminding everyone for the tenth time that this one was pure chaos, they're crazy out there so *use* it: "Don't stop," her features as if heat-changed behind thick stage makeup, its color the dry pink of spoiling meat. "They're only people. —Right, John Henry?" and Tess's rictus smile, all of them waiting for her to signal the beef at the doors: her job, somehow, from the very first: give the go.

Heat. And steam, wet smoke above their milling heads, they were eyes, eyes, mouths already yelling, hands already overhead. The room filled in minutes and there were, still, more, pushing, underfoot in the soundless whoop of strobes, painful screeching of miked metal twisting slowly past tolerance, long combat legs striped in black and chrome silver, leaping incredible to a soundtrack noise so dense it was blood music, terror and strange comfort, consuming and consummation all in one. Backlit vampire grin, the solo flamenco across a bed not of nails but of chipped and shivering wire, Tess's newest construct, still embryo but forced to service: *Mme Lazarus,* flipping endless its long file-nails, the looped montage of screams and the booming whip of light and Bibi creeping through the audience with a handful of rusty pins.

And that same audience responding in a brutal burst of energy, the loop from those who show to those who see a whining circle of current, faster and faster until the show's official end, scattergun Xenon bursts, a dazzle like the end of the world and it was suddenly flesh, hot moving wall and they were everywhere, fighting, shoving, trying to climb the constructs, trying to grab Bibi's arms, trying to take from Tess *Mme Lazarus's* black-taped control box. No longer content to be viewers, now they were participants, Tess kicking shins, pounding elbows and she scrambled like a cat upstairs, Jerome and Bibi and no one knew where the other three were. The building emptied shouts into the street, "Surgeons!" and breaking glass, yelling their heads off and sailing rocks at the windows.

Still where they tumbled, staring at each other: Jerome's jellied nose and shirt torn to the nipples, Bibi's makeup highlight for her growing bruises, bright and comic as a clown. Tess's underlip felt strange, sausage-swollen, her arms and legs ached as if she had been running for hours. Tiny glass droplets skittering across the floor like thrown roses.

And outside, still and continuous as the leathery coughing of beasts in the dark: "Surgeons!"

Cold, the morning air on her tired eyes; Jerome stretched like a puppy on half a sleeping bag, pale grease-

striped face too young in sleep. He had spent most of the
night making multiconductor cables, vinyl jacketed, Teflon
coated, silent shadow as Tess struggled with *Mme Lazarus,*
wanting more of her than just geek curiosity, just a pair of
moving arms and metal files. Still dissected on the worktable and Tess leaning her head against the glass, sighing,
then the voice in her ear: "John Henry doesn't *get* tired."

Out all night and still those clear pale eyes, handing Tess
a plastic cup of coffee. "I found us a place," she said,
stepping over Jerome to sit on the unmade couchbed, motioning for Tess to sit beside her; her smell like sweat and
other people's smoke, the peculiar dense aroma of clubs
now amplified in the room's chilled stillness.

"Guess where it is," and then instantly, "That gas station! Remember?" Muffled into her cup, "The one across
from the old foundry, that we wanted to use before?" and
from her pocket a beignet, miraculously unsquashed; she
broke it in half, gave the larger half to Tess. "I tried to get
the foundry, first, but the guy who owns it, nobody knows
where he is, and the holding company wants money before
they'll even talk. A damage deposit," her pinking grin, the
bruises gone to faint exotic wash beneath her eyes, fierce
prizefighter angle of her jaw. "So there's a for-rent sign on
the gas station, I called the number and the guy said yes
right away."

Wiping her mouth, still sore. Jerome twitching, bony
hands a-flex in sleep's deepest room. "You still want to do
it next month?"

"Before it gets too cold, yeah."

Next month already December, and snow: Jerome had
diddled the electric meter, but they would need more heat
soon; Bibi's scattered dayjobs, she was already paying
more than her half of the rent, Tess immersed so deeply
now in *Mme Lazarus* and hating more than ever the pickup

welding she had to do, on and off, the waste of time worse than anything. It was so *hard*, this work, this fresh new discipline, that to stop at all—even, sometimes, for the shows—was bare-wire frustration. If not for Jerome, so happy with the scutwork, she could not have done it at all.

And Bibi, in sudden chime: "You know what, we ought to start thinking about charging. To get in, I mean," and when Tess did not answer at once unique Bibi combination of diffidence and truculence, "Better idea?"

"No," stretching into a long yawn as if all her muscles woke at once; sharp sunny flare through the window, the ghost of summer's arc. Jerome sniffling into wakefulness in his tattered cocoon and her arm around Bibi, half a smile: "Of course we should charge them. By the pound."

Bibi: prominent in *AntiTrust* magazine, black-and-white stare and her theory of *tanzplagen*, the quote beneath her picture "Chaos must be met with greater chaos." Another photo, she and Tess like the gods of disaster, posing before the ringed rubble of the foundry: Bibi as changeling, heavy wire earrings and sharp new studs bored in either nostril, lips drawn back and Tess austere behind, all in dun gray and chapped cheeks stretched unsmiling against the freshet wind, fist light to her lips like the breath that breathes the secret. Paul bought a dozen copies; Raelynne said they looked like thugs. Jerome cut the picture out and taped it above the worktable until Tess made him take it down.

The article appeared a bare week before the new show, the last one, they decided, done for free; hard to keep people out of an outdoor show, anyway, and anyway they would need help to start charging, everyone was already pushed, time-squeezed between dayjobs, performances, rehearsals; even Jerome had acquired an assistant, Peter:

more silent than he, thinner and taller. They both lived on the first floor now, the dog woman having vacated without fuss or explanation: fast-food wrappers and their own worktable, Tess's contributions and what they could scrounge; they were excellent scroungers. Scrapyard duty, setup and teardown, ran errands, put up flyers; Tess had insisted they become full members of the group, "I can't shit without them," and their wordless shine, Bibi joking in private: our first children.

Not much private time, anymore, for jokes or anything else. Bibi the demon choreographer, besieging Tess at the worktable to show ideas, ask advice, slumped at last to sleep, Paul sometimes-quilt and Tess still up, working. *Mme Lazarus* far evolved, now, past her original sketchy persona, become the walking emblem of mastery, Tess's proof to herself of her own worthiness to play this harsh new game; evolution and culmination, she had to be *right*. Modification: the distorted landscape where function does not follow form but creates it. Centerpiece of the new show, *Crazy Brainchildren* and perhaps the *Madame* was in some gray sense an offspring, she had mocked the notion but perhaps: child of her blistered palms, blisters and burn sores, hour after hour behind the mask; deep green goggle-world from which she emerged with a diver's dazed care; surfacing. Even Bibi said she was working too hard, Bibi with her own frantic agenda, more than her share: spreading the word, seeking—what? Inspiration? Sandrine said she always conjured their most stringent costumes after nights in the piercing bars; what did Bibi see, what stringencies did she court from which she roamed home sweaty and bright as the false sparkle of the studs in her nostrils? "Come with me," but from behind the green Tess shook her head, no, she had work to do. Maybe after the show was over, take a breather, take some time; not enough time. The *Madame* had to be perfect.

CRAZY BRAINCHILDREN in fat black letters strung on wind-jittered wire between the empty gas station and the foundry gates, eerie parade sign. People had begun gathering two hours before the show, hands in pockets and the weather unseasonably brutal, wind tuned up a notch, another, the temperature going down.

Behind the store, abandoned stepvan in which they waited, stamping feet, cracking anxious jokes. Sandrine's last-minute makeup, slopping black under Paul's eyes, Raelynne's, long diagonals down chattering cheeks. Tess in cracked black and seam-split leather, going over it one more time: Bibi over her shoulder like a ghost familiar, scarecrow mummy in handmade cerements, fast and back and forth:

"—and the *Madame*," Bibi's runny nose, sore ears pinked from new piercings, for good luck she said. "Starting up *there*—"

Frowning, the construct still swathed; would it work? Tests, even last bitter midnight and her fingers frozen on the switch, putting *Mme Lazarus* through paces; Bibi had come out at last to bring her in. "Here," agreeing now, "and the stones—"

"And Peter's up here—Peter!" Baseball cap, red nose, peering around the stepvan door. "You ready?" and his solemn nod, tapping the neat square of the camcorder beneath his too-big parka. Bibi had brought it home with a shrug for its origin, obviously stolen somewhere but Tess had not asked, no time, she would ask later. As soon as the show was over.

Peter was pictures, Jerome the smoke machine that— already?—began its steady bellow of ugly oily smoke, impossible indoors but now it formed a fat delusive cloud, the crowd shouting as Paul cued up the music, amped-up carnival blare that would replay at increasingly faster speeds with a sampled track beneath featuring Paul's dead-baby shriek. Sandrine and Raelynne linking hands and out, Paul squeezing Bibi in a good-luck hug, brief nod to Tess and into the cold.

And their twin stare, co-conspirators in smoke and screech and suddenly Bibi was laughing, Tess's shoulders rock-tense under her grab and "Come on!" and out, Tess skinning off her gloves, Bibi climbing manic as a monkey atop the gas station, where the heads were.

Chainlink faces, shrinkwrapped wire tied with clothes hangers to the bolt-cut length of the fence, each one had taken Tess precious hours to sculpt from the balky wire. Bibi there, now, snip snip, tinsnips, cutting a nostril here, a sharp eye there, cut cut like the surgeon she was as below Paul and Sandrine bore a kicking Raelynne to the smoke-machine inferno, the trio disappearing and: Tess's cue to reappear behind the mobile doom of *Mme Lazarus,* and the instant skitter of thrown stones, Jerome's job. Somewhere close by, Peter: taping.

Control in cold hand, shouts and straining coughs, *Mme Lazarus* moving: exactly as meant to, off-balance rolling stride, files flipping in cold rotation, arms extending to catch at spectators, to snatch at the bits of smashed concrete ringing the thrice-roped performance area; Tess behind humble as an acolyte, priestling drab in skinned braids and black, the smoke making her slit eyes water. She had done it; made the *Madame* work, and work for real.

Stones in the air like dead birds. Bibi clipping above, Raelynne's rhythmic screams and now Paul and Sandrine fitting the torn wire faces to their own, the smoke iron blue, the veined blue of blood below the landscape of white flesh. Soundtrack groans and a sudden shriek when *Mme Lazarus* plucked too close, someone falling, not hurt but scared. More stones, more screams, the last face free and Bibi sailing it in vicious flying arc, bare-edged wire against the cold sky like a decapitated angel and her own banshee cry, leaping from the gas station roof to follow it down and landing graceless and sure beside the makeshift pyre where trussed Raelynne struggled and swore.

Mme Lazarus now bending to choose a yard-long tooth-pick of iron and an eerie moment as if the construct itself stood considering, *what to do* before turning toward Rae-lynne, rolling close to raise the spike, long iron in slippery grip and Raelynne below, Tess's lip caught in nervous bite

—careful now—

and bring it down *hard,* splinters of rotten wood and in perfectly, *perfectly,* Tess's bleeding grin and glee aloud: Yes! And Raelynne as untouched as she should be, miming freedom and pain and rolling over to choose from the lit-tered discards a warped-wire face, hold it up to her own, strange masquer, as she capered away.

And Tess's endless smile, wind-burned and the rest of the show a glare and a blur and cheers, Bibi beside her, wide cracked lips saying "Wave to the nice people" and grabbing her static arm to move it, once and twice and down, *Madame's* control still hot in her hand like the key to the kingdom of continuous light.

"You promised," dragging on her arm, put down the fucking tools for once and Tess's sigh, all right. All right. Bibi in her Madame Defarge chic, shiny new earrings, slip-pery little bells and needles and pulling her out the door.

"It's great," skittering into traffic, "wall-to-wall skin. They all know about the Surgeons, too," and on and on,

Tess's head against the cold window, half listening, half back with her new project, a smaller, faster construct all pinching fingers like a manic crab, a fierce chrome crab with fine-tuned eyes to see, search, in the smoke and the dark—and Bibi's hard little fist, whack against her shoulder; it hurt, too.

"Pay attention," little white grin. "I said that guy called again, the one from *Underground*."

Ugh. "What'd you tell him?" The stream of lights, billboards defaced and relettered like cryptic collage, half messages to make fever-dream sense of the sense of motion.

"I told him I'd call him back." Swinging around a dented delivery truck, scuttling back into traffic like an insect into webbing cracks. "You know, you can't keep avoiding shit like this."

"I know, I know," crossly, content with the elegance of wiring diagrams, the dripping sting of solder. The magazines had found them, the alternative press: the Surgeons were at the vanguard, now, they were "performance art" no matter how loudly Bibi said *tanzplagen*, no one could spell it anyway and anyway they had their own agenda: "fiercely feminist" or "reactionaries in an increasingly mechanized age" or "comic terrorists," it was all shit but they kept on printing it. And the pictures, dwarf and gargoyle, and the people who called and left messages, pornographic, worshipful, someone tied a half-filled condom to their outer door. Popularity was not hell, it was pudding, stuck to their skins, clotting in gears meant to roll in smooth silence absolute. Bibi could negotiate her way through this glue, but to Tess it was perpetual flounder: you said it yourself, reminding, I don't think like a performer. And Bibi back, astringent, that doesn't mean you can't *talk* like one.

Now their destination, past closed stores and empty buildings, false Victoriana and an unlocked door into the heat of a hundred bodies, two very bright lights. Harsh digitized reggae and Bibi seemed to know everyone, introducing Tess, plumaged people and so much *metal:* multiply pierced, shiny and bristling in silvery steel. Rings through lips and nipples, nostrils and ears, long black tattoos and indelible color spiraling up arms, down bare backs and legs, bewildering visual treat but it was the metal she liked best; and beside her Bibi's own sparkle, the flash of long silver rings, matte-studded nostrils like extruded drops of iron, flesh for the machine age.

A place was made for them, apparently something was just about to happen: the music adjusted and a thin muscled woman in white T-shirt and baggy sweats stepped forward, gently pushing people back from what seemed to be an examining table, carefully draped in clean white. On it, a bare-chested blond boy who resembled skinny Peter, all knobs and ribs and tiny pierced nipples small as a cat's.

"She's going to do a cutting," Bibi said in Tess's ear.

Stylized as a dance, the boy reclining and Tess saw the thin woman transfer a design, faintly Aztec in flavor, to the boy's back: venomous smiling bird and then the sharp edge, the scalpellike tool innocuous until: cutting, her gloved fingers very deft, the boy's eyes half-closed, breathing through parted lips. Lights surgery-bright and no one spoke, Bibi's consuming stare and Tess watching, only that, unsure of what to feel: it had to hurt, tears shiny in his eyes but the boy was not flinching; the woman's voice, calm and encouraging, moment to moment as the cutting went on, you're doing great, great, you can yell if you want to.

The design complete, and the careful press of a fresh paper towel to the cut, the image in perfect reversal, beautiful and fine as filigree: "That's a blood rubbing," Bibi again and the boy shifted, small motion of his muscles, and suddenly everyone was talking, smiling, congratulating the boy, who came to his feet slow and proud. The man on Tess's left bent to her, deep serious voice beneath heavy shock of white-blond hair, "Wasn't that something? Linda Joy never does hamburger cuttings—her stuff is always real pretty. It's something you're proud to have." And then, suddenly shy, "Are you really Tess Bajac?"

All the way home, Bibi's summation, now *that* was bodily expression, beside it plain dance was nothing; the static stalk of bone and the endless circuit of blood, that was the difference. If only there was a way to combine that intensity with pure movement, was there a way? The body itself, possibilities relentless, like remaking a machine each time, right, John Henry?

"She knew what she was doing," cold inward headshake at the thought of ignorant hands and a razor. "That woman, she knew exactly what she was doing."

"Well of course she did, it's her *vocation*." Rubbing one finger across her upper lip, "Maybe I'll ask her to do me. At a show." And then abruptly, her voice an octave bright as if to deflect attention from what she had just proposed, "That guy you were talking to, that big bleach-blond guy? He wants to join the Surgeons."

Do you fool me, hedgehog? Not at all. At one with the performing disregard, crawling fast and bloody over surfaces never meant for human touch, back to the very first show: Shit, it's only blood. Although it isn't; it never is. But I can walk that way, too. For a while. "Know anything about him?"

"Oh sure, I've seen him lots of times. He comes to all the shows, plus he's a regular with Linda Joy. His name is Andy, in case you forgot," and onto the idea of new members, how big should the Surgeons be; new blood, with one of her long grins. And Tess watching, alternate play of dark and light across those changing features, watching from the other side.

Andy was not a dancer, but he knew how to move, a big man light on his feet; instantly likeable, even Paul accepted him at once, jealous Paul whose moods were beginning to wear. After a night's rehearsal, Bibi flopping down in sweat and bad temper, complaining about Paul to Tess half listening, her abstract nod as she soldered a tricky circuit, the chrome crab must be able to turn completely around.

"I'm serious," popping ice into cups of scalding coffee, one for her, one for Tess. Outside the temperature kept going down, windows rippled with ice and shifty snow. "Paul's getting to be a real asshole," wanting more of her time, wanting to help with the decision making, to choreograph. "And it's not like he even wants to do this stuff, he says he does but I know he's lying. What he wants is to be my boyfriend," making of the word a dreadful sneer. Long swallow, the sweaty throat working. "And I don't want a boyfriend."

"What do you want?" Besides this question.

"I *want*," and a smile, "period," but beneath her flippancy Tess smelled impatience hungry as an ulcer, a ferocious disregard for what was possible, available, in favor of what might be, past the limits, past the dark. Since their visit to Linda Joy's Bibi had been back twice that Tess knew of, returning not less impatient but more, there was so much to do. Even in her sleep she chased it, bunched in the ratty blue blankets, mouth clenching on nightmare words for dreams and edges; sometimes she grew so loud that Tess would wake her, shaking her shoulders till those owl eyes opened in the dark, Bibi letting out a breath and sitting up to hold Tess's warm hand with her cold one, inexplicably cold though fresh from the fever-heat of the blanket sea.

In the morning, Tess back at the worktable and Bibi off, overseeing, interviewing, working on setup: another show, *Shock Loads* back downstairs but this time they would limit the crowd, they would charge admittance, Andy incredulous that they had waited so long. Jerome thought it was a wonderful idea, he and Peter had all sorts of plans, and there was this guy, Tess had met him, he came to all the shows.

"Right," from beneath the hood, distorted green-shade grin. The windows opened to the cold, stink and burn in the air and Tess happy, supremely so, bringing the Promethean gift of motion inherent in the liquid fire to her sculptures; she needed very little else; besides Bibi, who somehow in this new dissatisfaction burned brighter still. (And where was Bibi now? Linda Joy's?) "So what's he got to show me?" and Jerome at once, it's really torqued, this high-power carbon dioxide laser, it can burn a hole through eighth-of-an-inch plate.

"Tell him to come see me," and the Surgeons had another member: Nicky, shaggy salad hair and slippery overbite, enough bounce to be one of the dancers. Tess's techies, Raelynne called them, Tess's metal freaks who stayed obligingly apart from the sweaty grind of the dancers, planning elaborate carnivals of fire and steel; who thought of Tess as their leader. Their only leader, which disturbed her. It made Bibi laugh: "Who cares who they listen to? As long as they don't fry me in the middle of a show," and back into plans for *Shock Loads*.

Ambitious, there in the cold, the winter that already seemed to have lasted so very long, toes and fingers eternally numb, some tools unworkable in that temperature, or lack; Bibi alone did not complain about the icy floors, the

cavernous damp at rehearsals. And there were many rehearsals, there was a lot to do, four months' worth of
plans, ideas hatched cold as lizard's eggs there in the warehouse dark.

Biggest plan of all, of course, was the cutting: Bibi up-
front and on a table, spotlight as Linda Joy cut a long
ribbon of blood down her back, slim sinuosity and so *beautiful,* it would be very beautiful. See? showing the design to
a stubborn Tess, lips set and sarcastic: "Well, how about if I
burn myself, huh? How would that be? A nice big red
burn," and Bibi angry, stop making fun! I'm *not.* Yes you
are, and the longest silence ever, Tess banging furious and
Bibi stretched and equally enraged; silence almost till
morning, till Bibi's small weight on Tess's couchbed, cold
hand out in the dark: "Listen. Will you just do that? Will
you just listen a minute?"

Yes. And Bibi telling of watching Tess work, day after
day drenched in work, consumed and Bibi dry beside her,
dance was so *limiting,* there was only so much she could do
with it and here a way to make her own kind of fire, her
own consummation. To go further.

"It's not like I'm going to be killed or anything," strong
hand on her wrist; squeezing, and, "I don't *want* to do it
with you mad."

And eyes closed in the dark, pale morning seepage and
knowing Bibi would do it anyway, mad or not, furious or
not; burn or not and that was an empty threat, wasn't it?
Wasn't it? Then why say it?

Because I don't *want* her to do it. Because it isn't beautiful *because* it isn't beauty she's after.

What is she after?

Raising her gaze, taking both hands in a hard cold grip:
"All right. But I don't have to like it, all right?" and Bibi's
instant grin, arms tight around Tess's neck and then to

satisfied sleep while Tess lay awake, finally moving in slow silence to the worktable, to turn over and over in numb considering fingers the slick carapace of the crab.

They charged what seemed to Tess to be a ridiculous price, she argued against it but Bibi was adamant: you'll see. And she did: the big room was full, they could have filled it twice; but why be surprised? the magazine popularity, the notes and phone calls should have prepared her for such a concrete unreality: next time there would probably be even more. People talking, yelling; a feeling of anticipation; and the skeptics' contingent, they were easy to spot. Fine. Let them wait. A curtain all the way from the ceiling, black cataract of stain-rippled fabric and Tess and Bibi behind; everyone else in place, nervous flexing and jokes and Peter already filming, quiet circles like a tracking eye. Behind them all, Linda Joy, muscled wraith in white and white gloves and Tess to Bibi for the tenth time, "Are you sure?"

"Yes, I'm sure," squeezing Tess's shoulders, hands strong and dry and shaking. "Don't worry—it's at least as safe as that kid's fucking laser."

Pale eyes burning, excitement's white light, taking her place and Tess turning to Nicky: get ready. Overhead lights down, strobes on, soundtrack on—weedy groans, three ominous notes repeating—and the big curtain down to a roar, they were ready already. Tess backlit, her chrome crab walking beside *Mme Lazarus* like an evil pet, Bibi behind. On a table, beneath pure light.

It went so fast, *Mme Lazarus* as moveable menace and prop for the dancers, pursued and pursuing and working as well the crab, big shiny body and heavy steel-tipped pincers roaming close to the crowd, feinting, snapping, its ground-level mobility an unexpected asset: so much easier to sneak up on you, my dear. No eye for the background, trying instead to see what was happening to Bibi; but it was all too quick, the slim back bare and a ragged cheer at the long-drawn serpent of blood, spatter, the wet tension of Bibi's muscles, sweating, sweating in the path of the knife. Tess's own jaw in sympathy lock, ground it open as one of the watchers watching her, rolling eyes and a nudging elbow, big carroty burst of moussed hair and in a sudden jab of viciousness the crab was *pinching,* it was made to pinch and it *hurt,* the woman shrieking in painful polka and Tess drew back on the controls, sent the crab skittering another way. The knife in retreat and Bibi rising, queen cobra to flex and turn, showing it, *showing:* and from beneath the table the blood pellets, a river of blood, heavy and the crab deliberately through it, bloodprints, Linda Joy withdrawing into darkness and the drilling eye of the laser, bloody grinning Bibi and the crab clambering home at last as the soundtrack unwound to its last dry quivering scream. And the black curtain rising. And the whooping cries of the crowd as Bibi wrapped herself calm and careful in clean linen, sheet across her shoulders bleeding through in patterns complex and oblique, moving away and Tess turning at once to follow; she could feel, still, the heavy tension in her jaw, in the stretched ridge of her shoulders, as if she had carried something insupportable for a time insupportably long.

And combative in her path the woman who had been bitten, red scowling mouth and leather pantleg rucked to show the spot, already a puckered blue. Tess's gaze blinkless and absolutely flat, tension rising from shoulders to throat to the tunneled gray throb of her head, "So what's your point?"

"My *point* is, your machine injured me," loud and en-

couraged by attention, others were listening now. "This is
definitely an injury and I'm going to need—"

"Your ticket's a waiver. Read the fine print," dismissive
turn and the woman's escort, *hey bitch* and hand re-
straining on Tess's arm and before she knew she had done
it the crab's control box hard against his cheekbone, singular sound of slammed plastic and her grip at his throat,
dragging him eye-to-eye—he was just her size—and
"Don't you *ever* put a hand on me, motherfucker," the
watching circle now startled silent and from nowhere Andy
and Paul, still moist with fake blood and real sweat: pulling
them apart, what's the problem here? Huh? "Tess, hey,
what's the trouble?" Andy's gentle calm and Paul glower-
ing, Tess head down and turning away. Shaking.

Raelynne's bright voice, "Show's over, folks!" and somebody's laugh, and talk, motion, the doors closing and Bibi,
there: hand on her arm, looking up into her face with eyes
still not completely back: "What happened? That asshole
grabbed you, or what?"

"Nothing," hands in shameful jitter and Jerome there to
take the control box from her, hairline cracks, was it dam-
aged? Ruined? She would find out, put it on my worktable
but Jerome shook his head.

"Forget it—Tess, forget it, we'll take care of it." And
gone, her three as well as the others, melting back—even
Paul—to leave her beside draped Bibi, bloody back and
guiding hands, come on. "C'mon," smiling, a little, little
smiling teeth. "John Henry. Let's go home."

Late sun, the welding panels strange orange like construction cones, too bright; melting ice heavy as leaded
glass and Tess's frown, gaze on her work, solid skulls
a-jingle against a stiff steel bone: "Are you sure?"

"Linda Joy says he's okay, she's worked with him before.

Andreas," leftover hint of scabs like a zipper up her spine, the cutting stringent and beautiful; shower steam incongruous in the burgeoning cold. "Anyway it'll only be little cuts this time. —So how's the triplets coming?"

"Okay," and it was almost beginning to be so, stripped-down carcasses in the process of extreme modification, figures triumvirate and even harder than she thought but she had time, now, to make it look easy. No need for even pickup jobs; Jerome had picked up that slack, too, Rick's Auto Body three times a week and everything he got he plowed straight back into the Surgeons. The next show had nothing more concrete than a name—*Actual Torque*—and her trio of headless skeletal constructs, Bibi called them Deaths One, Two and Almost; and of course Bibi's plan for another cutting.

Little cuts this time and each symbolic, she had explained it all at least three times to a silent Tess still privately appalled by her own outburst at the last show: she had let worry and rage control her as surely as she had turned the crab on that woman, as surely as she had turned on the man. Bibi's body was simply that, Bibi's body. Not hers. If cutting was what she needed, then she would be cut. Simple. If she wanted to amputate her legs and hang them on meathooks from the ceiling, that was her prerogative, too. To think—or act—otherwise was foolish and worse; there was dissent enough without adding more.

And Bibi as usual, uncanny in her thoughts: "—don't know what to do about Paul." Through the inverted V of bent legs, strange stretching lotus shape and her head-shake inverted: Paul was getting harder and harder to take, he was forever walking out of rehearsals, and Sandrine as well now suddenly temperamental, complaining that the Surgeons were becoming more than half machine shop, this was supposed to be about *dance*. Metal versus flesh,

the engineered versus the organic, Tess had the same problems from the other side: Nicky most of all but even patient Jerome less so, *we* put in most of the grindwork, Tess,
we do most of the work and you know it. Did she know it?
The pure hot drip of solder, flat splash drying to thinnest
chrome shine; she knew *that.*

"I tell 'em they can all be replaced," and Bibi right side
up, blood in her cheeks. "Fuck 'em. Especially Paul. This's
the greatest thing any of them will ever do and they know
it. —Listen, I'm going to a club tonight, there's this *fou*
music thing I want to see. I forgot the name of it, but Andy
says they're pretty good. Want to come?"

Tapping Death Almost with the hilt of her soldering
gun, jingling skulls as small as charms: "Can't. Besides I
don't know what *fou* music is."

" 's like *art brut,* only music. Crazy people," and she
bared her teeth, comical glare and uncoiling in one long
reptile stretch, dressing backless and bright new piercing
jewelry, shiny surgical steel: beautiful, Bibi, pale hair
hacked shorter than ever, pale eyes now covered by heavy
cataract shades even though the sun was down. Tess in the
glow of her own sun, indoor burn and Andy at the door,
immense in heavy leather: "Knock knock—hey, hi, Tess,
how's it going? You ready, Bibi? Tess, you want to come?"

"Not her," Bibi tapping tart and fond across her back,
"you know Tess. Slave to the grind," and Tess's correcting
smile, "No, slave to the *burn,*" and the door closing again
on the dark coming on, stench of solder and singed plastic,
the blood-quiet drip from the smoldering tip of the gun.

"It won't work because you can't do it." Sickle-eyed
through the mask in matte afternoon shadow; deep in a
pleasing problem and here they were, in without knocking
and ringing her worktable with another bright idea. Trio

stare reminding of the Triple Deaths, she felt a dry smile that came nowhere near her mouth. "Do I have to pull rank? Is that what you want?"

Nicky's ragdoll hair in sullen shake, Peter picking at a hangnail. Only Jerome met her head on, glare for glare, only Jerome bold enough, mad enough to say, "It's not fair."

"Of course it's not fair." Flipping up her mask to point from one to another with the burnt flux tip, "It doesn't have to be fair, remember? And you don't have to stay." The limits of dominion were her limits, as far as such could be prosecuted, and she knew it; what authority she had they gave her and she knew that, too. "Now either help me with this, or leave me alone," and turning back, ticking off seconds and Jerome's sigh, angry hands taking the work from her, the others silent on the other side.

And Bibi breezing in, handful of flyers and new jacket jingling with zippers, "Hey," and the three in one collective motion removing the slippery jumble of cable, fragile as an intubated body, off the worktable and out the door. Staring after them, "What's their problem?" and Tess careful not to speak until the finite sound of the service elevator.

"Oh, they're pissed off at me, they want to try this new effect with the laser and I won't let them."

"Why not?"

"Too dangerous." Brief mind's-eye glimpse of the first show, the girl stumbling back behind the shielding panels. Crane's voice: How about the kid who got all cut up? No more of that, please, and thank you very much. "Where've you been?"

"Back to the Asylum. Look," new flyer in hand: ACTUAL TORQUE in heavy black sans serif on a background of pure arc flash, a woman's—Bibi's—bare back defined by lash marks and behind her a tall masked figure clenching a stylized joystick, connected by sparking cables to something angular and metallic just barely in frame. Tess stared at it with a vague discomfort; it seemed unnecessarily lurid, and it was so *big;* almost poster-size.

"That's you," Bibi's chewed nail on the figure. "I already put some up, at Greco's, and the Bar H, and Asylum's, somebody at Asylum's already asked where he could get tickets." Standing over Tess, now, hands on her shoulders: "Come with me tonight," and intercepting her shrug, "There's always work to do, that's what we *do.* Come on, you can take one night off. Besides you ought to see this guy, he's in that *fou* music thing, remember I told you? —Just come *on,*" dragging her arm like a little kid and Tess's long rare smile, briefest nod in counterpoint to the fresh-begun banging, big and hollow, from the three downstairs; for once, she thought, let someone else work while I play.

Asylum's smelled like a gym, mold and old sweat and the hundred secret stinks of working bodies. Rows of cheap folding chairs, some broken, some incongruous-new against the tired laminate of the floor, the stage where various instruments were being manipulated with varying degrees of violence and success.

A sawed-off cello. A drum kit played with the body. Two wildly out-of-tune bass guitars used inexpertly by a pair of blond women who looked like mother and daughter. And a long glittering stream of bells, silver, gold, cracked, split open to show clappers huge and bare as swollen knobs of flesh, the protruding tongues of the dead: played by a man, young man, eyes closed, lips pliant in choirboy half smile, the bells' dirty tethers hooked horse-collar and winding around his bare chest to hang down past his thighs as if extruded anew by each deliberate motion, each quick and shuddering jounce.

"His name is Michael," Bibi in her ear, warm breath and Tess barely nodded, caught by his motion, he was so obviously the only thing worth watching. The performance was as badly done as the lighting, cheap gelatinous primaries, it was all pretty worthless.

But not him, the bell ringer; see him now in his spastic crouch amidst the shrill tribal ring, sweat, he was sweating, the muscles of his legs bunched in effort and the bells in his hands like the jingling scales of lizards, descending sounds as the guitar-flogging women rolled like cannon-balls ("Hedgehogs," Tess in Bibi's ear) and the body-drummer used his elbows to thump to a flat finale.

No applause, but de rigueur comment, instant and earnest and Bibi pushing past it all, Tess a step behind to follow her over the stage. To corner the bell ringer, hand out, smiling: "I'm Bibi Bloss," shaking his hand and Tess remembered Bibi's hand in hers back in her party-store workspace: first hard handshake, the one that did not seem to test. "And this is Tess Bajac. We—"

"I know who you are." Close up he was very beautiful, strange haughty overbite in the long shy smile, long hair pulled back in messy plait, half-curled, half-straight, bright tarnished color of the silent bells. "You're the Surgeons. I've seen one of your shows—it was incredible." His hand hot on Tess's, fingers blunt and strong. "I'm Michael His-pard."

Bibi invited him out for coffee, a drink, but he declined, he had to clean up, there was work to do. Nodding to the Surgeons flyer, already scrolling at the edges: "I'll see you there," speaking carefully to both, diffident good-bye and gone, faint trickling jingle in his wake and Bibi's grin: "Pretty, huh?"

Very pretty. Tess glanced once more in the direction he had gone to see him, bells gathered careless against his bare chest, watching them leave. And then caught, abashed, ducking away this time for good and they both smiled, at him, at each other.

Out into the dark, moist wind and Bibi, nudging her: "Well? Aren't you glad you came?"

The only one worth watching; hair like summer and hot fingers, strong on her own. *I'll see you there;* will you? I'll see you, if you do. "Yeah," Tess said. "I think I am."

Spring heat, again unseasonable, sweating first thing in the morning and Paul's dramatic curse, bounding naked out of bed—he had a muscular ass, Paul, and shiny gold piercings newer than Bibi's—tearing on clothes while shrieking at Bibi who shrieked back, threw something; missed, and Tess hunched—still—at the worktable, yelling red-eyed Shut the fuck *up!* to the banging door, Paul's shouts in the street and Bibi slamming the window, hard; then with a shrug, apology, opening it wide again for Tess who socketed her gun, rubbed her eyes hard with the burned heels of her hands.

"You want coffee?"

Tess's nod, stepping to the shower and Bibi's commentary, half to herself and half-unheard in the shivering burn of the water. Full day's work ahead, *Actual Torque* actually on schedule but no thanks to Paul, or even Tess's three, all of whom seemed to have more pressing work elsewhere; true, they had pickup jobs but still their time seemed oddly fragmented; there when she needed them most, but only then. Maybe they were going to quit to form their own group.

The time between shows had lengthened in proportion to the planned complexities; maybe time was the key to all

the bickering. Bibi looking, bringing coffee, half smile pale
as a little ghoul, scratches across her breasts and neck, one
long and arrow-straight directing the eye down. Tess, gesturing with her own cup to the answering-machine light:
blinking; it was always blinking these days.

"That guy called again, from *AntiTrust.* He said you
were going to give him an interview before the—"

"I know, I know." Frowning, unconscious fingers rubbing the reddest of the scratches. "I don't have time, this
time. Shit! There's too much to do."

There *was* too much to do: the Triple Deaths first and
foremost, and almost done: the Claw Hammer, the Drill,
and the Guitar Pick, they could not walk but they could
move; motion so distorted it became ultimately hateful to
the eye, like the long-ago tape played at that first dance, a
rhythmless rhythm that put teeth on edge, made the heartbeat feel miscadenced, the breathing too fast or too slow.
Optimum distortion, Jerome called it; when he was there.
Which was seldom. "I think," Tess said, "Jerome's going to
quit on me."

"What? No," shaking that pale head, positive. "Not Jerome. He thinks you're God."

"Well, something's going on." Too tired to work, too
much to do; no time to waste. A week and a half, tickets
sold, supplies bought; strobes and smoke and the Triple
Deaths through their paces, everyone in black and
stretched rubber, rubber to burn, nauseating smoke another facet of discomfort: this time let's fuck them *up,*
Bibi's mantra and Tess agreed. The Surgeons were about
more than plain performance; or should be. Would be.

So: coffee drunk like medicine, Tess's head hung low
and Bibi toweling her dry, "Your hair's so *long,*" rubbing
vigorous to the point of pain: "There. If you're still asleep
now, you're dead," and into the shower herself as at the

door Paul, silent hands full of pastries, yellow crust and fat red fruit filling like split innards; bags down to strip and join Bibi in the wet and Tess back to the worktable, backhinge hurting, solder smoke like the rising funnel of incense in the church of the endless burn.

His name was Andreas, long hair and long fingernails and he was late, almost time for the performance before he came with his needles, his scalpels, his black rubber gloves. Unnecessarily deferential to Tess, jokey and fey with Bibi, who seemed to find him funny. Or something. Tess perched, vulture, atop one of the heavy black-sprayed crates, sore-eyed watch as one trio set up another: Nicky and Peter and Jerome, the Drill, the Claw Hammer, the Guitar Pick. Even she had to admit she was pleased: long ropy cables like necrotic veins, slippery oil and they moved as they were meant to: around the rusty drums meant for the rubber and the fire, around the splintered plywood table on which Bibi would be cut. More cabling from the ceiling, long U-shaped loops where the dancers would hang as frenzied as webbed flies until escape. Peter, as always, camera; Nicky and Jerome were music, smoke, backup for her with the constructs, ready to ready the portable welding gear if necessary, run patchup, fix cables. Turn on the fire extinguisher. Break windows. "Crowd control," and now she was talking out loud, "crowbars. Napalm. Paramedics. Paralegals. What the fuck are you looking at, dipshit?" and Andreas's placating shrug, moving off; I know right where you can stick those needles, asshole. —And why be angry at him, when it's her blood they're spilling?

Shut up.

Now black: except for lone deserted spots, the sound of the audience and everyone drifting into place, sullen Sandrine, Raelynne's friendly grimace as she passed trussed hard in thick radial black. Where was Paul? Bibi already stripped topless on the table, breasts half-covered with electrical tape; it would hurt like hell, coming off. The brownish smell of Betadine, at least he knew enough to clean up first, clean his scummy needles and his little cutting tools. Stop it. Concentrate on the show, on the triple dance of Triple Death. On your three stooges; where are they anyway? Peter had the camera on a tripod.

A tripod. "What the *fuck*—" but it was too late, the music was already coming on, car-wreck harmonics, the rhythmic rattle of pounded metal and Bibi's recorded voice stretched sonorous and bleak, the voice that groans from the heart of the pit: "Torque, from the Latin *torquere:* to twist—"

And the Triple Deaths in their own kind of motion, twisting, yes, the relentless systolic beat of the Claw Hammer against sheet metal, woundlike dents as big around as fists and the Guitar Pick's random strikes, toothed blade like the world's longest splinter, striking like lightning for the ground, for the watchers, for the dancers, for the spray-painted plywood constructs where the Drill was already in motion, groove upon gutter upon hole and Bibi's fresh cry, the needle at work and the box in Tess's hand sweaty, no room to look behind and

the sound of a machine

no sound she knew

and turning, staring, to see a lumbering concoction of iron and wire, ragged caterpillar tread despoiling by motion everything it passed, passed over, coming on in drowning noise and behind it Jerome: and Nicky: and Peter. Their new toy.

Fresh inexpert welds, half a look told her that and the second look told her it would probably burst from the stress of its own motion, shudder to pieces but no time, now, to really look it over, she had her own work to do. And anger, bright and inexplicable: a moment's black thought of turning the Triple Deaths in punishing combat on this secret toy, batter and drill and pick it to eternity and baby makes four; but it passed, inner shamed head-shake; she was angry at being left out, that was all: why hadn't they trusted her? Because she said no to the laser, because they felt overworked and overshadowed. Because it was theirs.

But anger, still, and in response Triple Death more fierce, and faster; I'll show you how to make a monster. Swung battering Hammer again and again and the lurch-ing grind of the Guitar Pick, music, hardcore, the whining drone of the Drill speed-splintering a plywood box twice its size, black needles of wood spitting everywhere and somebody's shriek, tough; her own hearing half-gone, blunted by the noise, the watchers scared and avid, staring; staring. Take a good look.

Bibi up off the table, slow burlesque turn and the danc-ers loose at last from their webbing, Sandrine rolling past, strange acrobat and Raelynne's howling mask, throwing rubber to burn on the deep drum-fire—not much time left, the smoke would start to get bad very shortly though every window was open and the blowers on—she felt Andreas pass her, grinning white teeth and black gloves but not gone; why not?

Paul passing her, too.

And a moment's worth of motion, bending all at once to throw himself into a crouch before paused Andreas who raised up a scalpel like a spike, big blade, long arc

all the way down his back

sheared rubber, ripped skin; blood. Too much blood. Paul breathing hard, muscles clenched motionless, An-

dreas gone for good into darkness and Bibi was seeing,
Bibi *saw:* bounding across the floor, still bleeding herself,
black-taped breasts and a face contorted, past Deaths and
nameless behemoth and the bleak internal surprise, so
much to be surprised by, tonight: to leap hard upon his
bloody back, jerk his head up by the hair, throat-tight victim ready for the knife and saying something in his ear—
and then off, down, his head jerked sideways as if she
would wrench it free with the power of her contempt. And
now in new wild motion, mad primate bounce up and onto
one of the constructs—the rubber smoke getting very bad,
now, sickening smell and visibility down to dream shapes
and the bright nightmare twinkle on the tip of the Drill—
but Tess could still see, see Bibi jump, again, a monster
leap upon the arched modified spine of the Triple Deaths:
jarred in the landing instant by juggernaut twist but holding on, clenched hands and one arm suddenly bared to the
relentless stroke of the Guitar Pick

oh Bibi *don't*

"Don't!"

and *torn,* blood, the Pick still striking and moving on and
Bibi's grip ripped loose to fall, hard, forcibly to the splin-
ter-strewn floor, facedown in the smoke and stink and the
greasy smear of blood on her head, back at a bad angle, a
broken twist; and did not move at all.

The crowd loved it.

"Just a tooth," trying to smile, mouth grotesquely swollen, "cracked a molar or something. And my arm, that's
all." The cutting on her shoulders smaller than Tess had
imagined, little red diagonals, they were nothing compared
to the rich gore on her arm, she was lucky to have an arm,

Tess felt like beating the shit out of her. Abrasions on her cheek, the side of her throat; she said nothing felt broken.

"Is Triple Death okay?" the slurred mouth frowning now, trying to look around. "I didn't think I—"

Before Tess could speak, Jerome; amends: "It's fine. We checked it over, no problem," not meeting Tess's eyes but she had no particular eyes for him anyway, not yet. All the Surgeons there, clustered around Tess's couchbed where Bibi lay in groggy antic state; except Paul. Who was still missing, had been since the end of the show, Tess's three instead bearing the unconscious Bibi through a rapturous crowd, Tess in the lead forcing a path and for one distracting moment the sight of unsmiling overbite, long summer hair. They took her upstairs, Sandrine all for calling the paramedics but Bibi waking on her own, no, no, I'm fine. I just need to lie down for a while. Peter with black tape and gauze from somewhere, Raelynne covering the bleeding gap and quiet in Tess's ear, " 'S okay, she's gonna be okay." Then louder, to Bibi, "Hey stupid—you want to ride bronco, get a job in a rodeo." Ripping more tape. "Or a whorehouse."

And late, later, with everyone gone and the mythos, the ethos, growing on the street with the indelible shimmer of virus, the two of them: sitting up, Bibi medicated to painlessness and content, floppy lips and butterfly stitches and Tess beside her, the cold anger of relief like a moving tumor in her belly, the cobra dance of rage: "What the fuck is *wrong* with you?"

One-shoulder shrug. "Lots," then darker, without the swollen smile, "but tonight I was mad."

Harshly, "At Paul."

Darker still, "Yeah. You saw what he did."

"You saw what Jerome and those guys did, that stupid machine, and *I* didn't do—"

Pulling sideways, half a smile: "You sure you didn't know about that beforehand?"

"What?" Momentarily distracted from her anger: another surprise in this night of endless surprises. "*No,* I didn't. I didn't know anything about it until I saw it out there tonight, and when I did I felt like running it over with Triple Death."

"Then why didn't you?"

"Because," and silence, unused to explaining herself and especially to Bibi sitting now patient in the long sorting minute, broken face waiting it out. Then, slow: "Because it would be wrong, that's why. It's their machine, they worked on it, they built it. Even though they were assholes to spring it on me that way, I still couldn't just destroy it, right in front of them."

"Really?" Turning a little on the couchbed and the long distorted grin, matte abrasion garish as some new tattoo and eyes as bright and sure as the oncoming tip of the needle, the striking arm of the Pick: "I could. I would have, too."

Late morning and Bibi in pain now, no more pills: mouth heavily ballooned and the bruises a festive smear, dried blood on her lips, her pillow, her torn forearm a warm festering color beyond the moist black-and-white square of taped gauze. Tess's red eyes dry; shaking keys, out for pills and something to eat even though Bibi did not want to eat, "My fucking *mouth* hurts," and Tess inexorable, "Live with it." Still angry: at Bibi's gratuitous injuries, at being disbelieved: *You sure you didn't know about that beforehand? Yes,* I'm sure. Partners were partners, no secrets; what secrets did Bibi have from her?

No talk between them, out to the car in the half rain, Bibi slumped sullen in the damp-smelling seat, head against the window and somebody's knock sudden to startle them both: green insect sunglasses, tentative overbite smile. "Hi," Michael Hispard's voice up close and soft unto whisper, sunglasses down to show the beautiful eyes, darker than Bibi's but still so pale, even in this uncertain light. "I just now quit my group."

Both staring, then Bibi's flat "Oh *yeah*," and Tess reaching behind to flip up the lock: "Hop in."

First the drugstore, over the counter and short of change, Michael there with a handful, silver still warm with his touch. On the way back to the car, diffident: "Is she gonna—is she okay?"

"She's never okay."

Next stop Javahouse, two brick stories and scrollwork balcony empty in the fitful rain above an awning bleached by pigeon shit and sun; the ironwork was pretty but unsound. Tess said, "That's going to crack one day," and Michael stopped at once, Tess almost ran into him, stopped to stare up.

"You think so?"

"I know so."

And Bibi, pushing rudely past them: "Then let's not *sit* there," and inside to warmth, dark wood, dark booths. Bibi took a table, changed her mind when the farthest booth became suddenly available. From there they could see the street through windows green like aquarium glass, like Michael's sunglasses; his hesitation, one long moment between sides before sliding in next to Tess; near enough to touch and smelling faintly of sweat, of damp denim, in his hair a sweet soap odor as if he had just shampooed. He sat with fingers linked around the sugar decanter, old-fashioned glass with a scratched chrome spout.

Bibi loudly impatient for the pills to start working, drinking her coffee through a straw and cursing when it slipped and spurted, brown dribble down her shirt; Michael adding lots of cream from a tiny metal jigger, ice-cold sweat down its silver sides. Tess rubbed her eyes, again, hard, stars against the itching lids. "So." Coffee hot in her mouth; someone's barking laugh loud and hard across the room. "Why'd you quit your band?"

"Because I want to be in the Surgeons." Looking first at Bibi, then Tess, earnest face and that strange mouth in appeal, "Any way you want to use me, any capacity. I can do a lot more than just play the bells, you know," and Tess felt her lips in sudden rubber twitch, the laugh unexpected and saw that it had tickled Bibi, too, both of them laughing out loud so people turned to look and Michael seemingly unruffled, his own smile slow and curious and small, and very unsurprised.

"Muybridge," Bibi said, "are you familiar with him?"

"His motion studies, sure," hunched still on Tess's couchbed, quart bottle of beer untouched between his sneakered feet. Around them nearly night, the sculpted shadows cast by *Archangel, Mme Lazarus,* the Triple Deaths newly cleaned and oiled in Tess's absence; her three buying goodwill with scutwork. They needed no passport back into her good graces, but she did not mean to tell them so, not yet. Now she would simply sit, swiveled at the worktable to watch: Bibi's rainbow-face raising painful eyebrows, Michael's answering nods and half smiles, dandelion hair, explaining why he left his old group; he was already calling it his old group.

"They had some good ideas," finally drinking some of the beer, it must be flat by now. "Like the whole *fou* basis, that's a terrific idea. They had this whole library of tapes, of brain-damaged kids, and people with autism, hebe-phrenics, sociopaths, people who'd had all these various kinds of strokes and brain injuries that destroyed different parts of their consciousness, like they had this one guy who could only hear certain instruments, he could hear a guitar but not a trumpet, or any kind of keyboard or drum, only string instruments, he—"

"So how come," Bibi's interested slur, fingers blind on her strawed bottle of juice, "how come you left?"

Palms up like a suffering saint. "You have to do something with ideas, or they rot. You guys," his warm gaze including Tess, "are *doing* stuff."

"Yeah, we're doing all kinds of stuff," and Bibi laughed, mouth immobile as a stroke patient's. "It's not always scripted, but we do it anyway. Right, John Henry?"

"Oh right," her own smile turned down, slow and dry. "Michael," curiously, "what do you want to do, with the Surgeons?"

"Whatever you—"

"No. What do *you* want to do?"

Answer immediate as his smile: "The music. For now."

They talked, the three of them, into the night, the first warm night and windows left open, cars and radios and radios in cars the counterpoint to Michael's questions about the Surgeons, the first shows. They talked about theory, about motion, Tess's bright passion and Bibi's litany of the knife, of the power of the body, it's an area we're just getting into; did Michael see Tess's stillness? No way to know. Tess changing the subject back to sheer motion, talking about dance, about Bibi's kamikaze choreography and making half light of her lunatic leaps; Michael smiled, then, but did not laugh; Bibi laughed.

Almost dawn, Bibi's doubled dose of pain pills and curling like a child on the couchbed, "I'm not really sleepy," and out, sore mouth falling open as if weighted by heavy bruises, injured arm stretched as far as pain would allow.

Michael carefully setting the beer bottle aside, standing to take Tess's hand in a careful clasp.

"Thanks," long lids suddenly down, his fingers rough at the tips, blunt hands, warm. "Tell Bibi thanks, too, when she wakes up." Picking up his jacket, old cuffless white denim worn at the seams, a rusted Sisters of Darkness button on the lapel. Again the earnest smile, strange overlay on that bent aristocratic bite. "You really won't be sorry."

Watching from the window to see him wheel out a broken-down red scooter, wheezing start and gone down the brightening streets, hair loose behind. She was still not tired, but lay down beside Bibi's warm hedgehog curl, eyes closed to dream at once of faces stretched pleading in mad wordless music, mouths spurting flowers like blood and plasma and in the rigid stamen of each flower a calm sad enucleated eye.

"Oh yeah," box of tapes under his arm, big weight-warped cardboard with HEVVY'S PEACHES in water-faded red along the longest sides, "I used to use a Yamaha DX-100 and a Korg sequencer, but that's low tech now. So we went to no tech, just a big jumped-up boom box." Examining their equipment, "But this is good, here. Real basic."

Jerome's slight smile, Nicky and Peter behind, showing the new kid around. Second floor and spring's insistent warmth, a singular closeness in the air as if the whole room were one big closet, a closed-up car waiting to have its windows rolled down. Tess to one side, making the chrome crab walk up and down a set of mockup stairs; legs struggling just as if it were real, flipping occasionally to lie in frantic empty crawl until she righted it again; have to fix that.

In the farthest corner, the trio's unnamed machine;

early today she had cemented the truce by critiquing the construct, fix this, see this here? Fix it. This's okay. Good job, "but next time tell me, all right? Don't make an ass-hole out of me."

Jerome, vehement, "We *never*—"

"Okay, okay," waving it off; forget it. No new work, today, just the crab and maybe a trip to the scrapyard; and then Michael, showing up with his big box.

Bibi had gone to the clinic, her arm infected now past ignoring; Tess had not offered to drive her but like a jack-in-the-box there was Paul, "just stopping by" and of course he would be glad to take her, of course, and Bibi very cool, "Why not? It's your fault I have to go." Tess's frown extravagant, *Oh bullshit* but no dent in his stare, mournful Paul who was still in the Surgeons but not Bibi's good graces, odds were he would never get back into those. Tess wanted to feel sorry for him; but not today, with his copy-cat piercings, his subservient smile; funny that he had been able to withstand so many vigorous fights only to crack under the silent treatment. Funny.

Nicky and Jerome now reworking their machine, Peter filming, leaving Michael to his tapes, bent sorting head and thorough; to play.

Tess at first unaware, busy: but: subtle sounds, and subtly terrible, someone's repetitive chuckle, mm-*hmm* like a sound from the bottom of a drain, a deep drain, mm-HMM and a guitar, three chords, over and over. MM-HMM. A car door slamming on something soft. It went on and on. No one else seemed to be listening. Michael kept going through the tapes, setting some aside, flipping past others. Three chords. The car door.

Light through the window, down the crab's smooth chrome skin, sweat at her hairline. Looking up to see Michael smiling at her, just a little, the way an angel might smile: one hand marking his place in the box of tapes.

MM-HMM.

"—seven categories of bodily modification," Bibi and Michael drinking watery vegetable soup, close together on the couchbed and Tess half listening from the worktable, the crab eviscerated anew.

"Contortion. Constriction. Deprivation," more soup through a straw, Michael with both hands around the mug as if he were a child, a child with cold hands. "Encumberments, penetration, fire—"

"Fire like how?"

"Like electric shock. Or branding. Or extreme steam, like heat baths and boxes. —And the last one's suspension."

"Like hanging."

"Exactly."

"Some of these can be simulated, can't they?"

Slurp slurp. "Oh sure," vigorously stirring with the bending plastic straw. "All of them, probably, if you went about it right. But I think the real thing is much more effective, don't you, John Henry?"

Gun in hand, not looking up. "Don't ask me," one sizzling drop, another. "I'm not doing any of them."

Bibi's shrug, Tess saw it from the corner of her eye. Talking—piercings, scarification, had Bibi ever seen the sundance ceremony? no?—until Bibi complained of pain, her arm hurt, her mouth hurt, she wanted to lie down and did, covers over her head despite the warmth, breathing shallow and ragged until she fell abruptly to true sleep; Tess suspecting her of taking too many pain pills, but saying nothing: she was a big girl, wasn't she? Wasn't she?

And in the slumbering silence Michael, dragging up the extra stool, come to sit beside her.

Nothing, for moments, only the sound of her own motions, the tiny scrape of tools, the gentle sound of the solder. Finally: "What do you like better," touching with relic care the motionless legs of the crab, "making sculpture? Or the shows?"

"Melting metal," making of the crab's wired legs a brief hideous frisson, like a corpse jerking back to hectic life; then nothing. "That's what I like."

Pale eyes unsurprised, watching her hands move. Bibi on the bed groaned once and softly in her codeine sleep as if touched by dreams whose malice she could neither measure nor control, bad arm in awkward flutter against the pale stained covers and at the unlocked door, Paul: peering in.

"She's sleeping," Tess annoyed, Paul's presence a concrete reminder of Bibi's bad behavior, it was unfair but that was how it was. "—And since when do you have a key to the big door?"

"Nicky let me in." Taking a seat beside the couchbed, beside his sleeping princess; dabbing with his sleeve the sweat on her slack face, looking up into Tess's irritable stare: "What the fuck's your problem?"

"She's still mad at you, you know," and then as his face fell her instant shame: why say it? Why hurt him? More gently, "Listen. Why don't you just let—"

"Why don't you just go to hell? And take him with you," nodding to Michael who seemingly took no offense, sat quietly still on his stool. Tess turning back to chrome and motion, let them do what they wanted, all of them, as long as they kept her out of it. Cut themselves up, hang from rafters, who gives a fuck. Heat would still rise, metal would still melt. Work would still get done.

* * *

Hotter everywhere, spring melting to summer, she had been here a year now. Eight shows, it seemed incredible, it *was* incredible; they could never work at that pace now, now when things took so much longer, required so much more precision and care. So much more discussion. So much more argument.

The worktable was her oasis, bent over the crab, or the arms of the Triple Deaths, or the new construct that she was calling, privately, the *Magistrate:* lozenge-shaped, a vacuum cleaner torso, the standard bag replaced with heavy sheer plastic: blood pellets would churn there, small plastic arms and legs—today Michael had brought her a shoebox full, they had spent a cheery hour sorting through headless doll bodies—two dozen plastic swords stolen from Bar Hernandez. Symbols of cutting; of *shearing.* And beyond the bag, which was after all the gimmick, the come-on: attached to the rolling torso itself long slim limbs like branches, tender as new growth until the blunt fury of their tips: scissors, alligator clips, miniature jaws with real steel teeth that opened and closed according to the whim of the user. With Jerome's patient help—and he was some helper, Jerome, more pure craftsman than she would ever be—the *Magistrate* would be horrifying in a most subtle way, six weeks' work or less and ready for the next show. Whenever that was; and surprising herself with her own disinterest, relishing less and less the decisions, the day-to-day managing of the performing entity called the Surgeons; it was far more than a good idea grown, it was a process, an ongoing motion whose path she could not, unlike Bibi, see either straight or clearly. The infighting, her three, Paul's problems; and the *people,* people all the time. Marketing, she called it in a particularly virulent moment,

I'm no good at marketing and Bibi nodding her head in cold agreement: You got that right.

And then off to see Andreas, Paul presumably tagging behind (and when was she going to forgive Paul? it was getting more ugly than ridiculous, this silent vendetta); Tess alone behind the screens with her three at noisy work on the floors below. And in-between Michael, making tapes; Paul's old chore and he still bitched about losing it though he had bitched incessantly at the having; turning his pique on Michael, who seemed barely to notice, who never complained: which made him a rarity. Andy and Sandrine, and Paul, of course Paul, habitually whining and it all came down to the machines, too much focus on the machines. Even Raelynne muttered, she was supposed to be *dancing,* not getting pinned and rolled over and pushed around by machine-shop zombies, naming no fucking names by the by and so on.

And the machine-shop zombies growing touchier, too, withdrawing more and more to their own worktables and Tess could not, did not, blame them; it was harder work for them than for anyone, arranging the effects, and of course they had their own work to do; in an angry moment Nicky had declared their next project to be a trio of constructs called Machine-Shop Zombies whose only function would be to follow the dancers, hurt, tease, and harass them, and Paul yelling So what else is new? Shoving, fistfight genesis and big halfhearted Andy somehow incapable of settling them down until Tess, pushing between with gas torch in hand and "How about if I burn off your hair? How about your *heads?*" and Paul cursing, shoving back and away and Tess feeling without looking Nicky's hand beneath her own, its grip loose and wet on the trigger.

To Bibi, then, that same night, back from Andreas with a headful of plans but Tess took her aside, just you and me:

let's talk. Let's go somewhere and talk and Paul moving as if to come along, Tess turning on him: "Go *do* something."

The barest snarl, and Bibi ignoring them both to listen to the messages on the machine; then, brisk to Tess, "Okay. Let's go."

Slow-starting, the smell of gas, Bibi: "Javahouse?"

"Anywhere. Anywhere you want." Tess's head against the window, eyes closed, unable to enjoy the solitude, all alone with Bibi; didn't all this use to be fun? Her first words, as they sat down, a back booth: "Are you having fun, Bibi?"

"Right now?"

"I'm serious. Is any of this fun anymore?"

Tapping the menu card, lips still faintly purple like some exotic cosmetic. "You mean the Surgeons? Of course it's fun."

Tess said nothing.

"You take everything too seriously." Tess silent still, and Bibi sighed, reaching across the table to squeeze her hand, then changing sides in the booth, good arm around Tess's tight shoulders. "Stop worrying, all right? They're just impatient, it's been too long since we had a show. Besides," reaching up to tug her hair, "*we're* the ones who matter, right? And we're doing just fine."

As if from very far away, "They matter, too, Bibi. Everyone matters."

"Maybe to you." Grinning and the coffee came, very hot, sweet. Cream like velvet, pouring cold from sweating silver. The cup was heavy and white in her hand, steam on its smooth lip. "Listen, I wanted to talk to you anyway, I was at Andreas's again today—"

Burned skin in her mouth. "I know."

"—and he said we shouldn't have any trouble doing what we want to do."

Who's we? but she didn't say it. Bright eyes pale as water, each ear hung heavy with gold and steel, crosses and chains thin as an eyelash, and round red rivets in each nostril like fresh jaunty blood blisters. Talking about knives and needles, about Nigerian scarification, about the *mensur,* facial wounds, it all became for Tess a river of talk like a burst blood pellet, a pellet as big as a wasps' nest, Bibi's bruised mouth moving with the rhythms of a beating heart.

And somewhere in the talk Bibi's hand warm on hers, telling her she really ought to try it, they could do it together, it was fantastically empowering and so on and on and on and all Tess could see past the moving mouth was the silence of her worktable, the panels screening out as well as in; and with this thought a strange sadness, as if she had hurt Bibi in some secret way both stringent and irreparable, the longest needle of all to scar them both. And then a kind of fear, and determination: propping up her chin, listening visibly, and nodding, and nodding some more: I see, she said. I see just what you mean. Thinking as Bibi spoke of her own body scarred, and the shiver visceral and harsh: never. Never never never. I don't bleed, hedgehog; I burn.

No title yet, nothing; there was nothing they could agree on. Tess lobbying for an indoor show, but they wanted to do explosions, her zombie trio, and she was less inclined these days to tell them no when already they had begun to assume the stance and moves of guerrillas in occupied territory. So: Jerome and Peter and their complicated gunpowder toys, blowups; and Nicky ready to spew ground glass with his new spray blaster. And in *this* corner, Andy and Sandrine and Raelynne, apparently going under the knife together; and even Paul, whose name was still anathema but whose blood was, apparently, at least good enough to be shed.

And Bibi doing some of the cutting, under the supposed supervision of Andreas, whose newfound presence at rehearsals was getting to Tess, getting on her fucking *nerves,* she tried to say nothing, tried to keep out of the way. Yes, Bibi had to learn how to cut, though the idea of taking up the discipline and the knife in the same month seemed just a bit optimistic; but why must it be giggly Andreas and his black corpsegrinder gloves, why not the calm professionalism of someone like Linda Joy? Why *not* Linda Joy? and Bibi's shrug, she's not interested, she doesn't care for performing.

Good for her. But Tess didn't say it, in fact said nothing; only nodded. She was getting good at that, nodding, the brisk nod, the solemn nod, she could do them all. And upstairs in record time, working again, they didn't need her down there anyway, did they? No. They did not.

And Michael, shy knock as he opened the door: "Could I come in for a minute? Just a minute," bringing a quart bottle of beer, sitting beside her on the other, broken, stool; to share it, very cold against her lips, somehow even colder going down. One of the *Magistrate's* arms dissected before them. "Are you using this in the next show?"

"No. It won't be ready yet." A lie; with Jerome's help it could have rolled directly from the table to a performance; but Jerome was busy with gunpowder, let him do what he wanted, everyone else was. "I'll just use the Triple Deaths again, tear some shit up."

His hand on hers, on the bottle. Softly, "You don't sound too enthused about it."

"I'm very enthused."

Looking once at her and then away, down, at blunt fingernails stained with some new makeup, some fantastic blood-based greasepaint, who the hell knew what they were cooking up now. "The Surgeons is as much you as it is Bibi. You know that."

Her silence, her slow considering disagreeing nod; right now the Surgeons seemed more everyone than her but what difference, really, should that make; she had only her own work to do, didn't she? Yes. Of course, and Michael pointing out with exquisite gentility that she seemed to be avoiding rehearsals lately, was that due to anything in particular and turning all at once on her stool so it rocked and jittered on the cusp of balance: to stare at him, stare at him hard: *"This,"* one hand in rapid pivot, "is *my* rehearsal."

"I understand that."

Sharp: "Do you?"

Silence. His gaze down, then up.

"Yes," he said, very calmly, very simply. "I think I do."

More silence. Hair white in the sunlight, dirty windows and pale eyes, his hand moving to slide beneath hers, squeeze upward. "I don't think of things," another squeeze, "as having sides. I try not to, anyway. I don't think it's a good idea. Do you?"

"Everything has sides," but she squeezed his hand back, hard, released it; the buttery swipe of tension in her grasp. "Front and back. Up and down."

"Right and wrong."

"Nicky and Paul," but she had to laugh, it was funny, wasn't it? Lots of things were funny, if you knew how to look. How to laugh. Not many laughs lately.

"I better let you get back to work," and already the soldering gun, his shape in moving elongation as shadowy as a bruise in motion, as oblique as a shadow cast by a body unseen; before he was fully gone she was back to silent motion, her own motion as long and measured as a dance.

So: not the *Magistrate* nor even the *Madame* again but the *Madame*'s new daughter, *Salome,* who was in fact a simple moving construct, nothing but pure spin, like a quark Peter said: that's one of the attributes, did you know that? Spin, and color, and charm. And strangeness.

Nicky: "What's a quark?"

And, on the other hand, in other hands: the needles. And the knife. And Andreas, his fussy smile and guiding fingers around Bibi's, Paul's guinea pig back stretched bare and painted disinfectant-brown: "Wear gloves," Andreas said. "Always. Wear gloves."

And Bibi, peevish, "But that makes it hard to feel what you're doing," and Andreas insisting, and Tess moving past all of them like a quality of silence, back in relief to the blunt ferocious juggernaut that was *Salome.* She had been very easy to make, pure point and shoot; in fact she was fun, in her own blitzkrieg way. The *Magistrate* now set aside; with *Salome* and the Triple Deaths she was ready, nothing to do but wait.

And listen to the sniping, Raelynne and Nicky, Andy and Jerome, and Bibi in motion, double-washed hands and the dull-nickel gleam of surgical steel; and see Paul bleed, and smile, pink flesh puffed around the seeking sites of the needle. And endless in the background like atmosphere itself the long ominous whistle of Michael's new sound-track, like sirens, thrown stones and running water, metal beaten till it sparks; the whistle Death uses to call us out to play.

Obscenely hot. Cloudy plastic sheeting like dried sweat on the windows, it had once been a kind of foreman's shack, empty now; only Tess, long fresh burn along her bare calf, head back and in one hand a cracked bicycle bottle filled with warm tap water, her hair so wet it was dripping, metronomic as blood on her shoulders; she was alone.

Heat aplenty, there on the foundry grounds, site of old burnings, old metallic immolations, at first Tess had thought it a wonderful kind of omen: the biggest burn of all, metal running rivers, pleased and impressed that Michael had secured the site without any sort of release or liability statement; Michael was good at things like that, liaison work, both sides of the street. Very good, and she was even able to get into the foundry itself, do a little scrounging, nothing that would ever be missed; no one was ever coming back here. Cathedral industrial and all around her the abandoned furnaces, cranes and ladles, heavy ghosts of hot metal, were there still gods in these machines? Dust and rust and reverence, out blinking into the daytime heat like Vulcan's daughter, born at the forge, born for the burn. It would take an act of will to go back into the warehouse, the workspace, to be among the bickering again.

Sweat prickling on her back like the tiniest needles, her shoulders in quick irritable motion to shrug it away. Thinking of Bibi, somewhere, where? Perhaps they had left already, she and Michael, gone back to work, back without her; good.

Their last talk so brief, yesterday at rehearsal and Bibi strangely stilted, Bibi barely there and it's hard, she said, all of it's hard. "I see stuff in my head, how I want it to be, but—" Glancing back over her shoulder, back at the big room: back to work and Tess urging, "Try to get done early," but shaking her head again: time's wasting, can you believe there's still no costumes, that half-ass Sandrine;

restless with some combination of excitement and nervous rage, Tess heard her curse in cantering dream long past dawn.

And waking to hot morning, the two of them off ostensibly to check the site, and Michael literally between them, unsmiling, gentle, sucking water from a waxy cup of melting ice. The show—what show? her own irritable question unasked, they were no closer to a show than they had been two weeks ago, two months—was to begin with a pair of small explosions, the skitter of scattershot plastics, beads like BB's and the dancers emerging one by one from a fat cocoon of heavy netting to crawl, and continue crawling, about an altar where priestess Bibi masked in black as a horned beetle would cut various designs onto their disinfected skin. Paul would receive the most extensive cutting, of course; and Andreas aboard as well, as backup. Of course.

And more explosions, growing progressively larger, mimicked by the spray from Nicky's scattergun, plastic to glass as the Triple Deaths prowled the edges of the crowd and *Salome* threw herself against a rusty cornucopia of found objects, trash barrels, scrap metal, treadless truck tires like giant rubber grommets. One last large explosion would coincide with an orchestrated *Salome*-crash into the Triple Deaths who would then seize and toss her, still thrashing, into an empty Dumpster, as the dancers returned in bloody triumph to their cocoon as Bibi mimed suicide atop the altar and the Triple Deaths faked one final headlong rush into the crowd. Who were to be sequestered behind crash barriers, one of Michael's tasks and would they be strong enough, was he sure and "Don't worry," his faint sweaty smile; everyone was always telling her not to worry; why was that?

Walking silent as trespassers through the city of rust, she

had mumbled something, some false brief excuse and turned away, down an avenue twisted as the shapes that formed it, old machines left to rot in slow unspectacular decay and pushing into this shack, get out of the sun for a minute, just a minute alone. And the minutes stretching, silence and time enough, now, for the sun to slip behind clouds, the morning's threatened rain and cupped mask of sweaty hands across her face, absurdly close to tears; why tears? Stop it, just stop, fist rubbing hard against her lips, *stop it* and the sudden noise, the door banging open: Bibi, impatient: "Where were you? We were looking for you."

Turning on her heel and Tess standing, slow, pushing out of the shack and into the first of the storm, dark water on split trunks and beams and iron bodies and on her own face, her shoulders, legs in deliberate step behind the other two who ran, it seemed, in tandem to the shelter of the waiting car.

Still no show, and the hot uneasy summer dragging on in a morass of shouts and silences, the group's first anniversary deliberately unmarked; only Michael seemed immune to the bad will; only Michael had a foot in both camps.

And Tess, pausing over and over in the shielded heat of the burn, silent in smoke and distracted once again by worry: was it somehow her fault, desires divisive to twist the Surgeons' energy down her paths particular; was it right to choose for others, too? Even Jerome, and Peter and Nicky, flashpoint emulation but should they be off on their own, was she their crutch? Should there even be a Surgeons anymore, had it served whatever purpose it might have had and thus earned the right to be dissolved? Or was it wrong to think of dissolution, was there a path that would accommodate them all? Bibi believed there was a way to do both, but not a reason; she wanted, she insisted, Tess to see it, too. Strange to think that this new brawling might in the end drive them closer together; but for now more sparks when they met: edges meeting: the tip of the flux, the point of the knife.

"I want you with me," stretched damp and dour across the couchbed, muffled through her laced fingers, "I want to take you with me. Tess, if you could only see! If you would just *try* it, once. Just once."

So little impetus to fight, again, the same old battle, so many reasons to say no; she chose the easiest. "And end up like Paul?"

Bibi's impatient headshake, but the pale stare did not rise to challenge; could not: for Paul the cutting gone awry and now the skin of his shoulders sausage-tight and red, heavy pus beneath. He was taking Bibi's old antibiotics; hot compresses, Raelynne said, tea bags to draw out the infection and he was trying that, too. Without complaint, which was somehow sadder; instead pleased by his illness's capacity to draw Bibi's strictest attention, not seeming to understand that she saw him without tenderness, a symbol of failure to be corrected.

"No," shortly. "Not like Paul. Oh, *shit,* John Henry," the smallest smile of all, "there's so much we could do. You know it?"

"I don't know anything," meant mea culpa but received as a rebuff, Bibi rising stone-faced to leave the room, leave the building, slamming back hours later half-raging, half in tears, bright new cutting on her shoulder, strange glyph like a pound sign split in half. Sitting down hard on the couchbed, humid hands on dirty knees: "We're both too good for this," and Tess beside to hug her, careful of the blood, unable to think of comfort, the single word that might restore balance, might bring again the ground to stand together. Trying for it, trying to talk about the *Magis-*

trate as if work's totem might heal, but all Bibi could think or talk of was her cutting; ending, again, mutually misunderstood.

Michael tried: with both, Tess was sure without being certain, using surely the same calm tactics of kindness and diffidence: brown ghost at rehearsals, fiddling with his handheld boombox, distant by miles from the sulks and stinks, noises human and mechanical; but. Afterward, one arm loose around Bibi, dandelion head poking up from under into her extravagant frown, talking; soft voice talking. Explicating? as he did on the floor above, arm now around Tess: disposable respirator hung fetishlike around his neck and his slow sweet banter, always the questions she most wanted to answer: Is it? Why? Show me. Beside the worktable to watch the thump and jitter, the frisky gush of sparks, saying very little, really, never very much at all but always the things she needed to hear: your work is good. Surgeons or no Surgeons, your work is good.

"Now? Bibi, we're not ready."

Tess's flat disbelief, and Bibi hunched, white-headed gargoyle on a chair broken backless, ticking points off her fingers: we need the work, *they* need to work, there's a new routine to try. And the money, too. "Anyway we can't let them sit around," peevish, her stare up, down, like searchlights sweeping a yard. "They get all fucking *twitchy.*"

"Translation," setting aside the tangle of cable, mouth in a frown and she felt above her lip a little mustache of sweat and dirt, it was unconscionably hot up here. Gray bandanna harsh against her face, rubbing, scraping, fist in echoing motion rubbing harder yet: "What you mean is, *you* want to work, you want to *cut,* right? Right? Just be honest."

Instantly defensive, up and off the chair: "What's wrong

with that? *You* work plenty, up here, you're always working. You do what you want and to hell with the shows."

"That's not true! That is not true and you know—"

"I know you're pretty fucking selfish, that's what I—"
and both at once aware of Paul and Michael, watching
from the doorway, Paul yellow-sick but grinning, Michael
obviously distressed. And Tess hectic with the same old
angers, slamming the cable down on the workbench, things
falling and to Bibi, up off the chair, "Time to take your
dog for a walk." Pushing past them all, downstairs with no
clear idea where she was heading, into the car and on the
way to the scrapyard; it was where she belonged, alone
with sharp edges, the slow corrosion of rust like the seeping blood of the dinosaurs at the bottom of the pit. She
stayed until it was dark, crawling planes and peaks of
scummy iron, crawling like an insect up the garden wall
until a guy with a flashlight chased her away, down and
through the gates: and waiting there in a funnel of street
light, Michael.

Head wrapped in white like a mummy, ugly sunglasses
around his neck on a braid of shoelace thong; unsmiling,
waiting on her mood.

"Do you want," and she saw his scooter, hurried slant
against the fence, "to go for coffee? Or a drink, or something?"

Silent, then "No"; then what *do* you want? I don't know.
I don't want to do a show now, things are too bad; bad
blood. I want to be left alone. I want to work; I want it to
be like it was. "No thanks," her smile artificial but she was
making the effort, anyway, and that was worth something.
Or ought to be. Michael's scooter a faithful tail, all the way
back until the last street: skittering abruptly left, the sick-
bug drone of his engine gone, lost in the night sounds.

Inside pause to note rehearsal, Michael's recorded

soundtracks and thump and bump and grind. And scratch. And scar.

No thanks.

Worktable at once but no desire to work, instead mechanically setting things to rights, scattered tools, the cans of flush and solvents upset. Across the room, half-dusk despite her light and Bibi's bed heaped full with costumes, black and red, rags and harnesses and long strips of rubber, leggings made of vinyl and bright snaps; just detritus yet all at once she crossed the room to sit a silent moment in that pile, mess and crumpled textures and smells, hands open as if in touch she might take more than was truly there; find the full in the empty, past in the present; what was needed from what sheer and simply was.

The next day like all the others, Jerome's near-constant clang two floors down and Sandrine screaming counterpoint down the stairwell "I can't work like this!" Bibi hurling an armful of big empty cans, props, stinky and rusty all the way down the stairs and Nicky writing names on them, SANDI and RAY and ANDY and PAUL in heavy black marker and then blowing them up. One by one. Under the windows.

And, late, Tess and Bibi in the shared quiet of exhaustion, for once not working or even fighting and then, abrupt: Raelynne, beer bottle and too much jewelry, clanking like Sandrine's totems and determined flop, even past Tess's frown, Bibi's austere half-lidded gaze.

"This troupe," without preamble, "this troupe is going to shit, and you want to know what the trouble is, I'll tell you. Be*sides* letting a bunch of dumbshit kids play with fuckin' dynamite, by the by and naming no names." Drunk, but not a lot; Dutch courage, they used to call that. "It's that blond-headed cuntstrummer, you want to know."

Bibi's head cocked like a puzzled dog's and Tess's eyes narrowed in instant disbelief: "You mean *Michael?*"

"Yeah," stubborn to Bibi's incredulous laugh, even Tess had to smile. If anyone was outside the problem it was Michael, the conciliator, the bridge between the groups; patient cyborg, half-metal and half-flesh. "Michael's the only one who *doesn't* bitch," and Bibi's nodding chime, Michael was the nice one.

"The only nice one," and to Tess a smile exclusionary, secret and Tess smiled back; how strangely dear Bibi was sometimes, you could want to murder her and then she would make a face like that: little hedgehog scarface with her nose grommets and studs and long bright earrings worked to look like razor wire. Did Bibi feel that way, too, looking at her? Yes? Maybe; maybe not?

Long sloppy swig and Raelynne insisting, "You guys, I'm *serious,*" but they were not, not anymore, Tess leaning forward, Bibi back and joking: Michael subversive, Michael the tool of long-gone Crane, Michael the secret love slave and Tess, deadpan, "We're probably the only ones who *haven't* fucked him," and Bibi's tickled screech, more and more silly and Raelynne finally pissed and shoving out the door, fine, fine. You all do what the hell you want, it's fine with me.

Slow subsiding smiles, headshakes and Bibi leaning low to stretch, bright eyes upside down: "Hey. Are you sure you haven't fucked him?"

Up and yawning to shut the door, "I'm sure." Pause. "How about you?"

"Oh yeah," about-face, right side up and grinning past the dangle of wires: "I'm sure you haven't fucked him, too."

* * *

The new flyer was completely black but for three things: Tess's fingers, Bibi's eyes, and THE MAGISTRATE OF SORROWS, red letters like stylized cuts, razor thin and staggered diagonal. They had not even bothered, this time, to post a time, a place; word of mouth would take care of that.

This time the *Magistrate* himself, itself, blood and suction, the bubble of plastic parts and the larger stretch and finger of the metal limbs, their shearing tips infinitely more manipulable than the blunt hammer-and-tongs of the Triple Deaths; they call that learning. Alligator clips a rusty smile; the fury of the scissors, heavy tinsnips and metal bite. There was a nursery rhyme once, German she thought, about the Scissor Man who came to thumbsucking children; the great red-legged Scissor Man, it had scared the shit out of her as a child and she hadn't even been a thumbsucker. That was there, in the *Magistrate,* nameless the lord of silver nightmares, the sound a knife makes in the dark; don't tell me, she thought, about knives.

Bibi of course had her cuttings, hinting at lots of plans but for once Tess was not anxious to hear them, did not want to listen or think about Nicky's piques and Paul's missed rehearsals, Bibi's disbelieving sneer, He *said* he was *sick.* Well; maybe he is. I am, too.

Smells. Sounds. Everything black this time, costumes and makeup, sketchy sets already in place upstairs, bare metal scaffolding, barely room enough for the *Magistrate* to move; smoke and blood the only colors. The scaffolding looked half-ass to Tess, complaining to Andy, arms folded huge to tell her she had two choices: either redo it herself or redo it herself. Just like almost everybody else he was doing his fucking best and in case anybody had forgotten he was a dancer and not a fucking ironworker in the first place, right? Right?

Mouth pursed a little, a little, poking him lightly in the chest with her finger, other hand calm on the heft of a chipping hammer; you're a big guy, Andy. Poke, poke. But I'm not all that small myself. Don't you think?

Hot in the room; long jittering whoop of a siren outside. Very carefully, "I don't think you really want to fuck with me, Tess."

As quietly, feeling the smile outside but not in, inside she felt nothing but a very small curiosity dry as a bleached insect, "I think you have that backwards. Andy."

And all at once Nicky at her side, pulling at her like a kid, c'mon Tess. Tess, come on, Jerome wants you.

Which turned out to be true: what was needed was her reluctant blessing on his ringleader plans, the ones he chose to talk about anyway: for *Salome,* and M-80s, and sound, look, he had pages of small-print specs: "Nicky showed me," hunched up on a tumble of boxes below in the first-floor workspace, the Zombie Birdhouse they called it. "Cops in Europe got 'em," pointing out a paragraph, "ultrasonics, it can send out two different frequencies at a time and it's really fuckin' *torqued* . . . 'course that's sort of dangerous, we're not doing that. What we want to do is a flat sixty seconds of a high-frequency scream, you can't really hear it but it's *there,* you feel it in your body." Dirty face, big smile, heat through the windows bright as light and the lingering miasma of dog piss; sounds good, Tess said. Or doesn't. Get it? but she didn't laugh and Jerome didn't either, slowly back to his worktable and she trudging up to hers, hammer still in hand. He came up later to help with the *Magistrate,* but all they talked was tech. She didn't feel like talking about anything. To anybody.

And then Michael would come, sit on the couchbed or maybe, if she wasn't burning, on the stool beside; and say nothing. Small smile, watching, making no comments or noise, sweat on his shoulders, water sometimes or sometimes beer. Head-turned watching and sometimes to Tess the thought unbidden, what would it be like? White-blond hair like ash, like vines between her fingers, O of a sweet red mouth and what would it be like to feel with her tongue its slippery sugary darkness, its black hole like the excise space left behind by a rotten tooth? Heat in her face, *am* I the only one who hasn't fucked him? Yet? and his silent hand on her arm, smiling; and gone, heat like a question left behind.

Bibi in and out, too, three interviews the week before the show, angry at Tess for refusing to do them with her but not angry enough not to do them alone; more messages on the machine, Tess ignoring them, setup work to do and ignoring that, too, instead out in the parking lot working the *Magistrate,* sweat-wet and oblivious behind the heavy Dumpster until people saw, people came, yelled, she had to push some guy in the face and Bibi scolding afterward, for fuck's sake Tess you *should* have known! They did not speak the rest of the day, Tess sleeping angry to wake, snagged weary in sweaty sheets and yes, Bibi was right: she should have known.

But: Bibi barely there and already gone, props to pick up and Tess left alone in the morning heat, below the sounds of beaten metal, the distant whooshing pop of something small exploding. Shitty instant coffee and half-closed stare to see taped over the toilet another stare, and fingers, THE MAGISTRATE OF SORROWS and chalked below in mocking caps THE WORLD'S LONGEST-RUNNING SORE.

"It's *full,*" for the twentieth time, Sandrine horrible and lush in heavy mesh, smiling as if she were high. Cobweb chain strung thin from earlobe to nostril, she and Rae-

lynne had added minuscule charms, skulls and curly daggers below identical bright-eyes; they both looked fucked
up. So did Andy, so did Andreas in the corner with pursed
lips and a rag, attending Paul: just finished vomiting and
too ill to even be there, black T-shirt loose and faintly
stained over the sick crouch of his shoulders.

And people, people, people, inside and outside and everywhere, some perching gargoyle on the opposite roof,
trying to see in; Nicky had said there were others on the
roof above them, trying to cut peepholes. Nicky now clustered triplet with Peter and Jerome, all of them headwrap-
ped in black, respirators hung bright against their chests
though Bibi had screamed about that, the respirators were
white for God's sake and Tess forced to defend them, they
need to breathe, Bibi, maybe you didn't think of that.

"The dancers need to breathe, too."

"Then give them respirators."

Each glaring at the other, Tess all bones and angles and
sparks, sparks under the skin, formicating shiver like
crawling insects, like the angry knurl of each separate and
particular element, fear and weariness, hot and cold. For
her tonight the whole room, the crowd, each one of them
in this loose twist had a distinct and unwholesome odor,
the smell that says This is not good. As if the rot inherent
in the group had begun to manifest, and rot stinks. Like
garbage; the silent fester of anger; like dried blood.

But for Bibi—Tess could tell just by looking—there were
no such tremors, never the underskin pavane: hands on
hips, clown mouth down, made up by Sandrine to look like
Marquesan tattoos, stark black bars across forehead and
eyes. Coldly, "The white ruins the symmetry of the *look.*"

"Tough shit."

And Andy, from the peanut gallery, the breathing circle
on the edge of a bubbling giggle, private giggle and leaning

in to say hey Tess how come you don't try the finger trick on *her?* Huh? Poke her a good one! and Sandrine's snicker; Raelynne's loose haw-haw, Andreas picking at the tips of his gloves, smile pointed down like a courtier and all of a sudden it was just too much, all of it, all of them, and leaning into Andy, his breath pure candy mouthwash and "Because I'd rather try it on you, fuckface," and shoving him hard, stiff hands smearing the makeup on his slack-muscled chest and from somewhere Andreas and Michael jumping tandem in between and Bibi's grip hard on Tess's forearm, snarling, *"Stop* it, *now!"*

Andy falling back, off balance and Andreas's unsteady grasp, Tess angrier than she had ever been, turning on Bibi: hands on her black shoulder blades to shove with all her force, knock her flat on her ass and Tess above, trembling: "Don't you ever grab me like that, Bibi. Ever."

Bibi surrounded now, tender black scowls to help her rise, turning silent away and Tess clenched hands, a sick taste under her tongue. Jerome saying something in her ear but she shook him off, go away, went herself away to a corner, where can you hide in a room full of people, a street full of people, fucking people everywhere oh God if only this were over. I said no show, I *said—*

And Michael all at once, hand light on her arm and a paper cup of water: "You want this? Tess? Are you thirsty?"

Equally vamped in makeup but still Michael, pale eyes and half a smile, chains across his bare chest; he was supposed to start up the soundtrack and then join the dancers, something about a tribal circle around the cutting altar; she had not listened. Tried to listen now, dry mouth and taking the water, taking his hand.

"Are you okay?"

Her slow nod a lie, sweat down her back and the warm

closeness of his shielding body; crowd sounds deeper now, louder, the coughing of beasts expectant. "You're working the *Magistrate,* right? But not *Salome?*"

The flat taste of bottled water, she drank it anyway. "No," draining the cup; crushing it. "I gave her to Jerome."

More gently still, "It's going to start soon, couple minutes. Are you sure you're okay?"

Mechanical as a construct, engineered response: "Fine," but his face even closer and his mouth very light on hers, faint moist feel of his tongue, "Then break a leg," and stepping back, gone, over to Bibi still encircled, cocooned, and Tess in dry confusion turning to walk somewhere, away, ending up beside Peter loading the last camera, the view from behind the stage area: "Hey," his grin unsteady, "you torqued?"

"Plenty." Her hands were still shaking. She did not want to look at Michael; or Bibi. Or the crowd. "Ready?" and in the instant the long feedback whistle of the soundtrack, lights cut and the yelling begun: *"Surgeons!"*

Peter's quick nudge, hurrying back to his bombs and Jerome moving swiftly past as: the drag of heavy curtain, I believe that's your cue: take up the *Magistrate*'s control: be ready. The dancers clambering along the scaffolding, Paul the last one to rise, coordination off like a drugged bug. Cut-down smoke machine pumping smells as rich as rotten meat, instant dead-food miasma and Bibi, turning in that instant, turning on Tess: to stare, lips back like a dog and no sound at all.

The soundtrack in earnest, barnyard groans and the beaten whistle of steam and Bibi stepping, goosestepping, ironic priestess in place, facing the crowd with a perfect flourish of black-gloved hands. She was all of a piece, solid and beautiful as a loaded gun; like a mirror that perfection and threat reflecting back to Tess her own ferocious sad apartness, outsider fighting in the end to get back out.

Shaking hands on the *Magistrate:* All right, she thought, sliding damp thumbs, fingertips: let's get it over with.

Half a dozen small explosions, grotesquely loud in this enclosure, echoes punctuation in the soundtrack growl and the stutter of strobes, two bodies like lizards crawling slow down the scaffolding—already swaying a little, what a *shitty* job Andy had done; never mind. Pay attention.

To the *Magistrate:* its first true show and see how easy to work, to manipulate, vacuum burble and plastic hands stuck in wet beseechment against the heavier plastic skin; reaching, vicious dandy, to pinch with alligator clips the long skirt of the curtain, pinch and twist and rip it like skin, tinsnips moving like the beak of a raptor, a killing bird, the vulture who tears forever at writhing Prometheus: *bring me fire.*

More bodies off the scaffolding to ring the cutting table, less stylized altar than butcher block and there the jitter begun of steel over twitching flesh, hot trails of blood mingled with the freshet spurt of blood pellets and they were sticky with it, they were slick and grinning and wet. The heavier groan of metal, metal twisting, *Salome* imprisoned in something like a drum and trying to batter her way out, the battering miked and sampled back into the larger shriek and another victim stripped for the knife

and the *Magistrate* moving to the very edge of the safety ropes, control box in her hands as warm as flesh and squeezing, tinsnips picking at the scaffolding itself, swinging like a beast on the loudest part of the crowd, everyone was yelling, Paul lumbering past for his turn on the table, poisoned yellow eyes like a plague victim and

hot, so hot in here, all the windows open and the blowers on full-bore and *hot* like the slippery cave of a beating heart, a dying heart in the heavy stench of rot, sweat in the grooves of her grin because she was smiling; why?

because this is fun

Isn't it?

Choral voices now, screaming, *Salome* hard against the imprisoning skin and a sudden bulge, battering juggernaut thump twinned with an explosion that made her ears ring. Half-deaf in the aftershock, heat and grease and atop the butcher's stage the strop of bleeding flesh, Bibi yowling something, bare blood-spattered breasts and the crowd screaming, screaming to urge her on

and now the rhythmic tidal motion of linked bodies: Andy and Sandrine and Raelynne and Paul and the *Magistrate*'s tinsnip fingers chewing, nipping, biting hard and past all the safety ropes, driving the crowd back—isn't this fun? isn't this what you paid to see?—and *Salome* rocking, the drum rocking, whine of working metal relentless

she's getting away

and uncontrolled—where is Jerome?

loose in a space this small

but no, not entirely, the thrust held back and slamming just past the altar, the block, the dancers' instinctive scatter and for a bald hysteric moment Tess wanted to laugh, how's that for a special effect? Stink in her nostrils and the stutter of the strobe; blood like oil and the crawling dancers now with

weapons?

some kind of blunt knives, hands and knees and approach like assassins, Tess's gaze narrow through the stench to see the dancers ring first Nicky, kick and slap then pushing and shoving at Peter, someone hit him and then Jerome, distracted at *Salome*'s control, trying to ward them away

and Bibi, halfway up the scaffolding to hang laughing

like a bat, like the wingless angel of chaos, laughing at everything and all the stupid half-fake blood

and Tess squeezing hard, heat and gristle like bone, metal, blank-faced advance on the dancers like death made manifest: You want to play? Play with this. Pulling, costumes ripping, the tines and snips and clips smeared with the pellet-blood, Cerberus nip at their slick new wounds, biting not to hurt but to frighten, to terrify, send them running, freed bodies, dogs in the path of a car, a train, an avalanche; you don't like the machines? They don't like you, either.

And now *Salome* working, resistless batter like a madman against the splinter of her chains, *let me out let me out* and Andy slamming up beside Jerome, shoving, the crowd uneasy now and back against the walls. Retreat, did they smell it, grudge match, grievance, what? What? Bibi black fruit astride the scaffolding tree, no more laughter, bloody arms and back and yelling something, yelling at Tess, big pale eyes in the strobing dark and Tess staring as one stares at an enemy unmasked

and on cue—was it?—the sound that was no sound at all, noise hot through the body and somebody pushing for the doors

as *Salome* now unguided slammed once more against the chains

and again

oh God it's loose

and hard into the first thing in her path—the scaffolding, but not bouncing off as she was made to, instead slamming to stick, intense vibration seen in Bibi's clinging body, electrocution-like jerk and Tess in the watching slapped free of anger by fear: *"Jerome!"* but of course he could not hear, no one could through that sound, hideous, noiseless, felt in the body and the audience moving, brute surge, the lunatic dance of panic at last begun and Tess wheeling at once, *hurry,* to aim the *Magistrate* to intercept the shock of stalled *Salome* against the teetering scaffolding, Bibi at last on the ground and "Get *clear!*" Tess's own screaming voice in her ears, like a train, like a truck rolling brakeless downhill Get CLEAR get CLEAR

and the noises mercifully off as Jerome on his knees snatching up *Salome*'s lost control, off but too late, the whole structure inexorable in a dance of its own: long skeleton reel of pipe and *"Get clear!"* through the shrieks of the trampling crowd, the dancers scattering, Peter and Nicky curled undercover in the loud enormity of falling metal

and Raelynne's siren shriek like the cry of the metal itself, the first pole striking final, striking flesh and fragile bone: Paul.

In the back of the head.

Blood, everywhere.

2

HYPNOTIZING

CHICKENS

There is a charge
For the eyeing of my scars
—Sylvia Plath

Paul had wanted to be cremated; in Bibi's voice the flat fiat of hysteria, face pale as her eyes, she had not slept for almost three days. Tess could not stand to be in the same room with her, had not been alone with her since the hours in the police station; on their return Bibi had gone up to their floor, while Tess turned left into the Zombie Birdhouse; and stayed there. Away from her tools and projects but for once there was no desire in her for tools or projects, nothing but the dry husk of disbelief like an alien new flavor: the falling metal, the heavy leak of blood.

The EMS tech said that Paul had died almost at once, brain death; token try at revival but he was already past resurrection, vegetable or not. No one had known whom to list as next of kin. Classified as indigent, his cremation was billed to the city; the ashes went to Bibi, in a little tin square half the size of a box of tissues, his name and date of death on a neat white label smeared by fingertips and tears.

To Tess's dull surprise there were no criminal charges, no legal punishments and it felt wrong, *wrong* that Paul should die and no one be held responsible. Responsibility and culpability, the road between sorrow and guilt; death: and no one, it seemed, was to blame.

Sick-hot day, afternoon, no one working. The canvased form of battered *Salome* in a corner; apparently they had carried it here; Tess had not touched it since the show, would not now, wished never to see it again. Let them tear it up for scrap. Now Peter, slow to start some busywork, Jerome leafing with half-closed eyes through a newspaper and all at once Sandrine's focusless stare around the Birdhouse door: "Bibi says," in a fucked-up voice, slow and blurry like a sleepwalker, like water through a clogging drain, "we're going to do the ashes in a while. In an hour, she says. Everybody meet upstairs."

Staring back, Tess, Jerome, Peter in various states of silence but Nicky: "Fuck if I will," startling them all, red-eyed and loud, the way a child cries. "Fuck it, she thinks she can run it like a show, like a fucking *Surgeons* show," and Sandrine shouting back through tears immediate, both of them shoving in the doorway until Jerome grabbed Nicky back and with his free hand slammed the door.

And Nicky weeping, "I didn't even like him, he was an *asshole*," Jerome leading him back to the long blanketed bench, better rest a minute, man, just take it easy. And Peter, young eyes old: "Tess. Are we going or not?"

As if through a distance, the desert of regret: when she spoke at last her voice was flat as the desert floor.

"Do what you want," she said. "I'm not in charge here anymore."

The next day Bibi moved out.

No argument, no discussion; no knowledge for Tess until the sounds began, the dragging and the dropping and the truck outside; Crane's friend, again? Not much—was there?—to carry but it seemed like a lot, many trips up and down and the cranky hum of the service elevator, Tess alone in the late afternoon heat of the Birdhouse looping listlessly through small twisted piles of solder and cable, pretending to work but: listening for the last trip, the empty elevator thump that would release her to move upstairs, animal-sniffing her way back into her own lair: what has been pissed on, scent-scarred, what left alone? Would Bibi send someone, Andy or Paul—Andy or Sandrine, to give the all-clear, a last message, fuck you all? Or just leave? Listen; in the silence clear as solvent, cables slim like veins through her cold fingertips and the endless headache knocking dull against her temples, mausoleum forehead: just listen.

And missed it, in the end: Nicky back from his scrapyard wander, bagful of crap and wires protruding, calling her name: "Tess, hey; Tess?" Cautious past the door as if the Birdhouse were her home, not his: "Tess? It's okay. She's gone."

"Are you sure?" a shaming question like a kid scared to look in the closet; big fucking baby, go see for yourself. Rising, distracted nod past Nicky, looking older now; they all did. Stairs, not elevator, climb into greater heat and see: the door politely closed but unlocked, a path left careful for the clearing: gone. Her bed. Her costumes and clothes, her piles of style books and underground rantzines, her tapes, her tiny cracked black coffeemaker, all the whirlwind detritus and only silence in its place. None of Tess's things were touched. On the worktable, slim oblong folded twice and inside her share, calculated to the minute, of the month's rent. No note; no nothing.

What did you expect, a sad good-bye? A forwarding address? Dust in the light from the windows, message light blinking monotonous: more calls for interviews, the decline and fall of *tanzplagen*, *AntiTrust* would be glad to pay

for an exclusive. Go fuck yourselves. And a message for
Bibi from Linda Joy, yes she would be glad to see her, just
come by anytime today.

The room infinitely smaller now; Tess sat on the
couchbed, door open, head in hands and did not cry but
felt in her chest the ache folded down through nights and
dry days expanding now, rising like vapor to fill her lungs
with poison, fill her throat with one long groan caustic as
slow corrosive, all the words unsaid and sorry, the unwept
tears to eat at last like acid until she was empty; and clean;
or dead.

Or worse.

Two days, she supposed and not unkindly, they would
give her two days to grieve, or scream, get it out of her
system. And, predictable as a construct *(really? would that
be* Salome *you were thinking of?)* here they came, Nicky,
Peter, and Jerome, rubbery stale beignets and coffee; they
knew, they said, that she liked beignets and coffee. The
plastic cup too hot to hold; bitter steam in her face at the
worktable, completely clean and sorted, everything was
clean, obsessively so, the kind you get from working nonstop for hours and hours pushing and moving and dragging
and sweeping, couchbed and sculpture and constructs and
panels and tools, mushroom clouds of dust to blind dry
eyes, to stick like gray cancer to your skin, you can get a
place pretty fucking clean if you do nothing else for two
days. No sleeping, no eating, now biting into one of the
beignets, wet cardboard taste: "Good," she said. "It's
good."

Three glances the same, back and back and forth and
Jerome, as usual: "Tess, listen. We just wanted to know if,
we wanted to see what you were gonna do, what your plans
are. You know."

No, I don't think I do. "Plans for what?" around the beignet, tumor-lump in the pouch of her cheek; force it down. "Plans for what?"

"For, you know," tilted coathanger shrug. "Work."

"You mean like a show? Like the Surgeons?" Expecting the name to taste bad but it was dull as the beignet, flat in her mouth as she shifted on the stool to better face them all. "The Surgeons are over. You guys are free to do whatever you want, work, put on shows, whatever. I'm not in charge of anything anymore."

"You said that before."

"I meant it."

Shifting themselves, now, answer in hand and unsure what else to say, nervous hands fiddling with the empty cups, the crumpled beignet bag, obviously uncomfortable in this new atmosphere where everything had changed. Peter's uncertain glance to Jerome, breaking the silence, "Well I started editing down those tapes"—then instant stutter back to quiet: taboo topic but Tess smiled, ugly little smile: "That one really ought to sell."

And Nicky, surprising them again: "Tess," very firmly, "none of that shit was your fault, and if everybody's too chickenshit to say it then I will. You're the one who tried— no," angrily to Jerome, rejecting some sort of covert signal, "I mean it. She didn't do shit, it's all their fault, those dumb fucks playing around with their stupid knives, that's how you lost the box and—"

"*Nicky,* shut—"

"—Paul had no fucking business even *being* there, man, as sick as he was, but *she* had to go and let—"

"Stop it," her own voice eerily conversational, up off the stool without knowing, or feeling, feeling nothing past the desire to hear none of this, now or ever. "Just stop, all right? It's over, and I don't want to talk about it, so I'm just going to work now," toward them, moving them with her motion (and memory, the *Magistrate*'s sweep toward the crowd, the dancers, I'll give you a special effect and she had gotten one, hadn't she? the most special one of all), "I'm going to be working all day so I'd appreciate it if you guys left now, okay? Thanks for the coffee," and out the door, stubborn Nicky turning for one last stare and then he was gone, too, the door closed, the room empty. Clean and square and lit by the calm hot oven light of day, all the time in the world now to work without worrying about interviews or shows, without talking to anyone, seeing anyone; do not disturb.

The light on over her worktable, fierce hunch to settle in, settle down: to what? To work and never mind why, if you kept looking for the why behind everything you might never work again, you might never bother to breathe again. So: head down and keep busy; and on the floor, on a strip of waxed paper her forgotten beignet, food for ants, for mold, for all the small erosions of heat and time, entropy's relentless remembrance and the slow organic rust of rot.

A small piece, she was working on a small piece this time, just big enough to fit comfortably on the worktable. No name or title, begun as a way to keep working, keep from thinking but a week into it she found it good, insectile stretch and impossible dancer's grace, a leggy thing that moved in disturbing ways.

At first like a cloud the gray encirclement of guilt, unsure if it was right to take pleasure in work, in anything; still not certain but now it was easier to breathe a little, to keep busy and find more than busywork in her light, with her solitude and tools; no one else had been to visit; she never answered the phone so that was not a problem. Up, wash, sometimes eat and work till sleep, sometimes fully clothed on the unopened couchbed, head back and the new construct stepping dainty through the surface of her dreams—when she remembered them; many were not good to remember.

And up, sometimes, in the night, unconscious focus for what waking told her was Bibi, the sound of Bibi's breathing, the whispers and cries from her side of the room, her dreams; what was she dreaming now, Bibi, did she wake, too, crying for Paul? For anyone? Don't think, Tess would say and sometimes aloud: "Don't think," in the dark like a prayer for poison. Pillow lumped and hot like a small body cooling; don't think; and sometimes she did not.

In the mornings it was the new construct again. Scale small, like the jitter of the crab but this was something different, made as her sculptures used to be made, for no application, no purpose beyond the fact of its existence. Here is a thing, black angles that can move like the shift and purl of remembered shadows, like the drip of dirty water in a cracked plastic bucket, like the smell of the room where the intern brought you the news. You can almost hold it in your two hands, this thing, but there is something in you that does not want to touch it, that does not want it to touch you: something that after contact makes you wipe your hand down the side of your leg. Something that Tess felt inside her, near her heart, drifting like a caul unmoored, slow and gray; every day. Every day from now on.

In the mirror she saw her face not older but somehow newly full of bones, as if her own mortality were pushing up against the tiring barrier of her skin; she spent very little time with the mirror these days. Hair in a long coarse tail, ragged T-shirts and barefoot over the metal shavings, summer's descent to mimic her own; descent into what?

Cold. Silence, although the downstairs Zombies provided plenty of companionable noise if she had been inclined to companionship; but it was her move and they were leaving her to it. Zombie Birdhouse, it was a sign on their door now, she passed it going and coming, scrapyard rendez-vous: the scrapyard, the one thing that had not yet failed her. Rust oasis, sometimes she spent hours there, up and down the piles with the absent balance of a goat, a wall-walking baboon, crawling like a hairy-legged spider up the carcasses of split hi-los, corroding drums as empty as old sacs, the sad pendulous sway of husked cranes; she had badly wanted a crane, just a little while ago, to help move around the heavier constructs, *Mme Lazarus* in particular; no need for it now. She had not worked with any of them, maintenance, nothing for the *Madame,* the crab, the Triple Deaths or *Magistrate; Salome* she wanted never to see again. Just the unnamed legs and small torso lying blandly on her table, sweet lubricant trickle as pink as flavored grease; this handle, here, this useless part of a larger use-lessness, industrial-quality steel-tank vacuum now pocked and filigreed with rust: this little handle might very well work on that nameless daddy longlegs; if it snaps off; there.

The one thing she stole, all the rest weighed and paid, not a lot this trip but later than usual, closing time and the bag heavy as thought on her shoulder—no more car—al-most completely dark and "Hey," from beyond the fence. Again, softer, "Hey," and she saw that it was Michael.

Beautiful; his usual beauty but unseen for weeks and so more painful and noteworthy: black bandanna printed with faded skulls and sleeveless black Stickler for Punish-ment T-shirt, bruised cheek and pale in the greenish wink of the streetlight: untouchable and strange as a stranger, as if the moment prior to conception might stand with sleep-tight eyes in the midst of life and say: This is how it was, before.

Around his eyes, circles, but his hands were warm as they touched hers, squeezed and did not release; her own hands in contrast seemed cool as lead. A smell like clean sweat and he was talking, head down and quiet and she asked him to say it again: "I said," reaching to take the bag from her, "she wants to see you."

From the place inside, instant the place with the caul; and terror; and what else? "I don't want to see her."

"She misses you."

"Bullshit."

"Tess," hands out, palms up, the sincerity of frustration and who asked you to come here? Who asked you? "She does, I know she does. She talks about you all the time."

Shaking inside, tremor like the shimmer of light over water, no plain point of emanation but from everywhere, marrow and substance; blood and guts. Taking back her bag, sharp and heavy the shift against her shoulder, slumped shoulders and edges through frayed canvas like a duelist's point, like a needle on flesh: "I bet she does," and it was hard to see, to look, she did not want to have to look at him. "All the time."

And now past them, seeming to startle Michael, who stepped not away but forward: the scrapyard manager, locking the gates and brief nod at Tess, not quite questioning: "You all set?"

"Sure," nodding back, false voice, "all set for now," and the harsh lunatic urge to cry, run; turning opposite away, as the man turned, to walk, hard, piston heels against the pavement and Michael's movement behind her, trying to gain and then abruptly stopping, she felt him cease as if in a finite pool, the ripple of chase subsiding and she walked harder, bag striking metronome against her body, banging

like a beating fist on an empty door. All the way home,
stripes of dark and light and dark again and inside to pass
the Birdhouse, empty: up the stairs and her heart had the
rhythm now, sharp against the shrinking wall of her chest.
Cluster of shadow past the calm worktable shine, magic
circle, white light in which problems could at least be pre-
sumed to be solved; for good; forever; where those same
shadows, pooled about the draped base of the *Madame,* of
the *Magistrate* and the Triple Deaths, stood less substantial
than memory or dreams: the ghosts of dreams, memory's
memories like the soot from roasted flesh, the smell of a
house burned to the ground.

Flat below her ribs the beaten ache of the heavy bag and
on her shoulder abrasion uneven, like a brand; a scar. The
bag at her feet, one step outside the light and suddenly she
was crying, crying so hard her knees bent, as if in her body
metal, iron, lead in the blood like a circulating poison, one
hand loose-fisted before her mouth; fence, shield, or neither. Pain correct and perfect as a rebus and crying until
she retched, nose and eyes and rising like a paralytic to
take the step into the light, to the table, to upend the bag
and try to work until she could; or slept, or fell out of her
chair or died with one slack hand soldered cold to the
table; inert as mud, as a husked plummy body on a
thoughtless slab, saved by silent death from the precisely
sliding needles of memory and thought.

Late morning, and through the windows the boxy glare
of Indian summer sun; cold here last night, the floor cold
still to shabby summer sneakers. Home with two paper
bags crumpled loose, sculpture shapes: dry muffins in one,
breakfast; and Bibi in the other.

Not *AntiTrust* but *Scuff,* no magazine Tess knew but on
the cover in red austere: DEATH OF A SURGEON, her own

foundry-face inset juxtaposed with a more recent photograph of Bibi in nun's high-collared black. Too expensive but she bought it anyway, home to scald her hurried mouth on coffee too hot to drink. The byline unfamiliar: a long piece, few pictures, one disorienting photograph of Paul, smiling teenager in front of someone's white brick house. The rest were crummy snapshots from Surgeons shows, blurry and poorly lit; *Tess Bajack,* said one of the captions, herself in smeared featureless motion, *and the ill-fated machine* Magistrate of Sorrows.

Ill-fated.

She read the article through. The phone rang twice: background voices, she did not listen. She read it again, more slowly, flipping back and forth; in the pages' middle Paul's picture, she had to keep passing him, back and forth his smiling face, no infection and no scars, no idea of what was to come. How many years ago? Six? Ten? Back and forth.

Into it for the third time and the phone again, Michael: "Tess, it's me, I know you're there so pick up, okay? Okay? I saw the article, I—" and taking up the phone like some rare instrument, putting it slowly to her head as if too wise for quick proximity: "What?" Outside the barking cry of a fire engine, right past her building and for a moment she couldn't hear him, "What?" again more strongly and his voice swooping back, too loud now: "—even *talk* to him, none of us did. Nobody even knows who this guy is, Andy thinks he might have met him at one of the skin parties but he's not sure. Anyway Andy didn't talk to him, I didn't talk to him. Nobody talked—"

Ill-fated. "What about Bibi?" Someone, a girl outside, laughing, another girl squealing some name, an insult and laughing back. Tit-rag: was that a new slur on the street?

Tit-rag, you old tit-rag, Bibi you fucking lying tit-rag, Bibi you *cunt*. "Did Bibi talk to him?"

His pause. "Will you believe what I tell you?"

"Did she talk to him?"

Breath in her lungs like a gas, the vapor between atmosphere and the dry airless air of space. The phone pressed to her ear and he spoke very quietly: "Why don't you ask her yourself?"

She did not want Bibi in the room, the careful new landscape so easily destroyed; I'll meet you, she said, and Michael said Javahouse, a choice Bibi would have made, was Bibi there with him now? Like a cartoon devil on his shoulder, whispering, snickering in her pointy horns and nun's blouse, a copy of the magazine rolled under her balancing arm? "Half an hour," Michael said; "I'll call her now."

Twenty minutes, drinking the cheapest coffee, starting down to her skin every time someone opened the door; the magazine before her, facedown on the table so the waiter couldn't see. And finally Michael, unshaven, ugly ripped shorts the color of dried snot and bending to touch her shoulder, a firm squeeze, was it meant to be heartening? Be brave. Buck up.

One hand tight on the magazine, as if she could feel Bibi's face inside. "So where is she?"

"Not coming." Biting his lip, pale underlip with a faint reddish mark, cold sore, blemish. "She said she didn't want to—she didn't want to talk about it."

Relief; and disappointment, strange such disappointment, how she had watched each brief emerging figure, is that her? No. And no. "She didn't want to talk to me, you mean. —Thanks," putting out her cup for more coffee, Michael upturning his, fat chipped china, pale lip now soft against the paler curve.

"Can't blame her for that." From one ear the faint dangle of silver, sickle-shape through the summery mess of his hair; still dandelion. "You really think it was her, don't you?"

Shrugging, a little, how loose her muscles felt, the same feeling she got after pushing metal, after burning hard for hours. "Who else?"

"I don't know." Magazine in hand, head down and Tess closed her eyes, thinking: ill-fated. Hazardous machinery, irresponsible use of same so close to the audience, the dancers forced to cooperate with effects that were, how exactly had they put it—right, "dangerously engineered": come *on*, who else could have said that, who else provide such a warm pathetic slant? Defenseless dancers versus Nazi Tess and her jackboot trio; bajac-boots; she even laughed a little, a little sour laugh and as Michael looked up, "I'd really like to think it wasn't her, I really would." Rubbing her eyes, aware at once of how dirty she felt, unshowered, how tired she was. "It was a fucking rotten thing to do to all of us. Paul, too," the name firm in her mouth, easy to say; surprise. "And when I see her I'll tell her so. If I ever do," sliding out of the booth. "I don't get out much anymore."

Michael still holding the magazine, reaching with his other hand to touch hers, that squeeze again and a simple sadness in those eyes: "You know, Tess, if you ever want company, I could come over. We don't have to talk or anything," a look as if nothing bad had ever happened, a smile that knew it had and in some way would keep happening, would happen forever. "If you want, you could show me some stuff, what you're working on now."

Her own smile, her new flat smile, magazine left behind; her work was her own now; stay that way. "Same as always," she said, still smiling. "Hazardous machinery."

* * *

See the prance of the daddy longlegs, the real thing, real long legs up the cold branch of the soldering pencil, a broken pencil, Jerome had promised to loan her his for now but Jerome was not home today, was out arranging the first Zombies performance, he was nervous and happy and had had, he told Tess solemnly, diarrhea all night long. "Chocolate squirts, man," running one hand over his skullcut, incongruous as the mustache he was growing, little pencil mustache, Nicky said he looked like a pimp. Nicky said that *Scuff* was for assholes anyway, it was nothing but a poser 'zine and everybody knew it except for a few tit-rag gallery geeks and the kind of people who still wore combat boots to clubs. "File under F-squared," his awkward half-embrace. "Fuck off and forget."

None of the three, in fact, seemed very upset or even interested in the article, of course they had their show to be interested in, their own nameless endeavor with scatterguns and bombs; they had asked her, oblique and sure of rejection, to be part of it, to be, in capitals, a Special Guest. She had refused, but only after a great display of consideration, after letting them think she had thought it all over and over; no, but: and thanking them as well, she appreciated it, wished them luck and of course she would come and watch. Next Saturday, they told her, and showed her the flyer, bright sinus green and staggered red letters, MACHINE-SHOP ZOMBIES and the date, an address in the neighborhood of Bar Hernandez, very close in fact to Bibi's original rehearsal warehouse.

Going there felt strange, stranger still to be at a performance yet a step apart, part of the audience: empty underpass parking lot on a humid night, everything glossed with moisture: sweaty hands, slick metal, sticky plastic litter to drift and catch like skin against her own. Wondering if anyone recognized her, hoping she would see no one she knew; would any of the Surgeons come?—stop thinking of them that way, they don't think of themselves that way; stop it. Innocuous in baggy black T-shirt, long shorts like a bike messenger, not at the fringe conspicuous but just beyond it, beyond the sundown sputter of arc lights and the nervy shift of the crowd.

Big crowd, at first surprising but then again (again) it was what Jerome had called spillover: the three of them remembered not for the Surgeons so much as for something disastrous and exciting, like the old buzz at the old shows: what might happen here? Unpredictability, of all commodities the hardest to fake.

They started out on time and with explosions, much more powerful than any they had used in previous shows (and stop comparing): preplanted explosive charges, she remembered Nicky telling her and here was Nicky himself, big rubber Halloween devil's head and she knew him as much from his walk as the scattergun, spewing chunks of ground glass as he played the nozzle back and forth, farmer and fireman, what do you want to be when you grow up? Another explosion and on the tinny soundtrack a woman screaming, no movie shriek but a real woman in real pain or fear, screaming her head off and here came Peter, another rubber mask but this one with the eyeholes gouged jagged, half the witch's face ripped free and spring-load eyeballs jouncing uselessly long as he advanced upon a misshapen heat-sculpted tower of heavy plastic, slick and pavement-gray, and in his hand shears, heavy-duty pneumatic metal shears, cuts up to eighteen-gauge rolled steel Peter had said with his usual laconic pride; sometimes it seemed he admired the scavenged tools most for shapes; engineered capabilities aside, as if one might enjoy a car for how it looks rather than how fast it can go, what distances it can travel.

Peter began to carve the plastic tower, the woman still screaming in the background at a slightly higher pitch, Nicky spraying long loops of glass against the ground, scattering dirt, small rocks, concrete chunks; they had not roped off the area and now sections of the crowd darted back and away to avoid the glass, pushing backward and for watching Tess memory sudden and sick, the crowd escaping battering *Salome,* Paul in the scaffolding shadow, why hadn't she grabbed him, grabbed the control, done something? Raelynne's scream; the woman's scream on the soundtrack, for one horrible moment she thought it might be the same, Peter had taped that show as well as all the others—calm down, calm *down,* one good listen shows that isn't Raelynne, her peculiar hog-calling screech, just some woman sampled from TV or something, they should have asked me: I could have screamed plenty.

Jerome, now: she had missed his entrance, big clown head complete with huge pink hair, embroiled with a black-dressed manlike construct that, with its own heavy Dracula-masked head, appeared almost a fourth member, the newest Zombie of them all: big articulated arm around Jerome's shoulders, Jerome struggling to get away, another huge explosion and some packing crates in a Dumpster started to burn, heavy resin scent weirdly pleasant and in the sudden orange flare she saw Michael, black cap and shirtless, moving mouth and beside him, Bibi.

Unconscious step forward and then consciously back; most certainly Bibi: hair chopped almost bald, long white T-shirt and some kind of short pants, knickers, her hand on Michael's arm now, she was yelling something into his ear. Staring, still and Tess found herself stepping farther back, as if she would hide, get lost in the crowd and another big explosion, brighter burn and staring like a deer in headlights as Bibi saw her, too. Shining, they called that; it was against the law. Because the deer was helpless, then, helpless and blind and she wanted to leave, right then, slip into the dark anonymous but she had promised Jerome she would not leave, would watch the whole show, stay till the end. More explosions; the woman's scream in her head now like tinnitus, a ringing inner ear to take her balance and her poise; it's just Bibi, for God's sake; she ought to be nervous to see *me*. After what she did; and thinking of that made it easier, made it imperative to stand hipshot and arms crossed, watching, staring and when after careful hesitation she searched the spot again they were gone.

Distracted now—were they crossing through the crowd? and the scream revved to a pitch impossible, loud blackboard shriek and the people near her were fidgeting, a few moving away and gone with hands to their ears and Jerome was apparently battling the construct, Nicky and Peter in tandem to free him and suddenly a bright terrible sizzling, Jerome's pink hair aflame: corona around his dewlapped mask, still dangerously enveloped by the articulated arms and without thinking Tess was through the crowd, elbows, kicking, shoving into the circle and over splattered glass but it was already over, his smothered head no longer burning and tearing off the mask in one convulsive motion: face very red, was it burned? and instantly an explosion so huge she bent instinctively, fetus-curl (hedgehog) and in the backwash found herself nearly deaf, saw Peter's mouth moving strongly and Nicky firing upward, fountaining burst of, what? more glass? No, plastic, some kind of tiny little balls, hit lightly in the face and she saw they were miniature eight balls: bad luck. Jerome was beside her, apparently he had been trying to talk to her but now he was simply dragging her away, off and now people were applauding, arms moving as if choreo-graphed; was the show over? Yes. And Jerome up close, not burned but still very red, shouting in her ear: "Can you hear me at all?" and digging from his own ears big brown-ish things like slugs: earplugs.

"Some," knowing she must be shouting back but help-less to stop. "Not a lot."

Overexcited and he wanted her to stay, steering her off again to a place past the performance area, behind a ware-house the sloping pit of a loading bay and Nicky and Peter there waiting among others, boys and a few girls and did she want something-something, she couldn't hear, it was already getting better but she shrugged and touched her ears: "Tomorrow," shaping the word, "okay?"

Nicky pantomimed driving, did she need a ride? and one of the boys beside her, taking her arm: this way. Nodding: then turning to Jerome to give him a quick hard hug, the same for Peter, for Nicky, sharp thumb's up and then mov-ing to follow the boy with the keys.

Big fat-tired Mitsubishi trike but with a doctored engine, the speedometer only went to eighty klicks but she knew they were going faster than that, leaning hard around the corners, lots of corners and all at once there, down her street to see another scooter, leaning against the building: two people waiting.

Michael and Bibi.

"Thanks," still too loud and a certain feeling, not antici-pation or fear, something: walking toward them and Bibi staring at her, ugly clothes, ugly haircut and new piercing in her upper lip, silver ring almost lost in the swelling around it, purple as a sore: staring at her.

Michael said something, we saw you at the show but Tess ignored him, staring back only at Bibi: who kept star-ing at her until finally: "Well? Can I come in?"

Up the stairs and Tess glad for the moment's darkness, glad not to have to look at Bibi; worse than I thought it would be, a jittering rhythm as if her heart had suddenly enlarged, grown too skittish for its space; it took her an extra moment to work the lock. Clearing her throat and she stood with one foot arched half-on her work stool: nowhere else to sit but the couchbed, uncomfortably far back against the wall, so Bibi stood. Facing her.

"I hear you're pissed off at me," and Tess's lunatic desire to laugh, *At least you can hear* but nothing here was really funny, was it? Was it? No. "About that article."

Her voice hollow in her head as if her head itself was hollow, the balancing foot in sudden jerking motion; keeping time to nothing, to her heart; stop it. "All I want to know is, did you talk to that guy?" Too loud. "The guy who wrote it?"

"No."

Silence; the ticking of blood. Bibi's lip looked infected, ugly. "Are you sure?"

With what seemed to be genuine irritation, "Why should I lie about it?" Pause. "Especially to you."

Still too loud: "Yeah, especially to me." Her own pause and then, magnet disbelief, "It was a pretty fucking rotten thing to do, Bibi, it—"

"Don't you listen? I *said* I—"

"—exploiting the *dead,* even you should realize that that's not—"

"Fuck you!" and Michael's aborted motion in the corner of her vision; one arm out, supplication? "You're the one who had to push it, with your stupid Zombies and their homemade M-80s, and *Salome,* what about *Salome?* If it's anybody's fault it's yours." Breathing hard, the little ring in her lip quivering, painful little shine. "I never said anything to anybody but you're the one who fucked everything up just to prove a fucking point, and that's what's unforgivable, that's what's really—"

"Me?" Yelling in earnest now, off the stool and above that tilted face, those unblinking eyes. "Who sent them out there with knives, Bibi? Who put them up to attacking—"

"Attacking, shit! *You're* the one who—"

"And Paul shouldn't even have been there, he was *sick,* you *made* him sick with your stupid cutting and you didn't even know what you—"

"Don't talk to me about Paul," very close now, very shrill. Dilated eyes. "Don't try to shit me that that's what this is all about, you never even *liked* Paul, you *hated* Paul, you thought he—"

"What difference does it make *what* I thought of him? He's dead, and you used him, you used him like you use everybody else. All of them, everybody—me—your own body, for God's sake, Bibi, your own *flesh* and *blood* and you don't even—"

"Oh right," and right in her face now, scorn like spitting iron. "Like it's any of your business, like you *care.* Like you cared about Paul," and wrist to forehead, anguish burlesqued: " 'Oh, poor Paul' when you couldn't even stand him, you used to make fun of him all the time. Why *shouldn't* he have been there? He wanted to."

"He wanted to because *you* wanted him to."

Silence. Close enough for Tess to see straight into her eyes, see the stringent beat of her heart, her own pulse rapid and sick and watching the sore lip rise into a faint and delicate sneer: "Well. He was mine anyway, wasn't he?"

More silence. Bibi staring at her; Michael starting to move, come forward

and in one motion abrupt Tess raising the stool, smashing it with all her strength against the wall, colt-legs cracking and "Get out" coming at Bibi with her hands out, *"Get out"*

and Michael trying to grab her hands, her arms, shoving him away with one stiff arm in half a punch and turning on Bibi again, swollen mouth pursed and staring and grabbing her, hard, grabbing her little shoulders and pushing her, dragging her out the door, *"Get out"* and down the stairs, wanting to throw her down the stairs, watch her tumble, watch her fall and get hurt and *"Get out of my house"* and into the street, still screaming, screaming over the heads of the people there, lots of people, she saw Jerome's wide eyes and Michael reaching to pull her back, clumsy, as Bibi on the scooter and gone, weaving a little to right herself and people staring, there must be a hundred people here. Nicky trying to speak to her but Tess turned, past them again and pounding up the stairs, Michael behind: "Tess, wait a minute, just—Tess, *wait* a minute! Don't—"

Slamming the door, hard but he got in anyway, she hadn't locked it, came to stand beside her, hand out as if to gentle: "Tess, just—"

"Don't," already crying, hoarse tears of rage and shoving him away, "don't." Crying into her fists, she had never been so angry, sick-angry, in another minute she would be on her hands and knees throwing up, throwing up blood. Michael behind her like an explanation, too lame and too late and finally she heard him turning, heard him finally go.

Then alone, and on her knees as if in dreadful prayer; and from the silence of her open mouth saliva, salt like tears and thin as spider's silk, depending in slow acid dwindle to the ground.

Warmth into cold, time not so much passage as absorption; there was the eloquence of the longlegs to work on, there were other things to do. She worked pickup every other afternoon, machine-shop grind but it was infused with the blessing of thoughtlessness, calm as medication and she needed that now. She found it best to think as little as possible; to feel if not nothing then nearly nothing at all. Thoughts of Bibi were as always inescapable, but she had learned a measure, an approximation of distance; a firewall between herself and the sheerest burn of all.

Michael called, and called, and then did not; no one else called her except strangers with whom she did not bother, or Jerome, hollering up the stairs: "Hey *Tess!*" at times some weird masculine approximation of Raelynne's re-membered screech; sometimes she answered, sometimes not. When she did it was to come down for a beer, for talk or sometimes silence, just to sit and watch what they had made; they were busy these days, they were in demand but, she found, curiously shy to admit it; did they think for a minute she would mind? be envious? Sitting in afternoon shadow, hair twisted wet from an after-work shower, she drank stale apple juice and with Nicky watched one of their videos on the new stolen TV.

"Peter's gettin' really good, isn't he?" and she nodded, he was: the cold eye of the natural documentarian, you ought to be in pictures. "We're selling 'em now. The tapes, I mean. You'd be surprised how much we make."

Juice sour in her mouth, "No," gentle shake, "I probably wouldn't." You are there, sort of; all the excitement with none of the risk. On the screen Jerome smashed a tower of red-painted heads shaped from scrap wire, with a flame-thrower set the tower ablaze. She drank more juice.

"Hey, you know, we got another show coming up, at the—"

"I know. You told me."

"Right." A pause; she knew what was coming. "Listen, if

you want to, you know, you're always welcome. Might
cheer you up a little, right?" and then earnest, close to her
face with the smell of mingled juice and beer and the
things no one else would say: "Tess, don't get pissed, but
listen: you got to forget a little, you know? I mean I know
that you're working on stuff and you got a job and everything, but it's like you're not even there anymore. I mean
it's over now, and anyway it's not like he was your best
friend or anything. Right?"

And she smiled without feeling, shook his shoulder
lightly; in fact it *was* her best friend she was mourning, the
best friend she had ever known. Horrible to know that in
brutal fact Paul's death was incidental to her pain, not
instrument but only circumstance; torment lay grounded
elsewhere but there was no explaining that to Nicky or
anyone, no trying to try so: "I know," she said, but with
such patent patience that Nicky went still with the silence
of confusion, opened his mouth once or twice and then left
her alone to finish watching, crash and smash, burning
metal and paint running like the river she had once hoped
to create, metal in liquid motion before motion turned on
her, turned on them all. And upstairs the slim presence of
the longlegs, dancer's legs, was she building Bibi's ghost?
Trapping the trappings, the beauty and the stretch, too
confused herself to stalk the black parts, the deeps where
the fire began, and hardest of all to admit even to her
secret self that she missed Bibi as well as mourned her,
missed her so dreadfully in the emptiness upstairs that now
all she wanted was the impossibility of Bibi back. Bibi the
cruel and the careless, Bibi who did not miss her, Bibi who
blamed her for Paul as if by doing so she herself might
evade the pale scar of responsibility, there on her head like
a brand.

Still: she was Bibi, endlessly, friend before enemy, love

before hate and even after in memory's stubborn colors: see her shadow, there, hedgehog ball and bright eyes, drawled jokes and small rages, her protectiveness when Tess was working, her willingness to carry more than her share. No way, perhaps, to balance this against that sore mouth saying "He was mine" but balance was not what she was after, was it? Balance was perfect, and perfectly empty, empty like a shed skin, something left behind.

So. How to keep up, or try to; pitiful nonchalance, what a sorry asshole she must seem. Must be. Michael she did not call, afraid in some obscure way that his concern had dwindled with the pressure of her obstinance; if he was no longer a friend, she could wait forever to find out; another loss she had no strength to bear but only fend from the prospect of bearing. She had had with Bibi no real mutual friends beyond the Surgeons, to half of whom her name was presumably anathema; the Zombie trio were her link to both past and present, Jerome and Peter, gregarious Nicky with a friend in every basement bar, every cheap nitro club. Her clumsy questions, who comes to the shows? Anybody I know? Yeah? No, Sandrine, I haven't seen her, and Raelynne's a barmaid? Really? And Bibi, what is she up to?

Working, they said, or said they heard; they heard a lot of things. Crosstown flat, cold water running bloody with rust and they said she was a regular at all the skin parties, the tattoo shops and bondage shops and S & M affairs, they said she even went to the shacktowns; was she crazy enough for that? Yes, they said, but others denied it, even Bibi wasn't nuts enough to hang there. Probably. Experiments, the malleability of flesh and skin, what was she piercing now, what food for her cuttings did she find? He was mine; and who was hers now, and how deeply, and with what bloody mess? Could she, Tess, buy her way back if she was willing to bleed for it? willing to take the knife? No. Plenty of pain, now; no more, not that kind; never.

Sometimes on her solitary trips Tess imagined she saw Bibi, arm in arm with someone, a boy, a woman, sometimes alone in that jaunty cold walk; in dread kept the figure in sight until sight proved her wrong: only someone who looked like her, walked like her, pale eyes and chopped hair but never Bibi all the way down.

And an afternoon, late after work, dragging home through gauntlet streets a burn damp with stink and sweat to burn some more and Jerome out front, talking; some guy, red plaid shirt and black bandanna and as he turned she saw it was Michael, half-blank, half-smiling, half–something else and he put out his hands to take hers in a touch begun tentative but gripping, then, till it hurt in her knuckles and bones and she was so glad to see him, so glad to see him again. For himself, surely; but he would know, wouldn't he? Better than anyone, he would know.

Dissembling, she had a little pride left anyway and up the stairs, gave him some ice water from the bicycle bottle in the squat refrigerator, showed him the longlegs but her mind was so far elsewhere that her hands shook on the stems of metal, how is she? how to ask? But kind, he was kind and he solved it for her, took her to sit on the couchbed and said, swift and simple, "You know, she hasn't ever got over that fight you guys had. She really misses you, Tess."

I miss her. I *miss* her. "She's a busy girl," her gaze away. "I hear she spends her time in the shacktowns now."

He made a face. "Shit. Have you ever been down there? All these little houses made out of shipping pallets and cardboard, and those toxic drums even the dumps won't take and they sit around there swapping needles and pissing on each other and half of them are just fucking crazy.

Sometimes I think *she's* crazy; you should hear her talk, sometimes. But she's not scared of anything." Half a smile. "Like you."

One bright cold drop of water unnoticed on his lower lip. Hands clenched austere between her knees, looking toward the window; had she so quickly run out of safe questions? "How is she?"

Michael's gentle shrug. "Skinny. She's lost a lot of weight."

"Less is more."

Headshake, less gentle. "You guys kill me, you know that? You're both saying the same things but you're saying them to me. Why don't you just break down and tell each other, huh? Why don't you just pick up the phone and—"

"Why doesn't she?"

"I don't know, you tell me. You're the only one who understands her anyway." Hand over eyes, slow blown breath; patience lost, try again. "Listen. Why don't you come with me tonight, and see her. Okay? Just see her, say hi, and leave. Or take it from there, or kill each other or whatever you want. What do you think of that?"

The opportunity: Will you? Heart fast from the temptation, near to scared laughter and less than half a smile, "What's it to you?" and his arm then around her, squeezing her tight.

"None of your business," head light against hers, soft little pressure, knock knock. "Hers either." And a big smile, sweet and slow. "Jeez. *Girls.*"

"This is it?" Crummy box-shaped row house with brick like acne, busted windows and six big kids in baggy jeans hanging outside the door; they were all, she saw, pierced in some way, ears and nostrils ringed over and over in interconnecting circles, shiny and complex. Tattoos and scars, waiting for Michael to chain his scooter and one of the kids laughed, called out, "Hey man, don't want it anyway."

"She doesn't really live here," past them up the wide unpainted steps into half-dark and heavy garbage smell. "Just visiting. Guy named Tony. You won't like him."

She didn't. Forever to answer the door, even her wet-palmed hammering knock and at first he pretended he didn't know Bibi; coy, then smiling, sure. Come on in. Big bare dewlap breasts, both nipples pierced and he told her about his cock piercing, 's called a Prince Albert, you ever heard of a Prince Albert?

"Yeah," staring down at him, he was a good four inches shorter than she. Dandruff like nits in his hair. "I know what that is."

"Wanna see it?"

"No."

"The chicks love it."

"I bet."

Michael, softly, with a certain coldness she had not seen in him before, "When do you expect her?"

That got a laugh. "Don't 'spect her at all, man, she just shows up whenever the fuck she feels like it, whenever she gets her shit together from those fuckin' shacktowns. I told her, you bring any of that shit here I'll ream your ass for you."

The idea of anyone reaming Bibi's ass was bemusing, Tess almost had to smile through the stuttering drive of her heart. Michael said something, low, she didn't hear because there were sounds in the hall, one of the outside kids laughing as the door swung crookedly to: Bibi, pushing in.

Purest white, virgin and martyr, white hair, white head-wrap like cerements and new white sneakers sparkling against the floor's red linoleum filth: shiny all over with

rings, studs, bright surgical steel like tiny surface manifes-
tations of a blunter core within; staring back at her; to save
her life Tess could not have spoken first.

Silence, and the kid at the door scraping slowly away.
Even ox Tony did not speak; incurious? or conscious of
currents, of plates shifting deep beneath the ground? Beside her Tess could feel Michael, tension, her own bones
thrumming in the space beneath her skin.

At last, dry: "Hi, Tess," and that pale gaze unsteady, up
and over and down to her hands; nails torn and rings on
every finger, coptic crosses, miniature skulls. Up to Tess
again. "Come to visit?"

"No," and from her own mouth, not loud but certain,
absolutely sure, "I came to take you home."

And instant as a blow what she would never have believed: the big pale blinkless eyes filling steadily with tears,
as out of place here as the coursing blood of angels, of
stripped seraphic veins. It was as if Bibi did not feel them,
heavy bright glycerin, her mouth moved on a word and
Tess felt her own tears, drove them back; they would not
be shed here no matter what.

"C'mon," she said, iron in her throat, out the door and
silent Michael behind them, the three of them in the half-
lit street and Bibi suddenly laughing, a shaky laugh, "We
can't all fit on that," and Tess unable to talk, biting hard at
her inner cheek, red from her mouth and Bibi in wonder
said "You're bleeding," and suddenly her face collapsed
into a terrible fist, as if everything not dead was pain and
Tess grabbed her, skinny little hedgehog, death's baby sister and hugged her tight, tight; and she did cry, then, Bibi,
silently onto Tess's shoulder, little chin digging in and without ever raising her head.

And Michael, half a pace away and Tess saw his smile,
small but so true, so informed with warm pleasure that her

tears ran as well for him: for his persistence, for his patience and the fruit of it, their joy.

"I don't have much stuff, anymore," nimble legs crossed high at the thigh, arms curling complicated as Shiva in some series of slow exercise as lovely, itself, as a dance. Square blocks of shadow, indigo drift across the plane of the floor, dust-sugared and striped with the terminus twist of cables, red and black and dirty blue. Michael had gone nearly after arrival, hugging them both swift and briefly, longest smile for Tess as he closed the door. Tess's hurried shower, aware she still stunk like work and Bibi nonstop, talking and talking, filling in all the time apart: and then I did this, and then I did that, and then I worked a couple weeks for Linda Joy, that was cool but we didn't really see eye to eye; so I left. And little chunks of time, a week dancing: Skeleton Fist, you know what that is? 'S a club. Sort of. And I did some work for this guy, he's a therapist, one of those free-lance clinics, you know—

From beneath the water: "What kind of therapist?"

"Mmm," bony little shrug, "sexuality. Deviant sexuality, I guess you could call it."

"What'd you do?"

"Referrals."

—and on and on, so much to happen in what was really such a short time, a short time that felt so long and now that it had ended felt like nothing at all. Toweling off, nonstop smile for Bibi on the couchbed: how she filled the room with just herself. "Anyway I've been moving around. I left that one flat, the bed and everything," a slim yawn, "all those magazines, I got rid of it all. Most of the clothes, too."

"What about that blue thing, that dumb Queen Mab

dress?" and Bibi's swift grin, fuck you and she poked Tess in passing with the stretch of one bare foot.

"Yeah, that, too, don't be a bitch. See, this's what I've got now—it's better than clothes," and she pulled free the white shirt, swiveling turn to display the long slim lines of scars precise, white runic tattoo as pale as her eyes and barely rimmed by faint receding pink; troubling, and beautiful, and strange. From over her shoulder: "I got it done after—you know, after, and a couple new piercings, too— my lip, you saw my lip." Sore purple hole healed now and she sounded nervous; how strange, to think of Bibi as nervous, and before Tess could speak Bibi's own lowest voice, soft as a floorboard groan: "It didn't make me happy, Tess. None of it. Not even this, at first," backhand brush of two fingers. "I did it to keep going. To just keep on going."

Hedgehog; it knows only one trick, one good one, and Bibi the hedgehog inside-out, baring the softest spots for the knife and the needle; nothing in the end left vulnerable to pain except the softest spots of all, where no needle can ever reach.

Head down, a little, shirt stretched on her crossed arms and she was so beautiful, pierced and shorn, pale as a ghost boned with steel and sharp metal and now her smile again, itself like a piercing: "So do I sleep with you, or use the floor, or what?"

"Anywhere you want," Tess said, "if you—" and her voice croaking loud and sudden and to her harsh astonishment came tears, hot and bitter as a caustic, an acid to burn for all the lost life, all the lost *time,* face grinding hard into the towel and Bibi instantly there, thin arms to hold her tight, saying shhh and John Henry and everything will be all right, now, you hear me? Everything is going to be all right.

* * *

And waking, the drifting line of blue dark and the fierce warmth of Bibi, there in the bed, curled caging around her larger limbs as naturally as a spider to prey; I have you, that touch said, I know exactly where you are. Thin scissoring thighs, shorn raptor's head like a pulled punch in the middle of her back and back to sleep, smiling, the room was cold around them but together they were warm.

Pulpy orange juice and hot beignets—Bibi's treat, juice on her lip and shreds of pulp like skin, curbside past the kiosk, their knees companionably close. She wore one of Tess's sweat shirts in a morning chill that had not faded, itself faded to a color like dirt and sleeves rolled high above the thick chain bracelet, it looked like iron vined with razor wire; real metal, pretty in a weird way on the bony stalk of her wrist. Big compound-eye sunglasses over the pale gaze, brushing crumbs disdainful from the sweat shirt: "Don't you have any real clothes?"

"Don't you?"

"No. Yeah. I have a bag at a friend's house, we should go and get it. —Let's go now," past the last of her beignet, crammed into her mouth like a child impatient. "It's not that far."

"What friend?" No napkin, wiping one hand against the other; such a feeling of looseness in her muscles, she felt so good. Squinting against the sun, "Not that guy, what's his name, Tony."

"No, not that asshole. You'll like this guy."

So: gone, not arm in arm but the distinct feeling of it, down the street and her own sudden idiotic grin, it was *good* to be together again, she had not realized how isolated she had become: as if, blinking into light she realized how long the dark had lasted, the changing of the seasons, the passing of a year; not that long but that was how it felt and Bibi, in uncanny chime: "I missed you, John Henry. I thought about you a lot." Slow sideways grin. "Mostly when I was going to do something bad."

"I bet."

Her friend lived, Bibi said, in a walk-up: eight flights of a walk-up, grit indescribable, pure urine stink at every step. Half the doors on each floor were either smashed or missing, there was garbage all over the floor. "It's kind of a sty."

"Who's your friend, the Ancient Mariner? The curse of the mummy?—*shit*," scraping dry at a desiccated turd tenacious on her shoe, hollow chummy voice suddenly above saying, "Don't fuck up the woodwork, man."

Lean death's head, skinny as Bibi and pierced in more places, thin nostrils ringed, rings in his lip, his ears: flashy and ugly and Bibi grabbing his hand in a complicated squeeze, turning with pride to say, "Matty, this is my friend Tess Bajac. Tess, this is—"

"Matty Regal," Tess said, slim memories revising now to include this monkey skullface. "I know you," without compliment. "I've seen your work."

"I've seen yours, too. You don't show much anymore, do you?"

"No. Do you?"

"I don't work in sculpture anymore," flat airless superiority like stating a fact to a feeb. "The whole art scene sucks."

So did your sculpture. "I remember you from the Isis," remembering more than that, a kind of pretentious academic reek clung to him still past the scent of deliberate déclassé, the kind of fuckhead who enjoyed writing artist's statements. In triplicate. "You did pretty well there, didn't you?"

"So did you."

"Wrong. I never sold a piece there."

"Jeez," Bibi said. "Just let me get my bag, okay? Matty, we're too busy to fight with you now," and in and out while they stared at each other, this is Bibi's *friend?* Jeez is right; and Bibi with her bag, dirty black nylon and Matty nudging her, you going to the Fist tonight? "No," shaking her head, one arm around Tess. "I told you, we're busy."

"Eating at the Y," and for a moment Tess did not even understand it as a question, did not understand at all until Bibi's sharp stare, "And how's that any of your fucking business?"

"Don't get touchy. I don't care who you screw."

And Tess, fouled by his smile, not wanting to resent it openly for fear of hurting Bibi's feelings, angry all over and down the stairs, silent, into the sun like an autoclave and Bibi's voice in her ear, "Don't be mad, it's just Matty." And then diffident, itself a surprise—Bibi shy?—"I hope you don't mind."

"Mind what?"

"If some people think we're lovers. They used to, before —I didn't know if you knew."

Another surprise: and a warm prickle, a throb at the base of her spine and memory, brief and strong as a smell: Bibi last night, small breasts pushed into her back; *So do I sleep with you or what?* and her own smile now, wide, confused: "No, I didn't know." Pause, try for a joking tone, is it a laughing matter or not? "Are we?"

Bibi's pause, far more subtle, six long strides and no smile at all. "Ask me again tonight."

So the thought, now, planted and growing in lush confusion; neither one brought it up but for Tess it was there: at night when they slept, in the morning when Bibi walked cat-naked to the shower, the stretch of her, the slim scarred tension of back and pointed breasts. All-day busy, and maybe that was better; it kept her from thinking too much, in a direction that deadpan Bibi had perhaps never intended. Or had. Who knew? In a strange way it was like the old Surgeons' gossip, who hadn't fucked Michael; it got her wondering: what would it be like?

But: busy: in differing directions, the routine established neatly and without plan: Bibi off nocturnal, Tess at the bodyshop or hunched in boneless ease before her worktable; she found that Bibi's presence (or absence, some nights till near morning) in some way—new and old—freed her, released her to the first days when the only thing surpassing hardest work was the gleeful exhibition to Bibi of same: look what I did! Slivering burn, again the resin drift of solder smoke and the turn of the screw: see: metal sinister, the longlegs in matte achievement; within a fortnight it was finished.

Up and down, small ball body and legs double-jointed, promenade in the oblong squares of cool sunlight in dainty steps, as if evil wore beauty's dress, its spangled cat's-eye smile. Bibi, wrapped in faded red cotton like a bright young beggar, sat on the couchbed and clapped her hands.

"It's beautiful. —No it isn't. It's worse than beautiful," and Tess paused, the smile only Bibi seemed able to call from her. "But what are you going to do with it?"

Shrug. "I don't know. Isn't it enough to just make it?"

"Oh, I get it: art." A little yawn, back of the hand; out late again last night; shacktowning? Why ask? A new bruise born on one of Bibi's cheekbones, almost theatrically dark; a beauty mark; she didn't ask about that, either. Gentle little landmines: each had her own; just let's don't spoil it, okay? Michael had called again, what he liked to call his checkup calls: How're you guys doing? and Tess's smile, could he hear it in her voice? Fine, she had told him. Fine. No mention of the landmines, the sense of walking warily, if with joy; why spoil it for him, either? He was so happy to see them back together, so proud of his part in it and justly so, would they ever have reconciled without him? Wanting to think so, but truth was stronger, gray with strength: no. No.

Bibi, sitting straighter on the couchbed: "So you're never going to show again?" Pause. "Or perform?"

No. "I don't know," pitter-patter, little devil's feet, the longlegs in minuet orbit around the couchbed. "No plans."

"Very existential." Another yawn, sweet pink gullet and the trembling silver of the ring; labrette, that was called, that kind of lip piercing; stick around long enough and you'll know them all. "Well, I have plans, for tonight. Linda Joy's doing a blood rubbing, and a friend of hers— of mine's getting her clit pierced, remember I told you? I asked you if you wanted to come, and you said you'd think about it, remember?"

Yes; and no. Bibi's hints over this particular cutting had become almost tedious; maybe this was some new manifestation of her personality since they had been apart: Bibi the Nag.

"I have to work this afternoon," longlegs's prance around to her side of the couchbed, turning her face away. "I don't know how late, and then there's stuff to do here," and Bibi's pounce, one arm hooking playfully hard around her neck: "Come on. You can take a night off, if you want to."

She could; and wouldn't, it must have showed on her face for Bibi at once, smile a little too bright: "Come *on,* Tess, just this once. It'll be fun. You can see some people you haven't seen in a while, Sandrine'll maybe be there, and Andy—"

"Andreas?"

"No." A discreet frown. "He doesn't, he's not really in the scene anymore. But you could see other people, and the piercing, it's really beautiful. The woman lies in the center, and some of her friends take turns holding—"

"Bibi, really, no."

Slow cool drain from pallor to anger, colorless, and when she spoke her voice was flat, fighting not to show it, not to let it go: "Tess, you know, I don't ask you for much, I haven't asked you for anything since, since we got back together. But I'm asking you to do this for me now."

"It means," skeptically, "that much to you, to—"

"Yes. Yes it does—"

"—for me to sit in a hot room with a bunch of strangers and watch some woman get a ring through her cunt?"

A slapped silence, and Tess instantly uneasy; as instantly, "Bibi, I'm sorry, I didn't mean that the way it sounded. I just—"

"You just." Flatter than ever but with a peak beneath, harsh; the spike through the ligament, the bone through the bloody wound. "You just hate everything I love. You hate everything," and up, even in her anger she was careful not to jostle the longlegs, poised below their feet like a patient pet. "You just don't care very much about me, Tess, that's what it comes down to so why don't you just leave me alone?" And up to skin out of ragged red, into black on black and gone, Tess calling out the window but she did not look back; Tess had not expected, much, that she would.

Hands flat on the glass, that hard skin no needle could pierce for pain or pleasure: watching her go. It was their deepest divide, visible everywhere, filigree roots in every talk they had, in the words they did not say; deeper even than the trauma of Paul's death. They did not discuss so much as orate around it, at first like crossing cracking ice, then as weeks passed without the emergence of fissures, bolder; yet still terribly careful to be kind.

Until today, her own clumsy impatience, she had hurt Bibi. Tight lips, closed eyes in self-disgust, remembering Bibi's care not to crush the longlegs, she could have stepped on it, cracked it like a breaking bone. And I hurt her, I said the one thing that would probably hurt her most except for coming right out and calling her a freak, a needle-happy sideshow freak.

Bibi thought, Tess knew, of her own machine continuance—especially now, when she would not even show, much less perform—as part of something she, Bibi, had left behind, having in itself no worth or deeper value other than the tangible object produced, producing in the end only the deadly pronouncement, Yeah; so? And to Tess Bibi's obsession with piercings and cuttings was a kind of unfortunate sidepath, a sideshow, a descent almost into— say it; you think it, don't you?: the freakish: it was *for* nothing, wasn't it, but the hectoring of limits? Which was interesting, certainly, and liberating in its way but ultimately a deader end: my friend got her clit pierced; yeah; so? Do you modify to improve, or empower, or simply to feed the greedy black scorn of the human boundaries that succor flesh to blood to the pulse and contraction of the emperor mind within? To her questions—rare, but she asked, she made herself ask—Bibi was purely elliptical: soft breath on her shoulder, quiet beside her in the dark: Tess, listen, it's not something I can explain in words, you have to do it, it's something you have to *feel.*

And for Tess the feel of Bibi's own desire, the need to share with her, to steep her in the bright blooded ecstasy of pain; in the service of the most capricious god of all, Change.

But I don't *want* to: the litany thought and again the brief imagining, What would it be like, to do it, to feel the sliding launch of the needle, the slippery edge of the knife in her skin, flesh parting wet and—no. Firm and visceral as the body's flinch from death: *no.* And a sigh, and Bibi's own sigh half a beat behind and the subject dropped as one abandons, with regret, a dead animal, a pet; to lie humped in the corner, stinking and dry-smiling, unconsumed and waiting for the inevitable: the slow red boon of the resurrecting touch.

Back from the body shop, she had stayed later than she meant, deliberate last to leave; back aching in a tired new way and the walk home had been horrendous, wind cold as December through her jeans jacket, sweat still combed through her hair. Hot, and shivering, pushing inside in the early dark past Jerome's outward-bound salute: Hey, and his hasty grin, "See you," and out; banging door and the building emptier, perhaps because she knew Bibi was gone.

Up the stairs, tired wash and the nagging unease of being at odds with Bibi; new-old habit fallen into with the discomfort of old pains; when would she come home? Maybe she wouldn't; maybe this was the end again. No. Please, not that bad and sitting at the worktable, mind like a leaf above currents, above the churn of hot air and the sound of feet on the stairs, she had not heard the door below: Jerome, or one of the others. She would send them away; no company now.

But the key in the lock; and Bibi, slamming in: hair wet and on end, her face bleached and drunk-looking; no, not drunk, enraged. Or crazy, burning crazy on fire and crossing to the worktable, to Tess, half-risen in alarm, and grabbed her hand—Bibi's own hands horribly cold, like a statue in winter, a corpse dug out of the ground—to push it hard against her crotch, against the damp black softness of her skirt.

"It's a ring," she said. "Through my cunt."

Tess stared, straight into pale eyes and felt against her hand the smallest hardness, it might have been a pebble, half a locket; broken heart. "It was my piercing," Bibi's voice, low as a growling dog, "it was *mine,* it was for *me* and I wanted you there. I wanted you *there!"* her voice cracking but she did not cry, kept grinding Tess's hand against her and suddenly with her free hand reached to wrench Tess's chin down, aiming her face to kiss her, very hard, grinding her teeth as she ground the captive hand and Tess grabbed her back, harder, arm around those shoulders tensed high and stiff as splitting bone and felt against her own breasts the soft crush of Bibi's, the frantic speed of her heart in her breathless chest and kept kissing her, dry mouth and the feel of Bibi's pierced lip, the hard dangle of the tiny ring there.

Tess's hand free, now; she kept it where it was, touching Bibi, stroking her, soft and wet and the hardness there, too, metal and flesh and Bibi's crying eyes closed, mouthing something, over and over and Tess pulling back just the slightest to hear, "I wanted you, I want you. I love you."

"Come here," pulling at her, Bibi almost stumbling, pulling her crying to the couchbed past dropped bag, Tess's shucked shoes and jacket, coverlets twisted and warm. "Come here with me," into warmth, skin and metal and desire, cold hands, wet face and parted lips.

Because I love you, too, hedgehog; spines and blood and all, I love you, too.

Waking, almost full dawn and Bibi's limbs clasped moist about her, sluggish sleepy smile, disengaging to go piss; on the sheets the tiniest spots of blood, small as punctuation, dry and spicy brown. When Tess got back into bed again Bibi folded about her, arms and legs, breasts and lean belly, blood and metal and wire. A soft fleshy smell at the back of her throat, rich as savored food; lying sleepless to watch the motion of Bibi's dreaming eyes beneath lightly shivering lids, turn her own body slightly to chart the areas of piercing, nose and lip and ears and now the new one, pink but seemingly unsore, small bright silver bead nestled like dripped mercury between Bibi's legs, nestled between her lips; the shaved skin seemed more irritated than the actual piercing itself. With one careful finger she parted Bibi's vulva, it was so beautiful, all of it, the pierced flesh not off-putting but arousing, erotic in an alien way; she felt like a hypocrite but true was true. And Bibi was Bibi; and Bibi was awake, maybe had been, lay looking at her with a long rare serpentine smile: "Kiss it," she said. "Kiss me."

Warm-cheeked, half-clumsy and she bent from the waist, Bibi's cool hand stroking her bare back, reaching to pull her lower, pull her all the way down, into heat, and moisture, and the slippery feel, the metal tang of consummated love.

Now everything was changed, heightened, everything burned with the heat Tess remembered from so long ago, forgotten days with long-gone lover Peter the sidewalk artist: but changed, charged; *torqued,* oh my yes. There was no one like Bibi, and to have Bibi focused this way upon her was like living beneath a glass in the sun, each day and motion in the day transformed by love. It was their first days bettered, it was being in love with your best friend.

"I love you," Bibi said; said it often, like a challenge. In the mornings, wet in the shower, late afternoon and Tess back from the body shop; in the growing stretch of darkness, the days short and shortening still. Bundled in coverlets, "I never loved anybody before," the feel of her breath on Tess's neck, lips moving so close they shivered the skin. "Have you?"

Her pause; she would not lie. "Yes."

Bibi's own pause indecipherable, then: "Have you ever been with a woman?"

"No."

"Good," fiercely, surprising Tess who rose up on one elbow till Bibi pulled her down: "Good," again. "I'm glad I'm your first." Silence. "First and last and only."

Bibi wanted them to be seen as a couple, she wanted everyone to know: her friends at the piercing parties, the people she knew from the clubs. Tess did not care who knew, not for secrecy's sake but sheer disinterest: her life was her own, and therefore beyond accounting; let people know, or think, whatever they liked.

Past noon, cold in the body shop and there came Bibi, beautiful and strange as some wild creature, backlit in the doorway and calling "Tess," blowing her a kiss and the guy in the next bay grinning, ugly with surprise: Oh I get it, she's the guy, right? and Tess in calm motion taking off her helmet, wanting to hit him once across the face, very hard, splinter of glass from the eye shield and out in the street, breathing hard in the cold: what business is it of theirs, anyway? and anyway what *difference* did it make? And Bibi's shrug, "Who gives a fuck? Kiss me," and she did, kissed her hard and then went quietly back inside to tell the foreman she was ready to quit. She was under-the-table labor, nonunion and he was getting her for peanuts; forget it, he said, just get back to work. But if you get your ass kicked afterward it's your own tough shit.

Nowhere else were they outwardly harassed, nowhere yet; and yet they seldom went out, Tess preferring to stay in, to work; if this chafed Bibi, she kept silent. But: cold night, true winter and Bibi had dragged her out, bright cheeks, ragged leather, to see a band; Crane's in it, that asshole, revving the feathery choke of her dying car around streets sullen with dirty new ice, can you believe it? Holding her hand tight through split-fingered gloves, hand in hand through the heavy turnstile doors and the first person they saw was Michael, himself bundled in heavy black leather: "Hey!" with genuine pleasure, angling them past the bouncer, sweaty little corner between the bar and the dance floor. Dirty sneakers, hair cut high around his ears, dull pewter shine of an earring shaped like the free-turning blade of an ax; a little thinner, maybe, maybe more beautiful still.

"Girls' night out, huh," brief kiss for Bibi, kissing Tess a little longer; his lips very warm, almost as if he had a fever, one hand light on her hip as he kissed her and if she was surprised Bibi was not: Bibi's fingers on Tess's chin, positioning her face for a loud, almost theatrical kiss: *"My girl,"* she said.

"Really? That's terrific," one-armed grab for both, hugging them now as a couple: his smile brightest it seemed for Tess and softly into her ear, his lips against her skin: "I'm so glad," and louder, "When did this happen?" Bibi said something, not soon enough and then he was insisting on buying them a drink, let's celebrate your good news. "Two tonics," Bibi said, "with lemon," and Tess hiding both her smile and her irritation; bossy child, like what I like and nothing but.

Which extended to her deepest choices, the extreme piercings and cuttings: where before she had only listed the seven disciplines, now she must explain them all in a welter of detail Tess neither wanted nor could bear; not from squeamishness or even boredom, Bibi enthusiastic was rarely boring and some of her more outré examples, such as fishhook piercing, or the fully functional bifurcated penis—it's great, she said, he says it gets hard on both sides—were interesting in and of themselves, but the whole idea was like the Bataille quote Bibi was forever intoning: "Human life is an experience to be carried as far as possible," but to Tess this did not go far enough. Yes, brute sensation, but I can get that from sticking my hand in a fire, so what? What does it prove, where does it lead, what does it *make?* Change: yes: right. Good. Change by all means. But change to accomplish, not merely to become and come on, Bibi, half of them do it just for sex reasons, you know that better than I do!

And Bibi would sulk, pulling away to lie sullen and cocooned on her side of the bed, Tess waiting it out, cold trench between them before she could reach across it and say, Come on. Bibi, come on; and Bibi finally turning, rolling close again to say, soft and sullen, "I wish sometimes you would just *try* to understand."

"I understand you," Tess would say, one hand brushing metal, always metal somewhere: in the morning, at her worktable, metal at the body shop, everywhere its slope and sheen but never less under her control than when lying warmed in the avenue of Bibi's flesh; she could burn her way straight through solid iron but stood helpless before Bibi's burn, her own fire, the coldest heat of all.

"Are you going to work again tonight?"

Tess's distracted half smile, gazing up for an instant; deep now in a new piece, a smaller piece yet but more intricate than anything she had ever tried before: a figure, half beast and half machine, its lines and jutting angles more disturbing even than the slender menace of the long-legs. Perhaps it was the humanity of it, the Everyman suggestion: this could be you, warped and bitterly shaped, this could be all of you: under pressure, under torture, going deeper down.

Bibi asked her again, more peremptory; Tess's shrug came automatic, she had been shrugging a lot lately. "There's a party at Linda Joy's, for Matty," and her own shrug more pointed, and pointed at Tess, "but I suppose that doesn't interest you, it's only a lot of people with rings through their noses, right? Just a bunch of freaks?"

"Bibi," tiredly, "that isn't—"

"Isn't it?" And gone. She was doing that, too, a lot.

Head bent again to the light, tiniest bright lava from the tip of the soldering gun; one of the figure's limbs spread delicate before her like a dissected human arm. Things were splitting again; bifurcating, small sour smile like sucking on contagion. Bibi had grown bored with staying in, watching her beloved work, the pursuit of the mastery of motion in metal; a smaller scale, a more intense arena and when Bibi was pissed off she called it sterile, it's all sterile. "You hate people," she would say, finger leveled like the blade of a knife; a needle. "That's why you work in metal, it's inorganic, it's not alive. That's why you like to be alone so much, you probably wish I would leave you alone more than I do."

And if it was not this, it was another of the arguments— Bibi was this, Tess was that, the whole like a dreary jewel with each facet more dry and painful than the last: Bibi's push for Tess to understand by doing, her forced empathy march at the end of which was the tip of the knife: you have to try it, just once, come on. "Just once," whispered, or stated, or wheedled or shrieked, Tess had already said no in more ways than she had dreamed existed; but Bibi did not seem to hear, or, hearing, understand. Why don't you understand sometimes, Tess staring at the sleeping face in the hours when she herself lay empty and awake, why don't you see that what works for you won't work for me, I don't want what you want; I don't love what you love. And I shouldn't have to, to love you.

Thinking, too, in those empty hours, ebbed resistance and the imaginings, one piercing, just once, to—what? Prove something? Shut Bibi up? but more forceful than ever the visceral No, stronger than any taboo, any hunger; stronger than love? Maybe. Yes. Heavy head on cocked wrist, watching sore-eyed over that breathing vortex, Bibi restless even in sleep: Not even for you.

But as the arguments grew more frequent, the happy times more scarce as the novelty of being lovers rubbed dry and finally disappeared entirely, Tess felt she was in a tumbler of stones, turning round and round and buffeted on all sides; they were so much their work that with no shared creation between them, no obsession like a child they had produced (or worse, competing obsessions like monstrous siblings; and in dreadful fantasy Tess could almost see them, Bibi's a rag doll, voodoo doll sprouting needles and everywhere sewed black and red with scars, and Tess's made all of metal, metal teeth, dull metal eyes and toolbox hands, each finger a screwdriver, a drill bit, a grinding wheel, all in constant empty motion), the center was splintering, and could not hold. Tess tried, or thought she tried her best to listen, to be sympathetic, but Bibi seemed more militant, less willing to accept her opinions or even her right to hold them because Tess did not know, Bibi said, what she was talking about, literally could not understand without the experience itself.

"When people've done it," sullen and smug at the same time, "they know better. If you would just once—"

"Bibi—no more. *Please.*"

That time, too, Bibi had banged out, still angry on return but wanting Tess, wanting to hold and kiss; and bite,

and scissor in long insistent legs; and finally fall silent to
sleep; to wake, and bring it up again. After these arguments Tess felt husked, abraded. Maybe Bibi was right;
maybe they were both right. Maybe there was not a way to
be together. But the idea of parting, again and with the
new cruelty of disappointed lovers, was so intolerable that
Tess could not hold it for long; but what else to do? Give
in, override that inner no? She would not be cut solely for
Bibi's sake; that way was resentment, sooner or later,
larger or smaller but destined as surely as cancer to grow
until it consumed in the end what it was engendered to
save. She became more silent, Bibi louder, as if the manifestation of their rages and sorrows must inevitably display
their differences, rub it in and in and in.

And now Bibi had a new tack, or perhaps it had been
there from the beginning, the very first beginning; perhaps
it was her vision of the Surgeons, and its failure to happen
her bedrock reason for the Surgeons' disintegration. She
brought it up from time to time, less obliquely with each
pass; last night they had even had a "talk" about it, though
Bibi had done most of the talking, starting by showing Tess
a magazine, a journal for piercers; see this? Bending over
her at the worktable, shutting out her light.

"See, this is what I was talking about. Look here," and
her finger jabbing sharp, some guy with hair as blond as
Michael's and his whole torso crossed and recrossed with
chains, all of them leading to and from various piercings,
all of it hung heavy with lead weights like miniature pears;
and some not so miniature, the whole collection must have
weighed a ton. Tess tried to take the magazine, a closer
look but no, Bibi was already taking it back.

"It's so powerful," she said, subliminally smug pleasure
that this was so. "I mean look at this, this guy's an invest-
ment banker and yet he's driven to do this, to modify him-

self this way. That's because it's *powerful,* it's been around forever, it's a basic human need which means they're going to do it anyway so they might as well have supervision, right? They ought to have someone telling them what to do so they don't fuck it up." A sigh. "That's what happened, I handled Paul all wrong," and Tess forbore to say You sure fucking did, in fact forbore to say anything at all. Metal drip, in the light; waiting.

"Someone has to be in control. The one with the strongest vision should be in—"

"That means," setting the soldering gun aside, "that means you, right?" Bibi's shrug, obvious; words like a smell in the air and Tess tried to keep her voice neutral, past the echo of the hammer of dread; old dread, like a sickness never cured and trace memory of Bibi, bleeding in the heavy light of a Surgeons show, hands wide and eyes too bright. "Sounds like fascism to me."

Another shrug, less interested; another example, probably, of Tess's chronic failure to understand. "Sounds like semantics to *me,* but *you* can call it anything you want."

Tess's own shrug, underskin shudder; something is wrong here. *Wrong.* "No one should have decisions like that made for them; and no one should make those decisions for other people. *I* wouldn't want—"

"The responsibility, right? Don't want," faintly jeering, "their blood on your hands? Because you're scared?"

"You're damn right I'm scared. You ought to be scared, too."

And Bibi, Tess thought, might with truth have said, I'm not scared of anything, but instead gave the shrug and with it the sense of the subject not dropped but locked away; there would be no more discussion of this with Tess; maybe she was saving it for someone more worthy, like, say, one of her old piercing cronies, Andy or Linda Joy. Or discredited Andreas. Or Matty Regal, whose name seemed to be cropping up more and more, Tess unsure if this was done simply to aggravate her or if Matty was really that close a friend; which would have been infinitely worse but there would be no questions, no asking because she knew there would be no answers or at least no true ones; which was the worst, the saddest thing of all.

So: alone and working, cold air seeping from spots she had not, last year, seemed to notice; of course last year they had heat, had Surgeons money instead of only her crummy pickup income; Bibi was at the moment, the long, stretching moment, between jobs; another bone to pick or leave alone, you choose. At least they still had electricity, a phone, though the calls were always for Bibi.

And then Michael, exception: "Hey," his voice so warm. Jingling background sounds. "How're you guys doing?"

"Okay." Liar. "Sort of."

"I just saw Bibi, a little bit ago. She was at—"

"I know."

"Well. Yeah. Anyway, I was coming your way, I thought you might like company."

She was going to say no, she had to work; and Bibi's anger if she found out, you couldn't come out with me but you could stay in and fuck off hanging out with Michael, and so on and on. "All right," was it less incriminating if she sounded unenthused? "Sure."

He brought coffee, two big plastic cups, half a half-stale roast beef submarine; lunch, though it was after dark. Dressed all in black, boots scuffed bald at the toes, gloves frayed; joking display, hard winter, huh? His lips were chapped, too; she felt their dryness as he kissed her, chaste kiss on the cheek.

"Working, huh?" standing beside her by the worktable, she noticed he did not remove his coat. Cold in here, isn't it? You should see how it is when we're fighting. "Can I see?" and bending over her, slow thorough examination and remembering in that instant Bibi's first look at her sculpture, that same single-minded thoroughness and Tess felt for a moment that she might cry, coughed instead, a watery cough worse than a sob and Michael peered sideways into her face. "Hey," very gently. "Hey, what's the matter?"

"Nothing," trying to shrug, or smile, something. "Working too hard, I guess."

"I thought," and she sensed the care behind the words, "maybe you two were working together again. Bibi says—"

"What?" too quickly, startling them both and Tess instantly abashed, unfocused stare past Michael's shrug, and his tone noncommittal: "She has a lot of plans, I guess."

"She has plans all right," touching the little construct, her hand past his. "I don't think I'm in them, though." And then that seemed so melodramatic she had to smile, tried to but instead produced such a half-assed effort that Michael bent from the piece to her and hugged her very hard.

"Is it that bad?" and the words begun before she could stop them, She's like a different person, Michael, she talks crazy sometimes Michael she's not the same, or she's more of the same I don't know I don't *know* if it's her or me . . . and then the lame smile, trying for a laugh, you always get my sad stories, don't you? Don't you? as if to force him to admit he was tired of them, tired of her as Bibi was tiring of her, as Bibi tired her out and "No," as gently but with reproof, "I'm your friend. I want all your stories, good and bad and sad, whatever you want to tell me. I'm your friend."

And she did not cry but felt a loosening, the comforting feel of pain if not absolved then set aside, a little, and told him what she felt she could: that she and Bibi were drifting apart again, that Bibi seemed angry all the time. That Bibi, maybe, had other plans.

"Like what?"

"Like bringing back the Surgeons. Or something like them." Something worse. "I don't know, I'm just guessing," the coffee cold now, faint powdered-cream skin riding faint on its surface. "I think it might have something to do with that scummy Matty Regal."

Michael's frown, the distaste one might show for roadkill; a bubo; an untended sore. "Yeah, he hangs around that scene, but he's such an asshole it's hard to imagine Bibi having anything to do with him." He drank his coffee, made a face. "This tastes like shit. —Did she say what she's planning on, with him? A new Surgeons, or what?"

"She wouldn't tell me. She knows I hate him." Sighing, brushing hair back from her face; vaguely aware of her looks, baggy sweat shirt, stained hands, horsetail hair messy all around and she sighed again. "I don't know, maybe I'm paranoid, maybe she does it just to bug me. I don't know," and her hair fell down again, tickling in her face; this time Michael brushed it away, settled its curve gently behind her ears.

"What about you?" leading her away from the worktable to sit on the unmade couchbed, lumpy pillows, blankets humped sad and cold. "What are you working on? That—" nodding back. "What is it?"

She told him, a little, the little she had been doing though in the telling it did not seem so little at all; maybe Bibi was right about that at least. "I guess I spend a lot of time with it, but I have to spend time at the body shop, too." Where she must watch, always, to make sure her tools were not stolen or sabotaged, where they called her

lezzy and cuntfucker behind her back and sometimes to
her face. "It's the only money we have, right now."

"Have you thought about having a show again? —Of
your sculptures, I mean," and his glance at the draped
forms, moving and unmoving; for Tess they might as well
have been buried, dead relics of a past she did not want to
remember, might never want to remember. She shrugged,
a Bibi-like shrug.

"No. I don't know." Little flutter inside of nausea, she
realized she was hungry, she had not eaten today at all.
Should she ask Michael if he wanted to go out, get something? but he was rising, squeezing her hands: have to go, I
have to meet some friends, do you know Skeleton Fist?

"It's a club," she said.

"Sort of, yeah. Anyway I promised I'd meet them at
midnight," and her surprise, was it so late already? Yes.
Time passed in talk; like it used to do with Bibi; don't
think about that now. "I'll call you tomorrow, if you want
me to. Maybe I can come over."

"We'll see," wanting to be gracious, he was always so
kind but it was, maybe, not something Bibi would endorse
or even allow; who knew? Reaching to squeeze his arm,
suddenly shy: "Thanks for coming," and he took her in his
arms, hugged her hard against his chest, held her so long
that she felt a different kind of shyness, he was holding her
the way a man holds a woman; wasn't he?

"Thanks," again, into his shoulder and he kissed her
cheek, as chastely but in another way not so at all: "I'll call
you tomorrow," his lips against her skin, against her lips
lightly; she watched him from the window, sure he could
not see, black figure on a bike, skidding once or twice and
gone.

And within half an hour Bibi back, Bibi's smothering
hug and Bibi's mouth on hers, unconscious trace of those

small Michael-kisses and Tess kissed her back very hard, shoulders in her hands and the metal at her mouth still slick with cold, all the piercings hard-centered with a deep unmelting frost. It was morning and past morning before Tess felt warm at all.

Michael's call came as he had promised, but showering Tess did not hear until Bibi came to stick her face nearly in the spray: "That was Michael," she said.

"Oh, yeah." The soap a mean sliver, working it hard to spring any lather at all. "He said he would call."

"Said it when?"

"Last night—" and the words fell as from a cliff; *last night.* Last night she had not told Bibi there had been any visitors at all.

And now, small head cocked, pale eyes narrow as the soap, you told *me* you were working, right? And louder, "Maybe you'd rather have a cock between your legs, maybe you're getting bored with me, is that right? Is it?" and Tess drawing back, underwater and startled in a way that had nothing to do with Bibi's jealousy but with her accusation: rather have a cock, what did that mean? It was not about cocks, cunts; making love to Bibi was not about making love to A Woman, it was making love to *Bibi,* Bibi of the indrawn breath and closed eyes and nipping teeth, the metal and the slippery scents. Just as making love to Michael would be not about a cock, A Man, but about— just Michael, just that.

"Bibi," shutting off the water; soap tears in her eyes, the cold skitter of gooseflesh. "Don't even start something that stupid. Don't even—"

"Stupid, you have a hell of a fucking nerve calling me stupid, you have a hell of a fucking nerve *any*way to—"

"Bibi, stop it!" Wet and naked and her heart pounding,

pounding, she tried to say something over Bibi's anger but it was impossible, it was like talking over a car wreck, a jackhammer jouncing over glass and broken jars. Yelling, calling her names, calling them both names and Tess's protests—Bibi for God's sake we talked about *you*—instantly made it worse: girding for the explosion and then suddenly Bibi's smile, long and carnivorous: "Well, I guess that's fair. Since *I* talked about you behind *your* back."

She knew. "To who?"

"To Matty. You should be flattered, he's very knowledgeable about your career."

"Really." This was worse than Bibi yelling, worse to sit and listen to her repeat Matty's screed, his opinion on Tess's work, Tess's mode of creation—she actually used that phrase: vintage Matty, mode of creation—and her own sidebar interpretations, how Tess might learn from Matty, how she might to her benefit use him as an example since her creativity seemed to be stalled—

"Who said *that?*"

Coolly, "I did."

—and Matty was of course having no such problems, his new votive service to art's deformed twin, obsession, she actually said that, too, although she had probably thought of that one herself; and on and on until Tess interrupted and in a few sentences, short sentences heavy as iron explained her theory of art-school fuckheads in general and Matty Regal in blunt and unsparing particular.

And quiet, cold ticking quiet and Tess realized she was freezing, her hair cold as forming ice in Bibi's slow gunsight stare: smiling a little, strange sulky triumph: "Well, Matty said you'd probably say something like that, so I guess you'll just have to wait and see."

Through a great tiredness, the same dry flatland: "What does that mean?"

Bibi's smile again, something older, colder than reptilian, cold as the oldest brain of all speaking, short wordless bursts, the back of the back of the skull: "Let's see," she said, "who can keep the most secrets. And be the most surprised in the end."

A silence, the silence of fundamental, tectonic change; a falling-out in the sense of plates shifting, where nothing is safe, not even the silent ground, the places we have been and always been. Tess felt it would not bear her, her weight or her presence. Where she had once lay cautionless to sleep was now a graveyard and worse than a graveyard; never close your eyes there again.

The phone's jittery chime, for Bibi; of course. Her cool chatter backdrop and Tess moving heavily, slowly, rubbing with great effort the towel up and down her body as if all her hollowed bones were filled with chilly lead, dragging to gravity, all the way down.

Now the veiled hostility, but no more big arguments, no real arguments at all unless you counted sniper fire; Bibi was immensely good at that, gifted. Gifted. Nothing as hideous as a death to point to which would at least have been concrete—it's good to be able to see what is killing you, it has its own relief, however dire—instead of this dreadful arid sterility, as if without shared work they could share nothing, not even love was strong enough to keep them together, instead seeming more readily to have driven them apart by placing in their hands the terrible weapons of lovers, who know where all the scars are, all the sick unhealable wounds. Bibi's absences more acute, and in their vacuum Tess worked: harder, not like last time to fill time but in an effort she did not herself yet comprehend; perhaps it was understanding, the effort to understand, make sense of, control.

The small figure on the worktable grew increasingly

more complex, almost rebuslike in the burden of its meaning: to Tess. Working from morning till her afternoon shift
at the body shop, they cut her hours, cut them again as the
winter dragged on, everything dragging, she was eating
crackers out of the box again while Bibi took her meals
elsewhere. She tried to save money on electricity, if they
cut that off she could not work, so: sat in the dark when
she wasn't working, early dark, dark when she got home; is
that a metaphor? Is it? Empty and dark, and Bibi always
gone, even when she was there she was far, far away, Tess
looking up at times to see her stare so absolute it pinned
her where she was, the stare that said more stringently
than any words, *I'm leaving; I'm already gone.*

And one afternoon like all the others, reluctantly ready
to go to work and Bibi stepping in, surprising Tess (instantly depressed by her own surprise): austere and distant, beautiful in a new black high-collared jacket; from
whom had she gotten it? but no way to ask, that right was
gone long ago, things were all the way down the hill now.

"I'm going," Bibi said, flat as a slap. Tiny steel skulls
around the rim of her ear, red ear bitten hard by the cold;
it was immensely cold, inside and out. "Matty will pick up
my stuff."

It took Tess a moment, not to register her words—there
was almost relief in the hearing—but to decide how to
react. Slowly she set aside the C-shapes of wire, sputtering
orange solder gun eye, as slowly rose from the stool.

"Well." Her hands were so chapped they were bleeding;
painlessly. Curiously painless all over. "Are you living with
him now?"

"We're not fucking, if that's what you mean. I don't have
much use for men anymore," and snotty, "although I know
you have a different point of view."

There was no need to respond to this—she and Bibi had

not made love for more than a month now and in that time Tess had not even so much as brushed against another human being; but: no need for any response at all, Bibi would say what she wanted to say, planned to say; Tess might have been a painted picture, a particularly dense piece of wall; a sculpture. Motionless, waiting for Bibi to continue but Bibi surprised her again, simply turned, black and white, and walked out

as Tess still standing, listening, her heart beginning to beat very hard

and walked back in again.

"Tess," holding out her hand, gloved hand, new slick leather around something bright: the keys. "Here. I don't want to keep anything of yours," and gone now this time for good, quick and quiet down the stairs and although Tess heard the door bang—not slam, simply bang—she did not move, stood in the same waiting posture and then suddenly turned, keys in hand and for a moment thought to hurl them, hard as a javelin to gouge a wound in the wall; but instead: pulling on her jacket, goggles in pocket and helmet in hand, ready to go to work and burn, and burn, and burn.

She would not, this time, cry for Bibi, would not miss her, would not mourn if it burned a hole straight through her body, straight down and finally to death. Instead she burned herself a new pattern: wake before the body shop, work there, sweating under her helmet, sweating out the hours and then at home a different fire, smaller, more focused and intense; working till bed, three or four in the ghostly morning, sleep like metal, inert, to rise; and repeat. Crouched over the beast-machine, she was sick of working for nothing, no purpose; sick of it. *Sick,* as the construct stretched geometric arms, crawled upright and monstrous and small across the table's landscape. She ripped the canvas from the other, older constructs, freed them to cold dusty light: *Mme Lazarus,* the Triple Deaths, the *Magistrate* and all the sculptures; only *Salome* lay entombed belowstairs, bloody juggernaut unretrievable; maybe the Zombies had scrapped her, cannibalized her as Tess would now cannibalize these others.

Which horrified Nicky. Hearing the rusty thump and clatter, mild up the stairs but almost comically aghast at the sight of Tess, acetylene torch in hand, constructs carved around her and scattered pieces like organs left to rot on the floor: "What are you *doing?*" as if she were a madwoman about to take her own life; what was left of it; don't joke.

"Tess, what are you doing?" at her side now and staring with such a woeful face that she set the torch aside, cracking knees and up to say, "I'm working again, that's all. Working."

"But all your stuff, you're tearing it up." *Mme Lazarus* stripped and gutted like a burned-out car, his gaze on the shell of her; back to Tess with a mournful accusatory eye. "If you didn't want it anymore, we could've taken it, stored it or something, but to just hack it up, I mean *shit,* Tess—"

I'm not just hacking it up. Or maybe I am. "Don't worry, Nicky. I'm going to make new stuff out of it." Because I'm tired of working for nothing; because I'm burning, burning inside and out and I don't want to eat and I don't want to sleep and I don't want to think about Bibi Bibi Bibi anymore; *fuck* Bibi. She knew that Bibi's advent had put her place strictly off limits to the Zombies; similarly Bibi's departure—and they knew, they were two floors down, how could they help knowing—would mean their return; good. She was ready, again, to speak the language of fire, of metal, of pig iron and slag and cables and snips and battering arms but this time battering small, so small, so *dense* that it was like cutting the burning metal at the molten heart of the world, solid iron shining like an underground star.

None of which she said to Nicky, underlip down and trying to kid him out of it, heavy-handed, she did not feel at all like joking but she tried. "C'mon Nicky, take it easy, I'm saving all the best parts," and she dangled a scrap of cable depending from which a rusty circlet of metal, some grommet like an eye on a twist of thready muscle rolling so grotesquely that it really did look like an eye and he laughed, a little dry but he laughed. And she laughed, too, entirely false, and Nicky started talking about a show they were thinking of having, they had thought—covert glance —about using, you know, the other one. *Salome.* Watching her eyes as if she might start climbing the walls.

"Go ahead," instead. "Use it. Do what you want with it, blow it up, I don't care," and happy now, perhaps they had wanted this permission for a while; they had never really needed it. He would tell Peter and Jerome, he said, they would all talk with her later, talk about *Salome* and the show. And she smiling, waving at him as she drew the goggles on; it would be good, to talk with them, she had not done much talking lately, not much to say in an empty room. Of course there are advantages to empty: no one to say stop working, no one to say you don't understand, no one in fact to say much of anything at all.

Except Michael.

Who came by, grave, sleepless, to see how she was; "I just heard," he said, perching quiet on the edge of the couchbed like a man come to visit the bereaved. "I was away. —How're you doing?"

"Fine," sweat and rust an interesting pox across her face, her neck, it was freezing outside; she had the windows open to let out the fumes, all the icicles melted from the windowframe. Brittle, herself, as an icicle: "Who'd you hear from?"

"Bibi."

Silence.

"I told her, I don't care about listening to right and wrong, don't make me choose sides because I won't. I'm your friend, too. I always will be." Hands on knees, frayed gloves gone and skin parched by cold to an iron red; red-eyed, rubbing at his face. "If I can do anything to help you, I wish—"

Harsh, "Like give me a shoulder to cry on? Well, I don't want to cry, Michael, and you can tell Bibi that, too, I don't *feel* like crying because *I'm not sad.*" Headache like a fever, full-bloom behind her eyes, what else did she tell you? Did she tell you we fought about you, that she was jealous, that she thought we were fucking, me and you? Did she? and "Tess, what's wrong?" alarmed, rising and Tess felt her mouth smiling, a smile like the blistered gash of a burn and she told him, sharp as a rusty edge, Bibi's screed, *maybe you'd rather have a cock between your legs* and when she was finished it took only a moment for the shame to set in, long embarrassed flush as if coming out of a sideshow hypnotist's trance: did I make an ass of myself? Did I bark like a dog, scratch like a chicken with my hands in the dirt? Without looking at him, "I'm sorry, Michael, I didn't—I'm sorry."

His silence, finally looking up at him and he was almost smiling, a strange little smile. Finally, "Was she right?"

White light through the window; hot all over, and the air cold against her skin. Opening her mouth, closing it and suddenly Michael laughed, that one-armed hug, loose and warm as ever: "Boy do you look *nervous.* Don't worry, I won't hold you to it," and somehow that was an insult, too,

Tess trying to explain, it was a *fight,* see, and I said and he laughed, more softly, kissed her cheek; his lips colder than his hands.

"Calm down, all right?" and his squeeze, little fissure of pain: her skin cracked open, blood on his hands like a bridge born between them, a lush tropical color like some exotic drink. They looked at the blood in a silence considering, and then like a broken spell Tess pulled her hands away, hunted up a towel, a rag for him to use; and he wiped his hands, slow and careful as if in the performance of a ritual where each step is necessary and necessarily done. And then kissed her again, more chaste than ever, and left: "Call me," from the doorway. "Hear? *Call me.*"

Yes, she said. I'll do that, and her covert gaze from the window, leaning back to see and not be seen; silly; if she wanted to watch and wave, why not?

No.

That night in bed she wept, wretched swirl of empty blankets, hands against her face and she bit down, dry skeleton teeth in the heel of her hand and sleepless till dawn, till the room turned cold with winter light and a perilous dust of snow beneath sills as cracked and porous as the skin of her hands.

" 'S like Le Cirque Archaos, you ever hear of them?" Nicky expert with duct tape, long nickel streamers down his T-shirted chest, hanging strips of silver skin; he tore one off, applied it to the peeling underside of a plastic breastplate tacked to an empty oil drum. "It's a sort of anticircus, like the Surgeons kind of but without art, you know? I saw the video, it was pretty torqued. —Where'd I put the—"

"Here." Tess handing him the heavy circle; he tore off another length and taped it to his chest. Cold in the Zombie workshop, almost as cold as her place. She had a terrible headache, it felt like a gopher was chewing its way out of her head. Just back and freshly fired from the body shop, not enough work and too much bad blood; jeered as she left and calm in the doorway, considering a 180-pivot to spray the bunch of them with fire; but that was a Bibi thing to do, wasn't it? Besides they could just as easily have burned her down, too, so why start? Save your energy: look for a new job. Or don't; freeze and starve. But she didn't want to freeze and starve, she didn't want the electricity cut off; she wanted to work, getting so close to completing this new piece, so different from the others, so tricky and oblique. Bad timing for eviction, though no doubt the Zombies would have taken her in if only to keep their former mentor off the street; but the workshop was so crowded with three, four would be unbearable. And they were busy, all of them, arranging shows or working their own pickup jobs or fucking one of the changeless coterie of girls, not women but girls in red slouch hats and leather jackets, girls with high-cut hair and black lipstick whom she sometimes saw running errands, pushing metal, hanging around the service elevator watching the Zombies trundle their machines, up and down, in and out.

So. Not to worry, she would just have to find something else, the grind in her stomach, she was already pared so close to the bone. But. It would be okay because it had to be, had to and Nicky saying something, Tess, hey. "Tess," nudging her and it was Michael in the doorway, stomping snow off his boots; smiling at her.

"You eat?" he said. "—Hi, Nicky." Beautiful now in a glacial way, dirty white parka, hair cut very very short all over and the thin sickle earring, silver in the shape of a scythe. Kissing her cheek, its cold dangle against her skin:

"I have a car today, you want to go out? Nicky," politely, "you want to come along?"

Gotta work, he said, lots to do before the show. "Next Friday, Tess, don't forget," and back to work ripping tape, Michael asking her questions about the Zombies' new show, keeping her talking until they sat curled in a half-booth before a steamy window, CHICKEN HUT in stick-on letters facing backward to the street; stringy chicken ka-bobs drenched in pink hot sauce, small fat cups of coffee; his thigh next to hers.

"And what about you?" Sauce on his lower lip. "What'd you do today?"

Trying to smile. "Got fired," and then in haste, before he could commiserate, pat her back, cheer her up, stupid, it was *stupid,* "It's not a big deal, Michael, really. I can get more work, I can always get—"

"But what about in the meantime?"

Dead chicken on a stick. "I have some money saved," a lie; a shrug. "I can get by okay."

Silence. He finished his chicken, his coffee, Tess trying to finish, she was so unhungry, her head hurt so bad. On the way back, stopped at a red light and he touched the keys in the ignition, set them swinging: clipped to the ring itself was another set of keys, Bibi's rejects; with the Zombies' permission she had given them to Michael, he was spending so much time with her now. Kindly time, simply sitting, reading or watching as she worked, saying little, just warm, just there.

He swung the keys again.

"I want to move in," he said.

"What?" Stupid; mouth open. She said it again: "What?"

"I said," green light, "I want to move in. I'm working a little, I can help you. Come on, Tess, you know you don't have any money saved, you told me a couple weeks ago you were behind on your electric bill, they'll cut it off and then how will you work? Especially with that piece so close to being done."

Silence. Her heart was pounding so hard she felt sick, head and heart, hurting everywhere and she didn't *want* him to move in, didn't want anyone, *if I can't have Bibi I don't*

"Hey," gently, not looking at her—and uncanny, so Bibi-like to know, "I'm not Bibi, okay? And I'm not going to try to be her either, so relax. All I want to do is help out a little, okay? I meant to say something before, but now—" Hands tight on the wheel; she leaned against the other door, slump and slope, eyes closed because she was going to be sick in a minute; or cry; something bad, something she didn't want to do. Something inside, hot like tears but dark, livid, a surging mess like puke, like bile, liquid anger and Michael said something else, she would be doing him a favor, too, it was overcrowded and something-something and she said, very quietly, very very quietly, "I don't want a roommate. I don't want anyone there."

Open eyes to see Michael looking at her, his face wiped blank. "All right," and then silence for the rest of the drive.

In the dashlight, door open and on his face a nonexpression so absolute that for a moment, slush to her ankles, head pounding, she could not properly interpret: then past her own misery to see more: not angry, or maybe angry too but—hurt. He was hurt. She had hurt him.

Standing in the slush, hot whisper of exhaust and she said his name, Michael, Michael I'm sorry. I'm sorry.

The car was still running.

Michael said nothing.

Keys lonely in the lock; dark all the way up the stairs.

She barely made it to the toilet before her whole dinner came up in one long blurt of pink and brown and she crouched with her face on the cold horsecollar seat and did not cry, stared at the wall where Bibi had tacked a postcard of the Empire State Building scaled by a giant skeleton and did not cry. And did not sleep again that night, restless beneath blankets slick with cold, light through the window on her worktable like the admonishing finger of a patienceless god.

Two weeks later, Michael moved in.

He parked the borrowed car beside the building, by the service elevator where Bibi had always parked, and brought as little as she had (and stop comparing them): clothes, books mostly—Ballard and Burroughs and Angela Carter, some photography monographs, Arbus and Witkin and Weegee, a strange German omnibus of surgical techniques with a lengthy appendix of failures—and a handful of toilet articles so strangely lavish—French moisturizer, heavy cream shampoo—that on seeing them Tess wanted to laugh: there was a dandy in there somewhere, past the cropped hair and dilapidated boots, the parka that looked like he had fished it from a Dumpster and probably had. He brought as well his silences, his small jokes, help when she needed it; money, and he seemed to know without asking how much was required. While the borrowed car was his he drove her around to body shops, tool shops, parked patient and he never asked for gas money or accepted when she offered; cheering like a child when she found another job: a machine shop, part-time and time enough time to do her real work. He never complained when she spent the night working, never mentioned the stink or the glare, only lay, stretched calm as an angel on a ratty red plaid bedroll unfurled at an angle to the couchbed. He brought the physical comfort of another body in the house, warm and moving (although he did not so much as hint there might be more ways to move, pleasing Tess who thought she had had enough of lovers lately, thank you, thank you so much). And, rarest, he brought to her, again without asking, the gift she wanted most but could not admit to wanting: news of Bibi.

Who was not idle: she spent, Michael said (and what a tale, gleaned from friends and almost-friends and hangers-on, Bibi knew everyone and everyone certainly knew her) much of her time now moving between the incongruity of plastic surgery clinics to the wet-cardboard reek of the shacktowns, where in the space that no one wanted, much experimentation occurred: where the limits of the body were pushed further and further back, where the philosophy of modification itself was stringently debated, sometimes with fists and grinning teeth: does one modify from love or hate of the body and its limits, for sheer sensation or more eloquent pursuits? —And Tess, passionate: "I *wanted* it to be more, for *her* sake. I did," and Michael's nod, arm around her shoulders; only that, a nod: he understood.

In her own body Bibi sought answers, her disciplines less spontaneous now but more extreme: where once she and Michael had listed for one another the seven categories of body play, the seven major avenues of expression, now she seemed bent on exceeding each. Contortion, constriction, encumberments and deprivation; the walling-away of the body in plaster, the encasing of warm flesh. Fire. Penetration. Suspension. In her own body, by the bindings, the piercings, the elegant tortures Bibi sought her own answers, as well as answers to questions only she would dare to ask (and Tess's pride, cold and obscure: there was no one like Bibi, exceeding limits no one else had guessed were there): proven by new disciplines, rigors she spoke of only obliquely and would not deign to share. Sinking deeper into her own flesh, she seemed to be transforming, in the eyes at least of others, into more, and less, than human, a creature shaped and bounded only by the edge of her desires.

More mythic than even in her Surgeons days, skinny body in black and red, always a new bandage, a new bruise or laceration: and always the same impatient brutality, as if to find her answers she must tan living flesh, break bones to heal them in humps deliberately grotesque and dire; nothing was safe from her, most especially herself.

They said (Michael said) she was becoming a fakir, that she slept in bindings, in bondage harnesses, with plaster drying on the rims of her eyes and mouth. They said she was learning how to pierce without bleeding, nothing but a faint plasma dribble to mark the tiny holes, a hundred avid mouths born pink and new on her thin skin. They said she performed the Sundance ceremony, hung from hooks through the skin of her chest, her breasts; painted her face with blood; went for days without eating or drinking anything other than lukewarm water. They said—that anonymous they—that when she spoke it was black genius; was all the way out there; was crazy as a shithouse rat.

And Tess, listening, hands knotted and thinking, thinking; worrying without thought, just the visceral turn of her guts: something is wrong here. Something is not safe: for her. For anybody connected with her; and who was connecting with Bibi, these days?

Of Matty Regal Michael said very little; they were maybe collaborating, "maybe," at her deep frown of distaste and dislike. "I don't really know."

"On what?" The resurrection of the Surgeons? Something worse? What?

"I don't know that either, but I think if it was going to be performance or anything like that we'd've heard about it, somebody always wants to tell you—anyway." Scratching at his neck, pale drift of stubble. "What're you going to work on today?"

Day off from her machine-shop job, boring mating of metal to metal but it paid better than the body shop with more free time; like today. Made to be spent at the worktable and she swallowed the end of her bad coffee, rose from the couchbed: "At it," she said. "All day, if I can."

He had errands, left to do them, left her in light and the small figure complete, now, but not done: because she was doing something new, creating as well an environment, the construct's home: thin steel corners and scratched discarded Lexan a smoky blue sky; air; element, the beast-machine made to move within that finite square. At first consideration the idea had seemed too limiting, but now she knew it was not, knew by hard practice that the movements engendered in that bound landscape were by its very circumscription that much more dense, and focused; and free. Terribly free, the way a whole life can be lived in one room. To see the construct pressed and moving against the Lexan gave a feeling she knew she had not conjured with her other works, the big *Madame,* the triune ferocity of the Triple Deaths. Her original genesis, of room-filling machines, huge lumbering sculpture made to move like dinosaurs now seemed exactly that: extinct, a scope unnecessary: what was needed was a distillation, tabletop constructs (and, perhaps, even smaller?) enclosed in boxes that would both enhance and define their function and meanings; more than art, each box must be memory, fear, sorrow, each box a microcosm of—what? The guilt in the night, the pain she still felt, would always feel? Did it matter, did she need to say the words even to herself? She could not think these things in words, or concepts, any more than she could think of breathing as sheer respiration, heart and blood as circulatory necessities; she knew without words, without conscious thought, knew by the turn of the fire, the slippery drip of silver solder, the slim heft of the hammer and the way it turned in her hand.

She articulated nothing; only worked. And Michael returned, to watch; through winter's cold decline, the snake dance of ice down the windows; reading sometimes, or sleeping, but mostly elbow-propped in the line of sight, the chitter of metal and sinuosities of smoke, Tess's sweat and smile past the goggles and the bright concentration of the burn.

She made three pieces, titled none of them; destroyed two and started over with more parts from the older pieces, the large feeding the small; forced nurture. And one night, Michael curled in red plaid and one bare foot extended, she working in her circle and realizing, as she put a piece through its paces, that for this piece at least she had not once wondered what Bibi might have thought of it; had not thought of Bibi at all. And was unsure if this was good or bad, knew only it encompassed a sadness immense, the sadness not of death but death's austere attendant, forgetfulness.

Cold. Still winter in the room.

A little sound: sleeping Michael, breathing in and out, warm breath, warm body under the blankets and suddenly Tess wanted to go to him, pull the blankets down and lie beside him, just lie there, her arms around him and her closed eyes quiet, breathing in his smell, breathing in and out. Just lie there.

Go on.

No.

If it were Bibi, you would do it.

If it were Bibi, she thought, I wouldn't have to; and back to work, this night a mortician, a taxidermist's tedious slow stripping of one part from another, the peeling-back of metal like the deliberate strop and shed of willing skin.

The Zombies were having another show, *Strategic Interventions;* Jerome's name, Nicky's choice of venue: cracked and empty bowl of concrete, built in the seventies for some purpose now unknown and used mostly by skateboarders in the summer. Now, slithers of ice, a strangely dry smell when standing in the center: dead center: Tess was standing there now, hands clenched in pockets, shivering in waves and talking through a little headset mike.

"How about now?" Peter's voice duplicated, large and small: loudspeakers in three corners and intimate through the headset, like the voices of God and conscience both talking out loud. "Is this okay?"

"Sounds good."

"Okay. How about now?"

"Too much feedback," tapping her ear, realizing he could not see the small gesture; amending, "Feedback through the headset," and the volume came down, her breath a slow trickle of smoke.

They had wanted her, nagged her to be in the show. We know you're working on stuff, declaration blunt and excited: come on, it'll be fun, all of us together again. Pinning her at her worktable—like old times, like old times, too, their awe when she showed the two finished constructs: one caged in blue Lexan and steel, animal and machine; the other in a prison prismatic, fake holography around a scrap skeleton, iron and plastic and wire crowned by the grievous skull of a bird.

"God, Tess, these're—" Nicky's hands reverent on the boxes, Ming care. Staring at the bird skull, its small dead geometry balanced against the weightlessness of the box's interior. "You do any more of these?"

"Just these two," and then they were really at her, come *on* Tess, this shit is great! The best ever, you gotta be in the show, you don't even have to do anything, just put these where people can see 'em. C'mon, it'll be—

No. Smiling; but no, she did not want to do that anymore; Michael silent behind her but she knew he agreed; he had told her so. No sense in forcing yourself—his nighttime hands on her shoulders, gentle to work the taut muscles loose; you'll show again when you're ready. In a month, or a year, or never, what difference does it make so long as you're happy with what you're doing?

But: the three of them so crestfallen, Nicky especially, that her rash agreement, she would *work* in the show, setting up, how's that? Okay?

Okay. So now, numb hands and wind-dry eyes and: "How 'bout this?" a whine like a drill straight through her head, she snatched off the headset and held it at arm's length as if it had burned her, scowling across the bowl and Peter's hands spread wide, Sorry.

And Michael then, with hot coffee, shooing her back to the van: "Take a break," the faintest kiss on her cheek. "I'll take a turn now."

It took longer than they had expected, wiring problems and now no time to eat dinner, the show due to start in less than an hour so: in the van, Jerome pulling out a bottle of vodka, label half-peeled like sunburned skin and "Have some," nudging Tess with the glass neck. "Warm you up."

"Fuck me up, you mean," but that was something Bibi would say, wasn't it? "Give it here," and she took the bottle, strange tasteless taste; not warm, but it seemed she felt the cold less, or maybe she was already numb. They all drank some, jammed together in the van, Michael's arm the closest heat, sure around her shoulders.

Sundown so early, the earth's rotation toward spring but it still got dark at six o'clock, dark now as she and Michael crawled out of the van, one last drink and over to one of the bonfires, strategic bonfires from which came smells like seared plastic and bubbling flesh; hideous smells at first but you got used to them, or maybe that was the numbness talking again. *Strategic Interventions* had begun, chattering feedback whistle and the idiot bounce of Jerome's pogos, directionless springloaded bullets standing maybe half a meter high, each bounce accompanied by a grunt or a coughing squeal: made to make noise upon impact. Just like human beings.

It was a good show: lots of noise, explosions, lots of threat for the audience; Tess caught herself scanning for Bibi and turned deliberately away. Pogos, and Peter's hideous looping screams, Nicky's propane altars and all of it overlaid for Tess like a strange template of the past, fires in the night and there should be bodies, leaping like the scattershot pogos; less nostalgia than brute memory, reminding her as well why she did not want to perform again; ever again. She sighed, or made some sound because: Michael, breath on her neck, "Hey," squeezing her upper arms, "what's the matter? What's wrong?"

"Nothing," lying. "Good show. Better than the Surgeons," and he did not reply; did not agree, probably, but so what? Only Bibi would really understand, see as she, Tess, saw now, with the double lens of memory; and Tess did not want to think about Bibi now. Ever. "Very good show," she said.

The audience thought so, too, cheers and the cheerful wild vandalism that usually followed a Zombies gig but there was so little here to vandalize (except the equipment, which would have earned the vandals something unenjoyable) that the energy instead turned partylike, a big party, Tess and Michael swept through it and into the van, crushed close with the Zombies and assistants and there was another bottle of vodka, its label intact: SANTA MARISA above a lolling señorita with heavy coconut breasts; since when did Mexico have anything to do with vodka? Since when have you had anything to do with it?

"It's a celebration," Tess's mutter less festive than defiant but one of the assistants heard and yelled, "A Zombies celebration!" and everyone laughed, Night of the Living Zombies, To Kill a Zombie, Death and the Zombie. Zombie V, The Final Countdown. Zombies in Love. Tess's head back, against Michael's shoulder; his arms around her and very warm.

Warmer still in the Zombie Birdhouse, there must have been a hundred people there; somebody put on Killbilly and Nicky loping by, drunk and shirtless and grinning: "Wanna dance?" Handing her a bottle of vodka; Santa Marisa metamorphosed into good old Brand X. Maybe it wasn't even vodka, maybe it was bleach. Industrial strength. She drank, held the bottle so Michael could drink, too. She could feel his hands, hotter even than the room around them, hottest of all against her waist, each finger a separate heat.

It's a celebration.

Killbilly into something else, someone's homemade tape, shrieks and bass-heavy laughter, a wrong-speed voice saying "Don't be nervous" over and over. Don't be nervous; don't be unhappy. Tired of being unhappy, sick and tired: over one thing and another, Bibi and work and money and so on and so on, Michael was right: things were looking up for her now. Weren't they? Certainly they were. Michael knew. The only one to see what she was trying to do (and a part of her undrunk mind speaking with the scornful clarity of perfect understanding, You're trying to make another Bibi out of him, aren't you? Well, it won't work) (shut up shut up shut up). His hands on her shoulders; shut up.

More people dancing. Almost completely dark in the room now, Jerome firing irregular bursts of orange fire at the ceiling. Her own admonishment, "Don't burn the fucking place down, Jerome," and his smiling slurred apology, firing out the window instead; Jerome was always so reasonable. Jerome was such a good friend. Not as good as Michael, but very good indeed. Michael's mouth grazing hers now, soft and sweet, his tongue touching hers just a little, just at the tip; warmth entering warmth, and everything wet inside.

More firing. Somebody else playing with a nailgun, and Michael's steering arms, let's go sit on the stairs for a while, somebody's gonna get hurt with that thing. Two big plastic tumblers filled with straight vodka and ice, ready to sit until, halfway up: two skinny sweaty shirtless girls, hissing and groaning like cats in their inexpert coupling. One of the girls had breasts like Bibi's, or maybe that was memory again, memory wrong; dark areolas, stiff little nipples; the other girl was kissing her neck, kissing and biting, Michael easing past them as if both they and the girls were conveniently invisible—such manners—and into their room.

Into the dark, and against the door; so cool in there, cold, his hands cold from carrying the drinks and his sweet wet vodka mouth, open on hers, on the dry twist of her neck. Kissing and biting like the girls on the stairs, nothing like Bibi, *nothing* and her own palms flat and up and down his back, up and down, feeling the cabling stretch of muscles, the unexpected lump of a scar and his fingers rising to

hook the raveling neck of her T-shirt, pull painfully down
until it tore, gone and his hands on her breasts, rough,
squeezing and his mouth in her neck, "Oh, God, Tess,"
pressing hard against her, pressing her up to the wall. Her
back bare, moist against the flaking paint and tearing open
the silvery square he gave her as with his other hand he
yanked down his jeans, raised his shirt and in one motion
she clothed him, skinned him in rubber the scent of which
mingled with his scent, his smell all over her, mouth,
hands, everywhere as he angled past her thighs, and inside.
All the way inside. His teeth on her throat like an animal,
lunging between her sweaty legs and she beat on his back
with her fists, harder, her head kept banging the wall and
she beat him in rhythmless fury, harder, harder, his pale
new curls in her hands now and dragging his panting
mouth to hers, kissing him blind and busy teeth now too
nipping at her lips, her lower lip, biting till it hurt: the pain
a spur and bucking now against his hips, *harder* and this
time she must have said it out loud because he groaned,
"Oh *Tess*" and she pulled him to her, hands, thighs, straining, blunt-nailed fingers digging at his back and coming
like a seizure, a sickness, fever's orgasm to burn her empty
and in the end she screamed, loud wet convulsion of sound
and in the echo of that instant she felt him come, driving
her back into the wall so it hurt, holding her there, pinned
like an insect and his eyes wild and blank as a bas-relief,
and she hung on him as if she were boneless, panting as he
did like a beast run to ground.

"I want to be everything," he said, voice wet, guttural in
the incubus dark; hands on her body like pinning circular
sculpture. "Everything for you."

She woke sick, shamed and bent almost in half, long
scouring puke and Michael there to help her back to bed.

Naked gooseflesh, flapping covers and it was hard to meet his eyes until, his hand deliberate, turning her face to kiss: deliberate, too, on her sewer mouth: "Hey," so sweetly. "It was bound to happen, Tess, don't be sorry."

"I'm not sorry," and he lay down beside her and closed his eyes, toothpaste breath tender on her wretched cheek. Herself sleepless, and memory edged by the vodka's erosion: show, party, sex, more sex on the floor, Michael saying Everything, over and over.

Everything for you; what was that? Lover? Friend? Assistant? She didn't want an assistant. Liaison, then; adviser, someone to help out when she needed it. Someone to talk to. Someone—that clear inner voice again and clearly sour, so much louder now without alcohol's winnowing filter—like Bibi. Bibi without tits, is that it?

No. Deeper burrow. No it is not.

Her expectation, then, for things to change; the shifting plates again, but this shift, if it truly came at all, was far subtler; to the surface eye there was little change at all. Winter's slow decline, and: lover now, his presence intensified; warmth, always, in the bed—their bed? Long legs hooked about hers, sweaty tangle of pale hair like a child's, a little child asleep. Skinned knuckles from carrying in some scrap for her, beaming, he had found it on the curb. He liked to find things for her, things she found useful, could incorporate into her art. He liked to make breakfast. He liked to fuck. A lot. He liked her to talk about her art; still part-time at the machine shop but full-time on the boxed sculptures, boxed figures; Michael had taken to calling them simply "the boxes," is that box done? are you going to make a new box? The third was done; the fourth taking shape, beautiful split chicken bones, the rubbery brace of heavy plastic: thin anemone spines of purest aluminum crossed with the unforgiving heft of heat-split iron, the whole terrible, and terribly sad; they were all sad, the boxes, their one shared characteristic a characteristic loss; full of emptiness. Why, Michael asked, one hand light on her shoulder, why are you so sad?

"I'm not." Voice distorted by the mask, fine dust everywhere. Delicate wire, tweezer-wound like a metal grapevine up the farthest spine. "The world's sad, Michael, not me."

"The world's not sad. The world's a lock," zipping his jacket, heavy plastic cap and hand on the door, outward bound; to where? Out. "The world's a lock and we're the key." Exit line; he liked those, too, exit lines, pronouncements. Had he always? or was it just the knowledge lent by intimacy that showed her things unseen before?

Bending to work again; and the phone. Ignoring it until she heard Bibi's name: her pounce belated, whoever it was had hung up. She hit the message button so hard it did not for a moment work at all, then the garbled end, man's voice she didn't recognize, something about a talk or a lecture. Bibi, giving a lecture? A demonstration, certainly and with knives, but a lecture? Podium Bibi, using her own body as a graph: nose, ears, lip and here's my labia piercing, as you can see the ring enters here—

Stop it.

Hand on the button to play it again and then instead: erase. Back to work. Get the fuck back to work.

And the slope of the chicken bones, marrowless, and in a moment's rage turning the heat gun on it all, turning it so high the plastic brace melted like ice, like skin in a furnace, a crematorium, melted to run and coat the coaxing wire and pool at the bottom, at the construct's feet like the heaviest blood in the world. Faint cooling bubbles; an ugly smell as, hammer in hand, she turned on the carcass of the

Triple Deaths and began methodically to strip it down, all the way back to iron, down past the memory of its bones.

"It wasn't a lecture," Michael said.

Half-distracted, "What wasn't," scrubbing her hands, thin seams of melted plastic beneath her nails; burns on her wrists bad enough to leave definite scars; her mind not on work, today. Something else, and Tess asked him to say it again.

"That message, on the machine." Unpacking a greasy bag of egg rolls and fried rice; cheap Thai beer. Paper napkins sticking to the cartons. "Bibi's thing, it wasn't a lecture, it was like a, an audition, I guess. Cattle call. She's starting a new group."

Gray soap trapped convulsive between her hands, and she squeezed; then forced her voice down to normal. "The new Surgeons, right?"

Frowning, sharp chopsticks poised in his hands; like needles. "I don't know, really. Supposed to be performance, like dance, but it's not about dance anymore. They're not asking for dancers, anyway."

"Who's they?"

"Bibi and Matty Regal, I guess. Some other people—you remember Andy, and—"

Matty Regal; *fuck.* "Sandrine, those guys?"

"No. Not that I know of. —I guess it's all about the body." Beckoning hand from the couchbed folded half-closed, "C'mon and eat."

Burns still stinging, sloppy with the chopsticks, she had not used them in a long time, not since she and Bibi had gone out to—stop it. Eat. A new Surgeons, but all about the body. Bibi's body, Bibi and Matty Regal, Matty like a rat familiar, smelly chittering grin; are you jealous? Is that it?

And then a cool internal pause.

Meat on the chopstick, the bifurcating spear. "Michael, where'd you hear all this?"

"The message." Nodding at the phone. "On the machine, it was a—"

"I erased that."

"No you didn't."

Yes I did. Did I? Remembering the minute, heatgun anger and suddenly unsure; she had had a hard time playing it, maybe she hadn't erased it.

Maybe she had.

"—mentioned something about it, too," a name she didn't know, woman's name, Michael had many friends. "She was even going to try out, I guess, but then she ran into Crane—remember him? Bibi's old—"

"I remember."

"Yeah, so anyway Crane gave her some story about the Surgeons and that Bibi was even more extreme now, so she —what's the matter?"

"Nothing." More extreme. How many little rings now, Bibi, how many scars, how much blood? Is all of it yours? Remembering Bibi's lectures to an audience of one, one at a worktable sitting silent in the storm of doctrine, they're going to do it anyway; it's so *powerful.* Like sex. Like religion. The freeing of primitive instincts, the *direction:* they have to be led. Bled? Sacrificial blood, Bibi slick to her elbows, covered with blood and honey and Matty behind like a nurse at the table, altar: scalpel please; knife please; ax. Please.

"Tess, what's the matter?" His frown, close enough to smell the ginger on his breath, the tang of the beer; he took her hands. "This shit with Bibi—I know you hate Matty, I hate him, too, he's an asshole, but Bibi's a big girl and she can do whatever she wants with whoever she wants. Even bring back the Surgeons, unless you feel like suing her for—"

"Oh *please*—"

"I know, it's absurd, that's what I mean. She's a free agent," squeezing her hands now, softly, "just like you." More softly, looking down so she had to look up: "Are you jealous? Still?"

Pale in the light from the worktable, two hundred certain watts and his eyes unblinking, staring down at their joined hands; Tess's burned skin like a brand: for lying. "No," leaning now, the Judas kiss. "I'm not jealous, it's just—I don't know what it is. I guess I think it's not a good idea," and looking past him at the light on the worktable proper, the figure of number five and the growing box around it: a female figure this time, and razor wire rusted like braille: what did it say, what cryptic sorrowing admonitions if only she could read? See your future in the wire.

Michael said something else, bright, released her hands to start eating again. Tess put her food aside, gray as flesh in the little cartons, the beer in her mouth like ash and water, a penitent's drink: the sour genesis of tears.

Rumors, it was all she had but there were always plenty of rumors, even for someone as isolated as Tess, about someone as fiercely flamboyant as Bibi. The Zombies heard some things, Michael heard things, too, and she encouraged him, all of them, to hear more: relentless and at the same time remorsefully conscious of use, it was ugly to use people, especially to do a job you ought to do yourself; and why not? Why not just pick up the phone and call her, say What are you doing now? Let's be buddies, Bibi, let's let bygones be bygones and how about I get in free to your shows? And incidentally, what kind of shows are they going to be? The kind they hold in basements and empty

buildings, the kind with half-closed eyes and mouths a little open, just a little, just to catch the smell? The kind
someone has to clean up after, careful motion of the rag
and the long broom, sweeping wet toward the slippery hole
of the grate in the center of the floor?

Filtering gossip, the half-heard, the improperly remembered and from it Tess made her own tapestry, her own
little puzzle and clue: picture this: Bibi had apparently
met, again, the inevitable limits, began to feel her own
experimentation on too small a scale, so voilà, new Surgeons, but not really Surgeons after all. This would be
performance, maybe even dance, too, but its essence was
to be the body transformed, the dark caperings of flesh
fantastic, bound and banded, pierced and scarred and
ridged with the needle's calligraphy of pain, and passion.
Around her she had begun to gather this group, more rig-
orous and exclusive than the Surgeons had ever been, had
begun, already, to train them to her own severe specifics,
while still, said Michael—quoting the vast they—continuing her own private experimentation; her body was the
vanguard.

Matty Regal was part of it, of course, and Andy, but no
others whom Tess knew, or knew she knew: perhaps she
had met them, at the few parties Bibi had dragged her to,
seen them at the shows, crouched and grinning, the ones
who screamed loudest for the needle, who pushed and
shoved at the sight of blood.

And Michael disdainful, he had met, he said, a few of
them, didn't know names but if *that* was Bibi's idea of—

"What are they like?" Avid as an open mouth and hating it, hating herself for the feigned tone, the lightly raised
eyebrow; you *liar.*

"Let's put it this way," leaning over her at the worktable, balancing his chin on her shoulder tensed true and

straight as a two-by-four: "She was better off with the Surgeons. A lot better. When she *thinks* 'jump,' they all go hop off a building. Metaphorically, unfortunately. And it isn't jump she's thinking, not anymore. . . . They're the last thing she needs now, Tess, and that's a fact." Musingly, half-lost with his lips on her neck, "I want you two to work together." Hands on her breasts. "Just the two of you, no baggage, nobody else to get in your way. *Then* you'd see some sparks." Thumbs kneading at her nipples and Tess half-aroused, half-irritated, she wanted to work: almost a smile: "Me and Bibi, yeah. And what would you do?"

She felt his smile against her skin, the stretch and pull of his lips, flesh to flesh: "Me? I'm the director." Fingertips light on her nipples, irresistible, her own loose grip on the heavy screwdriver, tilting upward like a phallic pun and his teeth were on her neck, canted sharp as a wolverine's: "Don't you know there's always more than one way to perform?"

Heavy rain. Electricity flicking on and off, a child's light-switch mischief, near midnight and Tess winding down: more tired, tonight, than usual, a long dark day and this piece was done, really, it was down to tinkering now. Woman figure, its skull the tiny sleekness of a rat, mummified rat, she had found it wedged behind the toilet behind a V-shaped spear of subdivided plaster, beheading it free of its starved body with one guillotine pinch of heavy-duty tinsnips and for some reason Michael had found this funny, laughed all the way out the door. Dirty gray fur merging with the slender steel of stick-figure shoulders, the rudimentary nervous system of thin-coated wire that made it, her, move. And she will: just press your hand against the razor wire, just exactly so; does it hurt? Mm-hmmm.

Noise at the door, rising expectant for Michael: but: Nicky. Two cans of Chinese beer, rain-slicked hair and he looked like a ferret, a wet ferret, an old-style greaser. "Hey," holding up the beer. "Got a minute?"

"Sure. Just finishing up," socketing the soldering pencil, neat sweep of plastic crumbs, slivers of wire into the basket; she left the big light on. Knee to knee with Nicky on the couchbed, raising the beer one to the other.

"To your stuff," and smiling, her headshake as she drank the toast. Foam on her lower lip. Something strange about Nicky; she realized he was nervous. About what?

"Tess, listen. I gotta ask you something." Silence. He drank his beer in long hectic swallows, a stalling drink, set the empty can at his feet. "Your stuff—it's really great, you know?"

"Right."

"Come on," and he *was* nervous, nervous enough to be angry. "It's fucking great and you know it. I want to," pause unto awkwardness and then, "I want you to show me."

"Show you what?"

Picking up the can, squinting away. Squeezing the can. "Show me how to do it."

Her silence, now, honestly nonplussed; Nicky was as good with metal as she, what would he need to learn from her? Technique? Approach? "Nicky," picking her way, "I don't know what you—"

"Like that," pointing, can forgetful in his hand, "that piece there, that's a genius piece, Tess, that's the maximum article, it's fucking torqued out of its mind! I want to do that. I want to make stuff like that. I want you to show me how." Pause. "Michael says—"

"Says what?"

"Just that, just—your work, it's great." Nicky was lying;

no, Nicky was not telling everything. Nicky was so nervous now he could not keep still, had to rise from the couchbed, fidgety bounce to the worktable to touch with still hands the barest edge of the razor wire. How big his hands were.

"So will you, or what?"

"Nicky, what can I teach you that you don't already know?"

"Just let me watch, then, all right? Just let—"

Unwilling, unable to think of what else to say: "All right, if you want to, I don't care but, Nicky, you should really—"

All smiles, bounding back to grab both her hands, big puppy spilling her beer unnoticed: "Tess, man, it'll be fucking great, you'll see," jumping bean and to the door, leaning back around it to say "See you tomorrow!" as if they might start at the first wink of dawn, cloppity-clop down the stairs, her new trick pony and what the hell, really, had all that really been about?

"What was that all about?" startling her but just Michael, wet cheeks and on the stairs unheard in Nicky's backwash, coming to kiss her and his lips were wet, too. Letting his jacket fall where it was, headshake like a dog out of water. "It's raining like a motherfucker out there. —What did he want, Tess?"

She told, faint bemused brevity and instantly surprised by his instant scorn: *"Nicky?"* heel-pushing off his boots. "His brain wouldn't even make a good sponge. What the fuck can Nicky learn from you?"

"What's the matter with you?" before him, head cocked, hands loose. "Why should you care?"

Slippery hands through hair dark with water, rubbing them dry against his thighs. His lips looked puffy, the bratty frown of a spoiled child; faint strawberry on his cheek shifty as a bruise concealed. "I don't *care,* that's not the point. I just don't think it helps you grow, that's all. I think it wastes your time."

"You're the one who sent him to me."

His underskin stillness, the sense of a square of silence over a big dark hole; and her own surprise uneasy, where had that picture come from? What hole? but he was talking, "What's that supposed to mean?"

Michael says. Michael says your work's great. "Something you told him. Something about my work. Don't you remember?"

"If I remember right," coming toward her, each step separate and particular, "the last thing I said to Nicky was where's the can opener, matey. I don't know what the fuck he's talking about." Close to her now, not smiling, taking her hands in hands as cold and slick as the endless spill of rain down the windows, black cataract and his voice very reasonable, very matter-of-fact: "You do what you want, Tess, but I'm telling you right now I think it's a waste of time. You don't grow, you know, you die."

Her pause, deliberate, deliberately long: It's my time to waste and I'll die if I want to but she didn't say it, said nothing, rain on the window, cold fingers around hers as she pulled her hand away, I have work to do tonight. All right?

All right?

"Whatever you want, honey," his smile, casual strip of his shirt, damp shirt, neck and armpits ringed with wet; hair half-wet, half-dry, pale and dark across his scalp like a changeable pelt, as if he were two creatures. "I think I'll just go to bed."

Nicky was serious; he meant to watch and the next day he did, initial distraction but the longer he sat there the blue of his jeans became the dun of the wall, his slouch the peripheral fade of a coatrack, a bent sculpted arm; even his questions came couched in a flat un-Nicky-like monotone, she could answer without thinking hard.

There were six of the boxes now, the seventh grown and building under Nicky's stare: this one a slanting tunnel of sullen steel burned dark around the round-mouth aperture, and inside no figure but a torso, studded, poisoned with eyes, all eyes, eyes in the armless armpits, eyes in the belly and groin, eyes made of tiny steel balls etched with the wide pupils of hysteria, the slanting glare of madness: and more eyes, couched in slits surprising, here and there up the sides of the tunnel, some gouged to blindness with big blunt-headed nails: see no evil. And then her capricious spray of heavy matte black, paint in blurts and spots and here and there, only a few eyes left open, only a little vision left to see, what? Nicky, watching, himself all eyes? Michael crossing like a smiling spirit, muffled and buffered in heavy black, long legs, new-old boots, bandaged wrist and an oversize black peacoat he claimed he had found in a club: don't let me bother you. Either of you. And Tess, her own thin smile back, saying nothing, she was saying nothing a lot these days. Except in bed.

Where his hands were often cold, his corpse feet oblong against her shins; bad circulation, he said, or said It's cold in here; warm me up. His erection like a lead splint, iron in her hands and she worked him hard, I'll make you warm; I'll burn you. Burning, sucking his bruisy lips, wet thighs all muscle; she had lost weight again, her visible bones cored with vanadium steel, her teeth socketed brittle as she rode him, rode him, hands on his shoulders, grip through his growing hair, growing longer, sweet little pubic curls and when she came she growled like an animal, grinding teeth; her fingers left marks in his skin. He liked her to leave marks. He had plenty of them, abrasions, skin in little half-moon bites—

"When did I do that?"

"Last week. On the floor, remember?"

—and she wanted to leave more, bite harder; burn; some things needed burning. Working all the time, she hated the machine shop, stupid robot work but they needed the money, they were living on what she made beyond Michael's vague income, his unspecified employments (he did not tell and she found without surprise she was uneager to learn; there was much about Michael she was content to leave alone). Working on her art, staring Nicky and, now, Bryan, one of Nicky's friends, sallow and always frowning, as if he were attempting to suck out her brain and all she knew through the strawlike tube of his concentration; lots of luck. She could have had more observers, more silent students—people were calling her, now, people she had not thought of for a year and more: gallery people, even, asking if she was showing at all. No, she said, if not polite then at least civil, a little, but sometimes less in her surprise: dismay: they wanted her to show, they wanted to see; they wanted, Michael said, to buy: commissions.

"What?"

"Calm down." Amused, in the dark, gently pushing her head back down onto the shelf of his shoulder; stroking her hair. "Some woman, her gallery specializes in outsider art—she heard about you. The other side of *tanzplagen,* she said, and—"

And Tess furious, hinge-backed off the bed and the other side of *shit,* that's what you'll get, and I'll take my own fucking phone calls, okay? Okay? Grabbing the topmost blanket to sit trembling at her worktable, would not come back to bed; slept there, head down and powdered faint with shavings, dreaming of nothing but black and blood and waking exhausted to emptiness; Michael gone, and she was late for work.

A rare rebellion: sick of work, spent the day instead with art: the eye-box now coated past paint with a thin skin of melted plastic as sickly as slick caucasian flesh, then scraped meticulous vision into less than 1 percent of the etched steel eyes, just finishing up when Nicky and Bryan at the door: unsmiling, unshowered, she stank and was starving, left them there to go for coffee and a red pepper sandwich, ate it on the corner with big angry bites, wind and dirt in her squinting face and then went back to work harder; harder. Knotted hands and knuckles like bad welds, dry eyes seeing past, what? The work she did, would do, the burns and the broken wire, the limbs like metal stretched tormented and why? Why so sad? You ought to be happy: love and work, isn't that the prescription? Don't you have both? Don't you?

Four messages on her machine.

Three were from galleries; one was for Michael. Someone she didn't know, man's voice from that wide and subtle network into which he disappeared, an hour here, half the night there but always home, sweetest smile voracious and his dick hard as metal; where have you been, bad boy? And to herself: Do you care?

Tell the truth.

In the silence of the worktable, her watchers ignored as she bent like a priest exhausted and still as gray silt beneath the desire not to know; not to admit that she knew what she knew.

Why don't you just get back to work.

Nicky; and Bryan; and now Nita, all wires, tendons, and narrow blue-eyed stare, the soldering pencil dwarfed in her huge knuckle-cracking hands, she had the largest

hands Tess had ever seen in a woman. A club friend of
Nicky's, sometimes-helper with the Zombie shows; she
talked hardly at all and thought Tess was God.

To have students at all was ludicrous in itself, almost
funny unless you considered Bibi: the mirror backward in
dreadful yin, her own actions eerie mimic of Bibi's fast-
growing coterie, a Surgeons split in two. Tess's new trio,
Bibi's—how many now? Five? Twenty-five? She would
want more, Bibi, would need more, but then her ambitions
were so much more flamboyant, her view so much more
encompassing; Tess trying, almost, not to teach at all, while
Bibi made a cult. An army. For what?

"Shows," Michael again, sharing the takeout food sup-
plied by Nita: good stuff, rich sweet Szechuan. "Suppos-
edly she wants to start doing stuff soon." His thigh warm
against her shoulder, Tess crouched on the floor like a
tired child, her plate beside her and untouched; not hungry. She had worked all night and into the morning, completing the eye-box, starting—again—another. She was so
tired she kept having the same thoughts over and over.
Paper napkins imprinted with Chinese astrological signs,
What Year Were You Born? The pig, the rat, the horse.
The dragon.

"Tess?" Nita's high, slightly hoarse voice, her earnest
smile: arms into coat sleeves, "You need anything else?"

"No. No, thanks, Nita. You sure you don't want any of
this?"

"No *thank* you," as if slightly shocked; and gone, missing
Michael's long smile, his toothy burlesque surprise: " 'No
thank you, Tess!' " hands to either side of his open mouth
and Tess poked him in the thigh with the end of her chopstick, poked him hard.

"Stop being such a prick."

"If you say so." Slippery gloss of sauce on his lower lip,

in the worktable light his hair, longer now, seemed almost white; beautiful gray-eyed albino; Bibi-eyed. Her demon lover. "I ran into Matty," spearing some vegetable shaped like half a heart. "He says they're about ready to start."

"Hurray."

"Tess." Setting his food aside, bending, angel from the clouds, to take her face in his hands. "Listen. Go out with me tonight."

"No."

"Yes." Firm. "You need to take a break. All you see is this room. And work. A bunch of dumb guys in helmets." Hard hands now on her shoulders, the flesh moving back and forth, back and forth, a tide, and coral bones beneath. "I'll show you a good time, little girl."

Shadows, the new box split left to right like a chambered brain. His sweetest smile.

"All right," and he kissed her, shards of food captured warm in his mouth, sauced tongue; shadows, everywhere. She took the kiss like medicine, scraped his taste off her teeth; and smiled.

Club, small as a bedroom: sweat humidity and hectic neon overheads jammed in one idiot sequence, plywood walls scabbed heavy with decals: KILLBILLY and MODE SAUVAGE, DOKTOR JEST in thin crimson caps, they had to push to get in. Michael, angel, white from head to toe, beatific smile and sharp elbow to clear the way: for Tess, paradoxically in gray, gray as his eyes, cerement gray at the bar and Michael wanted to buy her a vodka.

"For old times' sake," smiling.

"No," smiling back; she ordered ouzo. Syrup, heavy licorice taste and on her lips as Michael kissed her, vodka tongue in her mouth; bright eyes. Sharp music. The guy next to her was laughing the same laugh over and over, beer bottle jittering on the bar.

"—to dance?"

"No," again. Was it imagination or was her eye specially drawn to those who were pierced: there, bald and barechested, nipples ringed; or him, cockatoo hairdo, nose ring like a bull and some kind of gauntlets, or the woman in leather jeans with overlapping rings and, yes, the gauntlets again, leather wound on her arms and knuckles; must be a new fashion, must be—

A singular laugh: ice crystals, breaking; breaking glass. Bibi.

One tremendous lurch, heart in carwreck rhythm and: there, in the thready wash of neon, silhouette moving into moving light: *changed.* Grotesque new waspwaist, cinched hard past airlessness to some shocking constricture, where were her *bones?* Gone? Backlit and black and bristling shiny with hooks, spined with them, hooks in her ears and tusked tiny at nose and lip, anemone steel all over and down her bare back the thready spill of chains, ten, twenty, dozens like strange metal hair surrounding the raised scars, white ridges of hard tissue emphasized with red: makeup? or infection? Turning to speak to someone, a man beside her and in the turning saw—Tess watched her do it—Tess herself.

Michael, hand on her arm like the touch that pulls us back through sleep, through death on the operating table, the hand that holds the paddles that shock: "Tess. Take it easy, okay? Just—"

Tess did not answer. Bibi still now, waiting, moored and yet alone: wearing the gauntlets, too, wrapped and strapped like a boxer; breastlessly thin, clavicles in gaunt relief and bracketing her mouth the long swollen lozenges of a fresh scarring; she had done something to her mouth, too, something Tess could not put a name to, as if in subtle duplication of the ravages of stroke. Tess toward her through the press and mumble, Michael behind saying something but she didn't hear; didn't listen. Like the granting of a wish unspoken, red wish, her presence; and beside, beneath it all the strange singular pleasure: seeing Bibi again. Nerves like wires, arcing, sparking, and then Bibi before her, right before her, right before her eyes.

"Tess," and did not put out her hand. Heavy new rings, silver, one set with a cheap blue stone; birthstone. "How are you?"

"Busy."

"Me, too."

"I heard." Half-conscious of Michael behind her, breath on her neck like a fly on her skin: stop it. Forget him. "You're bringing back the Surgeons."

"No," that instant anger; remember? "You're wrong. It's nothing like the Surgeons." One hand raised to brush at her face, ring shaped like the blunt claws of a hammer; shaking. Bibi's hands were shaking. "It's way more than that, it's about *ritual*, it's—"

"*Tanzplagen,*" coldly. Michael's hand squeezing hers; shut up. "Blood dance, right? All the fun stuff you couldn't do before?"

And from behind Bibi, pop-up grin, "Why don't you come to a show?": Matty Regal, appropriately gauntleted, heavy with chains and hooks like Bibi, trying to be Bibi. "See for yourself," he said, and chiming, Bibi's own soft jeer: "See for yourself."

Now her hands were shaking, too. "I told you. I'm busy."

"Oh right, your private practice, art for art's sake. Right," bright sneer in the open, clot of smilers around her and then, abrupt, "I don't have time for this shit," and turning so quick she almost walked into Matty, Tess opposite away and in her throat constriction, the muscles tight and a feeling like burning, like something on fire. Anger; and swiveling to Michael's gaze, raised eyebrows and "Well. You really pissed her off."

"She pissed *me* off," shaking off his arm, let *go* of me. "I want to go home," and for the door, looking at no one, out in the street and Michael catching up, saying something and *this was your idea, asshole* but she didn't say that; instead, cold, "She didn't say anything to you. I thought you said you see her sometimes."

As if he were tired: "Hardly ever."

"Does she ever—" but she would not say it, would choke before she said it. "What do you talk about? When you talk?" And when exactly is that?

More tiredly still, "We talk about her, Tess. You ought to be able to figure that out for yourself."

No more talk, now, back through a night half-winter or maybe it was just because she was hot, she was burning the air around her, tearing open her coat and up the stairs, each footfall a driven nail, up and up and Michael behind her, saying nothing, silent in the wake of her heat. Burning.

And grabbing him as the door swung to, shoulders against the door—he was her size, just her size—kisses like biting, his kind of kisses, she could already feel him getting hard and she yanked at his clothes, just enough to open them, just enough to feel him against her and she fucked him that way, standing up, hips hard and driving him back against the door because he wasn't Bibi, could never be Bibi, good for him, good for *both* of them, *good.*

His breathless head against her shoulder, moist air. Was Bibi fucking Matty? *God.* She had said before she was not, but she was a liar, wasn't she? First and last and only; a liar then, too. Had she fucked Michael? Michael, too, was a liar, come to think of it; but don't think. He doesn't lie to you, does he? Does he? How should I know?

"Tess—"

Eyes closed. Tears against her lids; burning.

"What."

"You need to see her again. You need to have a—"

As if from a great distance, like a breath from her lungs: "No." Pushing him away, half-dizzy, yanking up her pants. To the worktable, tools' orderly scatter and the box upon it, just begun: metal hook-shiny, red-jacketed wire as slim and sweet as open veins.

Just get busy.

"—like this, see? So you get a clean weld. Not so fast," and Nita's earnest nod, if she listened any harder her head might explode, slow steam like a cracked reactor; calm down, Tess wanted to say, it's not the end of the world, it's just welding, it's just me. Okay? But of course to Nita, to the others, Tess was Tess-Capital T, Teacher Tess, grandly estranged and made by them to be so; her intrinsic value lay in the fact that she could never be just Tess.

The others; Nita's friends, willy-nilly her new students: six of them now, all of them all eyes on her every move: watching the boxes grow; watching them change. More than a figure boxed, now, more than metal: more, sometimes, than even she knew until they were done, till they had had time to sit and grow dust and cook a little: and then she would discover them, explorer's touch and mouth a little open: Oh. There in her hands the puzzle explicit, pain and hunger, sacrificial want: oh. I see. Bird bones, a curious twist of wire, a scrap of burned paper, a seed pod dried to mummification and strangely spiked: like Bibi's piercings, like Bibi herself; hedgehog.

Busy hedgehog: Michael had already brought home a
flyer. Flash new production values, slick black and mined
with hints of silver; she had named them Skinbound. In
goth lettering, lettering, too, around her flyer face seemingly more knife-sculpted, more painfully bizarre; her face
as well in *AntiTrust,* in *Scuff* a picture of them all: BEYOND
TANZPLAGEN, Bibi in unsmiling black and white surrounded
by shiteating grins, there must have been twenty of them,
all wearing the gauntlets: *cestus,* Bibi called it, from the
Latin for beat, worn lead-loaded, brass knuckles for the
boxers in ancient Rome. The marriage girdle, too, Venus's
girdle empowering the wearer to excite love. There was
more; Tess did not read it, tried not to remember the date
of the first show. Enough was enough. Wasn't it?

Now: "You don't want too much heat," and Nita's nod,
again, laser-blue stare somewhere behind the helmet glass.
"You try it now." Teacher Tess. Box on the worktable, Michael out somewhere, gone, he said he had a job this week.
Doing what? Soon she would be done here, send them
home; and work. Till she slept, and woke to work again; no
more machine shop; she had tuition now. Bibi would have
laughed till she screamed, but Michael insisted on it and
the others did not seem to mind, in fact agreed: Nicky said
it: "Otherwise you'd have to be out working. This way you
can stay home and teach us, right?"

Right. Michael's serious nod; they were all nodding;
they were all very serious. Tess had wanted to run out of
the room; but that would be selfish, wouldn't it? They all
seemed happy, anyway, and anyway she did her best to do
what they wanted. Didn't she?

And waking in the night, her own mouth open and
weeping, crying in her sleep and Michael warm and solid
beside her, solidly asleep, arms like lead and bare feet
dusty against sheets white as winding cloths; he had spent

half the night trying to talk her into seeing a Skinbound show; never. Never never never. You should see what she's doing, see for yourself; no, she had said. I don't want to know what she's doing.

"It could help you." Exasperated, trying not to show it, showing it when she said How in that particular dull dead voice, staring at her as if she was the crazy one, as if someone had drilled a hole in her head and let out all her brains. "In your art, that's how!" and louder as she said nothing, loudest in the vacuum of her silence until she had turned on him and threw the first thing that came to hand, a black-handled chipping hammer that struck a dent as deep as a quarter in the wall behind.

His injured shrug: Fine. "Fine," and showering, mute and beautiful his naked walk across the room, into bed like an angel atop a sarcophagus; the death of her career, probably. She had worked then, slow and laborious until a short stupid burn, the blistered skin of her thigh; then slept. To wake weeping, wake afresh to Michael's calm gravity, such sweet reason, hand in hers and asking Why.

"Are you afraid?" No. "Are you embarrassed?" No. "She doesn't have to know you're there, Tess, she won't even see you," that winning smile but he wasn't winning anything, not here, no use and after a while he stopped; gave up? Maybe. Hands on her throat, loose strangler's grip, mocking throttle that made her head rock back and forth, gently, gently on her neck.

"You're exasperating," hands a little tighter; kissing the side of her face. "You know that? If you don't grow, you die. And I won't let that happen. You know I only want what's best for you, don't you?"

"I know." Do you? He kissed her again, left as Nicky and Nita came in, hot coffee and opinions, yeah they had seen the flyer, who hadn't? "Fucking thing's everywhere,"

Nicky blowing noisy at his foam cup. "I even saw it in the pisser at Junk's last night."

Nita's nod, she had seen it there too, lots of people were talking about it, were planning on going. "They think it's like the Surgeons," and no one but Nita could pronounce that hearsay name with such juvenile reverence, "but *I* said—"

"Go if you want," Tess said. "Why not?"

Silence.

Nicky's incredulity, "Are *you* going?" and no, shaking her head, concentrating on the articulated metal hand motionless and adept on the moveable lid of this new box, new piece all of a piece: one metal finger snapped off at the knuckle, one ringed with a bolt painted circus blue. Inside the box was empty; for now. They were still talking, loud and she forced attention, forced herself to turn around.

"I'm not going," Nita firm and Nicky's echo, to them it was about loyalty; let them do what they wanted. She was in charge of nothing and no one, no wild and singular tribe; no one would ever dance, fight, die because of her; not now; not ever.

"Okay," the upturned tip of the soldering pencil, silvery drip of solder; machine blood, and their puzzled faces close; they would not ask, not again. "Let's get going here."

"Tess."

"No."

"Tess, you have to go."

Sullen, "I don't have to do anything." But die. And work. Cold water from the showerhead, why did he choose these moments to badger her? Wet and waterblind and naked; smart. "You go."

Calm with decision, beautiful—exceptionally so tonight, babychick curls and all in black, austere; not by any chance by chance. "I will. If you're too stubborn, if you can't put personal differences aside for the sake of your art, then I'll—"

"Don't *give* me—" but he wasn't hearing, listening, the water too loud and his pronouncement, he would be her eyes and ears if she refused to use her own; he would do that for her. How to summon energy to explain, how to say that to see Bibi's grotesque new circus would be not only to reopen wounds but to salt them with iron; she was tired, now, of pain, she wanted to work and be left alone.

Michael, coldly, "That's incredibly selfish."

"That's tough."

Nothing else. Rubbing her arms and legs, shiver in the steamless air and listening: gone. Wet hair down her back like a drowning victim, staring out the window, to the west: Battery View, a gallery, big gallery set up how? Heavy listing rags, black rags, altars? Scaffoldings? Bibi there already, crouched and grinning like a spider in the darkest corner of the room: changed how, now? and with what light in her eyes? Don't tread on me. And Matty Regal beside her, lesser demon, the jaunty smile of smaller wrong, and her massed troupe, pure Pavlovian sycophants swinging hooks and the shimmer of chains, ready for the lights and the needles, waiting for blood.

Percussive sounds; metal, falling. I'll give you all the blood you need.

Be careful, Bibi. No one tells you the truth anymore.

Be careful, Bibi, oh God be careful now.

The small cyanide twitch of the articulated fingers, the box lid moving up and down like the vicissitudes of a smile; Bibi's show had been titled *Force Majeure*. No real dance but a lot of movement, lots of the old fake blood; the bolt-ringed finger looked as if it had once been broken, set poorly to form a curious hornlike hump, calcification; what force shatters steel bones? Force majeure? All kinds of motion, choreographed frenzy of cuttings and bindings and Bibi, Michael said, had been beautiful; all in white like an angel on fire. She had opened the performance by cutting a long shallow trench in her own arm, the sleeve of her costume red and redder in the course of the show. The gallery had been standing room only; a lot of people to watch her bleed herself.

"She dedicated the show to Paul," Michael said; voice hoarse, he had been a long time coming home last night. Inside the box an emptiness, dry and white. Tess shifted on her stool, minute calibration of movement; the metal fingers flexed again. Could they crush bone? Incrementally?

"You know, you're not doing yourself any favors, Tess, by not—"

"Are you still talking?"

Closing up, now, in an instant, sealing door and through the crack the narrowed stare of disapproval, the brief pointed exhalation that means patience is gone. "You can be a real cunt sometimes, you know that?"

As weary, "Sticks and stones."

"Why do you *do* this?" Hands on her shoulders, not stroking, not squeezing; lying there. His hair still smelled like cigarette smoke. "It's like you hate me. Do you hate me? All I want is for you to keep growing, to get where you need to be."

The fingers twitched again, unsynchronized, spasmodic, as if the phantom limb to which they belonged had been victim of surging voltage, a killing jolt and Michael's lips very close to her ear: "Bibi knows where she needs to be; I saw that last night. And I know what you need."

The phone rang; neither moved. Matty Regal's voice, brisk and nasal: "You missed out, Bajac," and something else she didn't hear, the machine cycling into silence as dry and empty as the air in the box. Michael gazing at the phone, a curious blank gaze as if the space behind his eyes lay waiting for the shuffling thoughts to right themselves, like cards in a game; then to Tess, gravely: "He's an asshole. But he's right."

Quiet as if in the silent cavities of the body; Michael's hands on her shoulders like Art's policeman, you'll have to come with me now. Tess chose a tiny screwdriver, and screws as small as tears; her fingertips were numb. She did not speak or make a sound, and finally Michael turned away, slow creak of the couchbed, the susurration of blankets drawn high.

Outside, car doors, Nita and some of the others; it was already almost noon. They would want to talk about the show; they would be loud and opinionated; they would know what she needed, too. How did everyone get so *sure?* Light and heat; metal and blood; was everyone smarter than she was? Stronger? She had no business teaching anybody, no business being anything but alone with the things she understood: heat and liquid metal, tools and smoke and the confines of the helmet, the only world in which everything was both controllable and past prediction, hot with corrosion and yet perfectly clean, desirable, tender with the possibilities she could see as well as she saw silent Michael, distant as an iceberg, heard as well the steps on the stairs and the hand—she heard it—poised to knock, twice and strident, upon the door.

A longer wait between shows, spring bleeding into summer; Michael spent more time gone, Tess had lost ten pounds, she was never hungry. Nita and Nicky took her out to dinner, cafeteria Thai, her hands folded in the booth like a good little girl out for a treat too special to enjoy. Pink shrimp curled forlorn as fetuses, a plastic pitcher of ice water sweating dully on the gray laminate of the table. Upside-down plastic flowers nailed to the ceiling. Nicky told her Matty Regal was thinking of using sculpture in the next show; blunt fingers curling and uncurling his plastic straw and what did she think of that?

"Nicky, it's a free country," less mild than exhausted, she was sick of being asked for her opinion; wasn't Michael enough? The people at the next table were arguing over a movie. "Let him do what he wants."

Michael had ceased arguing, but his declamations were pervasive, like the genesis of fire, like rubbing skin to make a blister, to peel it finally back to flesh; he was getting to her, but not the way he wanted. Bibi's face on the cover of a musiczine, Bibi in an ad in the giveaway entertainment weekly; entertainment weekly? Bibi in a tabloid, lurid: SKINBOUND in cockeyed red, her lips red, teeth bare, strange little teeth. Two weeks from now; are you going, Tess? What do you think, Michael? Matty Regal using sculpture, Bibi using a knife: are there any volunteers from the audience? Is there a doctor in the house? Nicky and Nita, Bryan and the rest of them, she had trouble remembering their names sometimes, they were all faces: brown eyes, blue eyes, crooked glasses, funny spearmint grin in a circle around her, watching. See? Art. See the hand that catches, the fingers that squeeze, the box lid flapping like a singular terrified wing, wouldn't *you* want to get away?

But there's nothing *in* there.

That's the point. —But she didn't say that, tried to get them to see for themselves, make their own points; wasn't that what it was all about? Trying to smile, see you tomorrow. Sleeping alone; dreaming of Bibi and waking with her fingers curled between her legs, wanting her; estrangement, a word like a promontory cliff and no, Michael, I don't want to fuck you, no Michael I won't go to the show.

Others went: over three hundred people saw the second performance, paying customers; that kind of money would buy a lot of Betadine, sharpen a lot of knives. Jerome went, told Tess that no matter what, it was still a hell of a show, and Peter chiming in that there were even elements the Zombies might like to incorporate in their own work, certain effects, certain measures of crowd manipulation; Tess silent through this rushed hallway update, lips dry and thin as the smile on a stick figure and she wanted to ask Does anyone bleed? Who bleeds? Who cuts?

"It really is like a tribe," Jerome said, and Peter nodded, it's follow the leader, it's all Bibi's show. "She's really something, Tess. You might even want to—"

Brittle headshake, brittle smile. Back inside, locked door and again to work, finish the hand, the grasping hand atop the box of nothing, entropic box filled with everything we become, even the dust of the body's leavings swept away by time's disinterested breath; in the end we have no bodies, in the end we have, we are, nothing at all. Nothing.

And Michael, back from somewhere, where do you go, Michael? Little sweat curls at his temples, shirt damp beneath the sleeveless windbreaker, black as a dirty rag: running? Fucking? Appalling, to know that she did not want to find out, did not want to ask Are you seeing someone else?

Don't you care? not to him but to herself: don't you care?

No.

Why not?

And now, his hands on her arms, up and down the bare cool flesh, his touch was so very warm. "Tess—are you okay? You don't look good."

Swiveling on her stool, flat smile like a snake on a rock. "Maybe I need a tattoo. Or a scar."

His silence. They seemed to have two modes these days, silence and anger, punctuated with moments of a tenderness decayed: head on his shoulder, one nipple soft and thoughtful between his fingers; he would whisper to her, then, tell her how he admired her, yeah absolutely, admired her art, the relentless determination, he saw how she was withdrawing, saving her strength for her work: great, that's great. The nipple half-hard in his touch. Eyes half-closed, Tess sighting the ceiling, what was there to see? Smudges become faces, the faces of Goya dreams, Bacon's screaming pope screaming down at her. Michael's voice in her ear, insinuation, hand damp on her breast. You have great stuff in you, you have genius, Tess. I swear to God you are a genius. You just have to be willing to let go of everything, even yourself, even what you think is right and wrong, there is so *much* you could—

and shifting, still in his arms, her face half toward his in the unkind dark but no vision of him in her eyes: "Michael: don't start. Okay? No more commercials."

His hand falling away slowly from her like a shed limb; and silence as he slept, or seemed to, and Tess lay waiting, night rolling like a wheel toward sleep, toward morning, toward found meaning and its secret twin, forgetfulness, in the rarefied chamber austere of work, and work, and nothing but.

Michael's breathing, child-sweet, sleeping hands open like night-blooming flowers, small dull sore at the juncture of wrist and palm.

And now Bibi's face on the ceiling, outlined in shadows, running like metal, molten; like blood. Whose blood, Bibi? Do you miss me at all?

The next show on the heels of the last, it seemed to Tess too quickly: CATHERINE WHEEL in big aggressive letters, someone's bare breasts in bright silhouette and—again— Bibi's iconic stare; those eyes. Tacked to a magazine kiosk, the dull daytime door of a club, stuck to a hundred telephone poles; even on her worktable, spread under Michael's considering fingers; and to Tess's entering stare, his unsmiling touch tracing beneath Bibi's eyes: "Good production values," he said, "we could use something like this."

"For what?"

"For when you decide to stop punishing yourself and start having shows again."

That was past answering, so she said nothing, nothing when he told her, he said, what she ought to have known for herself: it was time to stop bullshitting around, take some responsibility for her art, *go see the fucking show.* One arm out like Mussolini, chin stuck out and declaiming, she was cheating herself, worse yet she was cheating her art by the way she—

Not loud, but harsh, jagged cadence of half-desperation: "Why don't *you* do it, then? Huh? Why don't you start making art instead of bitching at me?"

And Michael at once very still, pausing on the breath taken for reply but saying nothing, bas-relief; and a feeling beneath that silence; what feeling? His face so calm, beautiful as the moon or the surface of black water, and underneath the long slick splinters that can tear your skin to ribbons, rip up your hands, pierce your eyes if you fall; glass underwater, and what made her think of that? A memory: falling on the beach, falling underwater and the pain she had not guessed was there, slim and incredible, sliding deep into her knee; blood on the water, on her leg pulled forth lean and slick as a root. Screaming for her mother, her child's voice, screaming.

Then as if she had not spoken, his slow headshake and "If you won't do it for yourself, then see it for your students, do them a favor. They're what you care about, right?"

Tired, exquisitely tired and into her rubbing fist, fist against her lips, rubbing and rubbing as if she would wear away the need to speak: "They can go if they want, I'm not stopping them."

"Yes you are. By your attitude you are."

"They can do whatever they—"

"Because you don't go, they won't. They think they'd be betraying you or something, they think—"

"Then let them tell me! What are you telling me for?" Voice rising, but she forced it back down, monotone, monochromatic: gray. Fist to her lips again. "How do you know what they think anyway?"

As quietly as she, but with great emphasis: "I hear the things people don't say."

I bet you do but she didn't say that, didn't say anything, went about putting the screens into place again because she was ready for a burning, yes, today was the right time to burn something. River of metal and she Charon, pilot of the dead, the metal-cold, the empty boxes growing even smaller, now, little pieces you could hold in two hands, like a bomb: no lesser energy, in fact more, a laser's concentration, distillation, an immense subtlety needed to bring the power of pain to a place that small, to hold it in your hands like agony's particulate: the better to examine you, my dear. My darling. Why had she never made a box about love, made anything about love? Even in the happiest days with Bibi: why not?

Maybe you don't know how to love.

She had thought she loved Michael, but now, see him turning away—again, away from her, she had hurt him somehow by her words; the pain she had not intended like the spiked garden of glass underwater. But what to say to a turned back, how to make amends to a closing door?

He was reading *AntiTrust,* an ad for Bibi's show within, next to the ads for leather shops, for the all-night titty bars with double-digit cover; he did not look up when she said his name, said it twice, did not look up when Nita came in, Bryan, Edgar-Marc and the others like a pack of street dogs, scruffy, energetic, she had forgotten it was time for them, not time to burn. The hell with it; she would burn anyway.

To Nita: "Go downstairs," picking up her own helmet, "ask Nicky to bring all the helmets he has, goggles, whatever. —Where is Nicky, anyway?"

"On-site," Edgar-Marc's little-boy croak, a voice forever on the cusp of puberty. "He said to tell you."

The Zombies show upcoming; she had forgotten. Too many shows to remember. "All right, then. Nita, go on, Jerome or somebody is probably down there." Waiting in their amiable noise but she herself in silence, Michael's silence, watching him from the corner of her eye: graceful slouch across the unmade bed, had they really slept in that bed last night, warm and wordless, had he touched her with the tip of his penis, just lightly, just there on the inner skin of her thigh: like an insect with a flower, like a doctor with a needle? This won't hurt a bit. Had she held his panting head to her shoulder? whispered his name on orgasm's cusp, whose name? Whose eyes, in her mind's eye?

"I got these," Nita back with one helmet, a pair of

painter's goggles hung from her big hands like an ornament; useless, and Tess opening her mouth to say so when Michael, rising, still so very still but nodding to Nita, "I'll show you. Come on," and out the door, down to the second floor; he knew where everything was.

Edgar-Marc saying something, obviously happy with the presence of the screens; joyful pyromaniac, he liked to burn, he reminded Tess at times of herself, of Jerome. Jerome who went to Bibi's shows; maybe they all wanted to go, maybe Michael was right and she was holding them back. She ought to say something, make some disclaimer, hadn't she already told Nicky to go? And Nita? When Nita came back, she would make a point of telling her, telling all of them they had her imprimatur and more.

Readying for work, spreading out for their inspection her scrapyard bounty; the spent morning climbing hills of metal, creaking silence all around as if inorganic matter had found a way to grow; and wasn't rust growth, of a kind? the growth of decay? If you don't grow, you die; one of Michael's favorite sayings and now Michael returned, Nita behind and subdued with an armful of helmets; handing them out. A long strand of sunlight across the floor, warm and steady as a bridge, the bridge between now and never. She stared at it, so long that finally someone, Bryan, said something, hey Tess. Tess? And raising her gaze to cloak it, then, in heavy plastic and heavier glass, to hide from light in darkness and in darkness summon the brightest light of all.

Rain smeared across the windows, last night had been *Catherine Wheel* and Tess had slept poorly, slept alone, Michael's self-righteous kiss before leaving: I Am Doing This For You. Right. Her head aching, up too early and Michael still not back; fine; let him do what he wanted.

Alone in the shower, trying to masturbate and only sor-
rowful, thoughts falling heavy as water and Nita's knock
remedial, had Tess promised her this time? Probably. Anyway she didn't say no, set her to work on brazing,
busywork, keep those big hands moving and now, again,
the bright crash, Nita's anxious grab and "Shit, Tess, I'm
sorry," scrabbling tools from the floor, headlight eyes
dusted with gray; sleepless eyes.

"I'm sorry, I'm so fucking clumsy," setting herself to
haphazard rights. "I—" and a big yawn, prolonged and the
pink wash of her open mouth. "I was up real late last
night."

As tired: "Doing what?"

"I—" and the pause so long Tess knew: the show. She
had gone to Bibi's show. An absurd urge to smile, there
was something strangely touching about that flustered half
stare, hands still on the rearranged tools; maybe Michael
had been right, she had by her own avoidance come down
too hard. So: careful now, casual: "How was it?"

And Nita's smile, relieved, "Oh, Tess, it was really in-
tense, it was *redline.* I figured he, I mean I thought—did he
tell you?"

Frowning, the sludgy feel of her brain beginning to turn,
worm under rocks, under pressure: "Did who tell me? Tell
me what?"

"Michael," very unsure now, face flushing a deep dis-
comfortable red, big fingers busy unconscious with the
tools, the shiny edges. "Did he—"

"I haven't seen Michael since yesterday morning," and a
sudden idea, contracting like cold water, the words out of
her mouth as hard and flat as her hands on the worktable,
fingers tight: "What did he tell you?"

Silence; the nervous silence of fear.

"*Nita.* What did he tell you?"

Blue eyes blinking now, wide and dry with alarm: "He said you should know about the shows, it would help you, he said you wouldn't go for yourself and that I, that we should, like, be your eyes. We should see for you, he said, he said that I—"

As if from the bottom of a well: "Who went?"

The jitter of tools. "Me and Edgar-Marc. Jerome was there, too, but he wasn't with us, I don't even think he saw we were there."

"No," not even to Nita, of course it would be Nita, Nita and Edgar-Marc because they were the least sophisticated, weren't they, easy to manipulate, Tess's little helpers; anything for Tess. Anything can be a tool; Michael knew that, there wasn't much Michael didn't know, was there? Way ahead of me, and her flat hands were cramping, she felt like a piston's hammer the headache's singular pain, amplified by anger, red and black behind her eyes and poor Nita, still staring, waiting for Tess to—what?

"Hey," slowly. Approaching the way you approach a frightened dog, one hand out: it's okay. See? "Nita, it's all right, I'm not mad at you. Okay? Just tell me what Michael told you."

"Just, just what I said before, that we should go in your place. Because you wouldn't go for yourself. He said," still blinking, rapid flutter of crimping lids, "you needed to know. For your art."

"Did he say," as slowly, almost conversational, "why I wouldn't go myself?"

"He said he wasn't sure."

Standing in the silence like an alcove, a pocket of space outside considering time, standing so long that Nita had to call her name twice: "Tess?" Timidly. "Tess, are we still going to work today?"

Water in her eyes from the pain in her head; her mouth

felt oddly loose, as if she had been fighting, as if someone
had broken her jaw. Beside Nita, now, at the worktable,
hands blind against the shapes of making, the tools and the
wire and screws: "Sure," like an old woman, heavy and old
with a killing disease. "We'll work until Michael comes
back."

After five, and Nita fled, false thanks and glad to be
gone, her heavy welder's boots clunking briskly down and
out and Tess still at the worktable, its surface spread with
the silver clutter of punches and chisels, like tools for an
operation: strong, slim, impeccably cold. In hand the chipping hammer, one end beveled, one end a point blunt
enough to split bone. Heart beating tandem to the pain in
her head; waiting.

And Michael in, he must have passed Nita in the street:
pale hair wind-wild, T-shirt ripped a little, ripped along the
hem like a frieze, a fringe. Red around his lips, windburn
maybe, faint smile that widened briefly for her, a glossy
sliver of yellowish food caught between his teeth. Look
past that smile to see the thought that prompts it, the busy
factory of brain; what is in your head, Michael?

"What?" Pausing; she must have said it aloud. "What
did you say?"

"I said," her voice like the hammer, "how was the
show?"

Coolly, "Very instructive. Very intense."

"That's what Nita said."

Now: reaction, anger or denial, the gathering moment of
possible explanation but instead she saw the seamless stillness of a neutrality so absolute that it was as if she accused
a statue, a piece of her own sculpture, the heavy curve of a
light pole in the street: no expression in the reddened
mouth, that silent gaze and "You *bastard,*" advancing on

him, "how dare you go behind my back, how dare you use them that way?"

"How *dare* I? Listen to you," but without heat, her own rage blown back like the air from a smelting furnace, the blister and belch of running steel. "They don't belong to you, Tess, they have a right to do whatever they—"

"They have a right not to be lied to! Or used, to make a point, to—"

"What point? That you're afraid to go to Bibi's shows, that you're jealous of her?"

Hands shaking at her sides and in her grasp, still, the hammer; she slung it backward and away, sharp clatter and "Jealous? That doesn't even make any sense."

"Oh yes it does, I can see it, I can *smell* it on you," mouth much redder so close, red as a blister, as the burgeoning cast of a sore. "It makes you crazy that Skinbound's ten times as successful as the Surgeons ever were, you can't stand to see her succeed that way without you. So you denigrate what she does, you tell Nita and Nicky and the rest of them not to—"

"That's a lie!" Shouting now, harsh echo in tandem with the pain, anger and pain twin sisters, twin screaming harpies against the dry-rolling balls of her eyes. "That is a fucking—"

"You're the one who's using them." Roused now, pale-cheeked and the long eyes strangely bitter, voice like a hammer striking, chipping at iron and bone. "You talk about Bibi, about how she manipulates people, but you're the same way, you're worse, you want to control what your students see—students, that's a laugh, what're you teaching them? To be like you are, afraid? Afraid to go as far as you can go, as far as you have to go, to make your art? Bibi knows. Bibi's the one who isn't afraid."

Tears in her eyes now, hot, wanting to hit him, wanting

to throw him out, get out of my house. Another memory: Bibi: *he was mine anyway.* And her own voice, deadly: *Get out of my house.* "What do you know about it anyway? What can *you* tell *me* about making art?"

Silence.

All the heat in her body gathered in her chest, around her heart like suffocation's fist. Tears shiny as the scatter of screws and nails, the warmth of the room unfresh, like a spoiled taste, like biting deep into rotten fruit. Michael gazing at her, head tilted, very lightly, to one side.

"I'm not going to argue with you anymore," meeting her eyes, "I can't make you listen if you don't want to listen, I can't make you see." The red mouth twitching, calm pallor like a god defiled. "But I won't stand here and watch you lie to yourself and everybody around you, lie to *me* when you say you're serious about your work."

"How have I lied?" but now without emphasis, she knew he would not answer. Outside a coughing drone like a motor on the verge of stalling, like smoker's lungs coughing for life. The shiver of reaction in her muscles: machine tremor, run past all warnings, all redlines, all strength. Run it till it breaks.

"If you won't grow, you die. That's it, that's how it is. And I won't watch you make your little Skinner boxes, smaller and smaller, you're closing in on yourself, Tess. You're eating yourself alive."

More silence but this a differing quality, the silence of scales, of things in the balance. Were you ever mine, Michael? Her hands were cold, cold stiff fingers as if she had already died. "Then go, why don't you? Why don't you just go?"

"If I go," so calm, calm and beautiful, "I won't come back."

No tears, now, as if the heat of her body had dried them,

dried her inside and out. Downstairs, Nicky or somebody, the music kicking on bright and loud and the memory, dancing with Michael to Killbilly, his mouth on hers; fucking against the door, she had been happy that night. Another Bibi, is that what she had wanted? Why is your mouth so red?

Hands at her sides: "Just go," she said, and his shrug, faint headshake as if powerless before her most useless mistake. He changed his shoes, tied around his waist a sweat shirt, black sweat shirt with the cuffs torn off; that's mine, she almost said, but said nothing, did not move as he paused before her to kiss her lips: very lightly, very cold, the way death might kiss the maiden, the way life might leave the body: faintly, like a whisper heard from the simple rebus of dark, a voice you never knew but knew to fear.

Closing the door and Tess the sculpture now, incapable of motion, each leaving child of all the others and she did not cry, turning at last for the worktable but did not cry; did not work; sat silently sifting through the small bright galaxies of steel and whorled metal, of wire and solder and all their simple complexities, all of a piece, what they were and nothing else. Daylight to darkness, the lozenge of light overhead and finally she felt as if she might begin to weep; but did not, sat turning over and over the crooked gray haft of a screwdriver broken like a broken bone, over and over in her hand like a puzzle that she, if she were very true and careful, might in her lifetime begin at last to solve.

3

KISS THEM

FOR ME

Welcome to the Darwinian Monkeyhouse of the Iron Scream.
—Norman Spinrad

"—and a big black hood-thing, like an executioner, right? And he picks up this big meat mallet and—"

"What's a meat mallet?"

"It's, you know, a meat tenderizer. It's like a hammer only it has, like, *ridges* on it. Sharp ones, to pound the meat. Anyway, he picks up the hammer and starts beating the *shit* out of—"

And Tess, in motion, trying hard to stay unheard but they had good ears, her students, good reflexes for a nuance and now—Nita the storyteller, Nicky the questioner, Edgar-Marc and Bryan and the others, the boys whose names she always forgot—now they were industrious, busy with their boxes, looking up with false studious nods as she entered from the hot dampness of the hall.

A Skinbound show, last night: *Last of the Dancing Chickens,* someone had been thoughtful enough to paper the outer doors of her building with flyers: big clown mouths etched in acid-green, silvery dust of feathers sprinkling down on the silhouette of a woman's nude body, the neck grossly elongated, both arms triply jointed in a way less frightening than purely obscene; the body was not

Bibi's, but the face, even in silhouette, was unmistakable. On with the show; no questions of her students, who's going, who isn't; and she, alone, had slept to dream of Bibi, of coming home to find her curled asleep on the bed, pulling soft at the concealing covers but finding, when they were gone, a body but not Bibi's face at all, no face, nothing but blackness pure and absolute. Until it *smiled:* all blood and teeth, all conscious as the whistling arc, and so happy to be alive. And moving, flesh-dummy rising up from the bed with no human motion and Tess, then, waking with eyes wide open like an infant with night terrors, to find she had pissed herself, tiny warm dribble slick as ejaculate on the tight planes of her thighs. Shivering in the too-hot bathroom, washcloth loose in her fist and she wept, head against the bowl of the sink, wept until she felt she might sleep again but slept only poorly until Nicky, knocking, waking: come back in half an hour and he did, with Nita, and Edgar-Marc, and coffee. And talk they would not talk in front of her.

Now: leaning on the worktable, gaze on no one as they bent to their boxes: "So how was the show?"

Silence.

"Come on," smiling, how awful her smile must look. "I just want to know."

More silence until Nita, finally, clumsy with discomfort: "It was okay. I got there late, I guess there was some kind of ritual first, couple people from the audience got piercings."

Edgar-Marc, subdued: "I heard cuttings."

"Maybe, I don't know. Anyway they had like a dance? Like a tribal dance, Bi— they said. Everything was supposed to mean something, but if you didn't know what it was supposed to mean then you didn't really get it." Frowning. "I guess. Anyway then they hung this one guy up in a bondage harness and people took turns doing cuttings on themselves underneath him. And then he cut himself. On the chest, a big design like a stop sign, kind of. And this woman read like a statement, all about people getting skinned, that you had to skin them upside down." No one asked why; her circling gaze seemed to Tess to ask permission to continue; Tess, nodding, hating herself briefly for the authority to do so. "You have to do it that way so the blood stays in the head, like blood pressure? It keeps them conscious longer." More silence. "I guess that's supposed to be good."

Finally, Nicky: "So what about the meat-hammer guy?"

"Oh, yeah. That was earlier. He started beating up this big piece of, like, meat, like a skinned animal but they said before that they bought it, you know, at a butcher shop, that it wasn't really real. And while he was beating on it this other guy said a poem about power in the knife. It was really *intense.*"

No one spoke, then: "Beat your meat," from Nicky and everyone laughed, Tess's smile less for the joke than the tone, the moment of relaxation; and then the show was seemingly disposed of, they went as if by common consent onto something else. Exhaust breezes heavy through the open windows, Nita's fisty grip on the soldering gun and Edgar-Marc asking Tess why the pneumatic hand in his cast-iron box did not work. Poor Edgar-Marc, his hopeful croak and he was doomed, she knew, to be forever derivative, to be less even than a filter of the ideas he saw; she was careful to spend much time with him, more even than with Nicky, time most likely wasted but she owed it to somebody, some debt; she would help the ones she could, her students, living buffers between herself and the silence.

The new box, there, covered coyly with the corner of a

blue tarp but she did not feel coy, felt as if she nurtured in secret a living monster and must protect it from the light; but it had to be done: all teeth, smiling teeth, box like a mouth, like the hole in the ground from which issues the devil, the devil's secret grin pointing like a gun in your face when you raised the lid, flimsy lid and cheap black lacquer, she was working harder than ever now, Michael would call it obsession.

More silence, now that Michael was gone; and why, in retrospect, had it taken him so long to go? His own strange duplicities an anchor, maybe, but what about her? Weakness, tiredness, simple lethargy? Could it matter? What mattered now was work. She had not seen Michael once since he left, although Jerome had seen him removing his possessions; with heartbreaking courtesy had not mentioned it directly to Tess but caused himself to be overheard, so she might know that the danger of confrontation was safely past; she need not see Michael again. Gray eyes. Under the bed she found one of his shirts, soiled at the neck and chest, gluey little crusts like dried mucus; in heavy Goth lettering obscured by much washing, VEN-GEANCE IS MINE. She threw the shirt away. She was missing three of her books. She used to think it could not get any worse than those days, those early Bibiless days after Paul's death and the death of the Surgeons; now those thoughts were worth less than a laugh, her brief smile unamused: like remembering a toothache during a stab wound, I didn't know when I was well off. Now she had lost them both. Sleep like riding over rocks, jounced to near-constant wakefulness by this noise, that quiet creak, the gross amphetamine pounding of her own heart; eating little; working every conscious hour, with her students or alone, informed with dry ferocity and all of it symptomatic of a permanent despair; but what else to do?

And Nita, now, diffident smile and Tess, I think I'm
done; like a child with a crayon drawing: come see what I
did. Irregular planes of rusted steel, covered and stretched
with thornlike hooks, with razor wire: big and heavy, easily
a meter square; she liked to work big, Nita, every inch a
mile; Tess's old territory but now things were so entropic,
black hole's suction pulling everything tighter and tighter,
closer and closer to implosion's greedy lip; what then? Past
the threshold, what kind of—

"—think, Tess?"

"What?" Too startled, then, half a murmur, "I'm sorry. I
didn't hear, what did you say?"

"I said do you think this is good enough to show? Like
at a, you know, at a gallery?"

Nicky's sneer immediate, "Galleries're for shit," and
knocking gently at the heavy steel skin, "but you should
still show it. Somewhere. Where should she show it, Tess?"

Without thought, "At one of the Zombies shows," and
Nicky's pleased instant nod, sure, why not? "We got a
show coming up pretty soon, 's like a big warehouse-type
place. There's lots of room, we could all show our stuff."
Cautiously, "You, too, Tess. If you want," and both, all,
knowing she didn't, knowing the offer was courtesy only;
Tess accepting as such, a smile, no thanks. She did not
want to show anymore, ever, was not even fully comfortable with showing her work to her students, but after all
they had to see to learn, what she did as well as how she
did it; that was inevitable, and acceptable as such; further
viewing was not. Work was the thing that mattered, the
distillation, the capture unconscious of the living form, the
subtly moving edges of pain; when it's done, look at it: is it
good? Good. Now put it away and start something else.

They left her early, they had plans to make, down in the
Zombie Birdhouse and Nicky in charge—the parallels in-

escapable, she tried not to think of that, either, but it was hard not to remember: heat like a second skin and Bibi's feral glee infectious, egging her on, the both of them working in opposite tandem, as if their yoked thoughts rose to meet like vapor combustible, gas for the engine that drove the show, that drove them all, that drove Paul to death oh God why think of it again? Raelynne's scream, valkyrie in the falling metal; Bibi's devouring selfishness, even then— was it?—chased with the puckering glaze of corruption. He was mine, anyway; what kind of a mind thinks that way?

You loved her.

You *still*

"*Stop* it!" aloud, half-wild and shaking head as if by force to drive the thought away. Breathing hard through her nose, carefully around her students' work, tarp-covered and now: begin.

And so on; into the night, heavy with the rhythms of a slumbering drunk, smells assorted as garbage through the windows and still the air hot and close as the inside of a very small room, the chamber of an arrhythmic heart: metal burning bright and small and an observer, looking up from the street, might have seen the sparks and flashes, the gouty glare and presume from it weaponry, street armor in the service of chaos, and never know how, inside, the sweat beaded and ran, weary eyes behind the masking glass as fingers moved, crooked and sure and resistless, desperate as prayer at the bedside of incurable pain.

Now: new flyers beside the *Zombie ARThouse* blacks-and-reds: Bibi, too, was planning, working on another show, again someone had been thoughtful enough to gild her door. Michael? Why not, it was his style. Slouched on the curb, soda can rolling cold against her wet throat, gazing at the flyers' slippery blacks and browns, the lettering austere, all of it very professional and for some reason this brought half a laugh, dry as a cough into the small echoless depth of the can. More sweat on her forehead, God what a horrible day.

Down the street a car, small red car coming too close to the curb and Tess on her feet before the car lurched to a nervous stop and Bibi, out, not bothering to slam the door behind.

Seen at once in the hammering instant, Tess's first jumbled thought: *she's metal:* sun washed like animate light across the curves and slippery planes, the dangling lines strung like cobwebs from a spider made of steel. Still that hideous waspwaist, strapped black and so tight it hurt to look at, the whole of her more firmly sculpted yet somehow very much a work in progress, as if beneath her clothing her bones performed their own precision roundelay, hooking, unhooking, rejoining in new and secret ways as if she might at any moment turn and smile, arms waving like an insect, mouth restructured in the staring instant to the long mandibular sweep; I'll eat you up. Heavy scars pale as wax around her mouth, eyes hidden behind sunglasses unwieldy as welder's goggles: "Tess," one hand out, deliberately too far away to shake, to touch. "Hi."

"Hi," and the ferocious seismic jitter like a held-back scream, she wanted to run, she wanted to take her in her arms and say Bibi, oh Bibi oh God. Touch the brittle skin that looked as if it might split beneath the barest pressure, little head heavy with hooks and chains from ear to nose and nose to lip, like a child roped and buried in spun steel, gift of some cruel angel, evil fairy over the cradle: you will be as gods. The scars at her mouth heavy as a frown perpetual; a charm hung from the ring in her lip, little silver death's head, death's cherub with spiny silver wings.

"What, what're you," Tess dry-voiced, gesturing with the can but Bibi seemed barely to be listening, or listening as if through music, through the rushing inner cataract of blood.

"I saw the flyers," Bibi said, nodding up, one double-sized above the Zombie door. "For your show."

"It's not my show. My students—"

"Students," slowly, no mockery but something there, unreachable as a knife underwater. "Right, I—someone told me. Right," and a pause disconnected, the whole of her like a hidden picture, find the things that are wrong. Hands picking, digging at a cuticle already shredded skinless. Wrong speed, as if she was breathing some vapor different than air, methane, monoxide; breathing with something less than lungs; or more. Even her voice sounded different, as if the muscles used to make it had dried taut as jerky beneath her lessening skin. "Listen, I just wanted to tell you, it's not my fault. I wanted you to know that."

Plunging sense of wariness, worry, what now? and tried to ask, say something but Bibi in motion, back to the car, back with a handful of papers, folded pamphlets: she gave one to Tess. "Here," gravely, their fingers almost touching in the giving movement, "you should read this." URBAN PRIMITIVES in loud fluorescent green, the subtitle so smeared Tess could not make it out and now Bibi sitting down on the curb, ankles crossed, cheap boots coming apart at the soles. Boots. In this heat. If Tess touched her, would her hands be cold? "It explains a lot about what I'm doing, it talks about the rituals, all the religion behind it."

Tess paging to a random paragraph, half-scanning: machine culture deadens the soul, which in turn can be reclaimed only by the knife. The blood journey never ends. "Who wrote—"

"It's all about religion," and rubbing roughly at her face,

Tess's start involuntary, would she catch her hand in the heavy crisscross of wires and chains, rip something free; but no. Sunglasses off, blinking like a mole; a hedgehog. "I wanted—you know we never got a chance to talk, before."

Oh, Bibi. Tears in her eyes, so many things to say and saying nothing, gazing up and down, that wasted face and something canted wrong in the cast of her shoulders, her ribs; strange, like bones broken and set deliberate to angles unnatural, meant to cause pain. And Bibi's wise nod, "I had some surgery done, that's what you're seeing." Patting the region above the belt, heavy belt below the tiny waist. "It was something I couldn't really do myself. *By* myself."

Silence; Tess at worse than a loss and then Bibi again, asking if Tess had ever heard of the Popsicle man: frozen mummy, he's four thousand years old, like a mantra, four thousand years and you know what? He's *tattooed.* Like runes, it's power, they knew it: it's ancestral knowledge, passed down in the genes, maybe they're code for something, instructions, like Micronesian face tattoos, like a dream we should all be dreaming—"I dream of you," with sudden animation, her first real smile and so wrong, somehow, some way unspeakable. "You're always screaming."

"I bet," and Tess did not smile. "I bet I know why, too."

"You know it's really just another kind of engineering, body engineering, the kind of modifications plastic surgeons talk about . . . you ever hear of Interplast? Working on deformed people, congenital deformities. They don't do this kind of work, you know—most of them won't," with a sudden professorial air, stranger still in contrast to that weird blank scattering, that voice that seemed to speak from somewhere else. "They're afraid of malpractice, you know? You have to find the ones, you know, without licenses . . . but anyway, the people they work on, those deformed people? They're the ones, they're already tapping into the power. Without even knowing it. Like tapping into a vein, see?"

I see plenty; Tess's heart beating hard, one hand clenched tight and separate against her lip. Something is *wrong* with you, Bibi, *bad* wrong and nobody did it with a knife. "Listen," and without thinking she took Bibi's hand, little hand cold with rings, her own felt like leather around it, rough glove of flesh. "Bibi, listen a minute, I want to tell—"

And turning in the sunlight, sweat like blisters across her forehead, mascara clumped hard on her blinking lashes, hearing nothing but her own thoughts: "It's like bloodletting, the shows, that's what I'm trying to do. Like reclamation, that pamphlet tells a lot about it. But there are so many *limits!*" half-wail, frustration and she beat her free hand lightly against the curb, against her thigh. "I want to use some people with deformities, but I can't find anybody that'll do it. I told them I'd pay them, I said they—"

And sickened, without thinking: "Bibi, my God" (and the same tone she had used before, memory's turn like a snake's coiling but no time to retrieve it). "You can't use people that way."

"I don't mean making fun of them, nothing like that. You always do that, why do you always *do* that?" All at once shouting, her hand twisting in Tess's, twisting hard but she did not pull it free; perhaps she did not feel it; her eyes very wide, wide pupils fixed and fixed on Tess. "It's like bloodletting, I said! It's to understand!" and without even a breath, a viciousness sliding before her eyes like screens: "I don't know why I bother talking to *you* about it, what do you know about it?" and at once pain, Bibi's held fingers pinching hard, nipping like a handful of crabs, of biting spiders and Tess cried out and pulled her hand free, back to her body and Bibi, raging now, it's not a *circus,* it's not a *freak* show, it's catharsis! The SPIRIT, the POWER in the SPIRIT and screaming into her face, Tess up now and too alarmed to yell back, this was something more than anger, this was something wrong wrong *wrong*

and bitterly, "I tried to tell you, I *wanted* you to under- stand, he said not to but I *wanted* to," and abruptly tears, slippery as glycerin, as abruptly on her feet to shove past Tess and into car, crying loud as a child and gunning the engine so hard it stalled, the smell of gas and Tess grabbing at the passenger side door, "Bibi, don't—Bibi, *wait* a—"

and the car jerking forward and Tess, balance lost, one hand out in ludicrous empty grasp and then hard to her knees, falling on metal, gravel, broken glass, bare kneecap bright as fresh-cut meat. Staring at it and

"—you okay?" Three people, kids, two girls and a boy, hands wary and gentle to help her rise and back to the curb, arms and legs loose and silly as a puppet's. "Your leg's really fucked *up,"* and it was, jelly-thick, warmer than her sweat, hot as tears shed in anger and "No, I'm okay, I'm fine."

Resisting their hands to rise, heavy limp to the door and pull, back inside, leaning hard against the wall; and slowly as a victim take the stairs, one by one by one, toll like a bell or a circlet of beads, a brace of memories and all of it terrible with the feeling of having done terrible wrong.

And on the machine, message blinking: Michael. Cool as a voice anonymous, a stranger's voice free to say any- thing: "I hope I'll see you at the show," and nothing else, nothing but dial tone as she passed by to slump round- shouldered on the couchbed, to watch through dull eyes the blood on her leg dry to a thickening pattern, chiar- oscuro, secret and rough as graffiti, as the new-gathered guts of a box at last begun. And think of Bibi: screaming:

and crying: and something so wrong there were no words to pin it, nothing but the feeling, the way the wind from the pit brushes light as poison gas across your open sightless eyes.

Bandage white, absurdly so and pink at the center like the last chocolate in a gaudy box but the clinic doctor had warned her about infection, the cut was very deep. Keep it clean, the doctor said and she was trying, prim against the rust-scabbed door, HARDHAT AREA in slanted screwless red above her head. Hands in pockets, watching the crowd: easily two hundred people and most not Zombie regulars, word had gotten around and around.

Now Nita trying for cool beside her piece, Edgar-Marc in a semicircle of crushed cigarette butts, Jerome joking with Nicky, calling him Art. The others, her students, talking loud or slow or nervous, looking back and back again to where she stood, Tess Lodestone, their dim north star. Right. As they looked to her, she looked to the door, surreptitious swing of compass jaw, dreading, longing, would Bibi come? and what if she did? Again and again the scene in the street: something is wrong, wrong; past the inner echo, Raelynne screaming in the chopped-tree fall, was dead Paul driving Bibi, too? Reclamation; redemption; redemption from what? He was mine anyway. You can't just use people like that.

A hand on her arm, woman's hoarse voice: "Hey," and as if memory was summons Raelynne's smile, a Raelynne so different that Tess had trouble recognizing her: bleached hair skinned back in a punishing ponytail, heavy raccoon makeup; she had lost weight, too, skinny maybe as Bibi now. The voice, though, was the same, the same friendly nudge: "How you doin'? Looks like you hurt yourself, there."

"Yeah, I fell down. On some glass." Awkward, "So what do you think of it?"

"The show? 'S good, I guess; you know I don't care much for sculpture. I always liked what you did, though." Lighting a dark brown cigarette with a red plastic lighter: *Classy's* in scratched script down the side. "How come there's none of your stuff here?"

Shrugging, lying a little but not a lot, she had always been comfortable with Raelynne; that earliest rehearsal, Raelynne's easy twang, you can sit there. And Paul's hauteur; remember? Poor Paul. "What about you?" soundless wince as she bent her leg to give more weight to the lean. "What are you doing now?"

With a shrug: "Some titty dancing," and then the laugh, but toned down, way down, edged now with something dry: "You should see your face. Come on, Tess, I used to shake 'em for you and Bibi, remember? And this pays one *hell* of a lot better." Pause. "You ever see her anymore?"

"No," and not a lie at all. "Do you?"

"Nah, I'm done with all that." Long exhalation, a bitter scent. "I filled out my fantasies, I'm not goin' back and you better not either, Tess, she's messing with some real fuck-ups this time, makes poor old Paul look normal, you know? Stable . . . I mean those people worship her, you know it? All that tribal shit, power in the knife. You ask me, they're crazy as a shithouse rat, all of 'em." Toeing the butt to dark scraps. "Especially that Matty Regal guy, what a sack of snakes *he* is. And then there's—"

"Tess, hey," Jerome's wave, pinwheeling, "c'mere a minute," and Raelynne's hasty hug, you take care now, girlfriend, you stay off that leg and then gone, rangy hips and the bleached swing of her hair and Edgar-Marc there to offer the crutch of his arm: walk this way.

And afterward, the performance begun but she limping

out to the splurge of a cab: no one saw, busy smoke and bursting bottles, heavy clatter of rolling metal and all of it too much, tonight, ripe not with ghosts but their memories, less true pain than its nagging prescience: there is worse to come. In the dank backseat, cheap helpless dangle of the tree-shaped air freshener jouncing like fringe with each turn; through the window the presence of lightning, heavy in the deeps of the sky.

"Looks like rain," the cabbie said. Tess did not answer. The cabbie put on the radio, glittery Spanglish pop bright as the lightning, Tess's head against the window as loose and tired as the rolling wheels beneath her, the endless rolling circle of her thoughts.

"It's called *Sidestep to the Mind*." Nicky's slow reading voice, " 'The body as sidestep to the mind. In Jung—' " pronouncing it phonetically. "Jung?"

"Just read it."

"Okay. 'In Jung we learn that the dream is the theater: the dream of the mind unconscious, bringing us back to a more primitive reality, where we use our bodies not only as homes but as tools. Come experience with us that urban primitive vision.' And underneath, here," grimy pointer nail, "it says 'power in the knife.' What the fuck's that supposed to mean?"

"I don't know." Aspirin residue on the back of her tongue; weary swing of tired legs around the tripod of the stool. "Is there any more coffee left?"

"No. I could get some on my way out, if you—"

"No, no, that's okay. I have to go to the scrapyard anyway."

"The scrapyard's closed now, it's after six."

"Already?" It seemed she had just sat down, so little accomplished; so much to do. Half the morning spent with those two kids, girl and boy, red caps and earnest frowns, they had been at the *ARThouse* show, they wanted to work with her. Hand over one eye as if she had a headache, what kind of work do you do?

"Guerrilla art," the girl said, nasal and proud. Tess wrote down their phone numbers, said she would call; I'll call you, nodding and smiling at the door like the more loathsome kind of puppet. She had wanted to go to the scrapyard, sweat and stink, heavy boots and metal like the fins of prehistoric sharks; she had wanted to work. Now it was too late, after six and still hours before the poisoned sunset, heavy yellow, it had rained all night and would rain again this evening; already she could see the clouds. Bibi's show was not outdoors. "Are you going?" to Nicky, so quietly she had to say it again, forcing the words like a cough: "Are you going?"

"Are you?" Her sideways stare; he shrugged a little, as if to say Anything's possible. "You never know."

"Yes, I do. Have fun."

And alone then, Nicky's clattering echo and then street silence, the occasional car or curse like a smell through the open windows, sitting down to work and finding with weary surprise that she did not want to work: did not want to examine what this box, this particular new box with its snapped-bone interior and false gold-leaf sides, was leading to; someone, Bibi? Michael? had called them Skinner boxes. Was that true? and if so, to whom was the conditioning applied? Me, Tess thought, setting down the screwdriver she had been holding, thoughtful as an added finger. That's who it's working on.

Lying on the couchbed, the sheets matte with grime, dirty as her shoes, the windows, her tied-back hair, everything here was going to hell. Hands behind her head, she used to see Bibi lying so, bare to the waist, breasts pointing jaunty and one knee crossed and bouncing, just a little, too irregular to mark musical time. Marking thoughts, maybe; and what was Bibi thinking of now? Urban primitives. Power in the knife. *I tried to tell you,* her cry, *he said not to but I wanted to.* Who said? Matty, knee-jerk malice or something drier, darker, puffy fluid left rotting in a basement jar, the way the crawlspace smells; like Matty's smile.

She thought she would not sleep all night but the simple action of lying still, her tired mind in the same slow circles like lamed birds, slower and slower and she slept from light to light, waking as sore and dirty as if she had spent the night on the ground; still the rest had left her better and she woke to work at once, cleaning the worktable, sorting and sweeping, by the time her students arrived she had scraped the dirt from herself, too, clean and austere, half a smile on skeleton cheeks.

Only three today, Edgar-Marc and Nita, Nicky red-eyed and irritable, they were all less than pleasant though pleasant to her. Snapping at each other, Nicky and Nita especially and "Why don't you calm down, tit-rag?" and Nita's awkward shove, big hands in motion and Nicky's hop back to balance, murdering glare and Tess, sharp: "Quit it!" Silence. "What's the matter with you all today?"

"It's because—"

Nita, fierce: "Why don't you just shut up?"

"*You* shut up! It's because of the show, Tess," Nicky's stubborn supplication, going on fast and half-gabbling: the show a lampoon, one long mockery of Tess, her work, the art of her boxes reduced to cruel cardboard jokes with spastic plastic marionettes, the Tess character some guy on a stool with a welder's helmet and the others, freed now by Nicky's recitation, adding details: and this: and that, and this, too, it was fucking awful. Naming names and everyone had known, and everyone had laughed.

"Well," and a shrug: I don't care. She even said it aloud, "I don't care," into their wrathful silence, what difference did it make? She controlled nothing, nothing but herself; and her work. And as if to prove it worked harder still, drove them, too, as she rarely did, drove them hard until they were glad at last to go. And sat quiet in the silence they left behind, the box before her on the worktable like a split chrysalis of gold, its edges planed and burned and bent like elbows struggling in the greasy glue of birth, struggling to get up, and go on, until it was time to fall down again and die.

And the next day Nita's indignant gift, a review of the performance in no less than the city daily, all of them hunched horseshoe around Tess's bent reading head: "Read it out loud," Nicky said, he could not follow as fast as the others and so she did, monotone, " '—a disturbing and cruel duality, seeming to comment through the use of scarring and tattoo techniques on the brutality of modern life and the redemption offered by a renewal of so-called primitive cultural values.' " Silence; and in the silence went on, making her voice dry, driest, striving for no comment: " 'Although it can be understood as a supremely virulent form of metaphor (or, as in one segment a particularly vicious lampoon of her former partner, and co-founder of the Surgeons of the Demolition, Tess Bajac), ultimately this show is for and about nothing but violence and ugliness, and should be treated, and avoided, on that basis. What value there is here, is unquestionable: there is none.' Does however have tits," but no one laughed or even smiled, she had to do it herself. "For God's sake, you guys," but Nita shook her head, grim; it isn't funny, Tess.

And then she understood, a moment's surprise at her own surprise: of course, they were embarrassed for themselves, a slur on her was mud on all of them. Silently she read the rest, read it through and found buried in the artspeak a phrase that stopped her, hands tighter on the edges of the paper and there in black and white the words "something here is wrong"; the sentence again, read more slowly, "The viewer is left with the indelible impression that, past the shouts and the quotes, the blood theatrical and real, something here is not about performance, or even art; something here is wrong."

Is it that bad? Over and over, Is it that bad? in sorrow, and fear to see it written, mirrored, by an outsider, a mainstream critic moved by half-parts curiosity and duty, paid to go and see what there was to see. It must be very very bad if it was so evident, to someone who did not care.

Staring down at the paper, they were talking now, saying something and Bibi's name and "Cunt," Edgar-Marc's murmur, Nicky's narrow agreement and Tess surprised, again, at the leap of her anger; she wanted to yell at them, say Don't you talk about her that way. No. No. Folding the paper, oblong drop and "So," rising to set up the screens, act normal: let's forget about it, okay? Let's get to work; but no one had apparently the heart for it, sluggish and uninspired, preoccupied. She did not care, she had no heart for it either and sent them away, tomorrow will be better but they didn't leave, instead gathering below at Nicky's and Nicky back upstairs, diffident in the doorway: did she mind if they all took a few days off? Just to, you know, get a break?

"Sure," secretly grateful. "If you guys want a break, take one. And Nicky, please." Hand on his arm, squeezing a little; her hand cold, as if she had sustained a shock; did he feel it? No. "Don't take it so hard, all right?"

"Right," but patently not listening, if she was not man enough for a grudge then he would carry it for her. Music all day and into the night, half-heard, she was busy on her own now, the new box growing, something different about this one, something very dark beneath the gold. Frightened for Bibi, yes, but was she hurt, too; a little, after all? But honestly answering no, Bibi's power to wound lay grounded at a level so deep that these skinside skirmishes were even less than they appeared; Bibi could hurt her plenty, but not this way.

Now on the table the shiver, false pleated metal as friable as skin, she had not been wrong to think of it as a chrysalis, cold cocoon pregnant with black growth: inside thin strips of leather, old bootlaces dirty and twisted; a heat-ruined penny speared through the bent center, hypodermic length of wire; the eyeless corpse of a mummified mouse. And three drywall nails, heads rusted, tips still sharp and bright, each securing one paw, the broken fourth left free as if clutching for the shoelace, save me; help. The box, the cocoon, closed as prim as an evening bag, she even added the clasp it seemed to call for, heavy split shell-shape iced with corrosion, verdigris as green as plants underwater.

And while working, working hard, she found herself in a peculiar way missing Michael, whom she did not somehow miss otherwise; why was that? Bibi's leaving had gouged a void so great she had force-filled it with Michael, why did he leave no similar hole? Maybe he had never really been there to begin with. Maybe it's because you used him, the way you accuse Bibi of doing: making of the person a thing, an instrument, a tool; heat gun still on, burning heedless in her hand, guilty, guilty. Hot air blowing past her face, hot enough to make skin blister, wondering where Michael was, what he thought of Bibi's crude lampoon: did he think it was funny? juvenile? was he jealous? You only try to hurt the one you love. And what did he think of the deeper level, the wrongness? Nothing? Anything? Did he even think it was wrong?

Thump, thump, thump, machinery-sound from downstairs, Nicky moving stuff around; were they all still down there? Another, subtler thump from outside, the bass of approaching thunder; this summer somehow a perfect incubator for storms, heavy storms to flood sewers, gutters, snap weary glass like bone too old to carry its own weight, it seemed she was either waking or sleeping to the sound of rain against her windows. Maybe they would break, too, one night, shiver and split like skin parted by the moving scalpel, one of Bibi's knives come calling at last. Remembering Bibi's wild anger, in the street, the cruel surprise of her pinching fingers; and the heavy hand again against her heart: oh Bibi.

Open and close, the chrysalis. Dark outside, the artificial night of storms.

More darkness, working alone again, no storm this night but a tiredness immense, exacerbated first by another Bibi article, an interview so ugly and bizarre that reading it— fast and standing up, back to the kiosk like a thief—made her want to cry, cry out: Bibi in some fresh gibberish, talking about deformities: "It's like a blessing, you know," (and Tess could picture it, mouth moving in that new strenuous way) "it's better than being born normal. Because this way they're plugged in all at once, they know in their skin what I just now am coming to know in my heart: it's a bridge, it's where you have to be. To *know*," and it went on and on, explaining her theories devised in consultation with her "adviser," unnamed but almost certainly Matty. Unless she had a new disciple, fresh toy and a frightened thought: what would she do with someone like Paul, now?

And the guy behind the yardstick-sized counter, hey buy

it or put it back and she gave him the money, too expensive. Not enough money to waste, nowadays; not as much school to teach these past few weeks and then mostly they had wanted theory, maybe they were branching out. Nothing wrong with that. Except the money. Walking home, wondering how long it would be home, would she have to move? So what. Maybe better, in a new place, less money, less ghosts. Maybe.

Banging away, Nicky and somebody else, a couple somebodies: not Jerome and Peter, they were off for a month, a tour. Zombies on the road to four different cities, out in the street the horse trailer behind and a rental truck to follow, even pared down it was still a big show; she had not seen a Zombies show entire in months. Outsider, now; and Nicky, too, apparently self-excluded, invited but declining, he had his own work, Jerome said, his own shit to get done.

Asking driver's-side Jerome, sun on her neck and "What was it?" leaning in the pickup's window, her arms sticking to the hot maroon upholstery, peeling a little like sunburned skin. Jerome's sunglasses bound jaunty with duct tape, Peter still inside, last-minute gathering. "Did he say what it was?"

Jerome shrugged, shook his head. "No idea. I thought you might know."

Peter, struggling into view with a box of parts, the nose of a spreader baffle held under his chin: "Tess, hey," dumping the box in the back. "Jerome, man, you all set?"

"All set." One arm out to encircle her neck, sweaty half hug and a smile, not quite meeting her eyes as if he were again that young young break-in boy; I just wanted to see. "Wish us luck, hey?"

"Good luck," and to her own surprise she kissed him, kissed him hard on the cheek. "Have a great time. Come back heroes," and they all smiled at that, break a *neck* Peter said and Jerome starting the truck: deep tubercular rattle, squeezing her hand once more and gone, horse trailer and all. She had not even known until today that they were going. And why had Nicky turned it down?

Inside the brisk chug of an air compressor, knocking to no answer so she pushed open the door to see him bee-eyed, safety goggles and a respirator mask, the whole room reeked of paint. Beneath him on the floor a life-size mummy, a dummy, and in his hands some peculiar kind of harness, silver and black and, puzzled, "Nicky? Hey," and in the sight of her a start so guilty it startled her, too: coming forward and his scramble, like a child, to block her view: of what? What?

Naked white-haired dummy, heavy rings glued to the nippleless breasts, encircling the arms bent like broken, the legs unscrewed at the knees, big screws thick as thumbs, more rings at the smooth pubic valley and where the face should be an oval gouge; nothing. Empty.

And "Listen," his nervous gibber, he was talking but she did not listen, did not even hear beyond the buzz of sound. Everywhere, all over the room the lampoons so ugly and crude: a box here formed of stiff-bending bodies, clown-faced, silly and lewd; another box gaudy as foil enclosing some kind of food, green vegetable soft with gray-brown rot, scored and bulleted with rings, hooks, fish hooks where its painted eyes had been. Another, aluminum cube and each side a symbol, question mark, exclamation, dollar sign, fuck you in streamlined sans serif: inside it a pair of breasts spiked straight through with knitting needles, bleeding rivers of tacky red blood. Beside that an empty TV chassis scabbed with headless ballerina dolls, encircled in fake metal chains and some kind of writing, she could not read it, would not stop to read it now. A freestanding sculpture of a woman, badly done metal musculature made to move hydraulically, sloppy frowning mouth pierced with pins, hundreds of pins, each point a small and particular shine.

"Tess, listen, okay?" Nicky beside her, still wearing the goggles, his distorted eyes wide. "Will you just—"

and out of the room, she could not even look at him, would not stay with those hideous pieces staring her in the face; horrible, to know they had used their talents and her teachings, skill and knowledge wasted in this absurd and vicious way.

Upstairs she locked her door, turned off her machine; sat grim and still before her worktable as if she now must work to drive the ugliness away. Hands shaking on the drill, thinking of the magazine article, bending to prop it open to Bibi's thin and terrifying smile: and suddenly exhausted, blood like lead through her weary veins and she kissed the picture, set it where she could see it, eye to eye through the hours of work relentless, eye to eye, lit by sparks through the empty tunnel of night.

"No more."

Up all night, and she looked it, here in the light before them: semicircle of serious faces, nervous shuffling, miniature whispering sighs.

"When you do that kind of shit," staring around the circle, "you insult me. You insult yourself, too, and everything we do here." Burning feeling, somewhere past her ribs, the gassy feel of too much coffee, no food, anger's dull hangover. "I don't ever want to see that shit again."

Silence. Then Edgar-Marc, quiet: "So what're we supposed to do, just take it?"

Tess's silence, now, and them waiting in it like an empty room beyond which might lie an open field, an open grave,

the sleek gleam of the operating theater; she held it like
the last beat in a song, then, flat as her hands: "Take what?
Bad publicity? *Name*-calling?" and softly her chanting
whine: "She called me *names,* she was *mean* to me. Grow
up!" yelling, startling them, widening eyes and for a moment wished Bibi there to see it; she would have been
proud. See: I can manipulate people, too; and thinking
that took her anger, her edge, made her turn away to say
without looking, "You do what you want. But not here."

Leaving them then, trudge up the stairs and nobody followed. Only silence behind, not the wound but the puckering pocket of scar. She was sweeping under the worktable
when: the diffident knock: Nicky. Nita. Edgar-Marc.

No one said anything until Nicky, finally, "You get that
reversible drill to work yet?" and Nita, one hand out, past
the threshold and let me see it, I'll take a look at it. Edgar-
Marc saying nothing, quiet to stand before Tess and then:
"You want us to throw them out, or what?"

"Throw what out?"

Looking down, then at Nicky, Nita by the table with the
drill in her hand. "The, you know. The pieces."

"No," strongly, surprising them one more time. "Don't
ever throw your work away." Thinking—not the others,
but did Nicky know?—of juggernaut *Salome,* of the thrust
and brood of the Triple Deaths, the *Magistrate of Sorrows.*
"Keep it," flicking on the lights, white-green fluorescence
in the darkening wash of yet another storm. "Just keep it
covered."

The rest of them never came back, took their pieces and
gone. It was as if they had never been.

"Just once."

"No." Trying not to sound sullen, Nicky's aimless batting
fingers, skating the salt shaker past her and "Why not?"

for the twentieth time. That day. "Just once, she never even has to *see* you, she doesn't even have to know you're there."

"You sound like Michael."

An unhappy comparison, but he did not show annoyance; he was trying very hard. They were all trying, Edgar-Marc and Nita and her big hands still, side by side in the booth like kids in church. They had taken her out to dinner, Jimbalaya's, fake Cajun food drenched in no-brand red pepper, still it was better than the crackers and dry cheese she was used to eating. One pale chunk of chicken on the end of her fork, specimen.

"I don't want to go there, you know that's the last thing I ever want to see. I see enough anyway in the papers," sad and comic, Bibi's grainy stare in the back page of the entertainment section, I'll give you entertainment. *The industrial cabaret of Skinbound.* Step right up. Or down.

Nita now, and carefully, "But how can you tell us how to feel about it, Tess, when you haven't seen it for yourself?" and the automatic answer, I don't tell you how to feel, I just tell you what to do about it. Not to do. Maybe they were right, but even if they were she would still need more, a harsher spur: remembering Bibi in the magazine: industrial cabaret, industrial accidents, and now Nicky saying something, know thine enemy, right?

"She's not my enemy," but how could they be expected to understand that? The opposite of love is indifference, not hate, but how could they know that either? Nicky playing with a sugar packet, Nita mournful with her waterglass. Edgar-Marc gazing down at his fingernails, very dirty fingernails, lumpy and black, black as the clumped mascara on Bibi's staring eyes, staring at her that terrible day, there on the curb: how bad was it, then? And now, how much worse had it gotten? Bad enough to know at one remove, at a glance? A whiff? A sound, a whisper, what would it take to gauge and what would she do about it if she did know? Help her? stop her, what? Know thine enemy: Bibi's wrongness, that was the enemy, the depth and degree of Bibi's slide and "All right," like a line crossed and she said it again, "All right. Next show. When's the next show?"

Nicky careful not to show pleasure, careful not to crow but he couldn't help his smile, Nita's smile and Edgar-Marc's excited half-bounce, a kid before the circus, black circus of pain. *"Domination and Paradox,"* the salt spilling, Nicky's grin released, "and I'll even pay your way. Okay? Can't beat that, right?"

Domination and paradox. "Okay," slowly, already sorry. "All right."

Big place, warehouse, steel box already full of restless echoes, the movement of bodies, all kinds of bodies climbing slewed bleachers, tier to tier, peak to peak; some taking seats, some jumping halfway to land grinning and clumsy, too much energy; too much noise; already way too much of everything and they were hardly in the door. Tess kept looking around and around, as if she expected Bibi to pop out from behind a trash barrel, jack-in-the-box atop the bleachers yelling *Got you!* Ridiculous. Damp hands in pockets, she had changed clothes over and over, stupid, is this your first time? Come here often? Idiot. She was still sweating. Nicky on one side, Nita on the other and Edgar-Marc behind, they found her a place to sit and sat around her, honor guard, prison guard: don't worry, she wanted to say, I won't run away.

Heart too fast.

I won't run away.

The stage area unshrouded, nothing special, nothing

much at all: square scaffolded construction much like the bleachers around them, careless drape here and there, short lengths of orange nylon rope. Metal chemical drum upended, numbers stenciled bare across its peeling sides. Spotlights hung precarious and close above the drum; other lights, red gels higher up and above them the steady green burn of fluorescents, industrial constellation, what zodiac? No archers or twin fish, instead the dragon rampant, the scorpion, the headsman, the knife. The Red Empress, shaved head and bloody smile, scars thick as pearls up and down, up and down the thin bare arms as if gifted by disease as rare as that smile. Knife in hand and hand in glove, come to make chaos, come to make the water run red, turns staves to snakes with the faces of children, cut and bleed and

Nita, quizzical, "Hey Tess?"

and the lights went out.

Tremendous noise, one galloping roar and the sound of feet, hundreds of pairs of feet pounding against the bleachers, tremor through the wood and flimsy metal as if it were flesh and bone, Tess on her feet and Nicky trying to take her hand, to steady her but she did not want to be steadied, did not want to touch or be touched but simply to stand in the darkness, heartbeat wild and wait: wait for Bibi.

Who did not come. First a trio of boys, dancers, they moved like dancers anyway: bare chests and ragged leotards, perching and tumbling around the drum as the lights changed from red to blue and back again, slowly at first and then faster, faster till they flickered and the tallest of the boys snatched up by the others, borne to the drum like an altar and in their hands like magic some kind of knives

and the knives through the air and down without melodrama, so quickly Tess did not have time to look away ripping at his thighs, his pelvis

ripped his leotards free to show the tattoos on his thighs, red and black like necrotic roses, roses of flesh and the boys yelling something, all three, some bad tone poem about the will to dominate and half the audience yelling along, whooping and beating time, terrible seesaw rhythm become chant, becoming roar and the boys falling, bending in half and half again in limber prostration; Bibi, now?

No.

Now another dance, different dancers, women now in black robes moving only their hands, each outfitted with sheathing gloves ripped palmless and on their bare palms painted triangles, red and black, they kept talking about Egypt and the spicy smell of mummified flesh, greasy black grins and someone started beating the altar-drum, jack-handle drumstick and a big whooping pound

and a red spotlight

here she comes.

Her own heart beating as if in pain; hands wet and moving, clasping, releasing, in and out of her pockets as if they were stolen and she pledged to hide them, hiding them poorly; what would she look like? What would she do?

And the music, changing, hammering now an old, old rhythm, they might have played that rhythm on the lip of the volcano, on the edge of the bleeding cliffs, women rising, boys unbending to turn, see no evil, hear no evil, speak no evil and opening their mouths in sudden brutal light, glare-white to show

that they had no tongues

and fingers crammed into their mouths, pulling at the emptiness to fling out things black and wet, what the *fuck* and flying through the air and she saw they were dental dams, just dental dams, nothing worse than that and the light gone black again, her dazzled eyes needing a moment to adjust, and in that blinded instant Bibi came.

The Red Queen.

Face held up, pointed like a gun into the howling light to show every guttering bone, every sculpted shaft and plane: *honed,* and everywhere crossed and banded, everywhere silver, pinching steel-tipped fingers, metal scissoring at her hungry bloodless skin

and beautiful, so beautiful

and sick with it: the wrongness heavy as a coating, a syrup, the sugary shine of inner rot made manifest and as she opened those big eyes it seemed she saw everyone, everyone there, stark in the maelstrom of screams, the three boys at her feet and the boy next to Nicky howling "Bibi! Bibi! Bibi!" and Tess, the crawl of sweat down her cheeks, wanting to do something: run: scream: staring and staring and

others coming, now, sliding or leaping or creeping beside her, Tess thought she saw Andreas beneath half a mask, six or seven and all of them wearing masks, or horns, or animal ears, big jackass ears and the three boys masked now, too, all of them wearing dogs' heads, not rubber but fur, real fur, real snouts, taxidermist's work and for Tess the sudden sick sensation, what must it smell like, inside those heads, so tight over the wearers' own, so tight in all this heat? And Bibi calling out, miked voice clear and absolutely calm: "The paradox of domination is the paradox of freedom—"

dogs before her

"—the freedom—"

at her feet, snouts in grotesque snuffling motion up her legs, between her thighs

"—to be a slave—"

and she grabbed at them, one by one, pulled their heads

back, bent their bodies backward till it seemed their spines must crack and the soundtrack now informed with the shrieks of animals, cacophonic, unbearable, it was like being in the middle of a slaughterhouse, a slaughterhouse bounded by your own beating temples. Tess wanted to cover her ears but would not, would not move, would only stare as Bibi took a long razor, old-fashioned straight razor, dogs' heads bent back still and at their human throats, the blade

drawing a line, pink line, not even real blood yet, just pink, just the summery plasma drip and now they all had razors, mules and bulls and strange lion-headed cats and they were all cutting each other, merry slicing here and there, nicking and picking and Bibi turning

on the audience

and her stare, hands loose and coming forward and the sudden dreadful grin as if she saw Tess, *saw* her, came for her as she could and never would come for any other: because I love you, that awful grin, I *love* you, Tess, I want to *fuck* you, come to me now. Now

and her mouth open, to speak, to *say*

"Who will be my slave?" and one of the dancers, performers, coming from behind to offer a mask, pig mask, grinning sow mask and Bibi grabbing it up, grabbing a girl from the lunatic front-row surge, a crying blond girl in a ripped black bra and slamming the mask down over her head, spinning her balanceless to show the rest: slave: pig.

And pushing the girl before her, loose-limbed silly stagger and onto the drum, up, there you go, piggy, there you are and Bibi crying out, deeper voice now, Red Queen priestess on the shivering edge of the wound, "The power to take is better than the power to give, you have to give to get, you have to want it, do you want it?" The audience answering, maelstrom; but she was asking the girl.

"Do you want it?"

Crying, mumbling sounds picked up by Bibi's mike: indecipherable, the girl's glottal hiccups and groans and Bibi suddenly screaming DO YOU WANT IT in a voice to split skin and the girl as if released, shrieking back: "Yes!"

And the soundtrack now abruptly drums, kettledrums, and Bibi taking up this time not a razor, not a knife, not a weapon that Tess could see but the audience knew it at once, screamed their approval, screaming and Tess yelling to Nicky, yelling right in his ear What's she got? What's she got? and his bellow back, he had to say it twice before she understood. Fish hooks. Hooking up the flesh to cut it, cut it to leave a scar, leave marks and all the animal heads in motion now, whooping up and down, into the audience, climbing like evil children up the stairs at night and the bull's-head coming toward them, toward Tess, for a moment's horror she thought the mask would fall at her feet and she see behind it Paul, more bone even than Bibi, pared finer still and grinning eyes, bull's eyes, she had to fight the urge to run and saw, as the bull passed by her, others were running, too, here and there, some toward the stage, the drum, and some away, some jumping straight off the bleachers as they had done before in play but now in earnest, hitting the concrete floor badly as thrown fruit, a girl fell flat on her back but no one went to help her, no one went to see if she was all right, if she was trampled, if she was

hurt

and Bibi shouting something else, Tess did not hear but as surely as a hand in the dark felt the need, need in the strain and gloss of Bibi's movements, the tension in the muscles of her knife-ridden face and she screamed, really screamed, screamed like everything that was wrong coming out in one long terrible noise beyond succor or control

and borne on that noise Tess all at once in motion, pushing through the crowd, hysterical crowd, hysterical rum-
bling noises balanced on the rim of ecstasy and panic, she
had heard those sounds before oh God let me through.
Let me *through,* elbows out, she thought she felt a bone
give beneath her terrified assault, half-stumbling down the
bleachers themselves in motion, Nicky after her too late
and clogged by the others, impeded and she lost her balance entirely for a minute or two, felt the sensation of pure
helplessness as for those moments she rode the brute
whim of the crowd, crushed or borne it was all beyond her,
beyond control and she fell half on her feet, rose scrambling and shoving, sweat in her eyes, burning: Let me
through.

And Bibi howling, the pig-masked girl forgotten and
Bibi herself kicking over the drum, the girl bouncing more
or less out of the way and someone in a rubber frog mask
grabbing at Tess's arm; she smelled wet salty breath and
kicked out without thinking, aimed for the shin and was
punched for her trouble, not too hard in the stomach and
instead of punching back pushed hard, very hard, pushed
like an earthquake but it was no use, other people were
there, too, overrunning the performance area, overrunning
the masquers, the false animals as they bore Bibi away.

And then it was just noise, crazy yelling people and she
moved with the crowd's momentum until she could find a
hidey-hole, a slot to slip away; some kind of hi-lo ramp and
she crouched beside it, waiting till there was space, to
breathe, to move.

To find Bibi.

Backstage: keep walking and she did, past pallets and
heavy plastic drums, MASK AREA in unconscious irony and
beyond that, light and noise: the area they used for back-

stage apparently a kind of lunchroom, cafeteria gutted empty and there they all were, eight, twelve, talking too loud, sharing drinks on the long yellow tables. Somebody laughing, loose drunken whoops and Tess straining to see past the robes and masks discarded, shiny piercings dull in the crummy overheads: where is she?

And at the door, not Andreas but a boy pierced like him, one of the dog-boys, line on his throat stitched lightly with beaded blood, newer blood on his lower lip and dabbing, dabbing with a yellow Kleenex: "What?" Flat nasal vowels. "We're closed."

"Bibi. I have to see Bibi right now."

"Oh yeah, right," rolled eyes and pushing at the door, not even bothering with contempt and she grabbed him, grabbed his shoulders to shove him as hard as she could against the door, his head chattering back and "Yeah *right* you little fuck, I want to see Bibi and I want to see her right—"

"Tess," and now Andy, only his voice recognizable: beefier than ever, now, hair long and very dirty, chin and cheeks tattooed a dark slim blue. Bare chest scratchy with dried blood; he looked like he was developing breasts. "She doesn't want to see you, Tess. So go away, okay?"

The boy sagging, rising straighter to rub at his head, a monumental glare but Tess ignored him: "Andy," trying to see past him, so big he seemed to fill the door, "I have to talk to her. Just for a minute, all right? Tell her," her obvious fumbling, no good at duplicity's persuasion, "tell her I read the pamphlet, okay? Just tell her that."

"Tess—" and sighing, leaning against the doorframe. "I don't owe you shit, you know."

"Please." Staring him straight in the eyes, unused to asking favors and showing it. "If she says no, I'll leave, all right?" rising on tiptoe, trying to see past Andy's bulk to look directly into Michael's eyes, gray and calm and unsurprised; wrapped in black, pale hair caught in some kind of netting, messy plaits and one curl loose against the courtier's tilt of his cheekbone. Faintly scarred and laughing, the soft dry sound when something is amusing but not truly funny: a botched suicide, say, or a man being mauled by his own dog. Looking at nothing, and laughing.

And beside him, Bibi.

Head on his shoulder like a tantrum-worn child, eyes closed and slack lips drawn in exhaustion's pale frown, long as tragedy. Red and silver mingling with his dusty black, intimacy solid as a feeding vein and Andy saying something, shrugging, I guess you better go. Tess? you better—

Not even nodding, saying nothing, turning away past drums, empty barrels and black grease, past warning signs, all the signs were there. All of them, and all along. Am I stupid? or just naive?

And out at last into the dark where Edgar-Marc pounced on her, loud teetering croak: "She's here, you guys, I got her!" and the other two jogging up, Nicky saying something, angry, you scared the *shit* out of—

and stopping, stopping the others, hand up like a traffic cop. "Hey," roughly, still panting a little. "Tess. Are you all right?" Silence. "What happened in there?"

"Nothing," not looking. Her stomach hurt like an afterthought where she had been punched, bright little ache and sweaty all over, sweaty and cold in the night air and the three of them around her, sweatier than she; they had been running, nervous, looking for her. She tried to smile for them, blinking eyes so dry it seemed they would split like cherries, split wide open so she need never see again; what you don't see won't hurt you; oh you *asshole.*

"Who's an asshole?" and Nita's frown; had she spoken

aloud? Why not? Shout it from the rooftops. The Red
Queen, the Jack of Daggers; ace in the hole and the same
pale eyes between them, pale and gray, the color of needles and knives. Long midnight shiver down her clammy
back, shirt stuck messy like the hood of a burst blister and
the three of them, staring at her; "Who's an asshole,
Tess?"

I am. "Let's go home."

Nita's voice, distorted and loud, for a confused moment
Tess thought she was somehow in the room: "—TV, Tess,
turn it on now. Hurry!" and obeying the urgency, rising to
punch bleary at the button, "—animal rights activists later
this week. Troupe director Bibi Bloss—" and a hideous
still photograph, leaden and deranged, more freakish than
her real-life face "—reached for comment. In other news,
the city council's attempts to—"

and Nita, still on the phone, did you see it? Tess? Picking it up, feedback groan in her ear: Yes I saw it, some of
it. Headache, as if she had gone to sleep drunk. "What else
did they say? I didn't—"

"I guess," Nita's voice itself somewhat like feedback,
"some people, animal rights people? They were protesting
those dumb masks, they said they were made from real
animals."

And a laugh inside, the mirth of helplessness; instead, "I
have to go, Nita. Thanks," and sitting back hard on the
bed, head in hands: awake again to last night's knowledge:
she had gone to find out, hadn't she? And she had, but not
what she expected: instead Bibi and Michael, so much
deeper, so much more. It made so very much sense it was
hard to believe it hadn't happened earlier. Or had it? Why
not? She was blind, hammer and steel and all around her
the real fire, burning and spilling, sticking like napalm to

her hands, to her burning palms like a fire in the wilderness, Armageddon's light from a long way away. It takes a mask to make you see; and all at once she knew the bullface last night was Michael, knew in retrospect the grace of his ascent up the staggered slope of the bleachers; rubbing at her face, her eyes, she had thought of Paul, then, but it had been something dead after all, hadn't it? Something dead as love, their love, all three of them; hadn't it? Of course it had.

Shifting on the bed, this bed where she had slept with Bibi, with Michael, made love to them both: gray eyes open wide in the dark, mouths wet on her flesh and she had to get up, get out of the room, it was as if she could smell them, their scents commingled and slick as gloves against her hands, against the hot walls of her throat. Downstairs, hurrying as if pursued, masked man, the bull and the maiden, minotaur. Pushing at the Zombie door, using Nicky's key; nobody home.

On his worktable, some spread guts and she wanted to look at them, try to make sense, stop thinking: the familiar remedy, will it work again today? Her hands were shaking. Nicky kept it even colder than she did; heat rises. Fire burns. Like likes like, her mother used to say that. Gray eyes behind a mask, all kinds of masks, there were all kinds of— The door buzzer, sustained thrumming noise and she rose, robot, to peer through the peephole, who's there? A face she didn't know, long scowling stare and saying something, leaning on the buzzer again.

"Who is it?" before realizing they couldn't hear. Bending, trying to put more eye to the peephole: and seeing: Bibi. Behind heavy green glasses; Michael's old sunglasses. Two people with her, man and woman, all of them in fugitive black and gray.

Her throat clicking dry, hands clicking free the bolts, the

lock: the other two coming first, bodyguards. Bibi stepping behind, slipping off the glasses and Tess knew that she had not slept since the show, that brittle look around her eyes and something else; something worse, some stray wet shimmer like an insect caught in a basin, stepping in quick and dainty in bare feet wrapped like a dancer's, ballet dancer's, stopping when she got to Tess.

A smile, half grimace; so dreadfully thin, light as a mummy shriveled to infinite weightlessness; translucent skin, like paper, old onionskin that crackles at the touch. Her gaze kept moving, around and around, as if it did so without her consent or control.

"Did you see me on TV?" and they all laughed, Bibi shrill, breath in Tess's face strangely bitter, as if she had been eating bones. "Those assholes," petulant and bright, "I'll fix their fucking asses, next time I'll use a *live* dog, how would they like that? How would they fucking well—"

"No you won't." Not loud; gazing at Bibi as if there was nothing else in all the world to see. "You won't do that. You love animals, Bibi."

"Of course I love animals," more petulant still. "I would never hurt an animal. I'll skin them instead," and poking Tess, gently, with the tip of one finger, dirty little finger, dirty little girl, so resonant with that jarring inner wrong, as if her—what? craziness, what?—as if it were palpable, like a sore necrotic, like a broken neck. "So did you like the show?"

"No." Conscious of the other two, staring; conscious of the rhythm of her heart, the leaden beat of pain, pain. Why was Bibi so dirty? Why couldn't these fucking stooges get her to use a washcloth? comb her hair? Dirty and fey, little stick blown wild in the storm of her own desires and Tess felt her throat closing, the slow convulsion before great weeping so spoke instead and in a hurry: "What happened to that girl? The one you cut. What happened to her?"

And Bibi, distracted past some greater whirl of distraction, an inner buzz sharp as a spinning bit: "What? who, Kim? That's Kim, she's part of the troupe, kind of . . . hey, you should see what she does to herself. For fun," and laughing, harsh little hiccup of sound and then all at once grave as a surgeon with a cruel prognosis: "Okay, Tess. We're here to talk, right? So let's talk. All right? Let's talk. I'll go first."

Here to talk; says who? "I'd rather talk alone," looking at the other two, who stared back bland as cutouts, big one-dimensional dummies; Bibi ignored them, ignored Tess's request. Perching on a half-gutted red leather couch, stuffings' belch in the draft and stink and that bird-cocked head, haggard eyes: "So. I keep trying to tell you, but you keep not listening. Did the show tell you anything, Tess?"

Plenty; but nothing you want to hear; if you can even hear it, anymore. "Tell me what?"

"About the gates. —I knew you were up there, you know. I'm not stupid. I knew you were there."

As if trying to decipher a map coded in dialects she could not master, to a land where she could never be welcome: slowly now: "Bibi, I don't know what you mean. What gates?"

But her question lost, Bibi, too, intent on speaking, on her own wounded agenda. The modifications, carefully, like a teacher, ticking points on the bare air, the *modifications* are the *gates,* many gates for many people and there was still so much work left to do, only so much to be accomplished in the arena of her body, she had in fact done things in the past that made further modifications impossible in her own flesh; but there was always (a skeleton smile) the handy flesh of others. Wasn't there? So many people know about it now; did you know that? Tess? Did you?

Tess's mouth open, half a hundred answers and Paul's gaze somewhere in the silence of her own memory, Paul's arrogance, his infantile trust. Who had spoken for Paul? Not Paul; not anyone. Who speaks for—what was her name? Kim? Not Kim. What will happen here, in this vacuum of complicitous silence, what may have happened already?

But the rights of others, if they existed, did not seem at all a topic to Bibi, did not matter and never truly had. The body, she told Tess—thin, consumed, scarred with a thoroughness and complexity that left the careful eye wincing, scarred beneath eyes and on the backs of her hand, fat white careful scars like sleeping slugs, like insects yet unnamed, scars like brackets around the talking mouth— leaning far forward on the bleeding red couch like some mad angel of prey, as if she would fling her wingless body across unimaginable chasms—the body, she said, is the bridge.

"Don't you see?" so far forward, now, she might fall, tumble like a split bag of sticks. "Don't you see? If I can't use my own body, I have to use someone else's. I *have* to," and that last with a finishing nod of such black innocence that Tess wanted to scream. Instead, frantic logic twisting on the spot to fit Bibi's new madness, like metal heated to fill some bridgeless depth: like reasoning with the wet bubble of self-interest, Bibi's gaze a gray wall penetrable only perhaps by complexities as severe, and severely delusional: but helplessly Tess tried, tried to say All the world is not your playground, your meat market, your pick-and-choose to cut—Bibi, *listen!* and then suddenly in those gray eyes a new opacity, a darkness deeper and less fathomable; a place to be hurt in.

"Yeah," leaning back, then as abruptly forward, hinged doll-back and staring at Tess. "There's something else we need to talk about, I meant to tell you at the show but you left."

Exhausted, rubbing over and over at a ticcing eye. *You left;* leave it. "What?"

"That stuff you're doing," and anger spreading, cloud-like, diffuse as poison in water. "Why'd you have to do that? Why didn't you just tell me to my face?"

Already at a loss: "Tell you what?"

"Tell me what, shit. I *saw* them, Tess, he showed them to me—fucker couldn't wait to show them to me, naturally, but I'd've seen them anyway eventually. So why?"

Why what? and she said it aloud, confused, Bibi again unhearing, quick agitated bitterness, "And they're not even good *art*, they're fucked, the workmanship is fucked —I said, I said I was worried about you if you were producing such—"

"Bibi, wait, stop a minute." Bending to her, squatting as you would to a child, tired nervous child, there was some kind of new sore on her bottom lip, dark crust, and for Tess the monstrous hammer of pity and love so great she felt it like a blow: wretched face, twisted skin and body wrenched and prodded and pulled in ways that were, no matter what Bibi claimed, no path, no road to enlightenment, only the signposts to the dark and darker and going down; she was finding nothing or else there would never be such crippled animal need, need like heat from her skin like a furnace, she had cut and torn to no purpose but the purpose of pain and pain had given her nothing, *nothing;* it was as clear on her face as if she had shouted it, written it in letters carved from her own flesh. If there was beauty on the knife's road, she had found it in a way only she could; but if there was light, it was not for her.

Tears in Tess's eyes and Bibi shifting, some underskin twist like the turnings of her flesh and "No, don't, I don't want to see that, you're the one who's making fun of me and I don't—"

"What are you *talking* about?" shouting, finally, rising to turn away, turn back, hands to her head as if to keep it from splintering; tears down her cheeks. "I don't even know what you—"

"You know damn well what I mean: those fucking boxes! That vegetable thing, that dumb TV, don't tell me you didn't make those expressly—"

Vegetable thing; TV. What—and remembering with a swoop that was almost physical, swift dropping sensation as if all her breath had been sucked by vacuum from her falling body: those horrible boxes, horrible mimicry of that which was itself unworthy of parody or response; how had Bibi seen them? How in—

fucker couldn't wait to show them to me

Who? and where had they ended up, those disenfranchised relics carried by ex-students as terribly estranged, carried to—who? Who would want them? As if in terrible transfixion, panic's circular wiggle on the silent tip of the knife, thoughts round and round and Tess herself walking, round and round the room as if she could prove the offending sculptures were there, why weren't they there? Should we destroy them, who had said that? Nicky? Edgar-Marc? And she, no, never destroy your work, never do that

and Bibi staring at her from the couch, saying Why again and Tess pulling at a long sheet of matte gray plastic, cheap tarp and looking, see here they are, here they

and Bibi beside her now—how had she crossed the room so quickly?—quick little silver hand ripping at the sheet, to bare what lay under it, bring it up to the light: the gouge-face legless body, sprawled obscene in harness; hy-draulic dummy with its prim-pinned mouth. The spiked breasts in the icon cube, symbols: exclamation, question mark, dollar sign and why no death's head, where was it: here: and now, staring at her, anger and pain the clamor-ing handmaidens to the terrible red empress of need; and past those draperies as well the core, the human locus-heart and from it that high cracked infant's voice, saying

"You made *more?*"

"Bibi, for God's sake—they're not mine! I would *never* —Bibi, *listen* to me!" but she was not listening: as if unable to listen or hear, as if Tess spoke the language of a species of steel and she so patently a creature of the bleeding earth; and Tess saw like a box cracked open Bibi changed in ways past all sane charting, her angry soul grown only angrier with each turn of the knife, each pierce of the warm needle, grown now both wizened and monstrous, crouched resentful and wet as a tumor in the blind cave of her brain. Could no one see this? bodyguards, lapdogs, a troupe full of drooling yes-man sycophants crawling avid and openmouthed as if to catch the flecks and driftings of her very skin as it fell, queen, mother, master in adoration, those stupid fucks there in the corner, didn't anyone *see* this? "Bibi!" Shouting, as if down a well, a hole, a hole in the center of the earth's beating heart; her own heart, beating like falling down the stairs; runaway, arrhythmic. "Will you listen to me? I'm telling you they're not mine!"

Eyes turned on Tess now, stare like an animal on a choke-chain. Her hands, visibly shaking, her whole body one bright jitter, chains and hooks and slender silver rings. She opened her mouth twice before she could speak, working muscles and tight tendons suggestive horribly of feeding; and when she finally spoke her voice was ultima-tum.

"Then smash them."

Silence, the quiver before the stroke, the graceless blow that splits here from now, wrong from right, expediency from the moist blind obedience of love that sees only one road: and Tess at that crossroads: "Bibi," her own voice flat with fear, fear of Bibi there before her, with the power to burn every bridge Tess could build, burn it instantly as if it had never been. "Oh Bibi. You know I can't."

More silence, pause like power building, huge static to discharge in one surge like lightning; and Bibi blinkless, staring as if vindicated in a dreadful conclusion, a terminal diagnosis.

"He said you wouldn't."

"Who said?"

"Michael."

Staring now as if she, too, was blind, deaf, adrift on a vast confusion, and Bibi's sudden siren shriek, *"Michael!* Michael motherfucking *Hispard,* that's who, Tess, like you didn't know, like you—"

"Michael never even *saw* these things, he was gone before they ever—Bibi, stop it. Stop it!"

but she was screaming now, wild, one arm pumping up and down as if to drive her point like a metal stake into frozen ground and one part of Tess stood apart and silent, frightened in the way we fear fire, or the twist of a tornado across a flat ledge of ground: Bibi was completely out of control, completely gone in an escalation of rage and hysteria that no matter the cause was in itself horrible, and threatening, to watch. But why was Tess the only one staring, why weren't Bibi's bodyguards upset? *Because,* the calm of her answering logic, the voice that can speak in the midst of the whirlwind, *they see her like this all the time.*

And Bibi's mouth Kabuki, siren and that pumping arm, faster and faster, "I thought it would bring you back, that's what I did it for, having him there with me—you might follow him, I thought you loved him, I thought it would make you come back but you *didn't!* it was for *nothing! It was for nothing!"* in one long atonal screech, now the bodyguards were moving to her, were trying to calm her down. But it was like laying hands on a hurricane, on the face of motion itself, her screams were energy and now she wept, hideous sobs without tears and "Smash it!" shrieking, advancing on the torso, Nicky's work, Nicky's mean-spirited vision and "Smash it, Tess, smash the fucking thing, *smash it!"*

"I can't!" Someone else's work, someone else's rights, oh God Jesus must she always fight for other people, other people in the face of Bibi's naked rage, oh *God* and in agony she raised the nearest implement, long-handled chipping hammer to strike, nearly weeping, strike without heart at the misformed body, legless, escapeless, all for nothing for it did not soothe or placate, did not penetrate the juggernaut shell of Bibi's pain, her anger and her unconvinced disgust and Tess dropped the hammer, let it fall to try to take Bibi's arm, grab her, stop her but Bibi pushing her off, shoving her with such loathing violence that Tess fell, pratfall sprawl on her ass, her twisted arm; and screaming something, back over her shoulder like one last curse: and gone. Bodyguards trailing, tailing, trying to take her in hand and Tess risen from the floor, crying in big ugly sounds like an animal, is everything broken? Does everything have to be *broken?* and turning on the sculpture, her own rage now, frustration like a burning ulcer and she battered the torso as if it were living flesh, breaking it more, splitting it to chunks and pieces and then slinging the hammer aside to crouch, no longer even weeping, breathing hard and fast and heavy through constriction like a band, pain made metal clenching tight and tighter around the fist of her breaking heart.

Michael is the one.

Try to call him; he will not return your calls, he will evade you every way he knows how and he knows them all, he is a very clever boy, Michael, he knows how to get lost and stay there while being insultingly visible everywhere else: Tess had seen him three times this week alone, once on local TV, twice in print: skinny and beautiful in heavy black, almost burlesque his smile beatific, arms around Bibi who looked like a rabid wolf and took up half the page with her theories, the purity of primitive cultures, their unreason, their expression of *primum moveos,* the urge of man to transcend himself, to re-create. "Women have babies to try to satisfy this urge," the red-lettered quote, "but in the end everybody's got to remake herself, or himself, one shred of skin at a time." None of which sounded like Bibi, surely incapable now of a sentence this linear; it had come, Tess knew, from Michael.

Who had somehow shown to Bibi what she should never have seen; had lied, in the showing, about Tess, a monstrous lie. What other lies were there, the ones she knew— to Nita, be Tess's eyes—what others? Links of chain leading back to his hands, monstrous Michael whom she had— almost—loved.

Why?

She chased him, grim frenzy to confront confronting the wall of flesh impenetrable: there was no way to get to him, she did not know where he lived and when she assaulted the rehearsals was turned back each time more roughly, the last after what was escalating into a full-scale beating before Matty Regal, of all people, broke it up.

And grabbed her, dirty hand on her arm, lips scabbed as

if recovering from a monthlong fever; all of them dirty here, willfully unkempt as if ill with a proud disease: his breath in her face oddly fragrant, warm sweet coffee breath. "Tess," harshly. "Quit it."

Cuts on her hands, a long scrape down one arm; she had torn her jeans. Hair in her eyes. One of the boys she had hit was crying; she could hear him through the door. To Matty she said, "Fuck you."

"I'm serious," but not unkindly, pushing her sore back against the wall. "I know you don't like me, I don't give a shit, I don't like you either. But you're making it worse for her, do you realize that? Huh? Every time you come around she goes a little bit crazier, it takes Michael hours to calm her down."

"Calm her down?" Enraged, last flagging energies like a legless bug spinning circles on the floor, trying to sting the foot that has crushed it. "He's the one who's making her crazy! He's—"

"She *is* crazy." Mouth almost to her ear, that scented breath past her dry eyes. "She's a crazy saint. She can't leave herself alone, she's cutting on places that haven't even healed yet, she keeps talking about the skin being the gate, like she has to keep cutting to get somewhere—she is so *close*, Tess, I mean she is really on to something here, and the last thing she needs is you stirring her up. Just let her alone, all right? If you really care about her, let her alone."

Staring at him as if he, too, were crazy; maybe they all were. Maybe she was, too. The boy behind the door had stopped crying and was now cursing, drab repetition like a barking dog; someone else kept saying, "Uh-huh, uh-huh," each time he stopped for breath. Her own voice like a stranger's, "I just want her to—" and she stopped; what

did she want? For Bibi to come back, be safe? Not be
crazy? Love her again, what?

But she does love you

and it was true, she had seen it: still there, crippled,
twisted as Bibi herself, cut and broken and cut again; but
still there. Almost more terrible than anything else, what
in fact made it terrible: *she still loves you.* And yet in the
knowing some small and dreadful joy; for Bibi, too? Who
knew.

"I want her to be okay," she said, and Matty's face
closed, disgust: "She's past all that shit," and closing the
door, too, cracking it again to say if Tess came back, he
would not "step in" again. Step in. "Fuck you, Matty," she
said again, but there was no heat to it; there was no heat to
her. She walked home through the dregs of afternoon,
came to her building to find shit smeared on the door,
dogshit maybe, maybe not; Nicky was swearing, trying to
scrape at it with newspaper, a tilted L of cardboard. She
passed him without speech or comment, went up to lie on
the bed and stay there.

Too worn out to cry, the one question circling her like a
virus closing in, the sickness that brings death, why. Why?
As if questioning the fact of death itself. What had turned
him so against her, what lure? Hate, love, jealousy, what?
The brute sweetness of betrayal? The urge to punish? and
make no mistake, he was punishing Bibi as well, punishing
in fact all three, did he see that? She had made love to
them both, in this bed, their sweat on her hands, teeth
bare, hair gripped and flying, they had both talked to her
about love, about loving her; Jesus God; how it had hurt,
to think of them together and she the fool outside; this,
now, made nothing of that. Everything broken and she
without impetus to rise, to try in her own way for re-cre-
ation, to make not new but whole the wreckage around

her; she had lost purpose, thoroughly and completely, the way a limb is amputated.

Sleepless in bed, talking to no one: not Nicky or Nita or Edgar-Marc, not Jerome when he and Peter returned; not the phone when it rang which it did; infrequently, but she left the machine on: Bibi might call. Or Michael.

Two mornings, three, lying mute in T-shirt and panties like a body washed up on a beach and, like driftwood, another Bibi-interview, this one in an oversize magazine left at her door like a love offering, a way to rouse her. Sitting up at last to read it, cross-legged on the bed, turning the pages as if she must by rote verify the presence of each. Slick pop culture pretensions, galleries she had never visited, shows of work she despised, when had she last done work of her own? When would she work again? teach? Never?

And all at once the centerpiece, long article with small type, "Performance Art Ultima" and Bibi, there, even less presentable somehow though this was an earlier photograph: an earlier time as the words were still all hers, her white-hot rant, ramble and jumble and as Tess read she seemed to see, like palimpsests, the words Bibi might speak now, on this same subject, the way her eyes might look as she did; the probable cast of her smile. Less thought than pure knowledge, the contrast less immense than immensely skewed: as if the part of her that was still Bibi had had its last fling in these pages: the part that could still make a joke, take one, still slip from the hooked orbit of lesser passions and greeds called into service by the greater greeds and passions that were her, that made up Bibi as bricks make a wall; could still escape her guarding obsessions and be for moments free of the demands of that hunger now devouring her, dark yin to her yang. Were they still distinguishable, one from the other? or instead were they dominoes, grinless twins and each red-mouthed, hands out, hungry not for feeding but the flesh that hunger brings. She had been already crazy, in this article, but she was far beyond that now.

And I can't help her.

I can't help her at all anymore.

Crying, from beneath that twisting pity, twisting like an ulcer giving birth and little tears, very hot, moving lines down her dry cheeks. On the page Bibi's face, gray eyes the color of metal, the color of brittle hooks through flesh shy with blood's embarrassment; she was crying onto the magazine, one smearing hand to wipe the tears away.

Knocking, softly, at the door, two knocks and a pause; two knocks and no more.

She rose, unsteady from her days of lying flat, pulled on a pair of knee-length shorts half-folded on the floor. Face to the door, "Who is it?" and in the summoning breath knew exactly who it was.

A half smile, barely there: stepping in with that same grace, never less than beautiful; she had never hated anyone so much. Chains across his cheek, faint ceremonious scars beneath his gray Bibi-eyes. "I hear you're looking for me," he said, stepping past her; come inside.

Her heart, whipping rhythm, beating as if she were dying; she wanted to strip the bed of its sheet and strangle him with it, garrote his cock, his neck, fill his lying mouth choking-full. All the lies, out there in swift black crouch, what else was there that she didn't know? Helpless through her teeth: "I'd like to kill you."

His understanding instant; a small shrug. "Hey, I never forced anybody to do anything; they were a dissatisfied bunch. And anyway you're as much to blame as I am, you're the one who taught them how." Silence. "I don't lie to her, Tess. Like I never lied to you."

That itself was such a lie there was no answering it; saying nothing, she watched him sit down, herself stayed standing as if she were the stranger come to him in his home. He seemed to be waiting for her to say something, but she had nothing. What should she say: I hate you? Why did you do that? Would the answers mean anything more than the air used to form them, the thoughtless motion of tongue and lips? Finally, "You did a lot of things," she said. "I bet I don't know the half of it."

"I bet you don't either." Smiling wide but not in mockery, the way one old friend smiles to another over a successful practical joke: surely you're not still angry? About that? "I keep trying to tell you, there are more ways than one to perform. You didn't have one, and then you did, with Bibi. And now you don't have one again." Hands in pockets. He was not dirty, his hair was beautifully clean, soft messy strands escaping his braid. Thin chains shining like threads of metal, hardened veins. "But she does. She has one hell of a one, if that makes sense, and it should: you've seen the shows. Shit, half the shows are about you," and he laughed a little, shook his head very lightly. "You know, at first I wondered if you were sending them after all, those kids—you know, your girl, and that dumb beefstick kid—"

Gazing at him, almost without the urge to speak: as if at a hole, a chasm you had never guessed was there, you had almost stepped into it a thousand times, and finally you fell. Fell down. How had this *happened?* With effort, "What are—"

"—call those things, those beef sticks?—jerky, right. A big beef jerky." He laughed again. "If you weren't so pissed off at me, you'd see it was true. You could see a lot of things, if you weren't so pissed off. Incidentally I was trying to show you a way, there, with those kids, who do you think put them on to you, huh? As a teacher. You don't think they came up with that stuff themselves, do you? Bibi set herself up, and I was trying to set you up, too."

As if from a distance, somewhere past the airless clamor of rage: "Why didn't you set yourself up? You were in that group, that *fou* music thing. Why didn't you just—"

Impatiently, "Because they were stupid," as if she were as well. "You know that, you saw them. Why should I waste my time?"

"Why waste it," feeling sicker, now, a special red sickness, feeling as if she would like to get close to him, close enough to reach his face. "Why not just keep it all for your—"

"Fuck that," not looking at her, now, a point somewhere above her head. "I came here to talk, Tess, do you want to talk? I even have the password: Bibi sent me."

"Why didn't you?" ignoring him, ignoring his deliberate use of Bibi's name even though she wanted to slap it right out of his mouth, wanted to scream into his face *Don't you dare say her name, don't you dare say her name to me.* "Why didn't you just make your own group, lead your own—"

"She needs your help," too loud, too loud even for what he was trying to do; more than interruption, he wanted distraction, he wanted her to stop talking. Why? but still going on, Bibi Bibi Bibi until it worked, she wanted to scream again, she had to stop thinking, had to listen to make it stop. "What?" loathing him; showing it. "What did she send you to tell me that she couldn't tell me herself?"

"I told you. She needs your help," and smoothly, unbelievably, his solicitation, there were effects they would like to achieve, things they would like to do if Tess would only lend her expertise; maybe, legs crossed now, jaunty again, maybe they could trade? or she could be paid in cash, if that was what she wanted, they were very flexible after all.

Past disbelief, a moment's pause; then: "I want you to leave Bibi alone. That's what I want."

Shrugging, "It's not what she wants," and that long sweet smile, chain of memories connected to it like roots to a hungry vein; "Come on, Tess. I can't do that. I'm her right-hand man, how can I leave her?"

"You left me."

"That was different. You wouldn't grow. Bibi, now," and actually grinning, "Bibi won't *stop* growing, she—"

"Were you raised," measured, now, and almost close enough to touch, "by a wire monkey? Don't you care about anybody? Don't you care about anything at—"

"I care about Bibi. I care about her art. I used to care about your art but you—"

And she hit him, suckerpunch, he never saw it coming and in that instant of red surprise hit him again, in the face, in the mouth and this time he hit her back, tremendously hard, both of them two steps back and bleeding from the mouth: her ears were ringing.

"Don't play that shit with me," his glare: no more insouciance, no more shrugs and smiles: all deep-voiced carnivore and strangely this relaxed her, just a little, muscles loose and wire-bright. Deeper still: "I'll break your fucking neck."

"Get out of my house."

Past her, not even wiping at his mouth, self-possessed again and turning at the door: "No telling what I'll tell her, now," and gone, Tess wanting to scream at the door I wish I had killed you, I wish I had choked you when we were fucking, I wish

little red marks, all over him, little scratches, little bites

"Don't you remember? You did that last night"

and how long? How long, playing one against the other? I just want to work with you, oh the sincerity of it, little fawn eyes, pretty little boy: he tricked us both, Bibi, Bibi he made assholes out of us: and the dawning thought, swollen lips in a tiny blank circle, idea come whole and complete as if a piece of sculpture had leapt, dry and perfect, from her forehead: we have what he wants, Bibi. We have it and he doesn't and he *wants* it because *he can't work,* that's what's wrong with him. That's why he doesn't want to talk about the *fou* group or why he didn't start his own group—because he's empty inside, because he *can't.* He can't, lips moving, aching, she had said it out loud. Out loud to an empty room.

The wiped blood on her hand smeared subtle as a smile; more blood, in her veins, in her ringing ears and now a new internal buzzing, rhythmic wet buzzing as if her heart had been replaced by a cheap alarm. A motorcycle went by outside; downstairs, the music came on. Dancing with Michael; kissing Bibi. Gray eyes. Blood.

I'll tell her myself.

And tried; oh God how she tried. Tried to get in, day after anxious day at the rehearsal space to see Bibi; tried to leave a letter, a note, something, tried to offer them bribes, face pushed against the crack in the door like some grotesque parody of Lazarus at the gates: "Please," begging, she was begging openly. "If she doesn't want to see me, will you give her this? Please," to bored dirty kids who barely saw her, who shook their heads in slow instructioned cadence: She doesn't want to see you, she doesn't want to hear from you. Go away, in identical flat tonalities. Go away.

And Matty for once had not lied, he refused to "step in," refused to say anything when Tess, in a fight begun by her attempt to force her way in, calling Bibi Bibi Bibi, Bibi *listen* to me! was beaten half-dizzy, rib-kicked and the boy who did it saying, cold, "Will you get the fuck out of here already? I don't wanna hurt you, you stupid bitch, but you got to get *out* of here. Now."

And home, to hold her burning head, ice slippery behind bruised lips and thinking, thinking, who can help me? Who owes me? And finding, after rapid desperation calls, that no one was willing to take a message to Bibi; she had no real favors to call in, there was no one to help. But Nicky, who offered: and was refused. They'll kick your head in, too, and worse; but she didn't say that, it was too much like a challenge, instead said Don't do it, don't worry; I'll find another way.

And now the old engine, but with a fierce new speed: Tess was working again. Working on a box, for Bibi.

Hair like fur and sweat under the helmet, smoke and burning fumes, feral glitter of fountain sparks behind the orange screens: she knew they heard her, downstairs, even past the scorch and clamor of their own work, heard but said nothing or at least nothing to her. Was her desperation that evident? Yes? No time to think, or care. Not now.

And driven, ridden, by this urgency, she found beneath its goad a joy unlooked for, unexpected: she was glad, in the work, as glad as if risen from a sickbed, a wheelchair; a prison. In the making of this box, now, had come like an angel the old love for the melting metal, the wet running river of the burn: at first she thought it still the same but found it better: improved, in some way oblique and terrible, by her pain. A new surety, handling the metal as a surgeon handles the scalpel that cuts the flesh, and the flesh beneath; and surely a black new passion, rage and pity, love and hate and everything on fire.

Time-lapse hours; working. No rhythm but one, sunlight's chase up and down, the moon came out, exhausted she stood to watch its rise, earlier now, summer's humid hand relaxed and the cool fingers of winter coming on. The moon was as white as an innocent eye. There had been another Skinbound show, a wild one, bad; she had read about it only this morning. In the daily newspaper, right between the lines: more cruel and pointed, as if Bibi had somehow abdicated not control but interest in anything beyond her own centerpiece role, torturer and tortured all in one. The paper quoted some of those who had attended, all of whom sounded half-stunned, past bemusement and more than half-afraid; a police spokesperson was quoted as saying the shows were under investigation. Bibi herself was not quoted; but Michael was, clever Michael, saying everything right, art and censorship, the responsibility of the artist to be true to her vision, all of it instantly negated by the photo they chose to run, a grainy screaming openmouthed Bibi with bound arms, there was no explaining that image away, not even by Michael, smart Michael, smart cruel Michael who rode Bibi, now, like a jockey rides a lathering horse. All the more important that Bibi see the box made for her, see it and know him for what he was. Please, Tess's own internal prayer, please let her see it, please let me make it right.

And glad now, too, in the making, the burning, that she had not reached Bibi earlier, with her clumsy words, her badly written notes; she saw now that even had it reached Bibi it would have only made things worse; if they could get worse; anything can. Remember that.

A hinging ache in her back like a broken bone, so tired but this box could not be misinterpreted, it had to be perfect, absolute. Bibi's box, to tell in metal what she could not in words; the key, to bring Bibi if not back then to a place where real awareness was possible; the lock, to keep

Michael out once and for all, out in the greedy bleakness of his own impotence; I have your number now, fuckface. I know about you.

Surety now, and simplicity: cube-shape, twiglike, sparrowboned and seemingly defenseless but here and there the twinkle of razor wire, snipped to fragments small as rosebuds, snipped by her own hands: she had cut herself, twice, three times, cut and bled and left the blood thoughtfully to dry like a rusty second skin. Inside the cube would be the figure, and in its contemplation she felt almost frightened, unsure if skill could fashion what love and pain had borne in mind, her mind, tired; and afraid of so many things.

Working, in the burn and silence, telling no one, saying nothing; getting colder, nights and money going, soon it would be gone. But don't think, of that or anything else, don't think at all but only work, the box and what you have to do to get there: don't cry. Don't think of Bibi as Bibi, small and bloody and crazy, defiant as the ten-year-old with her skinny knife and gray-eyed stare; work, and if there are tears let them fall like alchemy's rain on the metal, fog the glass plate that hides your eyes from the glowing stare of the burn.

And the figure, in the beauty of that pain, taking final shape: not a woman, not a human figure at all but an animal: a hedgehog. Small and stylized, back down and belly bent exposed, its tiny paws open and claws choked and strangled with blond hair made of perfect plastic; beautiful false hair; beautiful eyes as false, gray glass transfixed by needles in the centers of the wounded paws. The animal's own eyes were gone, smooth sockets; burrows, last safety when all defenses fail.

Struggling, in a place where awareness of her own body had become remote as vision in eyes strained open for too long, where an arm can reach a mile, where the solder's tip is pinprick size. Working; unconscious of herself, of the physical hands that moved, opened, grasped, began the fire to burning; of the mouth that sucked tired air, over and over as if at the bottom of the sea.

And the phone rang, once and twice, three and four and she did not even hear it, heard nothing past the fierce and empty silence of her own working mind, concentration as the consuming splendor of disease and finally knocking, Nicky stepping in and gingerly around the door her name: "Tess." Over and over, *Tess* until she answered, turned on him with such a face that he had to step back: but firmly: "Tess, it's Bibi. She's here, she's been knocking for ten minutes. She wants to see you."

"Don't—wait, don't let her up here," trying to cover the piece, reaching wild for a fragment, something and Nicky turning away as if discreet before bodily nakedness; "Don't worry," his voice flat, speaking to the mad dog. "She's downstairs, she's waiting for you. But you have to hurry, Tess, I have to go."

And not even thanking him, pushing past him to hurry down the stairs and he left behind to close her door; her clattering desperation rush and down to meet at the bottom, Bibi.

Scarecrow, all in ragged blue: glasses and bandanna, blue fingerless gloves, ugly chipmunk swellings on either side of the cracked lips. Snot around her nostrils; black grommets in her earlobes, to let in the light. Medicinal smell; her hands were bandaged beneath the gloves. She looked like someone in the last stages of a killing disease.

"Tess," whispering, as if in continuation of secrets, "I found out, I had to tell you. I know what to do now."

Taking her hands, all bone, oh Jesus. Bruises under her eyes. "Bibi," trying to be calm. "Come inside, okay? I have

to show you something, you have to see. Okay? Just come
inside and—"

Not listening, "You know what?" still in that strange
whisper, her throat seeming to work oddly when she swallowed as if there was some impediment there; was there?
"You know what? He said you wouldn't see me, he said go
ahead and try. He thinks he can't be wrong. Like about
Tasha," a name Tess didn't know, Bibi's slow repetitive
headshake. "He was sure as hell wrong about her, wasn't
he? —But I wanted you to know," and now a nod as graceless, "it's going to happen pretty soon. Pretty pretty soon,
we don't want anyone to know but I told him, I'm telling
Tess, because I—I want you to know. That's why. I just
want you to understand," and counterpoint, the grunt and
bang of the service elevator as if the metal voice of her
Surgeons' past called to her now and Tess saw that Bibi
was weeping, did she herself know it, could her skin still
feel the tears? Delicate wire skeleton strung limp from the
chain across her cheek; tears passed it, touched it, laved it
and Tess kissed her, kissed her tears, please Bibi, *listen,* it's
important. I know about Michael. I tried to come and see
you, they wouldn't let me in, but I had to tell you, you have
to know. You have to come upstairs so I can show you—

"Oh yeah, I know about him, too," and incredibly a grin,
all teeth, still crying; still whispering. "He said you guys
had a fight. We fight, too," and the grin more luminous
still, teeth like hunger's avatars, sharp and slim and brittle
and then as suddenly no smile at all, hot serious hands on
Tess's hands and throbbing, as if twinned hearts lay captured in her clasp. "You know I really think I found it this
time, it's the very last door, it's the *key.* I just wish," with a
wistfulness unconscious that broke Tess's listening heart,
"you were there, so we could've found it together. But I
was mad at you," and looking up, sideways, half a child's

smile. "I wanted to kill you. I hated you. Sometimes I still—"

And Tess took her, bones and sticks and needles, into her arms, holding her against her breast, hummingbird heart and Bibi wriggling free, "I have to go, I just, I wanted to show him. Fucker thinks he's so smart. But you come, okay? I'll tell you when . . . John Henry," kissing her, now, kissing her lips, blood and a smell like infection, the gassy overlay of antibiotics, too many pills. "Come see me go," and out the door, Tess pushing after saying Wait Bibi *wait* and a car in front, red car she didn't recognize.

And Michael at the wheel: staring only at Bibi: "You had to come anyway, didn't you?" and Bibi all at once like an animal, scrambling in to hit him, hard, ineffectual, on the side of his head, hit him again as Tess grabbed for the door and the car accelerated, jerked her sideways and off like crack the whip and someone's head rising like a back-seat jack-in-the-box, someone else in the car and now too far to see anything whole, even Bibi, blue and red. John Henry. You come, okay?

Not even crying. John Henry, all the way up the stairs, leaden, dying woman's walk through the haze of frustration monstrous, she was *here,* she was so *close.* John Henry; opening her unlocked door.

Everything as she had left it, tools and screens and torches, everything in place.

Except the box.

The room now in shambles, waiting, breathing through her open mouth, breathing like an ox; she had looked everywhere, everywhere, sat now, impatience turned to stone before Nicky's door, and he returning to the instant grab, her hands on his shoulders, grabbing and squeezing like fear itself: where is it, Nicky, tell me, the box. The new box, where did—

"I don't—Tess, calm down, okay, I don't even know what you're talking about," and still her hands on him, hauling him upstairs to debris: tables upended, scrap rifled, tarps and tools and fragments scattered hectic as body parts after a bomb: "I can't find it," the voice of panic, "Nicky, I can't find it *anywhere*. Are you sure you didn't—"

"Tess, I swear to God, I never touched anything." Sweating. "I shut the door and then I left. Right when you went downstairs."

"No, you—no, it was a little while after," her mind as if a brushfire, here and there, the flash and tangle of thoughts, blurring, blowing. "You were packing stuff, or something, I—"

"No I didn't, I left when—"

"Nicky, I *heard* you, I heard the service elevator. When Bibi was—"

"I didn't use the elevator."

"But I heard—"

Elevator's grumble; red car. The same old easy locks.

"I'll kill him," and then she was running, pounding down the stairs to trip halfway and hit her knee so it bled, hot grind of pain in the moving bones but she ran and Nicky ran behind her, belated, yelling her name: Tess Tess Tess like the cry of carrion birds, dead feasting; Tess! all the way down to the street.

To realize she did not even know where they were, had gone, red car, backseat unknown. The rehearsal space? and now Nicky was beside her, panting, Tess what the *fuck* and she grabbed him by the elbow: "Get your car. Now."

"Will you just—"

"Get your *car!*"

As she was, barefoot, bleeding, Fury's stare through the nicotined windows, as if all she saw was red; Nicky driving, still panting, running lights and "What the hell happened? Tell me what—"

"The box, the one I made for Bibi. I was almost done," churn behind her breastbone, whirlpool of blood and the chemicals of rage, "and he took it. Just went up there and *took* it," and one fist against the dashboard, hitting hard then curling, instant, to her mouth, screams or tears, cry inarticulate; her muscles were on fire.

At the rehearsal space, Nicky's skirling stop before two girls, black jeans, black jackets, drinking from paper cups: the smaller one was chopped blond, pierced like Bibi. Tess out at once, trembling hands and when she spoke her voice was the growl of gears unmeshed, flesh caught in the bindings; the glimmer of bone like the glimmer of steel and both vulnerable, lost before such a rage as this.

"Where's Michael Hispard?"

The blonde opened her mouth, glanced at her friend. "He's not here now," drink forgotten, eyes the special blank of wariness. "Maybe he'll be back later." The friend, silent, then chiming forward, "You want to leave a message or something?"

"No." Forgetting them in the turning instant, back to the car and Nicky, half out of his seat, half out of her mind and she slammed the door to sit in the red silence, watching it turn internally black, blacker until everything was less than color, less than thought at all. They could be anywhere now, Bibi and the box, Michael serpentine and there to explain it all, explain it all away. It had been too late the minute she went downstairs; poor stupid self, poor decoy Bibi. Poor all of them.

"Forget it." Empty. "Take me home."

"Are you sure?"

Warm nausea, the spill and dribble of sickness in her mouth; jerking open the door to vomit, purling retch and leaning in, leaning back to sit quiet against the seat, eyes closed. Smell on the backs of her hands.

"I'm not going to find him," she said, and Nicky at a loss now, "But what about the box? What're you going to—"

"I don't know. Maybe make another one," but even in the speaking knew the enormity of the thought; there would be no replacement; she was incapable and it was so too late.

Nicky put the car in gear, acceleration gentle as if Tess were a china doll, a chrysalis cased in brittle membrane that could break without warning or hope. Back home, he helped her right the flush and scatter, tools on hooks, materials regathered and set in place. Halfway through she began to weep, slow animal tears and with great courtesy he did not notice them, kept working, silent, steady, hands in motion and as quietly gone, leaving her to sit at her worktable, methodically melting solder into pools as bright as the false blood of robots, the tricksy shine of crocodile tears.

In the morning, tacked to the door: elegance black and red and lettered in a script like flowing bones: SKIN UN-BOUND—BY INVITATION ONLY; and a handwritten date, and a time. The subdued matte gleam of a black carpet nail, and not the door facing the street but her own door, the door to her room: special as a bite, the scratch minute of a needle on which is inscribed your secret name; the one word written bitter on the landscape of your heart.

Paper folded slow beneath her fingers, and creased. And creased. And creased so tight it split the holding skin, paper cut and blood on the paper; blood on the dirt on the floor; and closing the door, slowly, never thinking to bother to turn the useless lock.

* * *

Nicky, angry, wanted to go, bodyguard, something; arguing in the hallway, "For fuck's sake at least take Nita, or *some*body, Tess, *shit,*" but she kept shaking her head, shaking her head, knee-cut jeans and long black T-shirt, heavy socks and welder's boots; dressed for a battle; was she? Was she afraid? Nicky was, kept after her and down the stairs, refusing to drive: arms crossed in the early darkness, lavender sundown smeared with black like oil.

"Nicky, come on. I have to go, don't do this."

Silence.

"I said don't *do* this, all right?"

"All right," sullen. "I'll get the fucking car."

Wordless in the car beside him, Tess as if wrapped in a membrane of building energy, the state beyond tension: so angry for so long it was as if anger, distilled to pass like goblins' blood beneath her skin, had worked changes subtle, alchemical, irrevocable in the shift and torque of her muscles and bones, in the process of breath; in thought itself. Hands and neurons, eyes and memories and rage; and she sat by Nicky as he cut corners, ran blind past wavering caution lights and in edgy monotony cursed every car he passed. She sat still as a contemplative in a garden's funeral dust: and thought of Michael: and Bibi: and the box.

All the way past the warehouse district, past storefronts, past even the shacktowns to a zone unremarkable, a place where that left standing seemed in error, not even decay but the process that comes after. Burned buildings, flat gray lots, a party store still viable; what had been an apartment building, housing something now that was not commerce, drugs or fucking; there were people outside.

"Stop there," Tess said.

"There isn't—"

"Just stop," and he did, rolling slow and she got out, some brief half-curious looks, maybe thirty people; no one she recognized. Closing the car door, no number on the building and the people in loose queue, moving toward the alcove, the door inside. By invitation only. Her hands, felt at a distance, were moist and very cold.

Not much talk, shuffling, a few half laughs but by and large they were too solemn for laughter, for the high spirits that accompany anticipation; more altar than circus ring, and they acted accordingly. Inside no light but flashlight jitter, no sign, no indicator but something there, just past the alcove, mounted gaudy as a trophy, lit from beneath with a trouble light the cord for which hung low and black as a ruptured vein.

The box.

And Tess stopping, staring, bodies pushing past unseen as shadows and her eyes opaque, as she might stare at a street wreck left where it had happened, instructive atrocity painted in black and spinless tire and bone: see what can happen, when you're not careful? See

her sculpture, raped of its frame, razor wire and bent sparrowbones: the blond hair gone, false gray eyes excised and in the sockets of the hedgehog itself a pair of human eyes, goggle-eyes wet and brown and smelly in the smooth metal clasp, small mouth jingly bright with safety pins circled tight as a cinching gag, the whole of it wrapped in hardware-store chain, the kind you use for a dog, and overdressed again in sloppy pink cellophane, like a candy grotesque; a sweet treat; a jest.

God, oh God; oh *Bibi.*

Her heart like lead, thickening in the airless feel, pressure: as if she had waited too long on the ocean's floor, far past all possibility of breath; all the people had pushed past her; she was alone. A man at the door, taped hands and heavy-handled flashlight, green T-shirt with HESITATION CUTS in clean white capitals just where his nipples must be, he must have been calling her: "—or out, last chance, okay? Either show me the invitation or get the fuck out, all right, lady, you listening or what?"

Producing the many-folded paper from her pocket, he did not unfold it, instead played the light across her and then followed her through. Dark inside, and claustrophobically small; muted red lights like the wet house of a beating heart. No chairs, no altars, no stage; just people, standing around, talking in quiet voices. There was a tape player on the bare floor, and as if on impulse the girl standing closest pressed Play.

Nothing, at first, or nothing Tess heard, still unable to do more than stand, wrapped and bounded by the shape of her anger, all her frantic haste come to nothing. And then a sound, a muttering, slow and guttural and dry, the sound perhaps made by disease as it creeps killing through the body, of death ancient in the whorl of the brain; the color of bones and sticks snapped black for burning, like the claiming smile on the face of the thing you fear. That; and red air, and the people grouping, without consensus, as if brute instinct forced them closer in the imperative of that sound.

Which did not cease, grew louder but not loud, just enough to stop all talking, to stop movement; over and over but not a loop, variations minute but quite distinct if you listened closely and there was no other way to hear it, listening as you listen to the approaching silence of the prowler, the noise the air makes as the knife divides it, elemental, a sound heard only once.

A woman's voice, whispering
very softly whispering
Bibi's voice.

And the red light, one bare crude spot on her face springing hectic from the darkness and that first look told Tess that Bibi was finally lost: the last edge at last behind her and her face pointing out of the dark like death's own finger: you and you and you. The whisper was not for effect: there was something hideously wrong with her mouth, her lips distended as if pulled by invisible wires and ringed somehow by a red so dark it was almost black, a necrotic color, the color of decay; when they moved it was with effort, sluggish and slow and Tess, watching, listening, felt as if her own mouth and lips were as split and ripped and spliced, as *ground:* more than her own life she wanted to spring for Bibi, drag her out, away, precious burden and gone. Gone. Home, but then the image of the violated sculpture like the corpse of a baby, a child, their child, there was for them no home together, could not and never be; and then her hands wanted Michael, wanted his face, his lying mouth; her hands and her blunt nails; her *teeth*

and Bibi speaking, that dry bloody whisper:

"There exist so-called primitive tribes who practice and have practiced a variety of rites that our modern society calls aberrant, and wrong: the piercings, the negation, the wearing of the Ituburi—the waist-binding—the sharpened sticks and the heavy stones. In Australia, in certain puberty rites, they used the tip of a flint to rip the penis open, from the head to the testicles. This was done to prove through the power of pain that *we are not our bodies.* That our bodies are subject to our wills. That with enough pain, and enough practice, you can *use* the body to transcend the body."

Red silence; and a smile on the wounded mouth.

"This is the lesson that we forget. This is the lesson of the knife," as if in a dream, that ruined whisper and moving forward, more than her face into the warmthless burn of the red light and she stood almost naked, washed in metal, ringed and pinned, circles of silver through ears and lip and nostrils, all of it strung with chains hung with special glyphs—the scorpion, the ram, the death's head pale as real bone—the chains running low as veins down her starvation belly to the rings in her vulva; rib bones visibly bruised, face bruised, her hair so matted-dirty it was like a little cap on her head; and held before her the slippery edge of the razor, small as her bandaged fingers, small as her grasping hand.

"We can learn the lesson again, but it isn't for fun, it isn't for pleasure, it's because we *need* to, because there's a place we need to get to and nothing else can take us there, not fucking or drugs or learning, not even the people we love can take us there. We have to go alone."

"On a carpet of blood."

And as if conjured from her words, the light gone bright and Tess saw the room much changed from her first notion, still narrow but two stories high with a hole in the ceiling as if for a fireman's pole: and in that empty circle, faces: staring down. Andreas. Matty Regal. Andy. Two women she did not recognize, all of them ferociously silent and intent, listening to Bibi as if to the voice of their own demanding hearts, one heart between them all and all desires the same: her voice: her hands: her will. Her knife, pointing up now in a gentle pedagogic gesture, patience: the lecture is almost done.

"There are all kinds of ways to get there, as many ways as there are people. I found the way that works for me, and for my friends. You're responsible to find your own way, but once you watch us, you might know—" and then nothing, a little silence as if she was listening to something inside her head, some music played by her thickening blood; and then smiling a smile so completely inhuman, as if the very muscles of her face had gone long and stiff and feral that Tess felt her hands clench without volition into fists, nails hard into her own skin as if digging for balance; help me.

Head up, the tip of the beckoning knife and "Andy?" and he jumped, heedless leap to gravity's harsh embrace but landed seemingly without hurt, hard on the balls of his feet to sway at once to balance. "Andreas?" Another leap. "Matty?" less leap than graceless fall, landing in a loose crouch half-caught by Andy's arm; and smiling.

"Michael?"

Head and heart, pounding, cold hands shaking and here he came, dropping down blithe as an angel, folded wings and lightly chained, the matte silver of surgical steel. Tess watched his vision touch her, saw him realize it was her: a slight tension in the pale half smile, a drawing-in as if in muscular anticipation of battle; of pain. In no other way did he acknowledge her, instead turning to Bibi to take in his own smooth touch her bandaged hand.

Still in the other, the razor; and Andy, already pulling off his shirt, his grimy sweat pants, kneeling in a classical pose. There was around his neck a ring of dirt; in his earlobes long delicate wires shaped like the patterns of myth, the *veves* of voodoo, each depending intricate as a chant to end in weights, crude and bulbous, seemingly too heavy for the wires to bear. He was sweating; Tess could smell it, heavy on the close red air.

She was sweating, too.

"Andy," Bibi's smile, distorted, as, gently freeing herself from Michael, bent graceful with the razor to stroke with its shining tip a series of lines across Andy's back, fresh red lines convergent with others, old scars, as deft and complex as the *veves* in his ears. Blood in the razor's wake and the minute sound of the tape resetting, and from Andy a sound very much like the sound on the tape, in the air, he was smiling, bleeding and smiling and the tip of his penis had begun lightly to protrude from his dirt-colored underwear; his earrings swung, pendulums to mark the time.

Andreas, now, in preparation, shirtless and bent before the knife and Bibi like a thoughtful nurse pushing back his hair to cut around his shoulders, his neck, cutting very deeply now, horse collar of blood and fluids, he was breathing hard, breathing through his open mouth and a heavy urine odor, he had pissed himself; from the pain? The women who had hovered like bats above were now beside him, acolytes maybe for Bibi or maybe subjects, too, ready for the cutting, holding his arms as he wept: "Oh," as if one word contained all thoughts or need for thinking, *"oh,"* over and over as the razor moved, deep roads and leading all to one direction, one red path and way

and the people around Tess merging, now, no plan or volition but moving closer till they were touching, hand to hand, back to back, all of them touching and touching her, too, the silent hysteria of the flesh as stringent as electricity's white focus and

Michael's smile, taking from Bibi the razor to present instead a different tool: curved at one end like a shepherd's crook, the razor at the other slim and clean and small. Placing it in her hand with another smile, no teeth, lingering and so false with loving-kindness that Tess began, at last, to move.

Through sound and flesh on a path of anger, rivets and black stones, triangles of metal matte with rust and sharp with tetanus to build a grudge piled mountain high: you *fuck,* and the movement of her own muscles hot somehow and separate, as if she could feel each one, warm red creatures in the landscape beneath her skin; did Bibi feel this way, when she was cutting?

You fuck.

And Matty, ritual strip to crouch naked at Bibi's feet, Michael half a step behind, still looking only at Bibi who smiled, now, mother and child, god and creation and her hands on Matty's neck, stroking, squeezing, her thumbs working the hollow diamond of giving skin at the juncture of neck and chest, pushing

as the watchers pushed closer, almost helplessly, mouth-breathing, hands empty and sweaty and wide

and Andreas gave a brisk loud groan and fell; fainted? as the two women dragged him sideways, blood like some farce map printed, coy and bold, across the filthy floor and Andy gripped his penis and wept, face all grimace and eyes seeing only inward, no room around him.

And Tess's motion.

And Michael's smile.

And the instrument in Bibi's hand rising to hook, sweet and sharp, into Matty's throat, intersection of bone and gristle and the blood popped bright as a brand-new joke, flipping the tool in her fingers to repeat the path of her incision as, cutting, she kissed his slack cheek, each closed eyelid and kept cutting

and cutting

and Tess's gaze meeting Michael's smile as she shoved through the circling wedge, wet flesh and open mouths and pushing *hard*

to see the blood, wild arterial leap to make Bibi wet with it, slick with it, and Matty's eyes open now, wide open as if waking to find himself in a place he had never dreamed of being, and from that place cried out, some word, something and Bibi's red hand jerking in sudden brutal need to

cut him open

wide open

and someone screamed

and in her own red moment Tess in motion, arms out to lunge for Bibi *stop it stop it Bibi NOW,* grab and find instead Michael before her, blocking her, grabbing her reaching arms

and she fell on him instead like iron onto stone.

Shrieks, piss smell, blood and blood and the sound of the door banging open, shut, red in the dark regained and Tess's hands on Michael's throat, face-to-face like lovers, all her rage, all her strength but he was stronger, choking her now, pushing her, forcing her back to the space by the door, hard against the wall and hit her head, hit it again

so hard it took her vision, made her blind, made her fall and in that fallen instant felt the flashlight, doorman's flashlight with the long incongruous heft, the phallic handle and as she rose, slow vision rising with her

Bibi's wet growl: inhuman: so terrible that Michael turned and congruent with his motion Tess swung the flashlight, all her muscle, only once.

No one else now in the room, tape still cycling and the door still closed. Tess sinking, hands and knees to vomit, small smelly burst accompanied by pain amazing, her throat and head one locus of cold red light. Spitting blood, and Michael, jigsaw position, bleeding from the ear; already a swelling above his temple, the point of impact, bulbous-smooth as a mushroom cap. The flashlight where she had dropped it, and he made a little noise, soft, like a fussy child in sleep.

"Bibi," rising, sick laborious whisper through that swollen throat, bending to touch Michael's neck; his pulse was strong. "We have to call 911, he's—I hurt him." Stupidly, "Bibi, I *hurt* him."

And Bibi's stare on Tess, now, milk-teeth bare like an

animal in the hungry act of feeding, red drizzled skin and metal warm with it, painted, runic and manic and bright
nothing in her eyes
as Bibi turned away, turned back to Matty; all done bleeding now; all gone.

"It didn't *work,*" to him, to Tess, to no one. "We were supposed to go together. He was supposed to take me, too."

Michael's sigh, as if in assent; the red room silent as a bubble of blood. Blood on her hands that moved to her lips, tasting it now, her face inexorable from dark puzzlement to a blank and growing rage that Tess, seeing, feared instinctively, as she would fear fire, fear death and

"He was *supposed* to take me, *too.*"

"Bibi—" Standing, trying to move toward her, trying to stop her as she bent, again, to Matty's body, bent to cut at the dead face, the hands, wild cuts as another would have hit with fists or open hands, cut and cut and screaming and Tess back to the wall, past Michael, crawling to the door through the screech and batter of Bibi's voice, screaming,
and screaming
"He was *supposed*—"

And then Nicky's arms around her, dragging her, bundling her into the car; Nicky had seen the exodus, had called 911. Tense idle a bare block away, waiting to watch them arrive; and then gone, grim-faced below the speed limit and beside him Tess's throat working, trying to cry out, vomit, something; hands on the door handle. "*Bibi,* oh Nicky, Bibi—and I hurt him, I *hurt* him, and she—we have to go back, Nicky, we have to get her to a—"

"The ambulance guys will get her. And you didn't hurt anybody," staring straight ahead. His hands on the wheel as motionless as time. "Whatever you did was self-defense and if anybody asks me that's what I'm gonna say. And I'm gonna say I saw everything, too."

Yellow light and cautious on the brake; light outside the window like the slow rumor of dawn. Her head against the cold plane of the glass as if on the breast of Love itself, throat corseted by pain and wanting more than anything else the last boon, the simple ability to cry.

Tess lives in the back of a storefront now, little room once pantry and storage, barely large enough to house her small necessities, sleeping bag and cardboard box, helmet and tanks and welding gear. The two windows, lozenge shaped, are covered with heavy yellowing plastic, reclosable with some effort; there is no heat but there is electricity. The boxes, the sculpture, stand out in the weather and the dark, rain and snow like the cold tears of the murdered, half-tarped like tragedy's mute survivors. At first she sat before them, knees bent past feeling, arms locked in supplicant's crouch as if they still held secrets she might need, but she has not, now, stripped the coverings for that purpose in weeks, weeks; already begun is rust's inexorable crawl.

She no longer sees anyone, Peter or Jerome, Nita, Edgar-Marc; only Nicky still comes around, tapping and calling, each time less sure; if Tess is present, which is most of the time, she hides, bent silent as dust until he is gone. Even loyalty has it limits; soon he will not come at all, tired at last of the endlessness of the action, dissatisfied, but sure that he has done all he could.

She never thinks of Michael, but sometimes she dreams, wakes from them not weeping but with the sense of having wept. He is not Paul, in these dreams, but sometimes he lies still beneath scaffolding; sometimes when the flashlight hits him his head shatters like old glass. His head, of course, is not shattered; a closed-head injury, the skull still safely pristine. Only the brain inside it is ruined, beaten by her blow and the subsequent pressure of blood and fluid to a state where thought is less impossible than flight, but as improbable. She does not wish more guilt upon herself, taking only what the dreams provide. Sometimes she forgets it was her hand that swung the flashlight, forgets the sound it made when it struck. Perhaps it is that sound that brings her tears, the screams that bring her finally to wake. His blood is on her hands, will always be, but only she and Nicky will ever know. Perhaps this is why she dreams.

Her visits to Bibi are as often as allowed: gray hospital room even smaller than her own and warm with a peculiar smell, as if Bibi is decomposing from the inside out; she does not know Tess, does not perhaps even recognize herself, her own moving hands, her labia, her feet; they have removed all the metal of her piercings, stripped her, Tess thinks, of her armor; all her scars are visible now, tiny puckerings and holes. She does not speak in words, as if she, too, is rusting into the moveless torpor of catatonia, life-in-death.

Her case will come to trial soon: dead Matty, why does he matter more than murdered Paul? They are equally dead. Tess has asked to be kept informed, but has no telephone; her post office box is paid for until the end of the year, but oh how slowly those wheels grind, "soon" might mean next year. They will plead insanity, the court-appointed lawyer—fat and brisk in navy blue, her breath the burnt-oven smell of chronic stomach distress—has promised Tess that Bibi will never spend any time in jail; she is already in jail, of course, but no one seems to notice that. Not even Bibi, who frets or wiggles or whispers in near silence, eyes rolled back in her head, suppurating lips now healed to cabled scars as pink as yarn, as baby booties, as the room of a ten-year-old girl who had once wanted to be a ballerina so much she cut off part of her own body to make the point. Point taken, now, but there is no one left but Tess to understand.

And she does; she can do that much, after all, and after each visit, each endless minute spent in the company of the only one she loves in all the world, Tess returns to damp gray stillness, her own stillness deepened to a pitch unimaginable, and with a surgeon's care assumes the hood and melts to slag another piece of work. Smoke, and heat; and the blister of light like Armageddon, infernal distillation past the underwater confines of the glass; last time it was the *Magistrate,* next time perhaps *Mater Intrinsecus,* or *Archangel,* that first attempt at motion; see, now, how far she has come, she herself can see it, like a light burning in the distance, white light pouring from an empty room. So much pain itself like burning, melting a place in her heart like that empty room, room for nothing but emptiness.

Aching back; sweat like blood in her eyes.

What will she burn, when all of them are gone?

> Since the soul in me is dead,
> Better save the skin.
> —Archpoet [translated by
>   Helen Waddell]

> We never know what is enough.
> —William Blake